PRAISE FOR

The Trials of Lila Dalton

'Now and again a new writer with a real feel for language and a genuine grasp of what makes a good psychological plot comes along. Enter L. J. Shepherd . . . It is a heady, ambitious mix of courtroom drama and dystopian mystery. But, thanks to Shepherd's formidable prose skills, she pulls off a winner'

Daily Mail

'Shepherd cranks up the menace, layering the story with one obstacle after another, revealing snippets of back-story, as evermore sinister forces circle . . . Writing with verve, Shepherd delivers a creative tour de force'

FT

'There's a fever-dream quality from the very start of this debut novel . . . an inventive and exciting read'

Guardian, The Best Recent
Crime and Thrillers

'Unputdownable from the first page. As the mystery deepens, readers will be on the edge of their seats, desperate to know what happens next'

Sophie Hannah, author of
The Couple at the Table

'Stuart Turton meets Agatha Christie – a locked room puzzle with hints of the supernatural, brilliantly told through the lens of the judicial system. A truly intriguing and intelligent mystery which had me gripped from the start'

Sarah Moorhead,
author of *The Treatment*

'A mind-blowing, audaciously inventive thriller'

Chris Whitaker, author of
We Begin at the End

© Charlotte Darlington Photography

L. J. SHEPHERD lives in Cardiff with her rescue cat, Coral. She studied English Literature at Christ Church, Oxford. After graduating, she decided to pursue a career in law.

She is now a Human Rights barrister instructed in high-profile public inquiries. Her debut, *The Trials of Lila Dalton*, is also published by Pushkin Vertigo.

ONE
OF
YOUR
NUMBER

L. J. SHEPHERD

Pushkin Vertigo
An imprint of Pushkin Press
Somerset House, Strand
London WC2R 1LA

First published by Pushkin Press in 2026

ISBN 13: 978-1-80533-505-4

A CIP catalogue record for this title is available from the British Library

The authorised representative in the EEA is eucomply OÜ,
Pärnu mnt. 139b-14, 11317, Tallinn, Estonia,
hello@eucompliancepartner.com, +33757690241

Designed and typeset by Tetragon, London
Printed and bound in the United Kingdom by Clays Ltd, Elcograf S.p.A.

Pushkin Press is committed to a sustainable future for our
business, our readers and our planet. This book is made from
paper from forests that support responsible forestry.

www.pushkinpress.com

3 5 7 9 8 6 4 2

To my cousin, Elaine

In the course of justice, none of us should see salvation.

The Merchant of Venice
Act IV, Scene I

THE ATTACK

Everyone likes to think they'll keep their cool in a crisis; that they alone will rise above the twin animal instincts of cowardice and selfishness to become the hero of the tale. Those people you read about in the newspapers, the ones who are brave enough to snatch the gun from the shooter, or who are smart enough to lie beneath a dead body and stay still until help comes—*Surely*, people think, *that will be me if I ever have to face my worst nightmare.* Of course we need to think this way. How do you get on a plane, navigate a busy train station at rush hour, or otherwise carry on inhabiting this burning hellscape of a planet without telling yourself it will all be okay? So, yeah: everyone likes to think they'll keep their cool in a crisis. And that is proof—if proof were needed—that all human beings tell lies, most of all to themselves.

Because no one *handles* a disaster well. There are lucky people, and then there are those who, by some fluke of fate or genetics or religious affiliation, manage not to be total idiots.

*

It was a Friday morning, and a jury of twelve sat in a room buried deep within the corridors of their local Crown Court.

At the time of the announcement, the jurors were sitting in their customary circle, deliberating.

Perhaps 'arguing' was a more accurate description of what they'd been doing, because their discussions had not been productive.

They were one hour in when the door opened.

This was unusual. Normally, the ushers knocked before entering. Deliberation was supposed to be carried out in the utmost privacy.

Heads turned; some jurors betrayed their annoyance at being interrupted in their hallowed duty. Others looked hopeful; perhaps someone had come to restock the biscuits.

At the door was an usher with plum-coloured hair. She was slightly out of breath and her eyes betrayed panic.

'There's been an attack.'

For a moment, none of them seemed able to comprehend what had been said.

The usher elaborated upon seeing their blank expressions. 'There's been a chemical attack.'

Mostly, people sat in stunned silence.

Only one person spoke. Her name was Vivienne, and she combined an eccentric dress sense with a flair for unusual proclamations. 'This is it,' she said. 'The end of the world.'

A bit dramatic, thought Leonie Vogt, who was more worried about how she'd chosen to dress for the apocalypse. It was an unspoken rule known to anyone who'd seen more than a handful of disaster movies: whatever you wear on the last day of civilization will be the outfit you wear for the rest of your life. Granted, in a post-apocalyptic world, that might not be too long.

At least Leonie's dress was khaki. The subtle print might even pass for camouflage.

One person stood up as though to leave.

'No,' said the usher. 'You've got to stay inside and keep calm.'

The phrase reminded Leonie of an irritating mug favoured by one of the other jurors.

The usher started handing out gas masks, pulling them from a bag as though handing out party favours. Apparently, since the Salisbury attack in 2018, the government had made tentative steps towards 'chemical attack planning', which seemed to be about as well-thought-out as their pandemic planning, so Leonie wasn't holding out much hope.

The usher dished out just four gas masks. Leonie looked pointedly at her eleven companions and then back at the usher, who didn't seem to see the funny side of it. Perhaps she was also in shock.

That was when it started.

Two of Leonie's number began arguing over whose chair the other was sitting in ('That's *my* chair,' 'There's no such thing as *your* chair, these are the court's chairs,' 'But I've sat in it all week!' 'So?' 'So it's *my* chair…').

As Leonie watched her fellow jurors, she thought about how wrong the movies had it. People didn't scream and run about with their arms flailing.

Eight out of the twelve were simply frozen, unable to take any decisive action or process what they'd just been told. That left only one other person who could redeem them all by behaving sensibly.

'I need to leave,' he said. An hour ago, he'd appointed himself foreperson, offering no one else the opportunity to put themselves forward. 'I need to make sure my family are okay.'

The usher let out the universally recognized sigh of someone in a customer-facing role when confronted with a twat. 'Sir, you can't leave the building. I've been told to make sure that no one leaves.'

'But my children—'

'Sir, we have a protocol to follow, and you mustn't leave the building.'

'Then I want my phone. Let me get my phone.'

'The phones will remain in the lockers until the building is secure.'

No one else had considered their phones. No one had thought to ask where in the city the chemical had been released, what type of chemical, or how. That's the other thing people can't do when disaster strikes. They can't think.

Leonie, however, wondered what else the usher was hiding from them, if only to protect them from themselves.

With the world as it was—the Doomsday Clock set at sixty seconds to midnight—Leonie had become morbidly curious about how to survive terrorist attacks. It was the eleventh hour: now or never for the world to find a way of saving itself. As a result, she found herself drawn to stories about how people reacted when confronted with their worst fears. One such article had told of people standing on the beach, watching the tsunami roll towards them, while others had been known to dawdle while being evacuated from a burning plane so they could take selfies. Some people injected themselves with the antidote to nerve gas without even being exposed to it. There were reports of people forgetting to open the filter on their masks. Imagine being killed, not by the enemy, but by your own stupidity.

A thud. She looked around. Sure enough, Tanbir, a shy young man who hadn't contributed at all to their deliberations had fallen sideways from his chair and landed heavily on the industrial carpet. He was wearing a gas mask.

The usher went straight over to help the poor guy. Leonie glanced at the pair who'd been arguing about the intricacies of chair possession rights and saw one of them eye up the seat left empty now that its owner was unconscious and on the floor.

Leonie took a moment to reflect. What was her reaction, if any? She guessed she was experiencing bystander syndrome. She didn't go over and help the unfortunate fool who'd cut off his air supply while having a panic attack and was only vaguely aware of the usher going over to administer first aid. After a while, he was propped up and blowing into a brown paper bag.

'This is it,' said one of the frozen people, now reanimated like a clockwork monkey, clashing her cymbals. 'The end of the world.'

There are twelve secrets of a productive morning. Leonie had read as much in a magazine, back when they could be found on coffee tables in dentists' waiting rooms.

Recently, she'd fallen back on gimmicky self-improvement techniques in a vain attempt at imposing some sort of meaning on her life.

Right now, she was on secret number four: exercise first thing.

It wasn't going well.

She was on her knees, forehead to the mat in 'child's pose' when Ollie, her geriatric cat, climbed onto her back and settled in for a snooze. Leonie had only ten seconds left on the timer before she would have to move onto secret number five, and only an hour in which to complete the final seven secrets before leaving for jury service.

'Ollie, come on.'

Ollie was snoring.

It would be too cruel to dislodge him. He'd cry, unable to understand why he couldn't continue lying in a happy ball on her back. Ollie was oblivious to the twelve secrets of a productive morning.

'Ollie, please—'

He refused to budge.

The timer went off. After cancelling the alarm, Leonie pillowed her hands, rested her head, and resolved to remain in child's pose for a while longer.

Though she tried to empty her mind, unhelpful thoughts kept intruding. *My hips hurt… This is murder for my knees… Ollie!*

Poor, ancient Ollie was the last relic of Leonie's imperfect but loving marriage. Every picture of Leonie's husband, Hamish, every piece of furniture they'd bought together, every record he'd loved had been cleansed from her life in the interests of attaining the fifth stage of grief: acceptance. She no longer lived in the home they'd once shared, which was a cluttered cottage void of straight lines. Instead, her new home was minimalistic, having been designed by a woman who claimed to be an expert in Scandi interiors.

But you can't just dispose of a cat the way you can possessions.

So there he was, the sole remaining witness to fifteen years of devotion and servitude. It was hard not to feel a little resentful towards him. In the same way that he was now sabotaging her carefully planned morning routine, he also sabotaged all of her attempts to get over Hamish. While everything else had been boxed away and sent off to charity shops, Ollie was the only thing left that could remind her of him. She missed Hamish's smile, his laugh, the way he held her. The way he'd put the towel in the tumble dryer while she was having a shower so it was warm when she got out. In the old house, she kept finding things he'd left behind. One time she came across an acid-green plectrum that Hamish had picked up at a gig. Their shared taste in music was part of the attraction. The early months of their relationship were a whirlwind of music and drugs and imbalanced neurochemicals. One look at the tiny guitar pick was enough to transport her back to the life they'd shared. That was why she got rid of it all in the end.

Now Leonie's hips were aflame, her knees were stretched beyond recognition, and she was sure that her forehead would be red and creased from where it had been resting on her hands. There was a wet patch on the small of her back—probably Ollie's drool.

She began to execute a manoeuvre far too advanced for her yogic abilities. She lifted her hands from the floor and reached behind for where Ollie lay snoozing.

'Come on, it's time to wake up now.'

She felt a sharp pain in her shoulder as it twinged. Ollie woke mid-snore and began to scratch at her arms. He landed inelegantly before trotting away, his tail poker-straight.

How had it come to this? Upsetting the only thing in the world who loved her in spite of her imperfections?

Leonie set about unfurling herself, every joint complaining.

Next, secret number five: eat a protein-rich breakfast. The liquidizer was probably her most-used kitchen appliance after her microwave. It did everything, as long as you wanted it in liquid form.

Hamish's death had brought about a significant change in her eating habits. The melancholy had worn away her taste buds. You'd think that would have helped her to lose weight, but instead she kept filling her mouth with food, hoping that this bite, the next mouthful, no, the next, would have some flavour, only to find herself eating increasingly sweet and salty food, to no avail.

But with her twelve secrets of a productive morning, Leonie had ensured that her breakfast was both nutritious and easy. Cooking was a lot of effort these days.

It had been ever since Hamish's death.

Why did she keep thinking of the loss like that? *Hamish's death.* It made it sound like a fact of life, some random consequence, the stars aligning. But it wasn't any of those things.

Secret number six: make time for creativity.

Leonie opened her notebook.

It had been years since she'd produced anything of any quality, but she kept squeezing her brain and hoping that something beautiful would fall from it.

The conventional wisdom was that creative outlets were cathartic, but Leonie's poetry was too wound up in Hamish. Separating her ideas from his influence would be like peeling a thick scab from healthy skin.

Perhaps she could just free flow, put her feelings into words.

Stuck in a rut.

She crossed it out. There was no artistry in that.

I'm on a train I can't get off.

I hate the world so let me… scoff?

Nothing good rhymed with off. This was dreadful. Her brain was now white noise. There was no point in carrying on, so she turned on the kitchen television to fill the emptiness.

As a juror sitting on one of the most notorious trials in recent history, Leonie had been encouraged to stay away from the news. *You must disregard any media reports on the case*, the judge had said. The trial was in its tenth and—she hoped—final week. In compliance with the judge's warning, she'd barely kept abreast of the current political situation. The first channel showed an image of the court where the trial was taking place.

'Today is the day that the twelve men and women of the jury will retire—'

She changed the channel, flicking through until she found a news item which had nothing to do with the trial.

A well-dressed presenter was delivering a news report in an ominous (maybe even a bit sexy?) tone of voice, concerning the escalating tensions between the UK and some other country they'd managed to piss off after the government had promised the world and delivered precisely nothing (is that sort of sultry, forcedly deep voice appropriate for this sort of content?). The presenter went on to explain how the incumbent PM had done little to alleviate the situation on his most recent visit to meet his counterpart.

She watched on with nagging anxiety. How had she missed this? For how long had this been going on? She'd finished her smoothie, but kept her gaze fixed on the screen.

Details, give me more details.

The presenter changed topics. Leonie checked the time; she was running late. Jettisoning the remaining secrets of a productive morning, she rushed upstairs to get ready.

When it came to brushing her teeth, she didn't complete the task in the allocated two minutes, but ten. The first eight minutes were spent staring at her Botox- and filler-ridden face, looking for flaws. There was also a significant amount of time spent having an argument in her head with one of the other jurors while she was supposed to be getting dressed.

She pulled on a silk shirt dress. The pattern was reminiscent of a dappled forest floor.

All in all, by the time she had to go, she was running fifteen minutes late.

Before leaving, she went to the French windows that opened out onto the garden.

'Ollie! Come inside, please!'

Ollie probably couldn't hear her, deaf as he was. She didn't have time to stand around shaking the Dreamies tub, so she left the window to the downstairs bathroom open.

When Leonie left the house, she was surprised by how quiet it was.

At this time, she'd usually expect to hear the sounds of car doors closing, children complaining, parents trying in vain to negotiate with teenagers.

Not this morning. It was a warm day between summer and autumn. The leaves of the golden ash tree at the bottom of the road fluttered to the ground, making prisms for shafts of sunlight. Leonie closed her eyes and enjoyed the heat on her face until a cloud passed over the sun. Her skin pricked with goose pimples, and she began walking to the bus stop.

When she got there, there was an older lady waiting, hands clasped over a wheeled shopping bag.

'Good morning,' said Leonie.

'Is it?' she asked, in a more confrontational tone than Leonie was prepared for.

'The sun's shining?'

'Mmm. Terrible times we live in, terrible times.'

'Are you talking about this morning's news?'

'We're asking for trouble, the way we're going. You'll see. It'll be World War Three next.'

'I'm sure it won't come to that.'

'Mmm.'

Leonie was glad when the bus came, also emptier than normal. Perhaps everyone had taken the last golden day of summer off work.

'Mmm,' said the woman again.

Luckily, this was all the woman had to say on the subject and took a seat at the back.

The bus jolted and pulled off. Leonie occupied herself with looking out of the window. As they left the leafy suburbs and entered the studenty part of town, the streets filled with litter, bars, and off-licences. Nearly everywhere she looked, she was confronted with the same symbol. It was the logo of a band playing that evening. The posters were black with a simple white line drawing of a cloud and three raindrops. The street lamps and bus stops were plastered with posters for the gig.

A line of schoolchildren wearing hi-vis vests with 'walking bus' printed across the back snaked towards the local primary school. If schools were already back, why was it still so quiet?

Even with the unseasonably mild day, she shivered. From nerves more than the temperature. Today was the day the case would be closed, and she and her fellow jurors would have to deliver a verdict.

The pressure had been mounting for weeks. Leonie *knew* that the accused was guilty but was worried that she was the only one on the jury who saw him for what he was. The thought of someone getting away with what he'd done was more than she could bear. He had to be convicted. Every time the spouse of one of his victims sobbed in court, Leonie projected her own feelings of grief about Hamish onto them.

The bus neared the city centre. She pushed the button and soon the bus began to slow until it eventually came to a shuddering halt.

'Thank you,' said Leonie to the driver.

He grunted in response.

She arrived at the rear entrance to the courthouse, which was a modern building made of dirty white stone with a large clock tower shaped like an obelisk protruding from the middle. It had the same austere solemnity as a war memorial.

The first thing that greeted Leonie upon entry to the court-house was an airport-style metal detector staffed by two security guards: one male, one female.

Leonie and the security guards were on first-name terms by this point, and she smiled warmly on seeing them before depositing her phone and handbag into the plastic tray.

After stepping through the metal detector, there was a cursory check of her bag. The female security guard waved the wand more in her general direction than at any specific parts of her body before returning her handbag to her.

'Thanks,' said Leonie, though really she wanted to say, 'I hope you don't let everyone off so lightly.' They were wrong to assume that, just because she was a juror, she wasn't a threat to anyone. The man in the dock, the serial killer, would have passed for an ordinary man, would have qualified for jury service, had he not gone on to murder innocent people in cold blood.

The truth is that those security guards were no better than anyone else at knowing who's dangerous and who's not. Leonie understood that better than anyone. She would quite happily have been subjected to a more thorough search if it meant she was safer. It pissed her off every time someone on the news moaned about data protection or loss of privacy. Try losing the love of your life. Then maybe they'd understand why it was so necessary. That might make it sound like she was in favour of a police state, which she wasn't, but losing someone changes you. Irretrievably.

Once through security, she walked through the sparsely decorated corridors. As the courthouse was built in the 1990s, it was just new enough to be soulless and just old enough to look dated.

She took a breath before going inside the retiring room, recalling her arguments, her strategies to get the other jurors to see it from the victims' perspectives. She needed to make them understand what this man was capable of. This was her chance to stop a killer from walking free.

The eerie quiet that had pervaded the streets on Leonie's journey into the city centre was dispelled the moment she entered the retiring room, where the hum of chatter filled the small space. Leonie was the last to arrive.

'It's all right for some.' Rob: gammon-skinned and beagle-eyed, he pointed out others' flaws with the fervour of a child recently promoted to milk monitor. Whether the crime was tardiness or gluttony or veganism (the last one being a particular bugbear of his), he would spend whole lunchtimes making sure everyone heard his views on the subject.

She knew Rob's incessant need to prod weak spots was a defence mechanism designed to shield his tender ego, but that didn't make it any less annoying.

Leonie ignored Rob's dig and took her seat next to the man who'd been her best friend throughout jury service. His name was Simbarashe, but he went by Sim. Leonie and Sim were part of a clique of young-ish, hip-ish jurors who appreciated things like modern technology and artisan coffee shops. Only neither Leonie nor Sim technically belonged to the 'young-ish' criterion; Sim was in his late thirties and Leonie could still just about taste the hangover left in the wake of her fortieth. This age difference led them to form their own sub-group.

'Morning,' said Leonie.

Sim smirked. 'Someone got their beauty sleep. You're glowing.'

It wasn't lost on Leonie that Rob's jibe irritated her but Sim's didn't, and that was a double standard. But Sim did it in that knowing 'we're both naughty kids and I'm saluting you for your insouciant rule-breaking' kind of way, whereas Rob was puritanical.

'Coffee?' she asked.

Sim raised his teacup. 'Herbal only for me at the minute.'

'You're so well behaved. I need my fix.'

Leonie made her way over to the tea and coffee station in the corner.

The retiring room was snug—just large enough for a table that could seat twelve. In the corner opposite the tea and coffee station was a coat stand. All the jurors' other possessions were to be placed in lockers before they entered the courtroom. The only things they would have on their person were their clothes. Everything else was provided for them by the government: locker keys, pens and pencils, notepaper, and folders for exhibits.

She overheard Rob holding court with the group of older jurors as she navigated the cramped room.

'And the left wanted us to disarm! Could you imagine if we'd voted in that pathetic excuse for a communist?'

There were nods. Maybe they agreed with him, maybe they couldn't be bothered to form their own opinions, so went along with whoever seemed to be expressing theirs most passionately.

'Force is the only way with these people. I hope the PM gives them both barrels.'

She squeezed past the younger jurors, all of whom sat in silence, looking at their phones. After catching a glimpse of news footage on one of the phones, Leonie began to stare. Images of news reporters standing in front of No. 10 Downing Street flashed up on the screen, spliced with footage of soldiers lining the borders of Baltic states. Journalists swaddled in thick coats with fur-lined hoods. Each image interrupted by incessant push notifications which were swiped away, into the never-ending to-do list on the phone's homepage. Leonie tore her eyes away from the screen and back to the task at hand: caffeine.

Steadfastly ignoring the plate of biscuits, she waited while the person in front of her finished adding sugar to his cup. It was Diren.

He was an outlier. Though part of neither faction, it was the oldish group he spent most of his time with. This wasn't motivated by enjoyment of their conversation or company; it seemed he found it easier to torment humourless people like Rob. That's not to say they had nothing in common. Diren often teased the younger jurors for being 'snowflakes'. Like Sim and Leonie, he was the wrong age for his chosen group. He was at least five years younger than Leonie.

Diren finished stirring the sugar into his coffee and waited a little too long before moving on.

'Morning,' he said, his gaze roving unapologetically over the curves of Leonie's figure. He had hazel eyes which were framed by thick lashes and dark eyebrows. 'Think we'll get out of here today?'

Leonie tried to arch her brow. 'Is that all you care about?'

'We're getting paid peanuts for being here.'

'But it's import—'

Luckily, the interaction was cut short by the usher—an indecently cheery man called Tom who had a salt-and-pepper ponytail—interrupting to say, 'Judge is ready for you, if you'd like to follow me.'

On their way to the courtroom, the usher took them to their lockers, where they deposited their belongings.

Once they had taken their seats, the judge turned to them. 'Ladies and gentlemen. Now the time has come when you will consider your verdicts. Counsel have made their closing speeches, and I have summarized the evidence you heard, which means your task is to reach a verdict. Before you return, there are some things I must remind you of: you should only discuss the case when all twelve of your number are together. If any of you are smokers and need to go out for some fresh air, you must stop discussing the case immediately. This is not trial by sub-committee. You must wait until all twelve of you are together before going on to deliberate.

'You may have heard of something called a "majority verdict". You must put all thoughts of this out of your mind for now and try to reach a verdict which is the verdict of you all. If a time were to come when the court could accept a majority verdict, then you'll be invited to come back into the courtroom. But please don't worry about this now.

'It might help if you appoint one of your number as foreperson, who will chair the discussions and make sure everyone gets their say. Don't worry if you disagree at the beginning; sometimes it's only through these debates that you will arrive at a unanimous verdict.

'It goes without saying that the directions I gave you at the outset still apply. Don't talk to anyone else about the case and don't do any of your own research. You have heard all of the evidence that will be called. Let's have the jury bailiffs sworn.'

Two people stood to give their promises to the court. The first was Tom the usher, a familiar face who had been with them throughout most of the trial. Leonie expected the second person to be Clare, who was their other regular usher. But Clare wasn't there. She'd been replaced by a woman with vibrantly dyed hair, the violet hue picked out by the halogen lamps. Something about the change in routine unsettled Leonie. It felt like an omen of bad tidings.

Before long, they were being led back into the retiring room. Leonie was reminded briefly of the children in their 'walking bus' tunics.

They sat down in a circle and began to deliberate.

If Leonie were to look back and find the root cause of the debacle that unfolded, she'd start with Rob electing himself foreperson (or 'fore*man*' as he put it). He did as good a job of ensuring everyone had their turn to speak as the Prime Minister seemed to be doing of easing tensions with psychopathic world leaders.

This was how he began: 'The problem with this case is that there's no direct evidence.'

Leonie looked at the other members of the youngish group. They didn't hold back.

'What do you mean?' asked one of them.

'Well,' blustered Rob, 'it's all circumstantial.'

The youngish group exchanged knowing looks.

One of the strange things about this trial had been how much the younger jurors knew about the subject at hand: serial killers. They'd watched countless documentaries and therefore knew about things like hunting patterns and profiling.

'Evidence is almost always circumstantial in murder cases,' said the one who had spoken up.

'Well, it shouldn't be,' said Rob.

'You can't really have direct evidence in a murder case—how are you going to hear from the victim?'

Leonie decided to enter the fray, selecting humour as her weapon of choice. 'Perhaps we should hold a seance and ask them?'

A ripple of sniggers. Sim nudged her in the ribs with his elbow.

'I've done several,' said Vivienne, who went by Viv. 'I know a good medium.'

Everyone stopped laughing. Awkward glances were exchanged.

Leonie had always regarded Viv with a degree of amusement. She was a woman of contradictions; she was deeply spiritual but combined fire and brimstone Christianity with New Age mysticism. She wasn't prim or proper. In fact, she always dressed as though she was ready for a night out, albeit a night out in the Eighties.

Rob, having been suitably shut down on the issue of direct and circumstantial evidence, went onto the second problem with the case. 'It all comes down to the expert evidence.' A pause. 'I'm fed up of experts.'

Leonie kept quiet, biding her time. Now wasn't the right moment. She didn't want to look like she was trying to persuade anyone. They'd push against her tide of certainty, just as they were doing with Rob.

To Leonie's surprise, it was Diren who challenged him.

'Tell us all what you do again.' Between his fingers, Diren played with a business card. Leonie remembered Rob handing them out weeks ago.

'I don't see how that's relevant—'

His protest was drowned by complaints from the younger jurors.

'All right, all right.' Deep breath. 'I'm an insurance adviser.'

Diren looked down at the business card. 'It says here that you're an insurance *expert*.'

Leonie understood why Diren was doing this. It had nothing to do with the case; he just loved seeing Rob squirm.

Rob blustered, 'Sales puff.'

Diren pressed his lips together as though stopping something from coming out.

That was Rob's second point down in flames.

She remembered the judge giving them a direction that their deliberations weren't supposed to be by 'sub-committee'. It made it so much harder to convince people when they were all together. Leonie was better one on one. She could approach each person and try to appeal to their individual perspectives. Group dynamics were trickier; should she try and appeal to the average juror? And what was that? The mean, the mode, the median? She wasn't even sure what those terms meant. They were leftovers from an education which had tried in vain to impress upon her the importance of maths. Her intelligence had always been more about words and people. But people were no longer themselves in groups. The group was a separate organism, with its own rules and patterns of behaviour.

'But I do think we should question expert evidence,' said Diren. 'Just like I'd question Rob's insurance expertise.' He winked at him—*We're still pals, mate, hones*t. 'The prosecution expert said that it was statistically unlikely that so many patients would die in one nurse's care. But who's to say he isn't the one in a thousand? What if the defendant is simply on the wrong side of the statistic?'

'That's exactly the point I was trying to make,' said Rob. It wasn't clear whether he was grateful for Diren's interjection or annoyed with him for better articulating his point. 'It's all…' He stopped short of saying 'circumstantial'.

The accused, Michael Quinn, was a nurse who worked at the city hospital. Twelve months ago, one of his patients had gone into cardiac arrest and died. After his collapse, one of the doctors took a blood sample and found an unusually high concentration of adrenaline. The police were called and they suspected Quinn of murdering the patient. When the other unexplained deaths in the hospital were reviewed, three other suspicious deaths were identified.

'We don't even know if adrenaline was the cause of death for the first three patients,' said Rob. 'They're taking two and two and getting five if you ask me.'

Leonie felt a surge of frustration. She had her arguments lined up, but they'd barely scratched the surface of the case.

'Perhaps,' she said, 'we should start from the beginning, and go through the evidence one piece at a time like we were told.'

'Rob's in charge, Leonie,' said one of the older jurors. Her name was Wynona, and she was Rob's closest ally. Throughout the discussion, she'd been nodding at everything Rob had said.

The first hour of deliberations was unproductive. At one point, Wynona got up to make herself a cup of tea without offering to make one for anyone else. While she was gone, Diren sat in her chair. When Wynona returned, she was furious.

Then the plum-haired usher entered. Told them about the chemical attack. Diren and Wynona bickered about chairs. Rob asked to leave so he could see his children. Leonie watched, impassive. Tanbir hit the deck, passed out on the carpet.

Viv stood up. 'This is it. The end of the world.'

The prosecution barrister stood to give her closing speech.

'A nurse is someone who is supposed to treat us. More than that, they are supposed to care for us.' She paused. Eyeballed each juror. Leonie almost winced when it was her turn. It was as though the prosecutor was able to see through the fillers, nose job, and expensive balayage to the real Leonie.

'Injured.' Pause. More staring. 'Anaesthetized. The most vulnerable we will ever be in our lives. We need to trust that those with the power to give us medicine use that power responsibly. You may be swayed by the emotional arguments about the NHS, the pressures it faces, the hardworking nurses who prop it up while getting so little pay. Who, in that chaotic environment, wouldn't make a mistake? After hours without a drink, without food, without rest, isn't it natural that the hand would slip? Members of the jury, you need not worry about this. This was no mistake. Michael Quinn was not in the profession to care for his patients. He was there for one reason only: to take advantage of them.'

Leonie chanced a sideways glance at the other jurors. They were bored now, tired. She looked back at the prosecution barrister, willed her to make a brilliant speech, one that would blow the defence out of the water.

'Let's start at the finale. The murder that ended this defendant's spree. The one that got him caught. Let's start with the murder of Hamish Ryan.'

Leonie had to brace herself to hear his name. Every time it was said aloud in court she held her breath, waiting for someone to find her out. Because here she was, sitting on the jury of the man accused of murdering her husband.

She was in contempt of court. Had been for ten weeks, from the moment she'd decided not to raise her hand when asked whether she knew any of the people involved in the case. She'd kept quiet, hidden behind her new name. No one had noticed. None of the junior police officers who'd spoken to her were there. Nor was the family liaison officer. It was a stroke of pure luck. These were the stars aligning, finally, in Leonie's favour. She wasn't religious and she didn't believe in fate until that moment, when the universe had answered her prayer. She had the chance to send a murderer to prison.

It was foolish and illegal and the most outrageous thing Leonie had ever done in her life, but it was also the most important.

THE ATTACK

Now Leonie's plan to convict the man who murdered her husband was unravelling.

Around her the frozen jurors started to thaw and were being noisy about it.

The plum-haired usher shouted, 'Will you *please* all sit down and be quiet?'

Leonie was sitting next to two younger jurors who started debating whether this was really happening.

'Is it real?' asked Lucas.

'Of course it's real, haven't you been watching the news?' replied Jade.

'I don't pay attention to "the news"'—said with air quotes—'I get all my stuff online.'

'Most of the stuff online is total bollocks. That's why you need to read from a respected outlet.'

'Yeah, whatever.'

Leonie went over to the usher. 'What kind of a chemical attack?'

The usher ignored her. She was being asked several questions at once. People were complaining. Rob and Wynona were demanding that they be allowed to leave. Everyone wanted to know more.

The usher was trying and failing to get the situation under control.

Leonie realized everyone had the same questions; they just needed to shut up to hear the answers.

She reached for the jug of water in the middle of the table

and banged a teaspoon against it. Standing on a chair, she bellowed, 'Will you all just be quiet for one minute?'

Everyone stopped talking to look at her.

She realized that her status as someone 'in between' the two groups gave her power. Neither group considered her out of their age range, so everyone had a modicum of respect for her. That was enough.

'Thank you,' she said, before turning to the usher. 'Can you tell us what kind of chemical attack? A bomb?'

'I don't know. They just said "chemical attack".'

'How was the chemical released?'

The others remained quiet, listening for the answer.

'No one's one hundred per cent sure at the moment, but they think it's in the air.'

Silence.

'Not left on someone's doorknob like last time?' clarified Leonie.

'Apparently people are collapsing in the city centre. There's no single object they all touched that they can trace it back to. So the consensus is they must be breathing it in, whatever it is.'

Leonie got down from the chair.

Meanwhile, the others shouted at the usher, at one another, at nothing in particular, just into the void. Some of them were getting their coats and making moves as though to leave.

Leonie walked away from them. She couldn't get a grip on what was happening. She should have paid more attention to the news, should have been better prepared. For fuck's sake, why did she do yoga that morning? She should have held Ollie a bit tighter, not thrown him unceremoniously from her back.

Ollie.

She'd left the bathroom window open for him that morning. Would the toxic air reach the suburbs? Was the last vestige of her life with Hamish slowly being poisoned?

A memory wormed its way into her thoughts: the day they picked Ollie up from the rescue. He was an old cat. At twelve, with a bite-sized chunk taken out of the right ear, he didn't appeal to many prospective adopters. He looked like an alley cat, but the moment they stroked him, he transformed from a jittering wreck into a purring ball of gratitude.

Leonie had wanted a cat as soon as they moved out of rented accommodation and into their first property. They took him back to the newly furnished house smelling of urine, having been cooped up in a cage in the rescue centre for years. She was worried that Hamish might not love Ollie as much as she did. But Hamish became just as enamoured. He didn't object to the smelly new addition getting his fur all over the sofa or on his expensive suits, and cuddled him just the same. Hamish fell asleep watching a film one time and Ollie curled up on his chest as though terrified that the first human who'd shown him love might leave him.

At the memory, a choked sob built up in her chest like a cough. She suppressed it and traced her finger along a scratch on her arm.

The other jurors were becoming more agitated. Some of them were almost ready to assault the usher in order to escape the room. To walk into what? Poisoned air? Leonie had always been fascinated by the inability of human beings to contemplate our own demise. We simply can't fathom that something as fundamental to our existence as air could be lethal. Or perhaps we can understand that other people might die, but not us. We're the hero of our own story, after all.

Leonie realized that what the other jurors needed was to see the attack for themselves, to understand that the threat was real.

She banged on the water jug again. 'Okay, let's just hold on for a second. If we had our phones—'

'I've been told to make sure you stay in here,' said the usher.

'But a halfway house would be to let people get their phones. Then they can speak to family members, make sure they're okay.'

'But the building hasn't been secured yet. The chemical attack pla—'

'We've got four gas masks,' interrupted Leonie. 'A team of people could go with, er…' She wasn't sure what to call the usher.

'Susan,' she said. 'Call me Susan.'

'Thank you. A team of people could go with Susan to the lockers and collect everyone's phones.'

People were nodding now, calmed by the prospect of imminent access to their devices.

'Right, so who's going to go to the lockers?'

'I'll do it,' said Diren, already taking a gas mask from Tanbir—the guy who'd passed out on the floor earlier.

'Me too,' said Rob.

Wynona also volunteered, apparently unable to behave independently of Rob.

Everyone handed over their locker keys and the volunteers left without any more debate.

People looked nervously at the door. Leonie stood by it,

feebly standing guard, worried that some of them would try to leave, but within a couple of minutes, the people who'd gone to the lockers returned.

Diren strolled into the middle of the room and dumped all the phones onto the table.

The jurors descended on the pile, snatching their devices away. Most of them were staring at their screens, pleading with them to switch on faster. Others were already calling loved ones. Leonie and Sim stood back and let the others go first. They both lived alone, and Leonie knew that Sim had a difficult relationship with his family.

As well as phones, those who'd gone to the lockers had brought back three chargers. Diren took one.

'What are you doing?' asked Sim.

'What are you on about?'

'Aren't we going to leave the chargers in the middle, so we have like a pool of communal ones for everyone to use?'

'Fuck off, this is mine. If you're all too stupid to be out the whole day without a charger, that's your fault.'

Leonie tried to appeal to Diren. 'Come on, don't be a prick. We're not supposed to have access to the internet while we're deliberating. Most people have their phones switched off in their lockers.'

Diren shrugged. 'Not my problem. I came prepared.'

Sim swiped his phone from the table, and muttered under his breath, 'Wanker.'

'What did you call me?'

Leonie got in between them. 'Stop it! We've not even been in this for five minutes.'

Diren pointed at Sim. 'Don't think that I won't hit you just because you're gay.'

'God, you're such a twat. I bet you voted for the idiot who got us into this mess.'

'Don't think so, mate.' Diren spread his arms wide. 'Don't vote, do I? No fucking point.' He turned his back on them.

Leonie rolled her eyes and put a hand on Sim's shoulder. 'Just leave it. He's not worth it.'

The two of them went to the corner with the coat stand. While they unlocked their phones, others were hanging up.

Leonie looked to Rob, who had just finished on the phone to his kids.

'It's the same where they are,' he was saying to anyone who would listen. 'The school is locked down and they've got gas masks to share between them.' Rob's voice broke. He turned away to stop the others from noticing how upset he was.

Leonie never thought she'd see Rob so vulnerable. Though he'd spent ten weeks being a sanctimonious prick, when it came down to it, he was just a stressed dad who wanted his kids to be okay. She felt guilty for thinking he was being too pushy with the usher earlier. Maybe that was the only sane reaction when your kids were in danger.

Most of the younger ones had taken to staring blank-faced into their screens.

'Do we know what it is yet?' asked Leonie while she waited for the interminably slow Wi-Fi to kick in on her own phone.

Tanbir was sitting close by. He mumbled, 'Seems like a nerve agent.'

'There's a video,' said someone else.

Leonie brought up X and saw that the name of their city was trending. She clicked on 'media', and the first post was a video.

The image was of a lorry. It drove slowly into the pedes-trianized area of the city centre—which was only half a mile away—and parked up. No one was driving it. Nothing happened, seemingly, until someone next to the lorry dropped to the floor. The person holding the camera started to run until the video cut out.

'How did they upload it?' asked Sim, who'd been watching over her shoulder as he didn't have a smartphone of his own. He'd lost his, so was resigned to using an old spare for now.

Elsewhere in the room, people were watching the same video. Identical audio bounced around the room in a tinny echo.

'Is that the only video there is?' asked Leonie.

'So far,' said one of the younger ones.

'Why aren't there more?' asked Leonie again.

'Maybe because no one sticks around long enough to upload it. That one was from a livestream.'

'So that's how it's in the air.'

'Probably through the exhaust pipe,' said Tanbir.

'And you said it was a nerve agent?'

'That's what they're saying online.'

'This is ridiculous,' said Wynona. She squared her shoulders as though preparing to ask for the manager. 'I'm leaving.'

Leonie and Sim exchanged a glance. They found her the most irritating of all the jurors.

'Fine,' said Leonie, snapping back at her. All of that effort to persuade the others to stay safe and Wynona thought she could take on a chemical attack.

'There hasn't been an explosion,' said Rob hopefully. 'We'd know if there had been a bomb.'

'There doesn't need to have been,' said Leonie. 'Think about the sarin attack in Tokyo. They just pierced the bag.'

Rob and Wynona shared a look. Leonie watched as Wynona's hand tightened around the gas mask in her grip. 'We don't know it's a nerve agent.'

'Maybe not,' said Diren, 'but I'd like to avoid my lungs turning to soup, if it's all the same.' There was a fire in his eyes. The chaos seemed to nourish his soul.

'How will us leaving make a difference to you?' asked Wynona.

'It will make the building less airtight. Normally, I'd say you're welcome to go on a suicide mission, but the more doors you open, the more the air from outside gets in and I'd like to avoid breathing in any of that shit.'

'You can't stop us,' said Rob.

'Yes, I can. And I won't hesitate.'

Rob turned to the usher. 'Listen to this.' He pointed at Diren while trying to get Susan's attention.

Susan seemed a little out of it. She was staring into space. 'We should be securing the room,' was all she said in response.

Leonie looked at her more closely. She looked drawn, haunted.

Leonie approached her, a gentle hand on her arm. 'Are you okay? What does the chemical attack plan say?'

At least they had a plan. She felt soothed by the fact there was a plan.

Susan held out black bin liners. 'We need to secure the windows with these. And we should put foam around the door.'

'You're locking us in?' asked Rob. 'That's against our human rights.'

Leonie stood in front of Susan, subtly shielding her. She was worried that the usher was experiencing shock.

'Get out, then,' said Diren. 'More oxygen for the rest of us.'

Leonie couldn't help but feel that Diren had a point. Rob was normally extremely sceptical about human rights, but seemed suddenly in favour of them now his were at risk.

She took Rob to one side while Wynona hovered nearby.

'Listen, I know you're worried, but your children will be safest at school. They'll have a plan, just like every public building. The best place for them now is exactly where they are.'

'But—'

'Think it through. How are you going to take them home without exposing them to the air? By the time you reach their school you could have breathed in enough to kill you. What good will you be to them then?'

To her surprise, Rob stopped trying to interrupt her. He pulled out his phone and began dialling his children for the second time. His eyes were watery. Leonie realized he just felt powerless, and the disgruntled middle-class customer act was all he had in his arsenal.

'Weird,' said Sim, who was at Leonie's side.

'What?'

'It's just weird seeing him cry.'

Leonie nodded as though agreeing. Privately, part of her felt like giving Rob a big hug.

She went over to Susan, who was standing holding a roll of bin bags in one hand and tape in the other.

'Is the rest of the building being secured?' asked Leonie.

'Staff and security are working on it as we speak.'

'Thanks.' Leonie hesitated. 'Er, Susan.'

Leonie took the roll of bin liners before turning to Sim. 'She said we need to secure the windows with these.'

'I've never seen you like this,' he said.

'Is that a good or a bad thing?'

'Normally, I'd say bad, because I have a mortal fear of bossy teachers, but I don't know. The assertiveness suits you.'

They shared a conspiratorial smile before Leonie went back to business. She looked around the room. 'Help me move this table. We'll need it to reach the windows.'

As Leonie and Sim struggled to move the furniture, some of the other jurors came over. Leonie left it to the younger ones to climb up and line the windows. She felt safer knowing there was another barrier between them and the air outside, even if a dark pall fell over the room.

Susan left, saying she'd be back when she heard more. Leonie looked after her, wondering where she was going, and what she had to do which was more important than look after her charges.

They waited.

An unpleasant buzzing sound started to whirr overhead.

The jurors looked around at one another.

'Is that…?' asked one of them.

'Helicopter,' said Rob. 'Cavalry are here.'

'Could be,' said Diren. 'Or it could be the press. They'll be over this like a rash.'

The noise from the helicopter was disconcerting. It should have made them feel less alone, but it made Leonie feel like she was under surveillance.

'Or…' said one of the younger jurors. 'It might not be one of ours.'

The constant droning from overhead gave Leonie a headache.

The younger jurors stared at their phones, constantly refreshing, hoping to be fed new updates. Meanwhile, the older jurors kept up a low, chuntering commentary. Leonie tried to block out their conversation, but snippets kept floating into her hearing.

'The army will be on top of this. They'll have rounded up the perpetrators by now.'

'What will America be doing?'

Everything they said was alarmist, reminiscing about the Cuban Missile Crisis or the time Andropov thought Reagan was going to nuke the USSR, so prepared for a pre-emptive strike.

Leonie did what everyone else was doing and doomscrolled. She searched for news and information, searching for confirmation that this was really happening. There was no content warning preventing her from watching the first video of someone dying. They writhed on the floor, drowning in their own lungs.

Adrenaline flooded her system and she started to feel hot. She was watching an actual person die a painful death in real time.

After the initial shock and revulsion of the first video, she found herself wanting to see more, as though seeing death would better prepare her for what would come next.

The internet did not disappoint.

Dead or unconscious bodies lay on the pavement, a white film coating their eyes, foam bubbling around their mouths.

Each refresh of her phone was like another toke on the pipe. The only video she could find of the attack itself was the one they had seen earlier, but there were now lots of pictures and videos of the aftermath.

People in hazmat suits established a cordon. Leonie realized that the courthouse was inside the perimeter of the cordon.

The Prime Minister had given a statement. All of the younger jurors watched it with their phones on silent, relying on subtitles. The only sound that could be heard was the older jurors' muttering. Jesus, didn't they realize no one in this decade spoke to each other any more? Couldn't they just do the decent thing and retreat into a screen-induced silence like the rest of them?

Leonie shared her phone with Sim so he too could watch the speech. The PM said that there had been a barbaric attack on the United Kingdom, which would not be tolerated. Twenty people were estimated dead, with hundreds thought to be injured.

Leonie thought about what this would mean for the hospitals. There was barely enough space in A&E on a normal day. How on earth were they going to cope with an influx of contaminated people?

The speech was only two minutes long. When it was over she clicked the 'What's Happening' bar on X. 'World War 3' and its abbreviation 'WW3' were trending, as were the words 'escalation', 'NATO', and 'conscription'.

She found herself bouncing between social media platforms in the hope that one of them would have a new piece of information. Really, she wanted a definitive answer to the question: is everything going to be okay?

Facebook had a mechanism where you could mark yourself safe during a disaster for the peace of mind of your friends and family members. Leonie thought back to the attacks in Paris. She'd woken up that morning to see posts from distant cousins saying *Je suis en sécurité*. Never did she think her quaint little British city would be caught up in something like this. She wondered what had provoked it. Conspiracy theories were appearing online and spreading like mould.

After a while it became clear that no new information would be forthcoming beyond 'a lethal nerve agent has been released by a truck'. She couldn't help googling the symptoms of nerve-agent poisoning: headaches, stomach pain, nausea, excessive sweating, and pupils like pinpoints.

Consulting the list of symptoms caused her to check in with her own body. Her stomach was cramping and she did feel headachey and nauseated. She reasoned that she always felt that way when hungry. All she'd had that morning was a stupid smoothie. Even though it had barely gone past 11 a.m., she was starving.

She looked up from her phone for a moment and took in the others. Apart from Diren, who looked positively nonchalant, everyone was on edge. It was strange to think that a short while ago their collective attention had been focused on the trial.

Even Leonie, whose every waking minute was caught up in thoughts of Hamish and, more often than not, the man accused of murdering him, had not thought about Michael Quinn since Susan had made the announcement about the attack.

Now that the stream of information had dried up and there was nothing left for them to do but sit around with their own thoughts, Leonie's drifted inexorably towards Hamish's murderer.

This trial had been one of the biggest stories in the news for weeks and now the murders would be swept aside by geo-political events, relegated to the status of footnote.

But it was more serious than that. There was a chance the whole thing could be deemed a mistrial. Then the case would have to be heard all over again by a different jury.

Quinn might not be convicted if tried by a jury that didn't have Leonie on it. She didn't trust anyone else to point out all of the key pieces of evidence and pull them together in a carefully woven tapestry. She deserved to be the one who sent him down. The universe owed her that much, didn't it?

This is not how it was supposed to happen.

She was supposed to come to court today and walk out the other side with a conviction.

Maybe there was a way through this that ensured Quinn was convicted.

The chemical attack would keep them in the retiring room. If she could persuade the jury to keep deliberating, maybe when they were finally released, they would have a verdict.

She just needed to make these morons stay put.

It had been half an hour since Susan had left them to their own devices. Leonie felt that she was faring better than some of the others. Her mission—to ensure that Quinn was found guilty—gave her a purpose that sustained her.

Right now, she was biding her time, trying to sense when would be the best moment to persuade the others that they should continue deliberating.

The problem was that people were continually messaging their loved ones, or else engaging in the social media merry-go-round. Leonie recognized the same cocktail of anxiety and boredom she'd felt during the pandemic. The ghoulish need to keep looking at the mortality statistics. The intense sense of claustrophobia.

She turned her attention to getting the others to focus on the case. Perhaps at some point the boredom would out-weigh the panic and they'd be glad of something to fill the time.

The twelve of them had taken their usual seats at the table. This boded well. It made it easier to slip back into their roles as jurors. The table was a long oblong shape. Rob sat at its head, furthest from the door and nearest to the tea and coffee table. To his right—on the side nearest the windows—was Wynona. To her right was Viv, then Tanbir, then Diren and finally a quiet lady called Jill.

At the opposite end of the table to Rob was a man called Anthony who always looked shattered. Leonie gathered he had small children.

Leonie and Sim sat in the corner nearest the door. To Sim's right were three of the younger jurors.

Leonie was just about to broach the subject of Quinn when Sim let out a frustrated sigh.

'I'm so annoyed that I don't have my phone,' he said.

'What would you be doing now if you had it?' asked Leonie.

'I don't know… sending ill-advised messages to my ex? Like, "Maybe now the world is ending we could hook up," or playing Wordle…'

'Wordle takes about two minutes.'

'Which is why they now have Quordle and Octordle… I'd be doing anything to take my mind off this. I'm so scared for my mates. I want to know they're okay.'

'You could send them an old-fashioned text?'

'All of their numbers were saved on my old phone.'

'I'm so sorry,' said Leonie. She reached for his fingers and gave them a squeeze.

While Leonie did feel awful for Sim, she was pleased that he was unable to message his ex.

'I thought it would get handed in at lost property eventually. I thought there'd be plenty of time to get it back. All the stuff we think we have time to sort out and then…'

'Hey, Sim?' said Diren.

Sim looked towards Diren with a catty expression. 'What?'

'You said you lost your phone?'

'Yeah, last week.'

Others started to listen in on the conversation.

'Huh,' said Diren. 'That's weird. When we got the phones, I noticed we had thirteen instead of twelve.'

Those listening in checked the middle of the table, but the phone wasn't there.

Sim narrowed his eyes. 'Right…'

'Is this it?' Diren pulled a phone out of his pocket.

Sim lunged for it. 'Yes, oh my God! You found it!'

At the sight of Sim's phone, Leonie felt the heat rise in her cheeks.

'Wait,' said Sim. 'Why didn't you put it on the table earlier with all the others?'

Diren smirked.

'Dude. Why didn't you put it on the table?'

'I wondered why you'd been using that brick all week. Then I saw your normal phone in the pile we got from the lockers. It seemed odd. Thought I should hold on to it for safe-keeping.'

'But why did you make me wait half an hour to get it back?' Sim was pressing the buttons on the side, willing it to turn on. With a grunt of frustration he said, 'It's dead.'

'Here.' Tanbir passed Sim his charger.

'Oh amazing, thank you.' Sim plugged his phone into a socket before turning back to Diren. 'Why did you hold on to it?'

It seemed Leonie hadn't been the only one waiting for the opportune moment. Diren had timed his revelation so that it would have the maximum impact.

He smiled and said, 'I just told you. I wanted to make sure it was yours.'

Sim was unconvinced. 'Did *you* steal my phone? Is this some weird reverse psychology?'

'I didn't steal it; I found it. You're welcome, by the way.'

'If it wasn't you, then whose locker did you get it from?'

Sweat began to gather in Leonie's armpits. She avoided Diren's eye.

'I can't remember,' said Diren.

Why was he protecting her?

'It's not difficult,' said Sim. 'Which locker had two phones in it?'

'I don't know. We just went in people's bags and picked out the phones. We weren't keeping tabs. It was only when we got back here I noticed it.'

Leonie was sure that Diren knew the phone had come from her locker, but she couldn't work out why he was keeping the knowledge to himself.

Sim turned towards the opposite end of the table. 'Rob, Wynona,' he said. 'Do you know whose locker this was in?' He held up his phone.

Rob was busy talking to his children. Wynona shook her head. 'No idea, sorry.'

Sim raised his voice and started to lose his temper. 'Someone in this room stole my phone.'

Leonie was struggling to keep her face from burning up. What an idiot she'd been to leave it in her locker rather than take it home.

It seemed stupid now she tried to justify it to herself, but she'd been feeling guilty about what she'd done and taking it home seemed like a further intrusion. She had no intention of looking through it. She only wanted to stop Sim from contacting his ex. He was no good for him. For weeks she'd subtly been trying to coax Sim out of the toxic cycle of sleeping with and then being rejected by a guy who didn't care about him, but he hadn't listened. It was so infuriating to see a friend in a cycle of self-destruction.

'We'll find out who took it,' she heard herself say. 'We'll work it out.'

Great, now she'd committed to solving the mystery of who stole Sim's phone.

Diren caught her eye for a fraction of a second, and with that look he confirmed it. He knew what she'd done.

Leonie arrived at court. Security waved her through and she stopped off at the lockers on her way to the retiring room.

Sim's phone was in the corner of her locker. She placed her bag in front of it.

'Morning,' said Sim. She hadn't noticed him behind her.

She slammed her locker door a bit too quickly. 'Jesus. You scared me.'

'In your own world?'

She waited while he put his things in his locker. 'Yeah… I'm kind of annoyed you jolted me out of it. It was nice there.'

'Where were you?'

'I wasn't really anywhere. Is there anything more delicious than vacantly staring into space?'

They walked along the corridor together.

'I can think of a few things… Triple-cooked fries for one.'

'You know what I mean. It's nice to switch your brain off. And you snapped me out of that.'

'I'm sorry. Do you want me to piss off? I can go hang out with, er… Anthony and Jill if you want?'

Leonie laughed. 'Too late. And please don't hang out with Jill and Anthony. Then I'll be left with Jade and Charlie.'

These were members of the younger, cool crowd. Charlie was a failed pop star who had been an *X Factor* finalist in the year no one watched it. Then there was Jade, a ghostly pale goth who dyed her hair silver.

'Yeah, they're insufferable,' agreed Sim. 'And it's sooo obvious Charlie fancies her.'

'Does he?'

'Of course! All the guys do. Apart from Diren. He's only got eyes for you.'

'But he's a douche.'

'True. We've both got awful taste in men.' Sim's face dropped.

Leonie's thoughts turned immediately to Sim's phone, which was safely stashed in her locker. She wondered if Sim had found a way of contacting his ex without it.

'All okay?' she asked.

'Yeah. No. I don't know. I can't wait for this trial to be over. It's so difficult because my thoughts keep straying from the trial and back to him. I really don't know what went wrong and I'm driving myself mad thinking about it. When I'm at work I can keep myself busy, but all we do here is just sit and listen to evidence. And then there are the times when we're just stuck in that room, waiting…'

Leonie found it hard not to resent him for being distracted.

'…With the posters all around the city as well.' Sim's ex was in a band. They were due to play an arena show on Friday.

'Yeah, I can imagine that's tough,' said Leonie. 'Please don't meet up with him. It won't end well.'

'I can't now my phone's gone… I thought about getting in touch through Facebook. He doesn't have any social media, though. Doesn't want groupies messaging him. The only way I could get to him would be by contacting the band, but how lame would that look? Maybe it's for the best.'

'I think so. You're amazing. You'll find someone else.'

'I'm going to get a new phone at the weekend. It's unlikely that my old one will ever turn up.'

Leonie flushed with shame. She hated the idea of Sim

wasting money because of her. Was there a way she could return the phone to him without him knowing?

'So, yeah… What I was going to say was, I don't know how you focus on this stuff.' Sim gestured at the corridor.

'The trial is interesting for me,' she said. 'It's like our own true crime podcast.'

'You've been taking loads of notes. You should be foreperson.'

'Eh, it doesn't matter. We all get an equal say.'

'But no one else has been paying as much attention.'

'I hope they have.'

'I never saw you as a swot but you're all over this case.'

'I wasn't a swot at school. If we knew each other back then, we'd definitely have been smoking behind the bike sheds.'

'Or doing weed on the sports field.'

'I didn't do drugs until after uni, actually.'

'So you were a swot!' he said.

'We probably shouldn't be talking about drugs in this place.'

'Good point. Do they have a statute of limitations in the UK?'

'I'm not sure. There's a lot less "pleading the fifth" than I thought there'd be.'

They arrived at the retiring room, which put an end to their conversation.

Rob, Wynona, Anthony and Jill were there already. Leonie thought she'd arrived in good time, but the older jurors had a different definition of 'on time', which involved being early.

Leonie and Sim took up their usual seats. Sim continued to talk about his heartbreak. She wanted to listen, she really did. It was the right thing to do. Sim needed to offload. But now she was in the retiring room all she could think about was the evidence they were about to receive. Today they would hear from the final witness.

The end of the trial was in sight. Soon, it would be over to the jury. After weeks of observing passively, the outcome of the trial would be in their hands.

The witness giving evidence today was a healthcare assistant working on the same ward as Michael Quinn. He'd been called by the defence to attest to the accused's good character. Apparently, this was allowed.

Leonie sat through thirty excruciating minutes hearing about how Quinn was a good man and an excellent nurse. As far as Leonie was concerned, the fact that he'd behaved well for thirty-five years did nothing to convince her that he was innocent.

The defence barrister was called Mr Ferguson. He finished up his questioning by asking, 'Is there anything else you want to say about the character of Michael Quinn?'

'Only that he was one of the best, most talented, most skilled nurses I ever worked with.'

Are people seriously buying this? thought Leonie.

'Thank you, no further questions.'

The prosecution barrister got to her feet. Leonie took a surreptitious breath, trying to calm her nerves.

'You said that Michael Quinn was talented and skilled.' Her voice was languid. 'What about caring? Was he a *caring* nurse?'

'Oh yes,' answered the witness.

The prosecution barrister looked down at her notebook and began reading from it, taking her time over each word. '"At this stage, they're just a slab of meat we've got to reanimate." Did you ever hear him say that?'

Leonie clocked the juror to her right, Viv, suppressing a shiver of disgust.

'Look, you don't understand,' began the witness. 'Saying this sort of thing isn't uncommon. It's gallows humour, you know? Sometimes you have to detach yourself from what's going on. You have to develop coping mechanisms…' His sentence trailed into nothing.

'Is that something *you* would say?'

The witness's eyes widened in panic. 'Oh God, no, no, never.'

'Because it's inappropriate?'

'Yes.' His response was assured, then he immediately realized what he had done. 'But it was a one-off. Maybe he was just stressed. We can all say daft things.'

'But you've just told me you wouldn't say something *that* daft.'

The witness looked at his lap. 'No.'

'Were you present on any of the occasions when a victim died?'

'Me? No, I wasn't.'

'So, you don't know what happened in the seconds before those patients went into cardiac arrest?'

'No, but I can tell you that Michael wouldn't have poisoned them.'

'You can say that with absolute certainty, can you?' Khan put particular emphasis on the words 'absolute' and 'certainty'.

'Of course!' answered the witness, too loudly and too quickly to be sincere.

Khan paused, flicked through the pages in front of her. 'I'm going to read out something that a witness said in evidence earlier in the trial. Okay?'

'Sure.'

'"Michael had this way of amassing followers. He did this mainly by collecting dirt on them and using it as a sort of blackmail. I don't know how, but he always seemed to know everyone's secrets. He had this way of making the owner of the secret think he kept their confidence while telling everyone else." I'm going to stop there. Does that sound like Michael Quinn to you?'

'Definitely not.'

'For context, this next bit of evidence was given in answer to the question "Can you give any examples?". Their response was: "Yes, there was a healthcare assistant on the ward, and I don't know how, but Quinn managed to find out that he had, er, used hospital premises in an unprofessional manner." As you can imagine, I then asked for further clarification and the witness continued: "He had sex with a member of agency staff in the, um, in the mortuary." I then asked if that was all, and the witness replied, "Well the rumour was that they made it a sort of threesome. Using the hand of one of the—"'

The jurors had already heard this evidence from the witness a few weeks ago, but there was still an audible gasp in the courtroom, barely drowned out by—

'That wasn't true!'

'What wasn't true?'

'I didn't… you know. That thing with the *hand*.'

'I'm not so interested in whether you co-opted the hand of a corpse into a sexual act, I'm more interested in whether Michael Quinn told others that you did.'

'I never heard about that.'

'Is that a yes or a no?'

'Well, if he did, I never heard about it.'

'So how did this witness come to hear about it?'

'I don't know.'

'Did Michael Quinn promise he wouldn't tell other people what had happened if you remained loyal to him?'

The witness answered quickly, as though he hadn't thought through what he was going to say. 'I don't know how that rumour spread.'

'Thank you, no further questions.'

*

They were back in the jury room, eating lunch, when Rob said, 'It sounds like Quinn will be a real loss to the profession.'

Leonie thought he must be joking, but when she checked his expression, he was po-faced and Rob didn't do deadpan jokes.

'Yeah, so long as you're not one of the patients he decides to murder,' said Charlie.

'You're supposed to keep an open mind,' Rob said haughtily.

'But Rob.' Leonie used her most patient voice. 'Didn't you think the witness seemed a bit too one-sided?'

'He's risking his job by coming to speak on Quinn's behalf. He wouldn't do that if he wasn't one hundred per cent certain.'

Leonie nodded. 'That's a good point, but we've got to balance that against the prosecution evidence where they showed that Quinn was very adept at manipulating people. He collected secrets and weaponized them.'

'But he didn't keep any of *his* secrets, because that rumour got out about him anyway.'

'Sure, but that might not be the only secret he had on him. Anyway, the other witnesses said he had this way of making people believe that something bad would happen to them if they didn't do as he asked.'

Rob let out a small 'hmph', which put an end to the discussion.

Leonie went back to her cheese and coleslaw sandwich with an uneasy feeling. *How is this so hard?*

The problem was that Quinn was superficially charming. That was why people were willing to come out to bat for him.

She realized that this was how it happened. This is how the Prime Minister in charge of the country was the worst possible person at the worst possible time. How people with a good story to tell and a modicum of charisma were able to get away with literal murder under people's noses. She still had until the end of the week to work out how to convince the others that Quinn was guilty.

Leonie had always taken it for granted that Diren thought she was a bit dim.

She wasn't, of course, but the fact she'd had a bit of work done was confirmation enough for most men.

On her first day of jury service, Diren had looked her up and down and made an inappropriate comment before returning to his preferred hobby of sowing discontent. It suited Leonie for people to underestimate her, so she allowed Diren to carry on assuming that she was an ex-trophy wife who, having been cruelly discarded for a younger model, had managed to get a Heather Mills-level settlement from her rich ex-husband.

But now Diren knew one of her secrets. And of all the jurors, he was the one most likely to manipulate the situation to his own advantage.

Sim was staring at the others, perhaps hoping one of them would crack under the pressure. As a result, most people were now avoiding his gaze.

Susan still hadn't returned. There was no new information available online. The new videos being uploaded were all taken from outside the cordon, or from inside a building within the cordon. There was nothing showing what was actually happening on the ground. The number of people injured or dead was uncertain. How long it would take for the city to be safe was also unknown.

Leonie could sense that the jurors were starting to get restless.

She put the problem with Sim to one side. If Diren wanted something in return for his silence, he'd have to be the one to open negotiations. Luckily, Leonie was the last person Sim would suspect of stealing his phone. She was the only one he wasn't glaring at.

She decided to return to her plan of getting the jurors to deliberate. The best way to convince the others to recommence deliberations was to persuade Rob. People tended to take his direction about what to discuss and when.

It was going to be almost impossible to broach the subject with the atmosphere as it was.

Leonie thought about breaking the impasse by getting herself some coffee or a biscuit—she was so hungry—but another juror beat her to it. It was Tanbir: a cynical man-child who seemed to have lived most of his life in the comfort of the internet and was frankly affronted by the prospect of having to do something which involved as much interaction with other people as jury service. Apparently oblivious to the tense atmosphere, he pushed his chair back so that it hit the wall behind him. Wynona tutted. He had his headphones in and he was bobbing his head gently to something or other. Could have been K-pop, could have been death metal—it was difficult to tell with Tanbir.

He sauntered over to the tea and coffee table—or did as close as he could to sauntering while navigating the tight space between the chairs and walls.

When he walked behind Rob's chair, Rob said pointedly, 'Leave some for the rest of us.'

'Stop bothering him,' said Charlie, who was the de facto leader of the youngish group. 'He's allowed coffee.'

Anthony stood up. 'I'm having some too, then.'

Leonie couldn't work out whether Anthony did this in a show of cross-generational solidarity, or whether they were already at the stage where people would panic-consume essentials like coffee and toilet paper just to stop others from getting there first.

Next to her, Sim took a break from scowling at everyone to stretch. He leant back and the front two legs of his chair lifted off the floor, revealing a couple of inches of toned torso in the process.

There was a crash from the other end of the room and a loud exclamation. 'Christ!' shouted Rob. 'Watch what you're doing.'

The tableau was thus: Tanbir was pouring coffee onto the table rather than into his cup. His gaze was fixed on Leonie and Sim's corner of the room. Leonie wondered if Sim's stretching had distracted him. Stood close behind Tanbir was Anthony, whose eyes were closed in a defeated expression. He must have really needed that coffee.

After Tanbir finished soaking the tablecloth, he made his way back to his seat, apparently unaware that his coffee cup was only half-full. He edged past Anthony on the way, head down and no longer bobbing.

Anthony looked mournfully at the spilt coffee. The guy was so permanently exhausted that Leonie could only imagine how annoyed he was to see precious caffeine go to waste.

Leonie looked to Tanbir to see his reaction. He was holding his cup with a confused expression, perhaps wondering whether his coffee had evaporated.

Anthony glared at Tanbir as he made his way back to his chair. Tanbir's face dropped.

People-watching was an activity Leonie and Sim loved doing together. He'd spot the body language—non-verbal exchanges being a speciality of his—while she'd analyse the phrases people used. They'd pore over the micro-battles and work out who won. The pettier the disagreement, the better. So far, they'd enjoyed dissecting the time Viv and Rob had discussed fate vs free will, with Viv stating that everything happens for a reason, but you can also change the course of events if you have enough resolve. She didn't seem to appreciate that these are two entirely contradictory statements. Rob nearly exploded. They particularly loved the occasion when Jill had told Lucas that she enjoyed a spot of 'dogging'. It had taken five minutes of Jill explaining what dogging involved to work out that she enjoyed showing pure breeds at shows.

Lucas was the final member of the jury. He looked like a hipster from fifteen years ago when 'hipster' was synonymous with good beards and disappointing sex. Some of the youngish group found him embarrassing because he was still wearing check shirts like it was 2010. His beard and beanie were doing a lot to cover up his weak chin and receding hairline. Tattoos snaked up his forearms. They mostly depicted characters from Star Wars.

'Ah man, this is so shit,' said Lucas.

Leonie thought that this was something of an understatement.

'I was supposed to be going to a gig tonight.'

'You're not the only one,' said Jade, pulling her hoodie away from her body by the kangaroo pocket. It was black and over-sized, falling to mid-thigh like a dress. It bore the same white line drawing that Leonie had spotted on the posters while in studentville: ☁

'You're going to see Acid Rain?' Lucas asked Jade.

Sim tensed. His ex played bass in the band.

Jade sounded put out when answering Lucas. 'Well, I was.'

'You got tickets?' he asked sceptically.

'Of course. I love them. I'm obsessed with them.'

'Huh.'

'What does that mean?' Jade asked.

'Do you only like the band because the lead singer is female? I mean, do you normally enjoy that sort of music?'

'I love that kind of music. I listen to it all the time.' She rolled up her sleeve to reveal a tattoo on her forearm.

'What's that?'

'Alien Pandemic lyrics. *Their* lead singer isn't female.'

Leonie recognized the band. Hamish adored them.

'Do you understand them?' asked Lucas.

'Of course I do,' said Jade, her tone suitably arch. 'Men don't have the monopoly on interpreting culture, you know.'

Lucas carried on arguing the point. His brand of performative feminism included saying the right stuff when he thought it would impress women he was romantically interested in while revealing his true feelings by insulting artists or books that women liked and gatekeeping hobbies which he saw as the preserve of men.

'Are you okay?' Leonie asked Sim in an undertone.

'Why did I have to fuck not only a rock star, but a massively famous one?'

Sim and the bassist—Amir—started dating right before Acid Rain blew up. Leonie could only imagine how tough their meteoric rise must have been for Sim. It was hard enough getting over someone who 'let's just be friends'-zoned you by WhatsApp, but to be confronted over and over again by that person's newfound success must have been torture. It was part of why Leonie had taken Sim's phone. He wasn't getting over it without help. The bigger Amir's band became, the more Sim was drawn back to him, and the more Amir didn't need Sim, given he had a whole world of options open to him now that he was a certified rock god.

'I think Tanbir's taken a shine to you,' said Leonie.

Sim smiled. 'What?'

'Yeah, I think you made him spill his coffee just now,' she whispered.

'Shut up.'

'I'm serious.'

'I didn't think he was gay.'

'Nor did I. Until now. Why else would he spill his coffee?'

'Because he lives on another planet?'

Leonie shrugged and smiled at Sim, hoping the thought of Tanbir having a crush on him would distract him from the issue of his phone long enough for Leonie to get a reprieve from the topic.

The coffee was gone.

The biscuits had all been eaten.

It was just over an hour since they'd been told about the attack and still they didn't know when the ordeal would end.

Leonie sensed that the jurors were starting to get fidgety.

'This is ridiculous,' said Rob. 'Where is she?'

Leonie assumed he was referring to Susan.

She didn't have the nerve to suggest they recommence their deliberations. Not when those with young children were still ringing them every five minutes and those without kids were glued to their phones, making sure their friends and family were safe, and giving reassurances about their own safety in return.

The more bored they became, surely the easier it would be to persuade them to think about the trial? But if she were to press the issue now, she might look, maybe not suspicious, but desperate. And desperate people were not persuasive. She had to find a way of getting Rob on his own. How to separate him from Wynona? The woman was like a barnacle. Speaking to Rob by himself could only be achieved if they left the room.

She had an idea.

'Maybe we could go and search for her?' suggested Leonie.

Rob looked nervous. She could tell he was also slightly annoyed at her for calling his bluff. He just wanted to complain about their predicament, not take any positive action to resolve it.

'I wouldn't know where to begin in this place,' said Rob. 'It's a maze.'

'Well, we can sit here and wait, or go and look for ourselves. We've got the masks to protect us.'

Rob looked torn.

'I'll come with you,' said Diren.

Leonie worried that this might put Rob off, as he did not like Diren. To her surprise, Rob said,

'Okay. I'll come.' It seemed as though Rob's dislike for Diren was outweighed by his need not to be outdone by him.

'I'll come as well,' said Wynona, before adding, 'we've got four masks,' as though worried someone might stop her.

Leonie had to wonder whether Wynona was in love with Rob or whether it was a mere meeting of minds.

They left the safety of the retiring room.

The corridors looked strange from behind the mask. The eye holes were like goggles and Leonie found the loss of her peripheral vision unnerving.

Immediately across from the retiring room was the door that took them into the courtroom. To the right were the lockers. Beyond that was a staircase which led down to the security desk where they were scanned every morning.

They walked in the opposite direction, which took them into the heart of the building. They didn't normally go this way, but it instinctively felt that this was the direction to go in if they wanted to find Susan. They passed through a pair of double doors with round windows like portholes. The trim was forest green. In fact, almost everything in the court building seemed to be green, though never the same shade. Only the walls above the dado rail were off-white, all the better to show up the grease stains.

Once through the double doors, they found themselves in another corridor at a right angle to the one they'd just come through. The wall was lined with windows, all of which were bin-bagged. To break up the monotony of the white wall opposite, someone had hung a series of framed prints. Monet. The colours had all faded to the same uniform blue. The ghostly shapes of bridges and lily pads were just discernible.

Somewhere in there was a metaphor. How justice is blind? Everyone the same in the eyes of the court? Something like that.

Leonie didn't stop to ponder the paintings for too long, as the others were walking on briskly ahead. She wondered what it had taken to get some art in the building. Someone would have had to wrangle a bit of precious budget to buy framed prints. Now they no longer imparted joy so much as frustration. She wondered if the person who had fought for their display ever walked past them. Were they proud of their contribution, or upset at the transience of it all?

At the end of this corridor were more double doors with porthole windows.

On the other side lay a choice. The corridor split in two.

They looked at one other.

'We should split up,' said Diren, his voice muffled but confident.

Leonie panicked. The whole point of suggesting this excursion had been to speak to Rob, and now they might be separated.

Rob pointed to the right to indicate he was going in that direction. Leonie went as though to go with him, but Diren put a hand around her shoulder and pulled her left.

'What are you doing?' asked Leonie.

'Come with me this way.'

She didn't argue. It seemed impossible to admit to Diren that she'd wanted to go with Rob. It would sound so false. Diren knew there was no love lost between them.

This was the worst of all worlds. Alone with Diren, where he was sure to strike up some sort of deal in return for his silence about Sim's phone, while the one person she needed to speak to was walking in the opposite direction.

The court building was unusually empty. Leonie knew that there were no other juries there that day, but no other cases at all? Why was it so barren?

She said as much to Diren. 'Where is everyone?'

'Everyone else will be doing what we should be doing. Staying put in their rooms, but I think some people might have left.'

'But we were told not to leave. And have you seen the pictures and videos? The bodies are sort of twisted. It looks like a painful death.'

'People are stupid. Incapable of recognizing the risk to themselves if it's invisible.'

Leonie was taken aback by the percipience of this. Just as he'd underestimated her, perhaps she'd been overly judgemental about Diren. Was it snobbery on her part because Diren wasn't university educated? She hated finding old prejudices she'd inherited from her parents. It was like being left a property in a will but finding rot in the foundations, or a hole in the roof.

'Do you know where we're going?' she asked.

'Right now? Following this corridor.'

'But we have no idea where Susan is. Or where she might be.'

'It was your idea to come and look for her,' he reminded her.

'That's because I needed to get out of that room.'

'Me too.'

'Talk about being able to cut the tension…' She let the sentence hang, bracing herself for the favour he was about to ask. The request never came. Was he toying with her on purpose? 'Oh, just get it over with, Diren.'

'Pardon?'

'I know what you want to say.'

She could almost hear the smirk in his voice. 'About what?'

'You know… What I did.'

'All I know is there were two phones in your locker. It's not for me to say how the other one got there.'

'I just… I thought I was doing him a favour, okay? Then it was obvious that it was extremely stupid and immoral, not to mention illegal, and I couldn't own up to it. Then the lie became bigger and bigger and it just… spiralled out of control.'

'You don't have to explain yourself to me. It's none of my business.'

'Then why did you make such a big deal of it, if not to torment me?'

'I just thought the guy deserved to have his phone back. In a way, I'm doing you a favour because now you haven't actually committed a crime. His phone is now unstolen.'

She sighed. It was very difficult in the gas mask, which sucked breath like a plastic bag.

'I do have to explain myself. To someone. I'm so ashamed of what I did. I didn't think it was healthy for him to be in touch with his ex. The guy is toxic. He was so cruel to Sim…'

'I'm not sure I need to know about all this.'

'Shut up. You love gossip.'

'You're right. I do.'

They walked a few more steps in silence.

Leonie asked, 'Why do you like getting under people's skin so much?'

He shrugged. 'Why do you like sticking your nose in other people's business so much?'

Touché. 'I just… I don't know. I guess I think I know what's best for people. Believe me, there are many times in my life where I wish a mate had intervened and stopped me from doing something unbelievably stupid.'

'So, you're a control freak.'

'I suppose so.'

'At least you admit it.'

'It doesn't make what I did right.'

'Of course it doesn't. It was an awful thing to do.'

This was not making her feel better.

'But we all do daft stuff,' said Diren. 'It doesn't matter that you did something bad, as long as you don't make a habit of it, let it become your whole personality. At least it's been put right now. No harm done.'

If only she could say the same for her other idiotic decisions; deciding to remain on the jury of the man accused of murdering her husband being the most recent example of such lunacy.

'Are you going to tell Sim?' she asked.

'Of course not. Why would I?'

'To stir up trouble.'

'I like causing trouble, but I like you too, Leonie, so I'll give you a free pass just this once.'

'Thank you,' she said. 'That's nice of you.'

He shrugged.

They reached the end of the corridor and were faced with another choice.

'What do you reckon?' asked Diren.

'Stick with left. Then if we need to find our way back, we know we always need to take the right-hand turn. It's easier to remember.'

'Good thinking. Left it is.'

'Was it a silly idea to come and look for Susan?'

'Probably. But you said you wanted to get out of that room.'

She had wanted to. But only so she could speak to Rob. Things had left her control and she was no closer to ensuring the jury came to a verdict. Of course she was worried about the attack, but she wasn't going to let it distract her from what she came to court to do.

After consistently turning left for the last four corridors, they came across a door that didn't open.

Leonie had to admit that she was fresh out of ideas.

'Thoughts?'

Diren shrugged. 'Go back and find the other two? It was never likely we were going to find Susan in this place. It *is* a maze.'

Leonie tried the door again, just in case it was stiff or there was a particular knack to opening it.

'There's no point. It's swipe access only.' Diren pointed at a black box next to the door.

Leonie let out a sigh of frustration. Then she sensed rather than saw something in her peripheral vision. It lingered in the black edges created by the gas mask. She turned and was greeted with something monstrous. A person without a face.

She looked again. It was just someone in a gas mask.

'Leonie?' It was Susan. 'What are you doing here? You're supposed to be in the retiring room.'

Leonie had a mind to ask Susan what *she* was doing here, and why she hadn't alerted them to her presence until she was breathing down their necks.

'We were looking for you,' said Diren. 'What's behind this door?'

'A part of the building that's out of bounds.'

'Why?'

'Because it's not for you. It's for the defendants and their family members. And lawyers. We don't like juries mixing with potential witnesses, for obvious reasons. Come away from there.'

'Are there defendants and family members on the other side of that door now?' asked Diren.

'No.'

'Where have they gone?'

'Out.'

'You said that we can't leave,' said Diren. 'But they have.'

'More fool them. Come on, I need to take you back to the retiring room.'

'We're not the only ones,' said Leonie. 'Rob and Wynona decided to look for you too.'

'Look for me? I've not been gone long.'

'It was at least an hour.'

She sighed. 'No patience.' She looked at Leonie as though she was disappointed in her.

Leonie looked down at her feet. It had been her idea to leave, after all. 'We need to let them know we've found you, that they can stop looking.'

Another huff of frustration. 'Where are they?'

'No idea.'

'What a well-thought-out little plan.'

Leonie felt a childish sense of shame.

'We'll have to Tannoy them.' Susan plucked at the card on the lanyard around her neck and held it to the black box. The light flashed green and the door unlocked. 'Follow me. I don't want you getting lost again.'

They walked through to the other side.

Stepping through the door felt like going through a portal, save that through the looking glass was a shoddier and less comfortable version of their world. There were no bins, no mirrors, no creature comforts. The shades of green were more garish and the attempts to make the space more impressive only made it look tackier.

Seeing this space so deserted unnerved Leonie. The court had an after-hours feeling, which was uncanny, given it was late morning. It was as stark a reminder as any that the world outside was not the one she'd left when she walked into this building.

'No one is here,' she said. It sounded ridiculous said aloud.

'No,' agreed Susan.

'Why?'

'People don't follow instructions,' she said pointedly.

'Where did they go?'

'The defendants either didn't answer their bail this morning, or left as soon as the emergency alert flashed up on their phones.'

'That means they'd have opened the doors to get out,' said Diren.

'We closed them,' said Susan.

'We?'

'The court staff. We were responsible for executing the chemical attack plan. But it's not ideal. The more airtight we can keep the building, the better.'

'Where's everyone else?' asked Leonie.

'There's an underground car park reserved for the judges. You can't get in or out without a pass. It's shuttered. They all left in their own cars, taking their lawyer pals with them. The security guards hopped in the prison van…'

'And we were the only trial left,' said Leonie. 'No other juries.'

The usher nodded.

'And the other ushers? Staff?'

'After making the building safe, some decided to take their chances.'

'What about… What about Quinn?' asked Leonie.

'He's still in his cell.'

'What happened to the people who left?'

'They haven't come back—'

'Which could mean they're safe—'

'But the only person who did is dead.'

*

They were walking across the mezzanine which comprised the main waiting area. Outside each courtroom was an L-shaped row of seats bolted to the floor. It was as though the courts and tribunals service was worried that people might steal chairs unless they were affixed. They looked uncomfortable: a hard wooden back with a sage-coloured fabric seat. Unidentifiable marks decorated the upholstery, white rings like mould in a Petri dish.

The lighting came from LED panels overhead, the chequerboard pattern mirroring the jigsaw of green-grey carpet tiles underfoot.

They emerged into another waiting area. There were more courtrooms here, as well as toilets and a number of unmarked doors. More rows of stained seats.

In the middle of the waiting area was a man lying on the floor, either dead or unconscious.

They stopped.

The body was a couple of paces away from the stairs. As they approached, Leonie realized that the man was no longer breathing. He had collapsed in an untidy pile, as though dumped unceremoniously.

The three of them looked down at him for a few moments. Leonie didn't know whether she should show some sign of respect. His white-filmed eyes were wide open and she had the urge to close them, but to touch him would be dangerous. Anything exposed to the air was potentially contaminated.

Diren dropped down next to her and she wondered if he was kneeling to show his condolences, but he was only tying his shoelace. 'I'll catch you up,' he said.

Leonie and Susan approached the stairs, giving the body a wide berth.

'Who was he?' asked Leonie as they skirted around him.

'An electrician.'

'Why did he come back?'

She thought for a few moments before answering. 'I don't know.'

The mezzanine had one staircase leading down to the atrium, which was like the nerve centre of the court building. It was pentagonal in shape, with corridors leading from four of the five sides: one towards the canteen, one for press and witness services, one for probation, and another towards the cells. At the base of the pentagon was a short flight of steps which led down to the lobby.

Diren appeared at her side. It was worrying how easily he'd crept up on her. The gas mask made it harder to hear. Mostly she heard her own amplified breathing. The mask also eclipsed enough of her peripheral vision to render her vulnerable.

Rather than going down one of the four corridors, they descended the steps leading to the front entrance.

Leonie was taken aback. There was so much glass. At the front of the building there was one large floor-to-ceiling window housing a revolving door which was no longer moving.

In between the revolving door and the security desk was a set of automatic doors.

She couldn't work out how anyone would even go about covering these windows because they were so large. She hoped that the fact that there were two lots of windows between them and the outside gave them enough protection.

The security cabin was also walled with glass. It was set off to the right of the entrance, opposite the metal detector and table. The arrangements here mirrored those in the vestibule where the jurors were searched each morning.

Leonie and Diren hung back, nervous about getting too close to the windows. Susan took a skeleton key from her belt and unlocked the security cabin. A voice came through the speakers as Susan spoke into the microphone.

'Please can Rob and Wynona return to the retiring room? I will meet you there. This is the usher.' She added, 'Er, Susan,' as an afterthought.

After locking up the security cabin, she led Diren and Leonie away. Rather than go back the way they came, they ducked into a side corridor and up a stairwell, which was shadowy and foreboding. There was little by way of light and the stairs themselves were uncovered metal. They were about to start their ascent when they heard a door bang shut. The sound came from somewhere above them.

Leonie jumped violently. Diren put his hand on the small of her back for reassurance. It had been over a year since a man had touched her like that. Not an accidental brush in the supermarket, or Sim's platonic hugs, but tenderly, protectively. Leonie chastized herself for feeling butterflies. She was in her forties, for fuck's sake. It had been well over a decade since she'd grown out of men like Diren—self-centred and all too aware of their own good looks. She'd experienced real, grown-up love. Sure, it was quiet and understated and needed regular attention to maintain, but it was ultimately so much more rewarding than any flash-in-the-pan romance. And anyway, Diren was a dick.

'What was that?' asked Leonie. 'I thought you said the court building was empty.'

It was impossible to discern Susan's expression. Too much of her face was hidden behind the mask.

'I'm not sure. Maybe a door had been left open and it just closed shut.'

Leonie knew that Susan was holding something back but wasn't sure how to call her out on the lie. 'Do doors just shut by themselves?'

'I'm sure it's nothing,' said Susan, and she led them up the stairs. Each step clanged underfoot. Leonie couldn't help but feel that she was alerting someone to their presence. Someone who was hiding out of sight.

*

Back in the retiring room, they removed their gas masks. Leonie gulped in air, but the room had the stuffy quality of a packed train carriage. She and Diren were confronted by a lot of questions. First, the others wanted to know where Rob and Wynona were. This remained a mystery to Leonie, but she assured everyone that they had split up on purpose and the pair of them were probably making their way back now.

Then they asked questions about what was happening, as though Leonie and Diren would know any more than them for having walked around the building. Those who had remained in the retiring room with nothing to do other than look at their phones were more likely to know what was going on outside than they were.

The jurors turned to Susan as the authority on when they could leave and what was happening.

Leonie broke away from the group crowding around Susan. She was thirsty, so sipped at some water. The jug in the middle of the table was almost empty.

Sim approached to ask if she was okay.

'Everything's fine.' She tried to sound breezy.

'Fine?'

'Yeah. Just weird, you know. No one's about. The place is empty.'

'What?'

Leonie relayed to him what Susan had said about everyone leaving. In the background, she could hear Susan explaining the same thing to the other jurors.

'Shit,' said Sim.

'Indeed.'

'So, what do we do now?'

'Wait, I guess. Deliberate, maybe.'

'Pardon?'

'I think we should get it over with. Otherwise we'll have to come back here on Monday. Relive the trauma of today.'

'If there is a Monday.' Sim's pessimism could be really irritating.

'Of course there will be. It won't stay in the air for that long. We will get through this.'

'I like your positive thinking.'

Leonie returned a pinched smile before sitting down in her usual seat. She reached for her file of notes and pulled them out, searching for inspiration as to how she would persuade the others of the case against Quinn.

After flicking through a few pages, Leonie had to admit that Rob had put his finger on why the case was difficult to be conclusive about. It really did all come down to expert evidence. The murders were unwitnessed. The scientific explanation for the death was key to the whole case.

Leonie had been making detailed notes throughout, not just when they were in the courtroom listening to the witnesses give evidence, but whenever they were waiting around. She had written out a timeline of the four deaths under suspicion and a list of facts that supported the prosecution case. She turned to the page of notes she'd made about Hamish's murder.

On 5th August last year at 23:34, the alarm had been pulled, alerting staff to the fact that the patient had gone into cardiac arrest. Hamish had been in a road traffic accident where he'd sustained a head injury and a fractured femur. He was recovering from an operation carried out a week earlier to stop the bleeding in his brain.

Leonie took a deep breath. She tried not to picture Hamish on the hospital bed, totally oblivious to what was about to happen to him.

When the alarm was pulled, nurses and doctors rushed to his bedside. They attempted to resuscitate him. They failed. He was pronounced dead at 23:58.

Tests revealed that Hamish had extraordinarily high levels of adrenaline in his blood. A lethal amount. The prosecution expert concluded that the only explanation for the results of the blood test was that Hamish had been purposely poisoned with adrenaline.

THREE DAYS BEFORE

On the whole, people in the courtroom paid scant attention to the jury. When they came and left was the only time that everyone looked at them properly.

Leonie hated this part.

Someone might see her in profile, or notice a mannerism of hers that jogged their memory. She could never be sure that there wasn't someone in the public gallery who might have known Hamish. He'd always had a difficult relationship with his family up in Scotland—who Leonie had only met a small handful of times—but what if a friend or distant cousin decided to attend the trial and recognized her from a picture on Instagram? What if they were in the public gallery right now, wondering why she looked familiar?

The changes to her appearance following Hamish's death were a welcome disguise. When she looked in the mirror, she was unrecognizable. In her grief, she'd gained at least three stone. She'd also stopped going to the hairdresser's. By the time she finally had the motivation to make an appointment, her pixie cut had grown out. She'd not only kept the length but added extensions and changed the colour. She'd wanted to shed her old self, sloughing anything that had been part of the Leonie who had belonged to Hamish.

The witness was already sitting in the witness box when the jury entered. His intelligent eyes surveyed the courtroom.

After the witness was sworn in, the defence barrister—Mr Ferguson KC—rose to his feet.

'Please could you give your full name and occupation?'

'Dr Ramon Casey, Consultant in Clinical Biochemistry and Chemical Endocrinology.'

Ferguson began laying down the groundwork. 'I'm going to ask you about the blood sample taken after Hamish Ryan went into cardiac arrest.'

Dr Casey nodded. 'The reason we're all here today. Quite astonishing.'

'Astonishing how?'

'That blood test is seriously flawed.'

'How so?'

'The blood test was taken *after* the resuscitation team gave the patient adrenaline.'

'What does this blood test prove?'

'It proves the patient had high levels of adrenaline in his blood, which is unsurprising, given we know adrenaline had been administered by the resuscitation team.'

'Does this blood test show that the high levels of adrenaline in the blood caused the cardiac arrest?'

'No. The crime scene had been disturbed. Administering adrenaline was the right decision clinically, as that's standard practice when responding to a cardiac arrest, but it drives a coach and horses through the theory that he was deliberately poisoned.'

'Dr Casey, I want you to consider a second plank of the prosecution case. That's the apparent lack of clinical reason for the patient going into cardiac arrest. Do you have any thoughts on that?'

'He had been in a road traffic accident the week before. When he arrived, he presented with a laceration to the head, internal bleeding, fracture of the femur. He was in a comatose state. His most serious injury was the fractured skull and subarachnoid haemorrhage, which is a bleed on the brain…'

Leonie had to stop herself from recoiling at how Hamish's brain was being described with no acknowledgement of his mind. None of his individuality was coming through in this evidence. She was sure that if the other jurors had known Hamish, they would care more about this case, would have paid closer attention to the forensic evidence. It meant that Leonie's task in the retiring room would be two-fold: a) she would have to make sure the others understood the importance of key pieces of evidence, and b) she would have to impress upon them how these were real people with families and loved ones.

'…He was recovering, but he was not a well man. There'd been a lot of stress on his heart. It's rare but not impossible for patients to die in those circumstances, even when their doctor thinks they're out of the woods.'

'Let's talk about the other patients. As we know, following the death of Hamish Ryan, all other cases where the victim unexpectedly went into cardiac arrest and died were reviewed. The prosecution expert has identified a cluster of three patients who died eight or so months prior. Is it unusual to see such a cluster of patients going into cardiac arrest for no apparent reason?'

'Until questions were raised about Hamish Ryan's blood test, no one suspected those patients of dying of anything other than the injuries and illnesses that caused them to be admitted to hospital in the first place. To now designate them as murders in retrospect seems… intellectually dishonest.'

'Do you consider the evidence presented by the prosecution to be indicative of unnatural death?'

'No. In my opinion, there is no evidence here whatsoever of murder. We've got one blood test containing large amounts of adrenaline—which you'd expect, given there was an attempt to resuscitate him—and previous deaths being looked at suspiciously on the back of one faulty blood test. It's a castle built on sand.'

'Thank you, Dr Casey. I don't have any further questions for you, but if you wait there, my learned friend might do.'

Leonie hated to admit it, but Dr Casey's evidence was dynamite.

The prosecution barrister, Ms Khan KC, got to her feet. She took her time, arranged her papers. 'Dr Casey, you say that the prosecution evidence rests on one blood test.'

'That seems to be the case.'

'What about the injection mark on the victim's right arm?'

'All that proves is that the *patient* had received an injection of some description.'

His emphasis of the word 'patient' was a low blow; barristers were supposed to use neutral language. 'Victim' implied that a crime had been committed. Leonie noted the ghost of a smirk playing across Dr Casey's lips. He was pleased to have got one over on Khan so soon.

Dr Casey continued, 'It does not prove that adrenaline was administered before the resuscitation team arrived.'

Khan recovered quickly and pushed on with her next question. 'Am I right to say that you've been provided with the patient's medical notes?'

'Yes.'

'Was there any suggestion within those notes that Mr Ryan had received an injection which would account for the mark on his arm?'

'An absence of evidence is not evidence of absence,' Dr Casey trotted out smugly.

Khan asked her next question almost patronizingly. 'Everything a patient is given goes in the medical notes. Is that right?'

'It should do. It doesn't mean it always does.'

Khan didn't push the point. Leonie wondered why not. There was no way an injection could have been given without it going into the medical notes; that was common sense, wasn't it? Instead, Khan moved onto her next point as though leaping across stepping stones.

'What about the empty syringe found in the sharps bin?'

'There's no forensic link between that and the injection mark in the patient's arm.'

'And the syringe of adrenaline missing from the arrest cart?'

'It might not be the same one found in the sharps bin.'

'Given the empty syringe in the sharps bin, the injection mark on the arm, and the missing syringe, is it reasonable to conclude that Hamish Ryan died of an adrenaline overdose?'

Dr Casey hesitated. 'It's a perfectly reasonable conclusion, but that does not mean that it's the only conclusion. There are other possibilities.'

Khan ignored that. Again, Leonie felt a frisson of frustration. *Anything is possible*, she thought. *Surely that doesn't mean that a killer should get off just because something is theoretically possible.*

Instead, Khan pushed on with her next line of questioning. 'In terms of the other three patients, is it normal to have three cardiac arrests in the space of a month for which there is no apparent clinical cause?'

Dr Casey hesitated for even longer this time. 'It would be unusual. But I come back to my point about it not proving—'

Khan interrupted. 'Dr Casey, I'm not interested in your opinion on whether or not the prosecution can prove its case. I'm only interested in your expert opinion. Is it unusual for there to be three deaths with no clinical cause in less than a month?'

Dr Casey's jaw tightened in frustration. It was clear he'd been backed into a corner. 'Yes,' he said. It would have been an exaggeration to say it was through gritted teeth, but he was certainly reluctant.

'Thank you, Dr Casey.'

*

'That put a bit of a dent in the prosecution case,' said Wynona, once they were back in the retiring room.

Leonie shared a look with Sim, and they rolled their eyes.

'What are you on about?' asked Charlie.

'It's all about one blood test,' she said. 'And that's faulty.'

'Haven't you been listening?' asked Charlie. 'He basically admitted at the end there that the fourth victim was probably given an overdose of adrenaline.'

'I don't remember him saying that,' said Wynona. 'And it's patient, not victim.'

'Wynona,' said Sim. 'You couldn't remember your PIN number last week, my love.' He said it gently, but it still garnered a laugh from the other jurors.

Wynona flushed. 'That was different.'

'He didn't say he was *sure*,' said Rob, who came back to that word all the time. He seemed to think reiterating the standard of proof made him sound clever. Like it hadn't been repeated a million times already.

'He didn't say that, you're right,' said Charlie. 'But the prosecution expert was. Anyway, Dr Casey said it's more likely than not that Hamish Ryan was given an overdose. It's not like he blew the prosecution case out of the water.'

'Hmm,' said Wynona. 'Well, I just have a different opinion.'

'What does that mean?' asked Charlie.

'I'm allowed to have an opinion.'

'Sure, but it's bullshit.'

'There's no need to swear,' said Rob.

'Christ,' said Sim in Leonie's ear. 'It's like being at my grandma's house. Except for the getting beaten with a shoe when I take the Lord's name in vain.'

Leonie smiled at Sim's joke but still felt unsettled by the discussion. The rift between the younger and older jurors yawned open, bad feeling filling the chasm.

TWO HOURS AFTER THE ATTACK

'What are you doing?'

Leonie looked up to see who had asked the question. The first thing to catch her eye was an R2-D2 tattoo on Lucas's forearm.

'I'm reading,' she said.

'Why?'

She had to tread carefully. Lucas would not understand. Even if he did, he would make a useless ally. No one liked him, not even the youngish group.

'I just can't bear looking at my phone any more,' said Leonie. 'Is it just me, or are we not getting any new information?'

'It seems to have dried up after the initial burst,' he agreed. This was uncharacteristically convivial of Lucas. He normally disagreed with people through force of habit. Leonie wondered if he'd been good at debating at school because he spoke with an irritating high-handedness that indicated he always thought he was right and everyone else was stupid.

Leonie nodded and went back to considering her notes, trying to find a way of piecing together the facts of the case so that they were compelling.

Lucas carried on speaking. 'Everything being posted now is just people inside buildings crying and screaming.' He said this scathingly, as though people who were openly emotional were distasteful.

'We just need to hold tight and wait for more news,' said Leonie.

'Yeah, I think that's right.'

She was suspicious about his congeniality. Then she spotted that he kept sneaking glances at Jade, hoping she'd notice him. That figured. He was doing that thing people sometimes did: talk to someone, anyone, to try and attract the attention of their crush. It was no use. Jade's eyes were glued to her phone and her chin was tucked into her Acid Rain hoodie.

The small exchange reminded her of how Leonie had behaved around Hamish before they started dating. They had met at her first job after university. It was enormously mundane work selling car insurance. Hamish had sat two rows of computers away with his back to her. Her job was so boring that she was able to do it while spending hours daydreaming about him. It was a wonder he hadn't gone bald from the amount of concentrated attention she'd paid to the back of his curly head.

She would look out for any clues about the things he liked to do outside of work; the band shirts he wore, pop culture references dropped into conversation, and any catchphrases he laughed at. Then, in her spare time, she would study his favourite bands and films and sitcoms in an attempt to feel closer to him, to nestle into his interests as though into his skin.

*

Leonie checked the time on her phone. There was still no sign of Rob and Wynona. Had they got lost?

'I'm starving,' said Diren. 'Who's up for going to the canteen to get some food?'

'I think we should wait until Rob and Wynona return first,' said Viv. Her loyalty to Rob and Wynona had always puzzled Leonie. Where Wynona and Rob were fastidiously conventional, Viv was as eccentric as they came.

'Why? Why do they get to decide when the rest of us eat?' asked Diren.

'Maybe we should send someone out to look for them instead?' suggested Anthony.

'And end up getting lost ourselves again?' said Diren.

'Who's to say you won't get lost finding your way to the canteen?'

'Because we just walked past it.'

'There's a problem with this plan,' said Leonie. 'That side of the court building is swipe access only, and we don't have a pass.'

'Actually, we do.' Diren pulled a pass from the inside of his jacket.

For a moment, Leonie wondered how Diren had got hold of it. Then she remembered: shoelaces.

'You fucking idiot,' said Leonie.

'What?'

'You got that off the electrician.'

'Which electrician?' asked Sim.

'The one person to have left the building and come back was an electrician,' Leonie explained to the others. 'He only made it to the top of the stairs before collapsing. He's dead.'

A fresh ripple of anxiety moved through the jurors.

'It was a good idea,' said Diren. 'You didn't think of it.'

'It was a reckless thing to do. You've touched the pass. What else have you touched? Shit, you touched me.'

'What? When?'

'I jumped at that noise and you touched my back.'

'I don't remember.'

Leonie flushed. 'Well, you did.'

'And? So what? Is this a feminism thing?'

'No. It's a nerve-agents-are-ridiculously-transferable thing.

We need to disinfect ourselves right now. If that engineer was outside, so was the lanyard. It could be coated in nerve agent.'

Diren looked chastened. 'You're right.'

'And we need to find somewhere to put that pass. Does anyone have a plastic bag, anything like that?'

Anthony cleared his throat. 'I've always got plastic bags kicking around.'

'Okay, when we get back from decontaminating, we can put the pass in a plastic bag so none of us come into contact with it by accident.'

Anthony nodded.

Leonie felt guilty acknowledging the rush of excitement she felt at being the voice of reason.

Once she and Diren had checked there were no windows in the toilet, they decided to take off their masks. Diren removed his jacket and started washing his hands thoroughly. Then he went to pull his grey t-shirt over his head, but Leonie blurted out—'No!'

He stopped and turned. 'What?'

'Not over your head.'

'Why?'

'Because if your t-shirt is contaminated and you pull it over your head, you're basically transferring the nerve agent onto your face, which is the last place you want it.'

'Oh,' he said. He dropped his arms and looked down at his torso.

'Get it in your eye, you'll be dead in hours. Get it in your—'

'Okay, okay, I get it.'

'You'll have to cut it off. Like they do… Like they do in RTAs…' Leonie paused. Hamish probably had his clothes cut off the night he was admitted.

'Have you got any scissors?' asked Diren.

'No, why?'

'You said I'd have to cut it off?'

'Oh. No, sorry.'

Diren grabbed two fistfuls of his t-shirt. It looked expensive. A logo of an animal's skull on the left breast confirmed as much. He tore at the cotton until he made a small hole. Then he kept pulling until only the collar was in place.

'Do you think there's lost property here?' she asked, averting her gaze from Diren's abs.

'No need. I brought some spare clothes.'

'Why?'

'My plan was to go to the gym when we finished here.' He ran a palm over his pec and looked at himself in the mirror before rinsing his hands again.

'Are you just going to stay like that?' Leonie was speaking to a tap to the right of Diren's body.

He smiled knowingly. 'How about you? What are you going to do?' He looked at her reflection as he spoke.

'Me?'

'Yeah, I touched you, remember?'

'Oh.' Leonie looked down at her dress. Was it contaminated?

'Not got any spares?' asked Diren.

'Just my coat.'

She wasn't looking at his face, but she could tell he was smirking.

'Maybe one of the other jurors has a spare gym kit I could borrow?'

He shook his head. 'I looked through everyone's stuff earlier. No one else brought spare clothes.'

'Why do you notice this stuff?'

'Basic survival techniques, isn't it? I always see who's packing.'

'Packing?'

He shrugged. 'I always check to see if anyone might have something on them that could be used as a weapon.'

'You're joking?'

'No way. It's the world we live in.'

She wanted to argue, to say that people were fundamentally good and kind. But he was right. Someone had just deployed a weapon of mass destruction in their city. This was living proof that their world wasn't safe.

'Can you get Sim for me? Ask him to bring my coat. It's on the peg.'

'If you want.'

'And use hand sanitizer. There's no way of knowing soap and water will do the trick.'

He left the bathroom.

*

Sim came into the bathroom two minutes later, removing his gas mask as he entered.

'Leonie, what happened? Why did Diren touch you?'

'It wasn't like that. It was sort of a reflex.'

Sim cocked an eyebrow.

Leonie shook her head. 'No, listen. The thing is, I heard something.' She corrected herself, 'We all heard it. It made me jump'

'What?'

'It was a door slamming somewhere close by.'

'But I thought you said—'

'That the building is empty? That's what we thought.'

Sim frowned. 'And now Rob and Wynona are nowhere to be seen.'

'The noise we heard could have been them,' suggested Leonie.

'Then why haven't they come back?'

Leonie didn't have an answer to that. 'Thanks for bringing my coat,' she said instead.

She unravelled the tie belt around her waist and started to undo the buttons on her dress until she could step out of it. After that she washed every inch of skin with soap and water and then coated herself with sanitizer just in case. When she was done, Sim came and wrapped her in the caramel trench coat like a parent wrapping their child in a beach towel.

'I look like a stripper,' she said.

'A very expensive one, though. What is this, McQueen?'

She mustered a wry smile. 'Let's go back to the others.' Her voice sounded more serious than she'd intended.

They put on their gas masks.

He pulled her into a one-armed embrace as they walked back to the retiring room. She was so happy he was here. At times throughout the trial she'd been sad to think they might not stay in touch. Maybe a couple of awkward meet-ups in coffee shops until the friendship spark fizzled out. Now she wasn't sure whether their friendship would survive to the end of the day.

When they got back to the retiring room, Leonie saw that Diren had changed his outfit. He wore a grey performance t-shirt and a black soft-shell jacket; a sporty version of the clothes he was wearing earlier.

There was something else she noticed. Rob and Wynona had returned.

Leonie approached them and spoke in an undertone. 'Where have you been? Did you get lost?'

Rob ignored Leonie and addressed the group as a whole: 'Listen, we saw someone in the corridors. That's why we took so long getting back. We hid in a side room for a while because they were acting strangely. But you should know there's someone in the building with us apart from Susan.'

'Who?'

'We couldn't see them properly,' said Wynona. 'But they ignored us when we called out. That's why we hid.'

'Are you sure it wasn't Susan?'

'Certain.'

'Who's coming to the canteen to get food, then?' asked Diren. 'With me and Leonie.'

'I'll come with you,' said Sim.

'What about this person walking the corridors?' asked Leonie. 'Is it a good idea to go out there?'

As though to undermine her, her stomach rumbled audibly.

'I'm starving,' said Diren. 'We need to get food.'

'I'll do it,' said Jade.

Diren looked sceptical but agreed.

'We'll need the lanyard,' said Sim. 'Anthony, did you say you had some bags?'

Anthony held out a reusable bag from a supermarket and some dog-poo bags. No wonder he always looked so shattered. Children *and* a dog. Diren used a poo bag to pick up the electrician's lanyard and deposit it into the plastic bag.

The four of them looked resolute and donned the gas masks before heading out of the retiring room.

They were near the heart of the court building, where everything was windowless and labyrinthine. Ten courtrooms on two floors, each with a room for the jury and a separate room for the judge. Walking past the other retiring rooms, Leonie felt like she was seeing into multiple universes, where alternate versions of the twelve of them sat deliberating. What would have happened if she'd been on a different jury? What if someone had been ill or her name hadn't been on the ballot? Each passing courtroom felt like a door into another timeline, where she could slip in and undo the crime she'd committed. Where she put up her hand and admitted to knowing the deceased, or where she was simply selected for a different jury that day. Maybe she could have been deciding whether someone was guilty of a boring crime, like benefit fraud or a low-level assault.

She kept looking behind her. Something about wearing the mask, having her peripheral vision cut off, made her feel as though there was always something behind her. It wasn't possible to trust her senses because all she could hear inside the mask was her pulse and her breath.

Since the start of this trial, she'd been dogged by a feeling of guilt. Every time she made eye contact with the judge, or a police officer looked her way, or someone said her name as though to ask a question, she thought she'd been found out. There were so many opportunities for people to recognize her, but it seemed as though she'd been lucky. And she was so close to the end, within touching distance of the finish line.

She wasn't religious, but since the chemical attack had been announced, she'd had this strange sense that something was punishing her, some higher power. Perhaps it was just the universe setting her straight, stopping her from committing a moral transgression as grave as sitting on the jury in the trial of the man accused of murdering her husband.

'Stop,' said Diren, voice muffled.

They did.

'Do you hear that?' he asked.

Leonie stopped, held her breath.

An eerie sound reached their ears. It was a woman singing with a hauntingly beautiful voice.

> It's time we said our goodbyes
> Why is it always fight or flight?
> The adrenaline has worn o-o-off
> I want to be alone this time…

Leonie could just about discern guitars thrumming in the background of the track. The sound was coming from a nearby corridor, but from which direction, it was difficult to tell.

After a couple of bars, the sound cut out. The earworm stayed in her mind, wriggling around.

'What was that?' asked Sim.

'Acid Rain,' said Jade, pointing to the ☔ symbol on her hoodie. 'It's the first single off the album. It's called "Adrenaline".'

'I know the song,' said Sim. 'But where's it coming from?'

To Leonie, it sounded like it was being played on a phone. 'Someone's ringtone?' she suggested.

'No one has songs as ringtones any more,' said Jade. 'It's not 2006.'

Leonie felt the comment like a gut punch. She could have dealt with ageing if it wasn't coupled with becoming so out of touch.

The singing had creeped Leonie out. She was struggling to breathe, the mask sapping the oxygen from her lungs.

'Adrenaline,' said Diren. 'That's…'

'An unlikely coincidence,' agreed Sim. 'What do we do now?'

'We keep going. If there's someone else in the building, we need to get to the food first before it's all gone.'

They were not far from the swipe-access door which would take them out onto the vast mezzanine waiting area.

Diren held the pass in the plastic shopping bag and swiped them through.

They skirted around the electrician's body before descending the stairs to the atrium. All the while, Leonie kept looking over her shoulder, worried that the person who had played the music was lying in wait for them. Or perhaps they were just watching.

When they arrived at the canteen, Leonie surveyed the scene. Circular tables were littered with half-eaten pastries. Cups of tea and coffee had been left to go cold. A couple of spindly-legged chairs lay toppled on the floor.

Leonie felt like a detective, assembling the clues to construct what had happened here. When people were told about the attack they probably froze, just as the jurors had done. Maybe some of them tried to finish their drinks. Others probably ran. Many would have followed, not knowing why. Some of them might have thought to take their pastries with them. For others, food would have been the last thing on their mind.

By the wall was a fridge. They salvaged what was left inside, stuffing any remaining sandwiches, drinks, or yoghurt pots into their pockets. Next, they approached the hot-food serving area, where metal vats were filled with overcooked bacon, eggs, and congealed baked beans.

Behind the serving counter was a large kitchen. Sim found a stash of blue-and-yellow Ikea bags underneath one of the work surfaces. They began loading what they could into them. Food that couldn't be contaminated was given the highest priority: anything sealed or tinned.

They left the kitchen, each with large bags slung over their shoulders. The rustling of the material and the jangling of the tins worried her. The sound would give away their location.

They made slow progress along the corridors, and Leonie's shoulders felt like they might snap with the weight.

She focused on the floor and started counting steps ten at a time.

Just ten more steps, she told herself. Then, once she'd managed the first set, it became easier to believe she could do the next ten and so on.

Finally, they turned the corner to go back towards the retiring room.

Sim was the first to go still.

Leonie looked around to see what had made him stop.

Above them, a body was hanging from the ceiling.

The usher's body. Susan's.

FOUR DAYS BEFORE

Quinn was already sitting in the witness box when they took their seats. He seemed more dangerous today. It was his first time out of the dock.

Leonie knew that he wasn't a physical threat. He was more like a virus, and words were his vectors. In the dock, he couldn't speak. In the witness box, speaking was sort of the point.

Quinn gave his oath on the Bible, looking every bit the choirboy. She hoped the other jurors could see through it.

Leonie studied Quinn. His frame was slight and he had small, delicate hands which you could quite easily imagine being dexterous. His head was coated with an even grey stubble, while overgrown facial hair made him look unkempt. During the course of the trial, they'd seen pictures of him in his nursing uniform, when he had been clean shaven and impeccably neat. Maybe the beard was all part of the act; presenting himself as a broken man, framed for crimes he didn't commit, in the hope the jury would take pity on him.

Leonie was sure she'd seen him at the hospital. When she'd visited Hamish, she hadn't been paying too much attention to the staff, but she thought she remembered Quinn. She hadn't seen him for what he really was. And he clearly hadn't paid much attention to her, because on the day she took her seat in the jury box, he raised no objection.

Sometimes, Leonie got it into her head that Quinn was watching her. And not just because she was one of the twelve. She sensed his eyes boring into her. Perhaps he had an inkling that he'd seen her before but couldn't think where. That was part of working in a hospital, coming across so many different relatives and names and faces. But would she have stayed in his mind? The wife of the man he intended to kill? Was he even planning to kill Hamish when she visited him? Perhaps his murders were spontaneous acts.

Looking at Quinn in the witness box, it was as clear as day what he was.

The way he held the Bible annoyed her. His thin wrists seemed as though they were buckling under its weight.

It's all an act.

She knew that—didn't need to remind herself—but somehow she needed that message to pass from her brain to the rest of the jury by osmosis.

Quinn took the oath. There was a coyness to his voice which would have been endearing had it belonged to anyone else. Part of his appeal was that he wasn't conventionally charming. Some people possessed an ineffable quality that made you want to be their friend. Whatever it was, Quinn had it.

Mr Ferguson KC stood up, hands resting on the lectern.

'Please can you give your full name?'

'Michael James Quinn.' His voice was sibilant, and his vowels drawn out in a way that was almost childish.

'When did you qualify as a nurse, Mr Quinn?'

'Two years, three months…' Quinn pretended to search for the number, 'three days ago.'

Ferguson asked, 'Have you ever tried to harm a patient?'

Quinn put on a decent show of being taken aback. He'd sat through nine weeks of evidence dedicated to proving that he'd done this on multiple occasions, so this performance surely wouldn't wash.

'Of course I haven't,' said Quinn, doing such a believable impression of bewilderment that it was indistinguishable from the real thing.

Leonie felt that this was the central problem with the task they'd been given. Of course, jurors were able to bring their worldly experience to bear when it came to determining whether normal people were lying; most people were terrible liars, but what happened when you came up against someone who was a good actor? Where was the safeguard for psychopathy?

'Have you ever been accused of murder before?'

'Of course not. The allegations are totally malicious.'

'Did you administer adrenaline to any of the following patients: Zane Chan, who died on the third of December of the previous year?'

'No.'

'Gail Bridges, who died fourth of January last year?'

'No.'

'Andrew Chapman who died thirteenth of January?'

'No.'

'Hamish Ryan, fifth of August?'

'No!' Quinn lost his temper slightly but recovered quickly. 'None whatsoever.' His voice was calmer now. 'That wouldn't be my job, that would be for the resus team.'

'Just to be clear, did you ever inject any of these patients with adrenaline?'

Quinn took a moment, which lasted for exactly the amount of time it took for his eyes to well up. 'No.' His voice broke in the middle of the syllable. It was a frighteningly quick turna-round of emotional state from anger to sadness.

'Let's go back to the fifth of August last year. It's half eight in the evening. What shift were you working?'

'I was doing nights. Seven to seven.'

'And were you caring for Hamish Ryan?'

Leonie felt an involuntary clench in her stomach at the word 'caring'.

'I was. He was on my ward.'

'What happened at a quarter to midnight?'

'I noticed that the patient was going into cardiac arrest, so I pulled the alarm—'

'A little slower, please, Mr Quinn.'

'Sorry,' said Quinn, giving the judge a bashful smile. 'I'm just nervous.'

'Keep things nice and steady,' said Ferguson in a sickly voice, which was pitched to put Quinn at ease, as though he was the victim in all this.

'So, I pulled the alarm by the side of his bed, which is what you do when a patient arrests. It notifies other staff. I obviously shouted for help as well, while I started on chest compressions.'

'Who was the first to arrive?'

'Well, this was weird, see, because Dr Bleasdale was there really quickly.'

Leonie saw Khan stop writing for a second to stare at Quinn, then she renewed her scribbling with extra fervour. Leonie felt a thrill of anticipation. She must have spotted something.

'Why is that weird?'

At this, Quinn's voice became gossipy. 'I don't know why she was the first one there. Doctors don't usually hang around on the ward, especially at night. But she was there quicker than anyone.'

'What happened?'

'She told me to step away. She was behaving very out of character.'

'What was unusual about her manner?'

'She was ordering people about. Telling me to back off. Why would she do that? Surely it wasn't in the patient's interests. When someone's in cardiac arrest, it's all hands on deck.'

'So, what did you do while your hands weren't on deck?'

'What could I do? I just had to stand and watch. Then straight after the resus team came, Dr Bleasdale started making all sorts of accusations about me.' Quinn took a tissue from the box in front of him and started dabbing at his eyes. 'And I didn't know I'd done anything wrong, and then the police…' Quinn waved a hand and resumed crying into his sodden tissue.

'Do we need a break, Mr Ferguson?' asked the judge.

For fuck's sake, thought Leonie. Quinn was the one being treated like the victim. Not Hamish. Who was standing up for Hamish?

'No, no, I'm all right,' said Quinn, dabbing at his eyes with the sleeves of his suit jacket. 'Carry on.'

'We're going to move onto the other three patients now. Zane Chan, Gail Bridges and Andrew Chapman. Did you ever administer adrenaline to any of those patients?'

'No!' said Quinn, apparently annoyed that it was being suggested again. As a little adjunct he added, 'And they don't have a shred of evidence to pretend that I did, either.'

That was cocky, and not in line with his previous demeanour. *It's boring for him to play it safe*, thought Leonie. He needed to be impulsive, to live life on the edge.

'You were on shift when they died, though?'

'Yes.'

'Do you have anything to say about that?'

'Well, I know this is difficult for people to hear, but patients die in hospital. It's sad but true.'

Leonie wondered if the others would see the lack of empathy in this response.

'How do you think they died?'

'Whatever was recorded at the time. It's only now everyone's decided to backtrack and rewrite history, rewrite medical records…' Quinn spoke as though falsifying medical records was more scandalous than what he'd been accused of.

'Did you murder any of the four deceased?'

'No!'

'Thank you, no further questions.'

Leonie was shocked by how short that had been. Was that really all he had to say for himself? She held her breath as Khan rose to her feet.

'Mr Quinn, you've been sat in this courtroom for many weeks now. You've heard all the evidence…' It seemed like a weak opener. Why was she stating the obvious? 'I'm giving you the opportunity to be honest. Is there anything you told the jury which you might have got wrong?'

Quinn's face was blank, clearly doing quick calculations behind that impassive face. 'No, I don't think so.'

'Are you sure about that?'

'Well, you obviously think there is, so what is it?'

'I'm asking you, Mr Quinn.'

'I've told the truth to the best of my knowledge. As far as I'm aware.'

That was instructive. He left open the potential for there being something about which he was mistaken, should it come back to bite him.

Khan looked down at her notepad. 'You've deliberately misled this jury, haven't you, Mr Quinn? You've just said that Dr Bleasdale was the first person at Hamish Ryan's bedside after you pulled the alarm. Do you remember saying that a moment ago?'

'Yes,' said Quinn, tight-lipped. He knew she had something, he just didn't know what.

'That's not what you said when you were interviewed by the police, was it?'

'How am I supposed to remember that? I was treated dreadfully by the police. No sleep, barely any food. It was awful. No one would remember anything that they said if they were subjected to what I was.'

'I take it you accept that you didn't tell the police that Dr Bleasdale was there first? You told a different story. Importantly, you said Dr Bleasdale arrived *after* the resus team.'

Leonie hoped that Khan would bring up what was said in the police interview because seeing it in black and white would be more convincing. It would prove that Quinn was lying.

'All right, maybe I did say that to the police,' said Quinn.

'Well, which is it then, Mr Quinn? Which version of events is the truth, and which version is the lie?'

'That's not fair.'

'It's a straightforward question. Were you lying to the police or were you lying to the jury?'

'Neither.'

'We'd like to know the truth. Did she get there before or after the resus team arrived?'

'Before.'

'Why did you lie to the police about that?'

'I wasn't lying, just confused.'

'It's quite an important point, isn't it? When Dr Bleasdale got there?'

'I don't see how,' said Quinn, brushing off the question.

Leonie recalled the song and dance he'd made of this point earlier. He'd been suggesting that there was something suspicious about Dr Bleasdale arriving first and now it had come back to bite him; he was pretending that it was of no consequence.

'If Dr Bleasdale arrived before the resus team, she'd have been able to take a sample of blood before he was given a shot of adrenaline. You said Dr Bleasdale got there first because you want to heap suspicion on her.'

'No, I don't.'

'When you were giving evidence earlier, you saw an opportunity to make everyone mistrustful of Dr Bleasdale and you took it, forgetting it's a different story from what you told the police.'

'Not at all, I just can't remember—'

'You can't remember?' asked Khan. 'When was your memory of the events of August fifth fresher? When you spoke to the police mere hours after Hamish Ryan died, or now, over a year later?'

'It's not as simple as that,' said Quinn. 'Just because the police interview was closer to the events doesn't mean my memory of them would be better.'

'Think about that answer, Mr Quinn. Memories fade with time, don't they? Everyone knows that. Please don't insult the intelligence of the jurors. It's more likely isn't it, that what you told the police was the truth, and what you told the jury today was a lie?'

'No,' said Quinn.

Khan put an end to that line of questioning, but Leonie's heart was still thrumming with excitement. Surely the others would see through his lies now.

'Okay then, Mr Quinn, I want to turn to your relationships with colleagues. Did you have any friends at work?'

Quinn shrugged. 'The relationships were professional. A mixture of happy times, stressed times…' Now he was off the topic of truth and lies, Quinn had returned to his previous chatty demeanour.

'What about people who you could rely on?'

'I tended to rely on myself.'

'What about Shelley Roberts?'

'What about her?'

Khan paused. Leonie and the others had heard evidence about Nurse Roberts's suicide, but until now Leonie hadn't been able to understand its significance.

'Nurse Roberts took her own life on the fifteenth of January. The day after the third victim died.'

Quinn's voice stayed measured. 'It was a tragedy.'

'Here are some of the text messages you sent to Nurse Roberts before her death.' Ms Khan placed one piece of paper after another down on the bench in front of her. She gave the judge and jury the page references and had the documents handed up to Quinn by Tom the usher.

Leonie, following Khan's page references, read the first of the messages.

QUINN: *I saw you drop that needle on the floor.*

ROBERTS: *What?*

QUINN: *I notice things. You didn't sanitize it—you just stuck it straight into that man's arm.*

ROBERTS: *You're confusing me with someone else.*

QUINN: *Haha, I know it was you. You know it too. It's tough coming to real nursing after being at the hospice, but my concern is for the patients.*

'That was on the second of December. Let's look at the messages from the nineteenth.'

QUINN: *Do you want me to help show you how to do a skin-prick test?*
ROBERTS: *Thanks—I was just flustered today.*
QUINN: *Yeah, well, it's not fair on the patients, is it.*
ROBERTS: *Please don't tell anyone.*
QUINN: *I won't. I know you can be a good nurse, you've just got to learn not to let your nerves get the better of you.*
ROBERTS: *I want that too.*

'What do you have to say about those, Mr Quinn?'

'I don't see anything there other than my concern for the patients.'

'Did you bully her?'

'I maintained standards, that's all.'

'I'm going to read out something that one of your colleagues heard you say to her. "If I was your patient, I'd ask for someone else too." That was on a day when a patient's family had asked for another nurse on the basis of Nurse Roberts's ethnicity, is that right?'

'I wasn't to know that,' said Quinn.

'You continued to be friendly with Nurse Roberts after this incident?'

'In a professional way, yes.'

'Did you hold any of her mistakes against her?'

'I don't know what you're implying.'

The judge interrupted, 'Yes, Ms Khan, tread carefully, please.'

Khan nodded to acknowledge the judge's request. Quinn smiled smugly.

'Was Nurse Roberts someone you relied upon?' asked Khan.

'God, no. She wasn't the best by a long shot.'

'After she died, the police were unable to find any evidence of suspicious cardiac arrests between the fourteenth of January and the fifth of August.'

Quinn shrugged. 'Maybe *she* was responsible for the first three.'

Khan's face remained neutral. 'Let's look at one last message. This one is from the thirteenth of January.'

QUINN: *How are you, sweets?*

ROBERTS: *I hate this job. I hate myself for fucking up the whole time.*

QUINN: *Do something else, then.*

ROBERTS: *Aren't you supposed to say something supportive like "hang in there"?*

QUINN: *I would if it was worth it.*

ROBERTS: *Lol*

QUINN: *It's not funny, Shel*

QUINN: *Patients are dying*

QUINN: *That's on you*

Khan let silence settle over the courtroom before she asked her next question. 'Do you accept having played a part in her death?'

Ferguson jumped to his feet. 'My Lord! I've let this questioning go on for quite long enough, but it seems to me that this is highly irrelevant. The accused is standing trial for four murders, not this nurse's suicide.'

Khan turned to face the judge. 'It's directly relevant, My Lord, to his modus operandi, his motives, his desire to ki—'

'Right!' shouted the judge. 'Jury out.'

Leonie and her fellow jurors were sent away with the usher. The jurors all knew it would be hours before they'd return to the courtroom, while the judge and barristers argued about Khan's line of questioning.

Leonie would be furious if Khan wasn't allowed to continue down that path. Quinn had shown no remorse for that poor nurse. He'd continued to criticize her and make out as though he was some sort of saint who only cared about the patients. Even if Khan wasn't allowed to carry on questioning Quinn about Nurse Roberts's suicide, Leonie would highlight that evidence during their conversations in the retiring room.

'I can't get a read on Quinn,' said Sim while they were making themselves tea and coffee ten minutes later.

'I think he's a creep,' said Leonie.

'Oh, definitely. I mean I can't get a read on his sexuality. He has kinda camp mannerisms, but I don't know… maybe my gaydar is off.'

They took their usual seats.

Rob was holding court. 'I don't see how he can be blamed for that other nurse's weakness.'

'You haven't got a clue what you're talking about,' said Diren.

Leonie was momentarily taken aback. Diren wasn't usually sympathetic to people talking about mental health problems.

'What was that?' asked Rob.

'You haven't got a fucking clue,' muttered Diren.

'Coward's way out,' said Rob.

Diren went as though to lunge for Rob, but Anthony was standing nearby and grabbed hold of Diren's shoulders. Diren seemed to come back to himself, but pointed aggressively in Rob's direction. 'Don't speak about things you don't know about.'

'That woman killed herself because of her problems. If she couldn't take the criticism, she had no business being a nurse.'

Leonie cringed. 'Jesus.'

Rob rounded on her. 'Come on, then. What's your take? We all know you'll have something to say.'

Leonie was stumped for a second. It was the last thing she wanted, to be known as someone who always had an opinion on the trial. Yet even someone as emotionally obtuse as Rob had spotted her eagerness to have her voice heard. However, Rob had asked her for her opinion, so she was sure as hell going to give it.

'I think he systematically bullied her, manipulated her, and put her down until she was a shell of her former self. Then when she was at her lowest, he persuaded her to help him kill patients. Look at the first three murders. They all happen between December and January. Then the fourth murder happens in August. Why the gap? It must be because he lost his accomplice. Then, lo and behold, he gets caught on the fourth murder, when she's no longer around. It's like he couldn't help himself and needed to take the risk.'

'Sounds too much like psychobabble for my liking,' said Wynona.

Leonie clenched her jaw, holding back a retort.

'It makes sense,' said Tanbir. 'The gap ties in perfectly with Roberts's suicide. And those messages spoke for themselves.'

'But she already had *issues*,' said Rob.

Diren shook his head and looked as though he was lumbering up to shout or lunge at him again.

'Okay, so what if she was more prone to feeling depressed?' said Tanbir. 'Quinn knew what buttons to press.'

At the end of the discussion, the jury were evenly split. All of Rob's acolytes agreed that it was unfair to pin a suicide on Quinn, while the rest of them thought it was the clearest evidence yet that Quinn was responsible for murdering his four patients. It gave him a motive: he was someone who liked to exercise influence over someone else's mortality.

They stared at the body.

The petechiae around the eyes, the blue lips.

'Fuck, fuck, fuck,' said Sim.

Diren turned away, looking as though he was about to be sick.

Leonie continued to stare. She felt a wrenching sensation. Almost like she was in a lift that was in free fall. She became unusually aware of her body but at the same time disconnected from it. Rubbing the tips of her fingers, she felt the ridges of her fingerprints like never before, yet she was outside of herself somehow, like she was watching all of this as a fly on the wall. It was the acute shock known only to those who are confronted with the unnatural death of someone they weren't expecting to die. At the same time as dealing with the shock of seeing Susan's body, she felt fearful. The jurors were institutionalized by this point, programmed to do as the court staff said. Without Tom or Susan, it felt as though the adults had gone home, leaving the children without appropriate supervision.

They couldn't just leave her there.

'We need to get her down,' she said.

'Fuck that,' said Sim. 'I don't want to touch a dead body.'

Leonie stared at him, mildly disgusted by his indifference to the woman who'd tried to keep them safe.

Meanwhile, Diren had his hand to the wall, bending over as though about to vomit.

'Are you okay?'

'Fine,' he said, though he clearly wasn't. His olive skin had turned a nasty shade of grey.

'Do you agree we should…?'

Diren nodded. 'Yes. But I can't.'

'It would be more respectful,' agreed Jade.

'Not out of respect, you fuckwit,' said Diren spitefully. 'She's staff, isn't she? She might have keys or a walkie-talkie or something else useful on her.'

'Brilliant,' said Sim, sounding a little hysterical. 'So we're not only going to touch the body, we're going to rob it?'

'Diren's right,' cut in Jade. 'We need to strip the body for anything useful.'

Leonie gulped and closed her eyes, feeling nausea rise up from her solar plexus. 'I'll do it.'

She felt she had no choice. It would be repulsive to leave her hanging there.

Leonie picked up the chair that Susan had kicked from under herself and used it to reach the curtain cord which had doubled as a ligature.

'Help,' she said curtly to the other three. Jade and Sim took a reluctant step forward but were otherwise no use.

She continued to work away at untying the cord.

Without warning, Susan's body sank into Leonie's arms, causing her to buckle under the weight. Jade came over to help put Susan down on the chair. The body was disconcertingly warm. Susan would not stay upright, so they allowed her to fall to the floor. Leonie cringed at the undignified way they were handling this.

She set about searching Susan's pockets. There was indeed another security pass, a mobile phone with a flat battery, and various other bits of detritus. She took the important stuff and discarded the rest.

She looked down at Susan and felt sick. None of it felt real.

She couldn't accept that she was really dead. And if she was, how could they just leave her here like this? She deserved something more dignified than being abandoned in the middle of a corridor.

'Shall we move her?' asked Leonie. 'Just out of the way?'

'It's not going to make the situation any better,' said Diren. 'I've got to get out of this mask.'

'I don't think we can just leave her here. It would be awful if one of the others finds her like we did. Just give me two minutes.'

Leonie asked Sim to open the nearest door. It was another retiring room, just like theirs. She and Jade dragged Susan's body inside. Jade left but Leonie stayed, staring at Susan, still processing what she was seeing. After taking time to close Susan's eyes, Leonie shut the door.

They arrived in the retiring room soon after. Leonie found immense relief in removing her mask, only to be greeted by the stuffy air and tense atmosphere.

The other jurors started rummaging in the food bags before they could even put them down. Diren pleaded with them to ration themselves.

Leonie didn't feel like eating. The image of Susan haunted her. It had nestled in the back of her head, voyeuristically watching over her unfiltered thoughts. She looked to Sim for comfort.

'What the hell just happened?'

He hugged her.

'Don't be so dramatic,' said Lucas as he plucked three packets of crisps from the nearest bag.

Chewbacca glared back at her from the top of Lucas's forearm, positioned between Princess Leia and Han Solo. Anger rose up, the urge to shout at Lucas overwhelming.

Diren took two bags of crisps out of Lucas's hands and placed them back in the bag. 'Don't be so greedy.'

Lucas skulked away.

The lazy prick had no business saying anything to her about being dramatic. He had no idea what she'd seen.

A conspiracy of silence between the four of them who'd found the body had formed. Whether it was out of shame for what they'd done, or because they didn't want to induce hysteria in the other jurors was unclear to Leonie, but she sensed that they felt as she did and didn't want the others to know about Susan.

'Come on,' said Sim. 'You need some food. Get some before it's all gone.'

'You go first.'

It took her some time to gather herself, but after a few moments, the nausea subsided. She took a tin of sweetcorn and walked over to where Sim was sitting. He was on the floor, back to the wall which had the coat stand in one corner and the door in the other. They instinctively felt the need to separate themselves from the others. Leonie noticed that Jade had done the same and was sitting against the adjacent wall.

Sim peeled back the ring-pull on a tin of tuna and popped open the jar of mayonnaise. Leonie did the same with her sweetcorn. Together they mixed the ingredients in one of the empty coffee cups and put the mix on crackers, sitting in companionable silence while they ate. On any normal day it would have been a pretty grim lunch, but Leonie wasn't in a position to be picky.

When they finished eating, she looked to Sim. 'I don't know where to begin with processing what just happened.'

'That music,' was all he said. Then, after a long pause, 'Who was playing Acid Rain?' He glanced up to the windows.

They were still covered with bin liners. The whirring of the helicopters overhead was still there, a constant drone like a headache at the base of their skulls. 'Maybe they know about me and Amir.'

How could he be so self-centred? The fact it was an Acid Rain song seemed incidental as far as she was concerned. More worrying was the fact that the song title was a reference to the murder weapon. Whoever was playing it was doing so with the intention of intimidating the jurors.

She could think of only one person who would do such a thing.

Quinn was brazen, impulsive, and too clever for his own good. They only had Susan's word for it that he was still in his cell.

Leonie was about to share her musings with Sim, but he spoke first.

'I don't trust anyone here,' he said, looking around at the other jurors. 'Someone here stole from me.'

'Yeah, it's pretty screwed up,' agreed Leonie.

Sim sucked on a carton of apple juice pensively. 'And then Susan…' He shivered. 'What the hell? Why would she do that?'

'I don't know—I haven't checked my phone since we got back. I'll see if there's any news that might have—you know, pushed her over the edge.'

'Maybe she's related to one of the people killed in the attack. Who knows how many people are dead? It could have been her kid or something.'

Leonie remembered how she felt on hearing about what had happened to Hamish. Police officers with dour expressions. 'I'm sorry to tell you that…'

Had she even heard the rest of the sentence?

Everything had been knocked from her so that she was an empty frame, no strength in her legs to carry her weight. The police officers had moved her into the living room. All she remembered was Ollie on her lap as police officers trampled through their clean house wearing outdoor shoes. She could barely register what she was being told. But she understood how Susan might have felt if she had received the worst news.

And yet somehow she knew Susan wouldn't have taken her own life. She couldn't communicate to the others how or why she knew that, but something about the scene wasn't right.

'Listen, Sim. I've got some doubts.'

His eyebrows lifted, not sceptically as others might, but curiously. It was that which had endeared her to Sim from the beginning. He was open to gossip, to thoughts, to jokes. He was never a source of reproach, only ever encouragement.

'Doubts about…?'

'It's like you said. Why *now*? Why would she take her life now?'

'Just playing devil's advocate. If someone is suicidal, they're not going to be logical.'

'She wasn't suicidal,' said Leonie. 'I'm sorry, I know there are loads of people who don't appear suicidal but go on to take their own lives, but she definitely wasn't.' She paused. 'I could just tell.'

'Instinct is powerful,' said Sim, 'but it's not really evidence.'

'Okay, well, why would she hang herself? She could just walk outside and kill herself just as easily. And say she wanted to take her own life, why would she do it in a place where we'd find her? She knew that was the route back to the retiring room from the canteen. She wasn't like that. All she's done this morning is make sure we're okay, ensure we're protected from what's going on outside. She'd have taken herself off somewhere quiet and private.'

'I think that's a good point,' said Sim.

'What if someone did it to her?' asked Leonie. 'Someone could have already strangled her and then staged it to make it look as though she'd done it.'

'Why—'

Diren approached them. 'Listen, I've been thinking. You know we searched the pockets?'

Leonie nodded.

He leaned in, making sure no one else could overhear. 'There was something missing.'

Leonie frowned, remembering the items they'd found in Susan's pockets. What wasn't there which should have been?

'Can't you remember? When we went to Tannoy for Rob and Wynona, she had a skeleton key that she used to get into the security cabin.'

Leonie did remember. The memory of Susan taking the key from her belt and letting herself into the glass box by the entrance was fresh, undisturbed by repeated recollection and untarnished by the passage of time.

'So, what does that mean?' asked Leonie, although a few explanations had already started to blossom in her own mind.

'Maybe she took her own life and someone searched the body afterwards, but if that's the case, they did so without lowering her down.'

'Tricky.'

'But not impossible. They just had to stand on the chair and root around in her pockets. Put the chair back how it was once finished.'

Leonie felt another surge of nausea as she pictured Susan's body swinging. The taste of tuna mayo and sweetcorn repeated in the back of her throat.

'Or someone took the keys before she died,' continued Diren.

'And killed her for them?'

Diren spread his hands.

'I think it was staged, too,' said Leonie. 'It's difficult for me to explain why, but the way the chair was positioned, her body hanging in the middle of the corridor. Right where she knew we'd walk—'

'People aren't themselves when they're suicidal,' said Diren, a little too quickly.

'I know that,' said Leonie.

'I'm just saying, let's stick to the facts, not clichés about how people might behave when thinking of taking their own life.'

'Noted.'

'Why didn't the person who took the skeleton key take the security pass as well?' asked Jade.

'They must already have a pass,' said Sim.

'So, a member of staff,' opined Diren.

Leonie thought back to her earlier theory. There was already a murderer in the building. He must have managed to get himself free somehow.

'Maybe,' she said. 'Or someone who was able to persuade a member of staff to give them a pass before it all kicked off.'

The others mulled this over.

'I think we should tell the others what happened to Susan,' said Leonie.

Diren shook his head. 'They'd freak out.'

'I'd want to know if I was one of them. Particularly now we know that the keys have been taken.'

'What are you lot whispering about?' asked Wynona, who was clearly trying to eavesdrop.

Leonie looked at Diren pointedly.

'What's the secret?' she asked. 'I heard you say something about Susan?'

More people had turned towards their corner of the room now, were listening in.

Leonie took a deep breath. 'Look, this will be a bit of a shock.' She knew there was no way to cushion the blow. 'But, we, er, came across Susan—Susan's body—on our way back from the canteen… and… And it looked like she'd taken her own life.'

This was met with stunned silence.

'That makes no sense,' said Rob. 'We'll be out of this mess soon enough.'

Diren began, 'People don't think rationally—'

'Maybe not,' cut in Lucas. He rearranged his beanie nervously. 'But maybe she knew something we don't.'

'She knew as much as us,' said Diren, exasperated.

'She still works—er—worked for the government, even if just as an usher. You never know what these people are told.'

Leonie rolled her eyes. '"These people." She wasn't MI5.'

'NATO are not going to take this lying down,' he replied forcefully. 'I reckon nukes are going to start flying soon.'

Even though this was an entirely baseless assumption, the effect it had on the others was instant.

'Lucas, seriously,' said Leonie firmly. 'Stop talking like that. It won't do anyone any good.'

'I notice you're not saying it's untrue.'

'I'm saying that it's a totally unfounded—'

He interrupted her. 'It's not. We just got attacked in a serious way. This is exactly what the alliance is for. If they're willing to do this to us, they're willing to do anything. First we had the biological weapon—'

'What do you mean? What biological weapon?'

'Er, the pandemic?'

'Don't be ridiculous.'

'Why did the WHO try to shut down the lab-leak story, then?'

'Mate, listen,' said Diren, placating him. 'I thought we massively overreacted to the pandemic, but you're taking it a bit far.'

'I'm just saying. They started with biological and now they're on chemical weapons—'

'A lab leak and a biological weapon are not the same thing,' said Tanbir. 'The former is an accident, the latter is a direct attack.'

'Sure,' said Lucas. '"Accidental."'

'The pandemic started in China. They're not the ones who've done this,' said Leonie.

'That's what they want you to think.'

'"They"? Who the hell are "they"? Can you hear yourself?'

'It's not a conspiracy theory if it's true.'

Leonie had had enough of this conversation.

Lucas's clinching remark: 'I think it'll go nuclear next. Maybe Susan was anticipating that.'

The doomscrolling recommenced. The jurors sought cast-iron confirmation that the conflict wasn't about to go nuclear. As always, the internet was ambivalent.

'The Prime Minister has made another announcement,' said Wynona, who started playing it loudly on her phone.

The others watched it on silent, the Prime Minister's lips moving out of sync with the audio blaring from Wynona's phone.

'My message to the people inside the perimeter is simple: do not go outside—'

'It's all about control,' said Lucas. People shushed him.

'You might think it's safe, but it isn't. The chemical used in the attack is highly transferable and does not degrade for thousands of years. What will commence now is one of the biggest clean-up jobs the British Army has ever had to undertake. Do not make their task any more difficult by going outside and exposing yourself to this nerve agent. Keep yourself and your families safe. Stay inside.'

'Get a new slogan already,' mumbled Lucas.

'Shut up!' shouted Rob.

'…MI5 confirmed to me this morning the identity of the people they suspect were responsible for the attack. I want to reassure members of the public that I will not rest until those people are brought to justice.'

A press conference followed the speech. The first reporter asked for confirmation as to which country had been responsible for the chemical attack. The Prime Minister replied that the security services were still carrying out investigations and hadn't reached a firm conclusion as yet.

'What will the UK do in response?' asked one of the journalists.

'We're considering our options.'

'Do those options include a military response?'

'Of course. We will respond with force.'

'With force? That suggests you will use weapons of mass destruction in response. Can you confirm that?'

'I'm not confirming anything about our military strategy right now. We have to consider who might be listening.'

One of the Prime Minister's aides walked onto the screen to whisper into his ear and the press conference was concluded shortly after.

'There you go,' said Lucas. 'I told you. This is escalating.'

'That idiot has always been a loose cannon,' said Leonie. 'Hence why we're in this mess.'

'That's not fair,' said Rob. 'We've got to respond with force or else they'll just do it again but worse.'

Three guesses as to who you voted for, thought Leonie.

'He's a messy-haired idiot,' said Charlie. 'That's why the press conference was cut short. They should never have let him go off script…'

The divide reopened with the younger generation railing against those who had voted in their own self-interest, while the older generation regarded the youth as a bunch of naive idealists who needed to grow up and get a reality check.

The idea this disparate group of people could ever reach a unanimous verdict seemed further away than ever.

Leonie spotted Sim walking towards the rear entrance of the court as she got off the bus.

'Hey.' He enveloped her in a hug.

'All okay?' she asked.

He was unnervingly happy for someone who was supposed to have broken up with their boyfriend. 'I'm *amazing*.'

Leonie's heart sank. There was only one person who made Sim act like this.

They crossed the threshold into the court building and started taking objects out of their pockets to place in the plastic security trays.

'Guess who got in touch last night?' Sim waggled his phone at her before placing it in the tray along with his belt.

She didn't want to play this game. 'Amir,' she said, deadpan.

'Right in one. He's going to message me later, tell me what fancy restaurant we're going to this evening.'

Much though she liked Sim, she found him insufferable in the hours before he was due to have sex.

Leonie wanted to ask if this was a good idea but decided to stay close-lipped. What was the point? They'd been through this time and time again.

The security guard gestured for Leonie to step through the metal detector, while Sim was busy putting all of his items into a grey tray. Once the security guard had passed the plastic wand over her outstretched limbs, she approached the table to claim her recently searched bag.

In the tray next to hers sat Sim's phone. A rash idea came

over her. She could take it and Sim would never get Amir's text. The affair would be at an end, and Sim might be able to get over him finally.

She noticed Viv come in through the rear entrance, in her usual daydream state. Sim was busy being given the plastic-wand treatment. The security guards were guffawing at Sim's joke. No one was looking.

She had less than a second. Without giving it proper thought, she swiped the phone and shoved it into her bag.

As she waited for Sim to collect his things, she thought, *What have I just done?*

She'd never stolen before. Not even when she was a teenager and her friends saw shoplifting as a mixture of cool and fair game.

Now was her chance to undo the wrong she'd committed. Sim would surely realize he hadn't picked up his phone. The moment he patted down his pockets to look for it, she would make a show of looking in her bag, say she'd picked it up by accident. But Sim didn't notice his phone was gone as he collected his belongings. He was too busy gabbling on about Amir and what they were going to do later. He wasn't paying attention.

As they walked up the stairs, Sim barely drew breath, recounting all of the romantic and funny things that he and Amir had ever done.

In her mind, Sim's phone was burning a hole in her bag. She shoved it in her locker and slammed the door, before Sim noticed.

It remained there for another week.

*

It was time for the final witness to be called in the prosecution's nine-week case. After that, Khan would hand over to the defence. Leonie was not looking forward to hearing Quinn's evidence. To cede control to him seemed dangerous. She was also concerned about her own ability to keep her emotions in check. With only a week or so left of the trial, she didn't want to ruin things now by giving away her true feelings towards Quinn.

Yesterday, Khan had asked questions of the Officer in the Case, more commonly known as the OIC. Detective Chief Inspector Juliet Burke's job was to prepare the case for trial.

Khan had begun by playing the video recording of Quinn's police interviews. They were fascinating to watch. The opportunity to hear a serial killer give his side of the story for the first time was compelling, even in these circumstances.

Quinn began the first interview mild-mannered, if aloof. He appeared confident and unconcerned by the questions. Leonie tried to imagine how she'd feel were she to be arrested by the police and accused of murder. She certainly wouldn't have exhibited Quinn's cool, calm manner. He didn't seem intimidated. Instead, he turned the interview on its head and started asking the interviewing officers what they knew about adrenaline, if they understood what it was like to work in a hospital, if they even had a clue what they were going on about. Then, as the interviews multiplied and grew longer, Quinn became more combative, even raising his voice.

By the end, he just kept repeating one phrase over and over, no longer able to sustain the conversational back and forth of the earlier interviews. All he could say was, 'I didn't do it. I didn't kill them.'

When the jurors returned to their retiring room, for some of them—particularly Lucas—it had been evidence of police harassment.

'They were goading him,' he'd said.

Lucas and a couple of others thought that Quinn's relaxed manner in the first interview was that of an innocent man who was unconcerned about being interviewed by the police because he knew he hadn't done anything. When one of the others reminded them of his angry reaction in the later interview, Lucas was able to bat that away. He said that he must have been flustered because he couldn't believe they were still suspicious of him.

Last night Leonie had stayed up until the early hours thinking of ways to persuade the others that Quinn's repetitive answers of 'I didn't kill them' in the second interview was evidence of his guilt. For her, it was evidence of him returning to script, unable to elaborate for fear that he would give himself away.

She was still mulling this over as they took their seats to hear the OIC be cross-examined by Ferguson.

The judge passed an eye over the jury, making sure they were settled. He then turned to Ferguson and gave him a nod.

'DCI Burke, the police were contacted by the hospital after Hamish Ryan's death. Is that right?'

'That was the first death which was brought to our attention, yes.'

'The jury have already heard the reasons why you considered Hamish Ryan's case to be suspicious, so I want to look at how the other three victims were identified. You started off with a pool of sixty deaths?'

'Yes, all deaths by cardiac arrest where there was no clear cause. Our medical experts then went through the autopsies and medical records of the patients and identified twelve which were considered high-priority. These cases were then looked at in greater detail and the experts all agreed on the three other cases which we then charged Mr Quinn for.'

'Thank you for that explanation. There's just one point I want to clarify with you. The sixty deaths you referred to. They were predetermined by a number of parameters, weren't they?'

'That's right.'

It was clear to Leonie that DCI Burke had received advice from other officers, or perhaps she'd learned from her own experience of interviewing criminals that the best way to avoid becoming tangled up in the web spun by the barrister was to give them as little thread as possible. She only gave as much information as was needed to address the question. Leonie thought it was a smart tactic. It was always the embellishments that got people into trouble.

'One of the parameters was whether Michael Quinn was on shift at the time of the death. Is that right?'

'Yes, but—' *Oh no*, thought Leonie. *Not a 'but'*. The OIC began to elaborate. 'We'd already established that Mr Quinn was the main suspect in the death of Hamish Ryan. We were trying to identify if it was a one-off.'

'Let me get this straight. There could have been other deaths in the hospital with the same pathology: cardiac arrest with no clear cause. But they weren't investigated because Nurse Quinn wasn't on shift at the time?'

Leonie could see how persuasive this line of questioning was.

'We suspected that Hamish Ryan had been murdered and the evidence said that Quinn had done it, so we were just looking to establish whether it was a one-off.'

Ferguson picked up a piece of paper and waved it in the air. 'Look at the bundle in front of you, DCI Burke.'

The detective flicked open the lever arch file.

'Turn to page 239. Here you'll see a case where there was a sudden cardiac arrest with no apparent cause. Nurse Quinn was not on shift. Why wasn't this investigated?'

'Look, I've already explained—'

'The prosecution case is that there were too many unexplained deaths when Nurse Quinn was on shift, but here's a death where he wasn't on shift. Why isn't *this* death suspicious?'

'Because we were looking to see if Quinn had used the same methodology more than once.'

'Now we're getting down to it, aren't we DCI Burke? The case I referred you to earlier was not considered to be suspicious merely because Nurse Quinn wasn't on shift. The selection of these cases was predetermined by whether Nurse Quinn had anything to do with them. Deaths where the patients didn't have contact with him are never regarded as suspicious.' Ferguson paused. 'Is it safe to say that you had it in for Quinn?'

'The only thing linking these deaths is Mr Quinn. He was the common denominator for every suspicious death on the ward.'

'Except for this patient.' Ferguson held the piece of paper aloft. 'How did this patient die?'

'It's irrelevant—'

Leonie clenched her teeth. That was a bad answer. It showed that the detective's mind was closed.

'Irrelevant!' said Ferguson, turning to the jury, sharing a knowing look with them.

I'm not on your side, thought Leonie, though she tried to keep her face neutral.

'We'll leave it to the jury to determine whether *they* think it's irrelevant that there was another death you decided not to inform them of.'

Khan stood up to intervene. 'My Lord, that isn't fair. That patient isn't in the jury bundle prepared by the prosecution.'

'I take your point, Ms Khan. Mr Ferguson? Try not to mislead the jury.'

'My deepest apologies, Your Honour, I just don't think it had been drawn to the jury's attention until now… No further questions.'

*

After DCI Burke's evidence, the judge sent them home early.

Leonie and Sim approached the lockers with opposite demeanours. Sim was bursting with excitement, thrilled at the prospect of seeing Amir's messages confirming the time and venue of their date. Meanwhile, a well of dread opened in the pit of Leonie's stomach.

Sim rooted around inside his locker calmly at first, then his movements became more frantic.

'What's the matter?'

'My phone,' he said. 'I haven't got it. Fuck. Did I leave it in the tray?'

Leonie clenched her teeth. 'I can't remember, sorry.' She hated lying, but what else could she do? Now she had the phone, now Amir wasn't able to take Sim on a date that evening, she may as well see it through. When the relationship was over, she'd find a way of returning Sim's phone to him.

'I'll have to ask lost property. Fuck!' He was seriously distressed.

Leonie went through the rigmarole of going with Sim to speak to the security guards at the back entrance, knowing it was all in vain. He asked whether a phone had been handed in. After several walkie-talkie conversations, they established that it hadn't been, but the security guard said they'd make a note that a phone was missing and would keep a look out in case it turned up.

'Best not to bring them to court, to be honest,' he said. 'It's not like you can use them, anyway.'

Sim's jaw tightened. 'Yeah, thanks.' Once out of earshot, he said to Leonie, 'Bit fucking late for that advice. Tosser.'

She nodded in agreement, overcome by a combination of guilt and relief.

'Anyway, we're getting off-topic,' said Sim. 'We found Susan's body, but we don't think she killed herself.'

'What makes you say that?'

'There were suspicious circumstances.'

'Like what?'

Sim looked to Leonie, who recounted how staged it had seemed, the unusual choice of location, and, fundamentally, the fact that the skeleton key had been taken but everything else had been left in her pockets.

'How do you know they were taken?'

'We, er, went through her pockets,' said Leonie, looking at the floor. 'Well, I did.'

Viv looked horrified. 'You did what? Why?'

'Because she was staff. She had access to passes and keys that could be useful.'

Rob cut in. 'So your main basis for saying that she might have been killed is that someone went through her pockets and took something, but you did just that.'

'I couldn't just leave her there. It was only after we let her down that I…'

This was met with a mixture of disgust and disbelief.

'I think we need to be realistic,' said Sim. 'Let's just keep an open mind about it.'

'And also,' said Leonie, 'we know there's an unidentified person roaming around the building. What if that person is Quinn?'

'Even if it is Quinn, what evidence is there to say he murdered Susan?' asked Lucas.

Leonie didn't have an answer to that. Quinn's MO was poison, not strangulation. But there was one similarity: he always took care to cover up the true cause of the deaths.

'You're jumping to conclusions with no proof,' said Lucas.

'What about Shelley Roberts? He bullied and manipulated Shelley Roberts until she took her own life. There's some similarity here.'

'I don't believe he had anything to do with that,' said Rob. 'Like I said before, she was predisposed to that weakness—'

'If you call people who take their own lives weak one more time…' said Diren. 'This coming from the guy who wasn't even brave enough to join us to get food from the canteen.'

'I would have come,' protested Rob. 'I'd only just got back myself.'

'You were scared of whoever is in the building. Admit it, it could have been him.'

'It didn't look like him,' said Rob.

'On your own account, it was impossible to tell.'

'If it's not Quinn,' said Leonie, 'who is it?'

Lucas started counting off options on his fingers. 'Another member of the staff? Surely the usher wasn't the only one who stayed put—'

'She had a name!' said Leonie, her temper rising. She regretted her loss of control instantly, because Lucas sneered at her.

'You're getting too emotional about this. You're not thinking straight.'

Her instinct was to shout back, but she refrained. It was exactly what he wanted. She took a breath and said calmly, 'Susan told us that the others had left. Why would she lie?'

'Why wouldn't she? She clearly wasn't giving us the full story. I never trusted her. She was too keen to keep us inside.'

'Not everything's a conspiracy, you know.'

'Says the woman who thinks the nurse is guilty of crimes he's not even accused of.'

When no one came to Leonie's aid, including Sim, she knew she'd lost the interaction. Still, she pressed on. 'I think we should discuss the case. Let's think about whether or not he's guilty first. Then we know what we're dealing with.'

'Easy,' said Lucas. 'Not guilty.'

'We haven't discussed it.'

'Don't need to. The evidence against him is crap.'

'Maybe now's not the right time to talk about the case,' said Rob.

'When is?' asked Leonie. 'It's not like we can leave. Let's at least do something useful with our time.'

'What's stopping us from leaving?' asked Lucas, asking the question of the whole group. 'The Prime Minister said that we mustn't leave the cordon because it's transferable. He said nothing about it staying in the air.'

The others' interest was piqued.

'Is it still in the air?' asked Rob, a note of hope in his voice.

'Wait a sec,' said Tanbir. He pulled out his phone and spoke into it. 'If a nerve agent is released in a city by being pumped out into the air by an exhaust pipe, how long will it stay in the air for?'

'For an exhaust pipe dispersal, most volatile agents would pose an immediate but short-term airborne hazard, lasting minutes to a few hours, depending on weather and dispersal efficiency. Subsequent contamination risks from deposited residues could persist longer.'

Tanbir looked at the rest of them as he spoke into his phone. 'It's fifteen degrees Celsius, sunny, with five miles per hour wind. I think the closest relative to this nerve agent is Novichok. How long would that stay in the air for?'

'It would remain airborne for between ten and sixty minutes before diluting to non-lethal concentrations after approximately an hour. However, in enclosed and shielded areas, the airborne threat could remain for two hours. The residual threat would be from contaminated surfaces, which would remain contaminated indefinitely until cleaned.'

'So we don't need these any more,' said Jade, holding up one of the gas masks. 'We can go outside.'

'As long as we don't touch anything,' said Wynona hopefully. 'That should be doable'

'Have you lost your mind?' asked Diren. 'How are you going to get out of an army-controlled cordon?'

Wynona's face dropped.

Diren waved at Tanbir. 'Ask it how long it took to clean up Salisbury.'

His phone replied, 'The cleanup after the Salisbury Novichok attack in March 2018 took about thirteen months to complete, with the area declared safe in April 2019. The operation involved decontamination across multiple sites exposed to the nerve agent.'

'Thirteen months,' said Diren. 'They won't keep us here for that length of time, but we'll have to wait until we can be evacuated.'

'Sod this, I want to leave,' said Rob.

'They're not going to let you,' said Sim. 'You may as well stick it out and be patient.'

'But my kids will be worried about me. They're outside of the cordon and they've been allowed to go home.'

'And your solution is to put yourself in more danger by leaving the building?'

'Let's just leave it another hour,' said Leonie. 'Just one more hour and let's see what the lie of the land is.'

Rob nodded his head reluctantly and the others agreed. One more hour was manageable.

'But if we can move around in the building without the need to wear masks,' said Diren, 'why don't we move to a bigger room? It's starting to feel a bit claustrophobic in here. We could go to the jury gallery, where we all had to sit on the first day.'

Leonie's instinct was to swat this idea away. If they could sit at this table, they would be more likely to deliberate. It was Pavlovian. But if they moved to a bigger room, they would likely split up into their cliques and it wouldn't feel as natural to discuss the case.

'The grass is always greener,' said Wynona, who, for all of her talk about leaving the building, was clearly unnerved by the thought of abandoning the place which had given them sanctuary for the last few hours.

'But the grass is literally greener over there,' said Diren. 'There will be fresh coffee and more space. I'm not being funny, but it stinks in here.'

Leonie had to agree with him. It smelled of tuna and crisps, not to mention that stale smell that humans always leave behind when cooped up for too long with no ventilation.

'Let's flip for it,' suggested Charlie. 'Anyone got a coin?'

'No, but I've got this,' said Jade, pulling a green plectrum from the pocket of her hoodie. Leonie was momentarily surprised to see the plec in her possession. Jade showed them both sides. On one side was the ♣ symbol, on the other was an X drawn in permanent marker.

'It's better to make decisions for actual reasons rather than at the whim of some stupid… whatever that is,' said Lucas.

'It's a plec,' said Jade with a silent 'duh' intoned.

Viv said, 'Actually, using a coin or a die is a good way of making decisions. Although it's not the outcome of the coin you should follow, but the feeling it gives you when it lands. It can be a good way of working out your true feelings.'

Jade flipped the plec and it landed on the X. 'Move it is.'

Leonie looked to see how the others felt about the idea of a move. As a general rule, the younger jurors looked pleased while the older jurors seemed chained to the room like it was safety.

However, they all picked up their coats, the Ikea bags, and the remaining items from their lockers, and walked down two corridors and up one staircase to the jury gallery.

Leonie and Sim walked side by side. Leonie was subdued, ruminating on Susan's death, the mysterious song played, and how on earth she was going to get the others to see things from her point of view.

'Hey, why aren't you happy?' asked Sim.

'I don't know,' she lied. 'I just… I don't want to come back on Monday. Not after this.'

'I get you. Maybe they'll discharge us, given the circumstances.' He smiled broadly at the thought. 'And Leonie?'

'What?'

'I'm ringing him.'

Leonie stopped walking. 'Pardon?' Jade bumped into her, due to her abrupt stop. She apologized and carried on walking.

'I've been thinking. It's no longer lethal in the air. We're not going to die any more. It feels—I don't know—like a sign?'

'A sign that you've lost your mind. How many times have we had this conversation?' Leonie was getting sick of repeating herself.

Sim carried on jabbering—too fast to catch his breath. 'Do you know what I've been thinking about this whole time? He's here. He's in this city. We've been saved. Don't you sort of think that's unusual? It means something, right?'

'Slow down, you sound crazy. Playing here is a homecoming gig for them. You can't possibly think that Amir being in the same city as you has had any bearing on your survival.'

'Amir?' asked Jade, who had clearly been eavesdropping. 'Do you mean Amir Bernard?' She had that fangirl mania in her eyes.

'Yes,' said Sim, proudly. 'He was my boyfriend.'

'From Acid Rain?'

Sim nodded. The smug look on his face was killing Leonie. How could he be so naive?

'*You* dated Amir Bernard? Are you kidding?'

'No need to sound *so* surprised,' said Sim good-naturedly.

'Sim,' said Leonie. She was loath to be the bad guy, but someone had to set him straight.

'Be happy for me, please. I've realized what I want. I love him. That's why I can't stop thinking about him. There was a fucking chemical attack and all I wanted was to know that he was okay… I'm ringing him.'

Leonie had the urge to rip the phone from his grip. It was like Sim had lust-induced amnesia when it came to Amir.

'Wait,' she said. 'Think this through. How many times has he let you down in the past? How many times has he treated you like you're nothing to him? Listen to me. You are an amazing, wonderful, hilarious man. You deserve everything in life. He can't give you that. He just can't.'

'Don't ruin this for me.'

'If what I'm saying didn't have a modicum of truth, it wouldn't ruin it for you. But you know I'm right.'

'Seriously, do you have to be such a buzzkill?' He was starting to sound vicious.

'Fine. Knock yourself out. Get your heart broken *again*. But when it happens—and it will—I don't want to hear a thing about it.'

He looked at her defiantly before pressing the call button.

Leonie felt a surge of frustration. She hadn't handled that well.

Sim's voice changed when the person at the other end of the line answered. 'Yeah, I know… Jury service… Yeah… It's so random.'

How was being on jury service when the attack happened any more random than being at the bank or the petrol station or anywhere else, for that matter?

'…Oh my God! You lucky bugger. I wish I could go in the jacuzzi while there's a chemical attack going on… I'm guessing the gig isn't going ahead? Ah, that's a shame. Look, if you stick around, maybe we could…'

Leonie couldn't listen to this. She walked ahead and left Sim to his own stupid decisions while Jade listened in, desperate to overhear the sacred words of Amir Bernard. It was difficult to say who she hated more in that moment.

In her attempt to put distance between her and Sim, she caught up with Diren.

'I'm guessing he's getting back together with that guy, then.'

'Yep,' said Leonie shortly.

'Too bad.'

'Not my problem.'

Diren raised his eyebrows sceptically.

Leonie gave him a dangerous look, but didn't rise to the bait.

They hadn't been in the jury gallery since the very first day of jury service. After coming up the staircase, they entered via two double doors into a corridor. Here was where they had given their names before being led into the main waiting room, which seated over 100 people. It was so much lighter up here. The windows hadn't been lined with bin bags, but Leonie supposed that didn't matter as much any more.

It was a much larger space. There was even a small canteen on the other side of the room.

Already, they felt more comfortable, putting their feet up on seats. Anthony was first to the new coffee machine. When he poured himself a cup, Leonie saw that the coffee had a tar-like consistency and the lack of steam made her suspect it had gone cold, but as he drank it down, Leonie thought she saw his soul return.

Sim sat with the younger jurors, mostly talking to Jade. Leonie didn't want to be near him at the moment.

She decided to take herself into a corner, which put her equidistant between the older and younger jurors. Diren, too, had chosen to sit apart. He was on a row of seats nearest to the short flight of steps that led up to the mini canteen.

Leonie could hear both sets of conversations. She tuned into the older jurors first, who were discussing the status of their children, grandchildren, and so on. It seemed that most of their relatives were either inside the cordon and safe, or outside of the cordon and at home, waiting for them to return while watching the disaster unfold on television.

Rob was speaking into his phone. 'I won't, I won't.' He turned to the others. 'Promised them I won't leave until we're evacuated.'

The others agreed that this was sensible.

Now, she just needed to bridge the gap between the two groups in the hope she could get them to deliberate.

She tuned into the younger jurors' conversation next.

'So, you're into music, then?' Lucas asked Jade, presumably off the back of the earlier discussion about her tattoo.

'Yeah,' she answered. 'In a big way.'

'Heavy stuff?'

'*Really* heavy stuff. Like death metal. Screamo. It's all, like, so cool.'

Leonie smiled to herself. It was a long time since she'd had awkward, stilted conversations with the object of her affections.

In those first few months of working in the same office as Hamish, she would watch his movements, make a mental note about what times he tended to make himself a cup of tea so that she could be in the kitchen when he walked in. She didn't want to follow him in there. That would look stalkerish. Her meticulous planning did not bear fruit. She would stand in the kitchen, stirring her tea for minutes, hoping he would walk in.

Then one day, her boss had informed her that she needed training on the new database. Hamish was a permanent employee whereas Leonie was only working as a temp. She wheeled her chair over to Hamish's desk so that she could see his computer screen.

It had been impossible to concentrate on the training he was delivering. Though eye contact was the done thing when someone was speaking to you, she found it almost impossible to hold Hamish's gaze. Instead, she averted her eyes to the desk, where she saw the song he'd been listening to on his mp3 player.

'Tool,' she said.

'What did you just call me?' he joked.

She panicked. 'No, I wasn't calling you a tool, I just saw what you were listening to… I love that band.'

'*You've* heard of Tool?'

She chose to ignore the incredulity in his voice. 'Yeah, well…' She wondered whether she should recite one of the facts she'd learned about their songs while revising the topic of Hamish's likes and dislikes. Maybe she should say something about the time signatures, lyrical patterns, or the use of the Fibonacci sequence.

As an amateur poet, she appreciated the economy of words and skilful use of meter. As he stared at his computer, blandly reading the words from the screen to deliver the training, she wondered whether she should tell him all of the things she felt when she listened to the Ænima album, as she'd taken to doing when she cooled down on the treadmill at the gym. As the chord progressions floated around her endorphin-filled brain, she found herself thinking about Hamish and the lyrics and how they were about pleasure and numbness and satisfaction while also frustrating the listener, never quite giving them the crescendo they craved.

Hamish took a break from delivering training to respond to an email. She took a deep breath. *Be interesting,* she told herself. *Don't be lame.*

'Are you a lyrics guy or is melody more your thing?' she asked, trying too hard to sound casual.

'I think the two are inextricable. Or should be. They are in the best songs, anyway.'

'I think I prefer lyrics,' she said. 'I, er, write poetry, actually.'

He turned away from the screen to face her. She felt a jolt in her stomach.

Stop blushing.

'Yeah?' he seemed genuinely intrigued. 'So how do Tool compare to, I don't know, Keats?'

'You're asking the wrong person. I didn't study poetry. I just like writing it.'

'Can you do something well without studying it first?'

'Maybe not particle physics, but poetry is just about inspiration and emotions. I understand the basics of meter and rhythm. After that, you've just got to let go.'

'That's so cool,' he said. 'I wish I could do that.'

'Do you write?'

'Sort of… I write music. That's what I want to do, anyway.'

She rushed to capitalize on this commonality. 'I never feel more like myself than when I'm writing.'

'Can you make money from poetry?'

'I'm not sure. I'm not interested in monetizing it. But I don't want to work here forever, either.'

'I hate the whole nine-to-five grind. I'm in a band but we can't get a break. At this point, it's just a very expensive hobby.'

'What do you do? In the band?'

'I'm a songwriter but I also play lead guitar.'

'Like George Harrison!'

'The Beatle no one wants to be.'

Leonie sensed the bitterness in Hamish's voice.

Not long into the first one-on-one conversation she and Hamish had ever had, their boss came over to ask them how they were progressing with the training, putting an end to their chat.

But after that, Hamish would come and place his tray opposite hers during their forty-five-minute lunch break. And
they would talk about desire and ambition and imaginative
pursuits. He invited her to a gig where his band was playing.
Their first date.

The band was awful. Their name was Something Cool. It
sounded as though they'd sat around thinking of band names
and decided to go with the placeholder for lack of any better
ideas. The lyrics were similarly uninspired. Hamish played well,
and the lead singer had a good voice, but there was no magic.
It sounded like a mediocre imitation of more successful bands.

Not that this mattered to Leonie. She spent the whole gig
staring at Hamish's beautiful, sweaty face, relishing the opportunity to stare at more than the back of his head. And the best
part was that no one questioned her. Everyone was staring at
Something Cool.

When the gig was over, he found her in the crowd.

'That was amazing,' she lied.

'Yeah?'

She launched into a carefully constructed fiction of why
their lyrics were good and how she loved the riffs.

His smile broadened and she melted. She'd have told lies
all night just to make him smile like that. When she stopped
to draw breath, they kissed for the first time.

She grabbed the sides of his face as though worried he
would escape.

Leonie hadn't felt a spark like that before or since.

So, she looked across at the younger ones: Charlie and
Lucas both vying for Jade's attention, while Tanbir, who was
sitting next to Sim, had his arms pressed into his sides to avoid
accidental contact with the object of his affections. He had

the chance to have a stumbling, gushing, heart-pounding conversation with him. Instead, he sat there, wasting it, listening to his headphones in an attempt to block out sensory input, when he could be drinking in the proximity of his crush.

She wanted to grab him by the shoulders and tell him to take the chance, because those intense feelings wouldn't come back, to warn him that every infatuation was slightly less powerful than the first, that the law of diminishing returns applied to love as much as economics.

But all she could think about was how hard she'd tried to sound cool when talking to Hamish, recalling facts about a band she only half liked.

*

'I write song lyrics,' said Jade. 'It's what I really want to do.'

'Nice,' said Charlie.

'What about you?' Lucas asked him. There was a clear challenge in his voice. 'Do you like heavy metal?'

Charlie shook his head. 'No, mate. I'm a pop man, myself.'

'Pop?' Lucas sounded disgusted. He smirked at Jade, hoping she'd join in.

She didn't. Instead, she said, 'Charlie was pretty close to making it big at one stage, weren't you?'

'Er, sort of. You could say that.'

'Go on, then,' said Lucas.

Charlie's was a cautionary tale about chasing fame and the ruthlessness of an industry that had no shortage of talent or willing bodies to be fed into the meat grinder. Leonie knew all about that. She remembered the wall of rejection Hamish had faced on trying to get into the music industry.

'…The fans said I ruined their favourite song, that it was sacrilege and that *X Factor* was shit and that I should be burnt at the stake or something for daring to cover that song. It wasn't even me who picked it anyway. My mentor decided every little thing about me, from my hair to my clothes to my "brand". What they want is a simulation of authenticity. The real thing would be too messy. I was supposed to have this whiter-than-white image, so later, when it came out that I'd done drugs…' He ruffled his blond mop as he spoke, eyes not moving from the floor.

He continued to talk about therapy and rehab and the embarrassment of being the cliché of a reality-TV star who didn't quite make it.

'Did your mentor help you at all?' asked Jade.

'She just ghosted me. During the show, she made out like I was on a fast track to LA and a record deal. Nothing came of any of it. So, yeah. Now I work in a supermarket. How tragic is that? The most impressive thing I've done since *X Factor* was that I was a key worker during the pandemic. But I wasn't like a hero or anything. We had a paramedic living on my street and people used to clap for her when she left for work. Once—even though I was wearing my uniform—this lady told me I was breaking the rules because I was out of the house.'

'I'm so sorry,' said Jade. 'That's—it's just awful. No one deserves to be treated like that.'

Charlie nodded, still looking at the table.

There it was. Her in.

'Maybe that's one of the reasons why he was a nurse,' said Leonie. 'Sorry for eavesdropping, Charlie, I couldn't help it. But I wonder if that's why Quinn was a nurse? Because he liked the idea of people admiring him?'

She knew it was tenuous, embarrassingly so, but it seemed like they might take the bait. Sim looked frosty but didn't shoot her down. Lucas, who might have accused her of being obsessed again, didn't say anything.

'Don't you think that might have been a motive?' asked Leonie.

'I don't think we should discuss it between ourselves,' said Lucas. 'We're only supposed to talk about it when all twelve of us are together, remember?'

'Quite right,' said Leonie. She called over her shoulder. 'Hey, we were just having a thought about the case. Can we gather round to discuss for a moment?'

The older jurors looked at one another, and they all rearranged the chairs into a circle. Once they were settled, Leonie said,

'I was just wondering whether one of Quinn's motives for becoming a nurse in the first place was that he liked the status it gave him. He wanted to be admired.'

'Then why wouldn't he become a doctor?' asked Rob.

'Medical school is hard to get into. It takes a lot of time and money, which makes it more difficult for working-class people like Quinn. Becoming a nurse is challenging, too, but it's not as closed off.'

Rob rubbed his chin. 'Maybe.'

'Anyway, it ties in with what the nurse said. Caroline Harris said that Quinn always thought he was better than everyone else.'

FOURTEEN DAYS BEFORE

Leonie arrived in the retiring room to find only one other person present: Jade. A silver necklace swathed her slender neck. The pendant bore a heart impaled by a crossbar.

'Morning,' said Leonie as she hung up her trench coat.

Jade was too preoccupied with the notepad she was poring over to respond. A pale hand tucked a tendril of peroxide-grey hair behind her ear.

Leonie was curious to see what she was scribbling. As a teenager, Leonie had made her first tentative steps into the world of poetry. Her early work wasn't exactly Emily Dickinson. It was juvenile stuff, mostly about boys she fancied. She never shared her poems with anyone, and never intended for them to be published. Still, she took the discipline seriously, editing her poems until they worked, ruthlessly culling words that didn't serve her.

Leonie walked behind Jade as she made her way to the tea and coffee table, peering at Jade's notebook as she went.

> *I hope they all feel sick when they look at me.*
> *Next time I walk past the nurse's station they'll need pepto bismol.*
> *Which isn't even real medicine.*
> *I hope you all remember to take your meds.*
> *This is a taste of your own.*

The above had been read out by the prosecutor the previous day. These were taken from scraps of paper stuffed into Shelley

Roberts's diary, found soon after her death. They were mere fragments, never intended to be read or heard by anyone.

Except Jade had decided to amend them. On lined paper provided by the court for the purpose of taking notes about the evidence, Jade had written *Song Ideas*. There was a sub-heading: *Pepto Bismol/Take Your Meds* and an arrow leading away from it with a note: *Pepto Bismol sounds like a great song title but could be sued by Big Pharma? Take your meds a bit too similar to Placebo? Note: check legal ramifications.*

Below the song title(s), Jade had copied out the quotes from Roberts's diary and edited them into a shaky iambic pentameter:

> *You're going to feel sick when you see me*
> *Next time I walk on by you'll be seething*
> *I hope you remember to take your meds*
> *Because this will be a taste of your own*
> *I hope you remember to take your meds*

Leonie read this mutilation of Roberts's personal reflections, horrified that the diaries of a suicidal woman were being manipulated by Jade for 'Song Ideas'.

'What are you doing?' asked Leonie.

Jade jumped and hastily stuffed the notes back into her folder.

'Just playing around with some ideas.'

'They're not your ideas.'

Jade cast around for an explanation. 'I'm a songwriter. I get inspiration from weird places.'

'Do you think it's… ethical to copy evidence from the case? She was a real woman. These could have been the last things she thought before…'

Jade's cheeks flushed. 'I didn't think of it like that.'

Leonie took in Jade's all-black clothing and concluded that there must be some morbid allure for her.

At that moment, Tanbir came through the door and Leonie ended the conversation, turning to the tea and coffee table.

Throughout the day, Leonie would catch Jade looking at her as though anticipating reproach.

*

As they were waiting for the witness to finish giving the oath, Leonie became distracted by the two jurors in front of her.

'I saw this and thought of you,' whispered Charlie. Between his index finger and thumb, he held a green plectrum.

Jade took it from him and turned it over, inspecting it. On one side was a rain cloud with three raindrops, on the other was an X drawn in permanent marker.

'Thanks,' said Jade.

Leonie didn't catch all of Charlie's response, but she managed to hear the words 'charity shop'.

Leonie stared at the plec in Jade's clutch. It opened up a whole universe of memories for her.

Khan stood to ask her questions and Leonie had to drag her attention away from that dark well of memories where the early months of her relationship with Hamish dwelt.

Sitting in the witness box was a short, curvy woman whose brown hair was wound in tight ringlets. She had a round, pretty face with long eyelashes framing dark eyes.

The first question, as always, was the witness's name, which she gave as Caroline Harris.

'And your occupation?'

'Staff nurse.'

'On which ward?'

'The acute short-stay ward.'

'Please could you outline your relationship to Michael Quinn?'

'We were colleagues,' the witness said simply.

'How did he approach his work as a nurse?'

'At first, he seemed to be very proficient. But as time went on, I started to become concerned. He could be… it's difficult to explain because he wasn't slapdash. He never did things without meaning to. But he didn't always do things properly and I could never understand why. Any feedback you gave to him seemed to go straight over his head. He'd shrug it off…' The witness trailed off, seemed to lose confidence. She looked up at Khan, her cheeks dimpled by a sorry smile.

'Could you give some examples of times when he didn't follow procedure?'

'He'd go too far in giving medical advice, for one. He seemed to think that he was… Well, the sort of expertise he was dishing out, you'd need to be either a nurse practitioner or a doctor, and he was neither. He'd only just qualified as a nurse… And there were times when he'd leave it late to alert the doctor to an emergency because he wanted to handle it all on his own.'

'How was his patient care?'

Harris pulled a face. 'It was variable. He had the capacity to be very caring and nice to patients. I saw it myself. But sometimes I would hear conversations from behind a curtain—I shouldn't have been listening, really—but I would think to myself, "I wouldn't speak to a patient like that."'

'What did you hear?'

'I'll never forget this one time, I heard a patient ask for help with going to the toilet. Michael said, "Well, you'll have to wait your turn I'm afraid, I need to go as well."'

People in the courtroom gasped at that. The judge's eye swept over the courtroom and honed back in on the witness. It seemed to focus everyone else's attention.

She continued, 'I mean, I get it, we're all rushed off our feet, no chance to stop for the toilet, but there was something odd about it. It's part of nursing that the patient comes first. It's not good enough to tell them to wait their turn. I mean, consultants can say that, of course, but nurses can't.'

There was something so eminently likeable about Caroline Harris. Qualities that might be irritating in other people, like naivety, or accepting that consultants could behave badly and nurses couldn't, weren't annoying in her case. With her, it seemed to be a point of principle that her behaviour would be impeccable, no matter what.

'What about relationships with other staff members?'

Harris let out a deep breath. 'He was a bully. There's no other way of putting it. He wasn't a bully in the sense of, you know, someone who is loud or throws their weight around. He was capable of being very charming when he wanted to be. But he was unnecessarily cruel.'

'What do you mean by that?'

The witness's face furrowed, the dimples in her cheeks deepened. 'He… knew what buttons to press. It was like he had this innate sense of where someone's weak spots are. And he absolutely loved salacious gossip. Sexual preferences, marriage difficulties, financial problems… all of that. He'd store it and then use it as leverage. Not explicitly, but he'd use innuendo or double meanings. Make the person aware that he knew their secret and if they wanted him to keep it, they'd comply with his request to swap shifts, or help a particularly difficult patient.'

'Can you be more specific?'

'So, in my case, at the time when we worked together, I was pregnant. I felt like he honed in on that. He would always come across as really friendly and affectionate—touching my bump and so on. But then he'd talk constantly about my pregnancy. About the risks, the dangers. It was just this weak spot he would prod. And it all came across in a way that it looked like he was helping but really he was just meddling. He offered to come and see me after the birth. It sent shivers down my spine, quite frankly. The last thing I wanted was a random colleague anywhere near me at that time. And then when it got closer to the birth, he had all of these opinions about the labour and whether to induce, and the percentage of people who haemorrhage and so on. I mean, we're all medical professionals, we know the risks. But I never understood why he would go on and on about them. It was like he was wearing me down or something. And one thing I know for certain is that I saw this manipulation of other staff members too.'

'Who in particular?'

'Shelley Roberts. She was a very shy woman. Perfectly competent, but she was prone to thinking that she wasn't. Often, if she became too self-conscious, she would make mistakes. And…' Harris let out a dark laugh entirely out of character. She looked up at the ceiling as she said, 'She was exactly what he was looking for.'

'What do you mean by that?'

'She was someone he could bully.'

'Did you say something about it?'

'I took both of them aside separately and suggested that perhaps they should try to work with other people. Neither would take my advice. Sometimes Shelley would look at her phone and her face would just drop and I knew she'd received a text from him.'

'Did you ever suspect that the relationship was romantic?'

'Never. It wasn't like that. It was a friendship, but a very one-sided one.'

'Is there anything else you wanted to say about Shelley Roberts?'

'I saw her once, putting something in the sharps bin. I said, "What's that, Shelley?" She said, "Nothing." Five minutes later, Michael pulled the alarm signalling there'd been a cardiac arrest. Andrew Chapman. I didn't put it all together at the time, but now it's plain as day. She was being used by him. He ground her down and made her into his… minion, I suppose.'

'Thank you, Ms Harris. If you could wait there, my learned friend, Mr Ferguson, may have a few questions for you.'

Ferguson asked, 'You didn't actually see Nurse Quinn kill any patients, did you?'

'No, I never said I did.' The witness displayed the preternatural calmness of someone who had spent a career dealing with emergencies.

'The behaviour you've described doesn't mean that Quinn murdered anyone, does it?'

Khan got to her feet to interrupt. 'My Lord, that's comment. If we could stick to factual questions?'

The judge nodded. 'Quite right.' He looked to Ferguson. 'Let's stick to the facts, shall we?'

Ferguson looked irritated. 'But, My Lord, the difficulty with this witness is that she doesn't give any factual evidence, it's all conjecture.'

The judge consulted his notebook where he'd been making handwritten notes. 'I've got written down here that this witness made a number of assertions about the facts. That Quinn gossiped about others, that he could breach professional boundaries. If your client disagrees with any of that, please put his case to this witness.'

'My Lord.' Ferguson turned his attention away from the judge and towards the witness. His lips were tight as he asked his next question. 'You accused Nurse Quinn of liking gossip.'

'Yes.'

'That doesn't make him a bully, does it?'

'It was how he used the gossip.'

'Your evidence was vague on that—'

'My Lord.' Khan was on her feet again.

'Mr Ferguson. We've had this discussion. Facts, please.'

Even more disgruntled than before, Ferguson turned to Harris. 'Let's talk about Nurse Quinn's friendship with Ms Roberts. You said that, even after talking to both of them separately, they remained inseparable.'

'That's right.'

'You went on to say that *he* was exerting control over *her*.'

'Yes.'

'Did you ever consider that it could have been Ms Roberts controlling Mr Quinn?'

Caroline Harris suppressed a scoff. 'No, Shelley wasn't like that. It was Michael who was always cruel to her.'

'What evidence do you have that their reason for continuing the friendship was because he was controlling her?'

'Well, none—not directly—but it's the only thing that makes sense.'

'You also gave evidence that you saw Ms Roberts deposit something in the sharps bin in the minutes before Nurse

Quinn pulled the alarm indicating that someone had gone into cardiac arrest. Let's be clear about this, are you saying that Nurse Quinn asked her to do that for him?'

'Yes, that's what I think. I think she was helping him because he was psychologically abusing her and she couldn't live with the guilt of what he'd made her do, and that's why she killed herself.'

'Let's unpack that,' said Ferguson. 'You see Ms Roberts deposit something into the sharps box?'

'Yes.'

'Nurse Quinn is the one who raises the alarm?'

'Yes.'

'And then a short while after this, Ms Roberts takes her own life?'

'Yes.'

'Well, isn't there an equally plausible explanation for that set of circumstances: Ms Roberts is murdering patients, hence why she is the one you see deposit the syringe, and out of guilt she takes her own life?'

'No, Shelley didn't have it in her. She would never—'

'And Nurse Quinn, because he's so concerned about patients, is the one to pull the alarm to ensure help is on its way when there's a patient in need.'

'He was always the one to pull the alarm. So many patients, so many cardiac arrests. We had loads while he was working with us. And then Shelley takes her own life. I think she was helping him but she didn't know what he was doing, fully. Or she did and couldn't live with the guilt.'

'You can't know, can you, why Ms Roberts took her own life?'

'No, but—'

'And it's incredibly complex isn't it, because suicide can happen without anyone knowing about someone's inner turmoil?'

'Of course, but if it was Shelley who killed the first three patients, who killed Hamish Ryan?'

'Well, Ms Harris, ordinarily I might posit that Mr Ryan died of unforeseen health complications but given the results of the blood sample I would suggest that someone came in off the ward. Someone with a grudge against Mr Ryan, who wanted him gone.'

'That's ludicrous.'

'Can you say for definite no one could have come onto the ward late at night?'

'Not definitely, but still.'

'So someone could have entered the ward without being seen?'

'Yes, but how would they know where the adrenaline was?'

'Your answer is that it's possible.'

'Possible, but not likely.'

'My Lord, no further questions.'

The judge sent them away for the day. Today's evidence had been a turning point for Leonie. Before now, there'd just been evidence of murder. Now, whether Quinn committed all of the murders or not, Leonie knew for certain that they had a full-blown psychopath on their hands. If he hadn't harmed anyone yet, he would do soon. He was a dangerous man and she decided it was best he went away for life.

FIVE HOURS AFTER THE ATTACK

'So are we doing this, then?' asked Rob. 'Are we deliberating?'

'I think we should,' said Viv. 'Something to pass the time.'

Rob was happy to take charge. 'Perhaps we should start with the murder weapon, so-called.'

Leonie didn't want to begin there. She wanted to start with Quinn's psychology. Then she could at least show them how he was capable of murder before meticulously setting out each piece of evidence which confirmed he went on to fulfil this latent psychological ability. However, she had just won one battle and wasn't going to inveigle herself in another for the moment.

'Okay,' said Rob. 'The police became involved after Hamish Ryan's death, so I suggest we decide that count on the indictment first.'

Leonie tensed involuntarily, as she always did when Hamish was mentioned.

'If he's guilty of that murder, let's go on to consider the others. If he's not, then… I don't see how we could find him guilty of the others, given there's less evidence for those.'

Again, that wasn't how Leonie wanted to look at it. She thought it best to look at the murders in the round. All of those deaths in that one hospital. All of those cardiac arrests with no clear cause. Surely that was part and parcel of the evidence?

'Okay, so: did Hamish Ryan die because of an adrenaline overdose?' asked Rob.

Leonie couldn't resist answering first. 'By the end of it, his own defence team agreed that he did.'

Lucas shook his head. 'That's not what they said.'

Leonie turned to the notes she'd made during Caroline Harris's evidence.

'Caroline Harris was asked who killed Hamish Ryan if it wasn't Quinn. Mr Ferguson replied, "I would suggest that someone came in off the ward." That's their case. That he was murdered, but Quinn didn't do it.'

'Dr Casey didn't agree,' said Lucas.

Leonie flicked through to find her notes of Dr Casey's evidence. 'This is what Dr Casey said. Ms Khan asked, "Is it reasonable to conclude that Hamish Ryan died of an adrenaline overdose?" and Dr Casey replied, "Even if that were the case, who says it's Nurse Quinn?"' She stopped to look up. 'See? The defence case was that someone else injected Hamish Ryan with adrenaline, but they don't fundamentally question that it happened.'

'You mention the mark on his arm. I don't understand why the defence barrister didn't ask...' Lucas trailed off. 'Why would a trained nurse inject adrenaline into the vein if there was already a cannula in place?'

Leonie had to admit that it was a good question, one that she was going to have to give some thought to if she wanted to convince the others.

'It sort of looks like maybe he's being framed?' said Lucas, in that irritating rising inflection of his.

'Don't be ridiculous,' said Leonie too quickly.

'Go on, then, why didn't he use the line that's already in the vein? Why risk injecting it into another vein and leaving an incriminating mark?'

Leonie had backed herself into a corner. Now she had to answer a difficult question before she'd had time to think it through. 'Motive is not the most important thing here. We've got to look at means and opportunity. He had both of those.'

'Let's stick a pin in that… no pun intended,' said Charlie. 'We're getting away from Rob's question. Does everyone accept that Hamish Ryan was killed by an adrenaline overdose?'

Lucas answered 'no' immediately, while Leonie answered 'yes'. The others were more uncertain.

'Look at it this way,' said Charlie. 'If it wasn't adrenaline that killed Hamish Ryan, what was it?'

Leonie expected Lucas to have a quick retort, but he said nothing. She wondered whether he was conducting the same calculation she was about answering too many questions too quickly.

'Could have been anything,' said Rob.

'Exactly,' agreed Wynona.

'He was ill, wasn't he? Recovering from a car accident that near enough killed him, so it's no surprise he died not long after.'

'It wasn't "not long after",' said Leonie, her temper rising. 'It was weeks later.'

'I'm just not *sure*,' said Rob.

Leonie could have screamed. That word again; the get out clause for deep thought. She made a gesture somewhere between surrender and frustration.

Rob, Wynona and Lucas glared back at her.

'Dr Bleasdale said there was no clinical reason for him to go into cardiac arrest,' said Charlie. 'I come back to—'

'Stop talking!' said Diren.

Charlie stopped, mouth open.

Leonie wanted to know what had caught Diren's attention. His posture was uptight and his eyes were fixed on the windows.

'There's someone out there,' he said. 'Maybe they've come to get us.'

They all rushed over to the other side of the room and crowded around the large windows that faced out onto the side street below. Their range of vision was narrow, limited to the building opposite. If they craned their heads and got up close to the glass, they could see either end of the street. At one end was the main road.

Driving along it they saw an army vehicle filled with people in hazmat suits. Some of them carried weapons. One of them held a loudspeaker and was yelling instructions into it.

'Shh,' said Wynona. There was lots of shushing of one another. It made it harder to hear what was coming from the loudspeaker.

'Stay inside. You must remain inside the building. Do not come outside unless you are given specific instructions to do so.' It was discernible but muffled.

They saw people crowding in the windows of the building opposite, their hands splayed against the glass. Leonie became aware that they were almost a mirror image. However, the people in the building opposite seemed more desperate. They were pressing themselves up against the window, apparently shouting down at the army vehicle. 'Let us out,' they mouthed. 'Please. Let us out.'

Leonie watched as they appeared in window frames closer to the main road, trying to get nearer to the vehicle blaring out its message.

The vehicle crawled along the main road, oblivious to the plights of those in the buildings, until it was out of sight. Moments later, the sound from the loudspeaker dwindled until it was drowned out by the droning of the helicopters.

Leonie watched the people in the buildings opposite retreat from the windows, defeated.

The jurors looked at one another, sobered. Never once did anyone think they'd be in a situation where their streets would be patrolled by soldiers in hazmat suits carrying guns. Leonie thought back to this morning. The world seemed so normal. How had it slipped so far into chaos in such a short period of time?

'We need to see this through,' said Leonie. 'Let's try to reach a verdict. We can't leave the building, so let's just make the most of a shit situation.'

The other jurors looked at each other sceptically. It took them a while to take their seats and focus on what Leonie was saying, but once they got going, Leonie sensed they were glad to concentrate on anything that took their mind away from the situation outside.

Leonie began, 'We were talking about adrenaline, but I think we should focus on—'

'It's Rob's job to decide how the discussion is structured,' said Wynona.

Rob nodded portentously. 'Let's go back to cause of death for Hamish Ryan. Thoughts, anyone?'

'Obviously he was poisoned with adrenaline,' said Charlie. 'What other explanation is there?'

'The accused doesn't have to prove his innocence; it's for the prosecution to prove his guilt,' recited Wynona. Leonie wondered whether she would ever have anything material to contribute to the discussion, or whether her role would be confined to reminding the others of facts they already knew.

'Let's go back to the evidence,' said Jade. 'Why was there a syringe of adrenaline missing if it wasn't used?'

'I bet stuff goes missing all the time in hospital,' said Tanbir. 'Those records weren't exactly watertight.'

Leonie had thought Tanbir would be on her side.

'But,' said Tanbir, 'It's pretty open and shut. There's just no other convincing explanation for someone to spontaneously go into cardiac arrest. Plus, the mark on his arm, the missing syringe, and the corresponding syringe in the sharps bin… It all adds up.'

'Not to mention the shit ton of adrenaline in his blood,' said Jade.

Lucas said, 'But we don't know that the mark was definitely from an injection of adrenaline.'

'We're allowed to draw inferences from the evidence. It's just common sense,' said Leonie.

'No. They have to prove it, like with CCTV or something.'

'But this happened in a hospital,' said Leonie. 'There was no CCTV on the ward.'

'They still have to prove it.'

'So, if someone accuses someone of rape in an area not captured by CCTV, you're going to acquit them, are you?'

Lucas looked shifty. 'Well, if there was DNA or…'

'What if DNA didn't prove anything? What if he accepts that sex happened but the question then becomes consent? What then?'

Rob stepped in. 'How is this relevant?'

'It's a point of principle,' said Leonie. 'There has to come a time when you use your judgement. You look at the evidence and you make a decision. Just falling back on "well, if there's no CCTV or DNA there's no crime" is stupid. How would anyone have been convicted before 1990?'

'But the judge said—'

'We all know that,' said Sim, cutting Wynona off. 'The judge told us like a million times. What Leonie is saying is that the evidence presented is pretty obvious. At some point you've got to take a leap. Two plus two is four. That's what she's saying.'

Lucas still looked unconvinced. 'I can't be sure unless there's proof.'

It took all of Leonie's strength not to scream. She looked to Sim, who had his thinking face on.

'Okay,' said Sim tentatively. 'You're asking the prosecution to prove a negative. It's like asking atheists to disprove the existence of God.'

Leonie secretly thought that was a pretty good analogy but could immediately see the pitfall of his approach.

Wynona looked offended. 'There's no need to bring religion into it.'

'I don't need evidence of God,' said Viv. 'Spirituality is all around us.'

They were getting side-tracked.

'Whatever,' said Lucas. 'I'm not religious at all. The only proof that the fourth patient died because of adrenaline is the blood test. The whole case rests on that. Do you agree?'

'No,' said Leonie. 'That's just one piece of evidence in a wider picture.'

'For me to be sure, there needs to be some piece of scientific evidence which proves the adrenaline in his blood was as a result of an injection of adrenaline before he went into cardiac arrest. That's the bottom line.'

'This is where it's all about experts,' said Rob, throwing his hands up in the air as though to say 'we're done for'.

Leonie went quiet for a moment, hoping someone else would respond. She looked over to Tanbir, whose youthful features were arranged into a frown. 'On its own, the amount of adrenaline in the blood isn't enough.'

Leonie's posture sank.

Tanbir looked directly at her. 'Which is why I think Leonie's right. It's one piece of crucial evidence in a much bigger picture. To ignore everything else and to focus only on that is… like only eating the vegetables in a Sunday roast and then criticizing the meal as a whole.'

Leonie could have kissed him. He was talking in Rob's language now. Rob was a meat-and-two veg sort of fellow. Sure enough, he nodded along.

'I don't really like Sunday roast,' said Viv.

'We're not talking about Sunday roast,' said Sim irritably.

'We are. He just said.'

'It's a metaphor,' said Sim.

Leonie ignored them and looked over at Lucas, who was still determined to acquit Quinn, whether through ignorance or deliberate obstinacy, she couldn't tell.

'That's not good enough for me,' he said.

'Okay, well, let's focus on the blood test,' said Leonie. 'There was much more adrenaline in the blood sample than could be accounted for after just one injection of adrenaline, which is all he was given by the resuscitation team.'

'How can we possibly rely on a blood test that doesn't prove anything more than what we already know, which is that the resus team gave him adrenaline?' asked Lucas.

'It's just maths,' said Leonie.

Lucas shook his head and rolled his eyes.

'Let's take a vote,' said Rob. 'Hands up who is sure that the cause of Hamish Ryan's death was an overdose of adrenaline?'

Leonie, Sim, Charlie, Jade, Diren and Jill all raised their hands instantly. Tanbir raised his tentatively but then lowered it. They were almost evenly split. Viv, Rob, Wynona, Anthony and Lucas kept their hands down.

'I need more discussion,' said Viv.

'Okay,' said Leonie patiently. 'Why doesn't the evidence we've discussed so far convince you that Hamish died because of an adrenaline overdose?'

Viv scratched her cheek and frowned. 'I suppose I think all of that evidence probably does mean he died because of an injection of adrenaline. But am I sure?' She looked towards the windows as though searching for inspiration. 'Well, if I'm not sure I'm sure, then I can't be sure.'

'Ri-i-ght,' said Leonie. 'It's just that the prosecution only have to prove guilty beyond reasonable doubt and I'm just wondering where the *reasonable* doubt is? What possible other explanation is there for this extraordinary set of facts other than adrenaline overdose?'

'The scientists could be wrong,' said Rob.

'And you'd be in a position to know that, would you?' asked Sim.

'Why wouldn't I be?'

'You don't have any medical training.'

'I've spent a lot of time in hospitals, I'll have you know.' A large red blotch appeared on his jugular notch.

'Let's just calm down,' said Viv. 'And be respectful of each other's feelings.'

Leonie didn't understand how Sim's comment could be construed as offensive, but Viv carried on speaking crossly towards Sim.

'What with Rob's son—'

'Not now,' said Rob.

'I'm just saying.'

'*Not now.*'

Viv took the hint and left it at that.

After a mere ten minutes of discussion, they were already at each other's throats.

'Coffee break?' asked Viv.

'Coffee break' turned out to be a euphemism. There was no more coffee left, so they settled for sharing the same tea bag, which they brewed in a large pot found in the disused canteen adjoining the jury gallery. There was just enough for each of them to have a cup of weak, milkless tea.

As Leonie approached Viv, the decanter of the lousy tea, she crossed paths with Sim.

'Look,' she said. 'I'm sorry. I shouldn't interfere or tell you what to do with your life.'

Sim's face relaxed. 'You were right anyway. The twat's left me on read.'

'Oh.' She reached out for his arm and squeezed. 'I'm sorry.'

That was all it took for their friendship to resume.

After that, they found a quiet corner where they sat together, cupping mugs to warm their hands as Sim explained how he'd had a flurry of messages from Amir, only for them to dry up.

'It's the same thing every time. He keeps me coming back for more, then drops me like a stone.'

Though she was irritated to be hearing this story for the umpteenth time, she listened sympathetically, relieved to have Sim's company.

Looking out at the other jurors over the tops of their teacups, they resumed their position as aloof observers, never acknowledging that their snarky sense of humour belied a belief that they were superior somehow, because they weren't as out of touch and politically incorrect as the older jurors, nor were they as earnest and try-hard as the younger jurors. Leonie felt uneasy about this supposed superiority. She was just as eager as any of them, except she tried hard to appear nonchalant. As she surveyed the others, her eyes rested on Jade, who self-consciously played with the long pieces of hair lining her face.

Leonie, too, had tried to fit in when she was younger. Never more so than when she and Hamish first started dating. She would have done almost anything, including reinventing her personality, to keep him.

Never before had she been out with someone so good-looking. Hamish was boyishly handsome. He had bright eyes—blue in some lights, green in others—and the curly, floppy hair that was in fashion at the time. She was in her early twenties. Back then, she was plain-looking, in the absence of cosmetic enhancements; pale-skinned with no discernible curves. No one could ever have accused her of being sexy. Big tits and long, tanned legs like the women from the shaving adverts were in vogue, but Hamish said he liked her appearance.

'I hate that whole makeup and fake-tan thing,' he'd said.

Since reading *The Secret History* as a teenager, Leonie dressed like it was eternally autumn and she was on a college campus. In the office she wore thick black tights, brogues, and cable-knit tank tops. It suited the whole 'I'm an undiscovered poet' thing she had going on.

But when Hamish invited her on a night out to his favourite rock club, Subculture, she wanted to look more alternative, not really believing him when he said he had a 'thing' for the nerdy look.

Girls in rock clubs were edgy. Most of them had tattoos and facial piercings. They wore black leather dresses and fishnet tights.

On the night of their date at Subculture, Leonie experimented with eyeliner, black lipstick, and spiked her short hair with wax. She had to buy a new outfit for the occasion, going for a plaid red skirt and black crop top.

'Wow, you look great,' said Hamish upon seeing her.

So much for 'I hate makeup', thought Leonie. Men thought they hated makeup when really they hated a certain type of poorly applied makeup.

He held her hand and led her onto the dance floor. It was dark and sweaty, with a small mosh pit churning in the middle. They stayed on the outskirts. He continually checked to see if she was okay and he put a protective arm around her when one of the moshers came careering into them.

'Sorry dude,' the mosher had said, before diving back into the heap of bodies.

She smiled at how polite it all was. In between songs, those in the pit shook hands or hugged one another.

The atmosphere was great. She didn't feel at all self-conscious. Not everyone was dressed as Leonie had imagined. Some people were just in a plain shirt and normal jeans. The only time she felt observed was when she caught the jealous looks of other women, probably wondering how she had managed to bag someone as good-looking as Hamish. She felt like she'd won a prize.

They met up with Hamish's friends, a married couple who were five years older than them. Leonie was relieved to see that the woman, Amy, had a smattering of winged eyeliner but otherwise looked normal in black jeans and a band t-shirt. When she tucked her hair behind her ears, Leonie spotted some helix piercings. She was down to earth and friendly, while her husband, Josh, grinned broadly.

At around 2 a.m., Amy and Josh invited them back to their house.

In the taxi, Josh sat in the front. He turned around to look at Leonie, who was squashed in the middle between Hamish and Amy.

'Hamish tells me you're into Tool?'

'Yeah, I like them a lot.' She hoped she sounded convincing.

'They're my favourite band,' said Amy.

'They're all right,' said Josh. 'But there's only one way to listen to Tool. How are you doing it at the moment?'

'Er…' Leonie paused. Was this a trick question? 'With headphones?'

Josh threw his head back and laughed as though she'd just told an enormously funny joke. She smiled like that had been her intention.

'We've got amazing *speakers*.' He winked and shot a surreptitious look at the taxi driver.

Leonie felt a prickle of nerves. She'd never taken drugs and didn't know whether she wanted her first time to be in front of Hamish, in case she did something monumentally stupid or embarrassing.

Amy and Josh's house was a normal three-bed semi in suburbia. They had cute dogs and an extended kitchen. Only the odd band poster or piece of gothic artwork on the otherwise magnolia walls hinted that Amy and Josh flirted with an alternative lifestyle. In the bright overhead lighting, the subtle aubergine tint in Amy's dark hair became more noticeable. The lighting also picked out the purple bags under Josh's eyes.

From the garage, Josh brought out four bean bags and his big speakers.

'Won't the neighbours mind?' asked Leonie.

Josh looked unconcerned. 'We have to listen to them cheering the bloody *football*.'

Leonie didn't want to point out that football matches tended to be finished before 10 p.m.

Josh reached into the back of a kitchen cupboard and pulled out a brown paper bag.

'Mate, I'm just going to pop into the lounge to have a quick chat with Lee,' said Hamish. Leonie liked it when he used this nickname for her.

Josh wiggled his eyebrows suggestively. Amy hit him on the arm and called him a twat, which comforted Leonie.

'We've got a bed upstairs if you want to use it, mate.'

Hamish laughed it off and called him a dirty bastard.

In the living room, Hamish closed the door behind him. 'Listen, if you don't feel comfortable with this, you don't have to do anything. We can call a taxi and head home. I'll say I've got a headache or need to be up early or something. I promise I won't think any less of you, nor will Josh and Amy. They're cool. Sorry, I should have made sure you were okay with this before inviting you back.'

Leonie felt at once touched by Hamish's attentiveness while terrified that if she took up his offer, he may never ask her out on another date.

'No, it's fine,' she said. 'I'm looking forward to it.'

Her heart started to beat rapidly, as if she'd already taken something. She wasn't even sure what drug they were about to take.

In the kitchen, Josh's first word was, 'Mushrooms!'

Leonie took one to start off with. After that, they hung out in the kitchen. Amy and Josh's dogs wagged their tails and busied around their feet, demanding fuss and play. It was a while before Leonie started to feel any effects from the shroom.

After half an hour, Josh put on the Lateralus album. They sank into the bean bags and let the hallucinogenics and psychedelic music wash over them. Leonie slipped into a giggly but relaxed state. She took another mushroom. Amy and Josh's dogs mimicked their owners by finding their beds in the corner and settling down.

'*This* is how you listen to Tool,' said Josh.

Leonie laughed, following the train of sound until her laughter seemed to get caught up in it. She closed her eyes. The colours behind her eyelids and the notes coming from the speakers were indistinguishable. She slipped into the music and got lost there.

The sound of Sim's voice babbling away next to her, and the low hum of the other jurors brought her back to the present.

'Leonie?'

Sim had asked her a question and her automatic 'hm' response had clearly been unsatisfactory.

'Sorry,' she said. 'Miles away.'

'Daydreaming again?'

She took a moment to answer. 'I'm thinking about the case.'

Sim looked uncomfortable.

'I don't know why the others can't see it,' she said.

'See what?' Sim had a far-off look in his eye, like the case was much less interesting than the great love story of Sim and Amir.

'That Hamish'—she almost forgot to use his full name—'Ryan died because of an adrenaline overdose.'

Sim considered this. 'I think some people just like to be contrary.' In an undertone he added, 'Especially the likes of

Lucas. So alternative he can't find someone guilty in case it makes him look too mainstream.'

Leonie wanted to laugh at Sim's joke; she knew he was only trying to lighten her mood. 'I wish I knew how to get across what I want to say.'

'I understand what you're trying to say. The thing is, you can't persuade people who don't want to be persuaded.'

Leonie frowned. It sounded a lot like giving up to her.

'Anyway, I've been thinking about who took my phone.'

'Oh yeah?'

'I reckon it was Viv.'

'Shut up. Seriously?'

'Yep. That cow's always been holier than thou.'

Leonie felt torn. Given their newly repaired friendship, she was loath to do anything that would jeopardize it. On the other hand, she couldn't think of anyone less deserving of Sim's ire than Viv, who only ever seemed to want people to get along. As a compromise, she merely raised her eyebrows as far as they would go.

'Yeah, on the day I first noticed it missing, I remember that she was right behind me when we were going through security.'

And I was right in front of you, thought Leonie, praying that none of this showed on her face.

Luckily, their discussion was cut short. There was a noise overhead, as though someone was smashing a broomstick into the floor.

'What the hell?' said Sim.

Leonie looked over to Diren, not wanting to think too hard about why she always looked to him in times of danger.

TWENTY-ONE DAYS BEFORE

It was nearly the end of the lunch break, and the jurors still hadn't heard a single live witness or entered the courtroom. They had spent all morning sitting around.

The ban on electronic items in the retiring room and courtroom—'we take no responsibility for items left unattended'—seemed to cause some of the younger jurors physical pain.

For weeks, the evidence had been very heavy and difficult to disentangle. It was all about adrenaline, specifically about proving that the amount of adrenaline in Hamish's blood was indicative of intentional poisoning, and therefore murder. Leonie laid out all of her notes and was trying to tabulate the various pieces of evidence on one page—a route map to the vast and sprawling evidential landscape—but Sim was distracting her.

He'd come to court puffy-eyed. Sometimes he would be on the brink of tears, at which point he'd make an excuse to go to the toilet.

Leonie recognized his grief as a pale imitation of her own. It had taken her a long time to get to the point where she could even cry. At the beginning, it had just been shock. It was incomprehensible to her that Hamish had simply ceased to exist. Only upon seeing his body had she understood that it was real. Then came the weeks of staying inside the house, being unable to leave. Even now, she found the outside world difficult to cope with. Other people drank her low reserves of energy, with their constant need for attention and tolerance and forgiveness.

Frankly, Sim was testing her patience.

'Was he really that special?' She was unable to keep the irritation from her voice.

He looked affronted. 'Yes. Haven't you been listening?'

She stopped trying to tabulate the evidence. 'Yes, Sim, I've been listening. But what you've described is a relationship with a mortal man, not some god-like creature who came from the sea.'

'But Amir *is* a god-like creature.'

Leonie suppressed an exasperated sigh. 'The sooner you realize that he's a fallible human being, the easier it'll be to get over him.'

'Is that what you did with your ex?'

Leonie hesitated. 'Yes.' Rather than get enmeshed in the tricky story of being a widow, she had told everyone that she was a divorcee.

'How long did it take?'

'I'm still not over him, but it gets easier. I promise.'

'What, because of *time*?' The last word said with scepticism.

'Time helps, but there are other things. We're attracted to people who have an abundance of whatever quality we see ourselves as lacking. So, rather than thinking about how to get Amir back so he can fill whatever absence you perceive in your own life, think about why he's so attractive to you, and work on filling your life with that instead.'

Sim looked dissatisfied with this reasoning. 'Did I tell you about the time we went to the zoo?'

'And he loved the animals? You'll find other guys who love animals. It's quite a common trait.'

'He had a deep connection with them. I've never seen anything like it. And what about that time he kissed me in the rain? Even though those dickheads tried to throw things at us? He kissed me *in the rain,* Leonie. You can't tell me that's not true love.'

It's a ploy, is what she wanted to say. Instead she went for, 'I'm not saying it wasn't true love from your perspective, but the way he's treated you—'

Their conversation was cut short by Tom, the usher, coming into the room to say that the judge was ready for them.

*

The witness in the box had an unnaturally upright posture. She was thin, with straight, wispy hair and glasses. Her clothes weren't fashionable, but they were neat.

Once the jurors were settled, the judge greeted them with the usual pleasantries and then handed over to Khan.

'Please can you give your full name?'

'Doctor Helen Bleasdale.'

'And your occupation?'

'I'm a consultant in emergency medicine.'

'I want to go back to the fifth of August last year. The day when one of your patients, Hamish Ryan, died.'

Dr Bleasdale had small but empathetic eyes. 'Yes.'

'Can you tell us when you first became aware that Mr Ryan's condition was critical?'

'When the crash call was put out. My first thought was "not another one".'

'What do you mean by that?'

'We'd had an unusual number of deaths on the ward, and when the alarm was pulled I just remember thinking, "Oh God, not again."'

'Did you have any suspicion about what might have been responsible for the cardiac arrest?'

'No. I approach every arrest with the same mindset: why has the patient crashed? I'm always on the lookout for medical reasons for collapses.'

Just then, for no reason that Leonie could determine, Dr Bleasdale looked over at the jury box. Leonie felt that familiar shiver run down her spine. Dr Bleasdale's gaze didn't linger long, however, and she turned back to Khan.

Leonie remembered the doctor. They'd not spoken, but she recalled seeing her looking tired and dishevelled, huge bags under her eyes and a limp where her sensible shoes had given her blisters.

'What happened when you attended at Mr Ryan's bed?'

'The resus team were resuscitating the patient.'

'What happened next?'

'I took a blood sample. I asked a number of questions first but there didn't seem to be any reason for the patient to have crashed. I'd checked on Mr Ryan earlier and he was fine. That was the moment I thought the arrest might have been… induced.'

'Okay,' said Khan. 'What do you mean by "he was fine"?'

'He was recovering. When he came in, he was in a coma, but he recovered from that following surgery. He was nearly fit to be discharged—we just needed to keep him in for another couple of days because his blood pressure was a bit on the low side, but otherwise he was doing well. Cardiac arrests can happen at any time, but there is always a cause. There was nothing in Mr Ryan's clinical presentation which would explain his collapse.'

'You said earlier that you suspected the cardiac arrest had been induced. Why?'

'The deaths always seemed to happen when one nurse was on shift.' Dr Bleasdale turned slightly, as though to look at Quinn, but she didn't seem able to meet his eye.

'What happened after you heard the alarm pulled on the fifth of August?'

'I ran over there as fast as I could. I suspected Quinn, had done for a while. I thought, "This is my chance to catch him". I thought, "I'm not having any more patients die on me. I'm not letting him carry on with this."'

'Carry on with what?'

'Hamish Ryan's wasn't the first suspicious death. There had been a few where I wasn't sure of the cause.'

'Okay, so you run over to Hamish Ryan's bed. What happened next?'

'I told one of the HCAs to guard over the sharps bin and not to move until I told her to.'

'Why did you do that?'

'In case the drug he was using was in the bin. If there was to be an investigation, I knew we'd have to preserve evidence. I put some gloves on and looked in the sharps bin. Inside was an empty syringe of adrenaline, the sort we keep on the arrest carts.'

'And then?'

'I asked someone to call the police. When the police arrived, I showed them what had happened. I also went and got the chart I'd made.'

'The chart of what?'

'Adrenaline had been going missing for a while, so I had instructed one of my most experienced nurses to make a written record of the amount of adrenaline in the arrest cart.'

'What else did you do on that day to preserve evidence?'

'I took some of Mr Ryan's blood.'

'Why?'

'To see if adrenaline caused the cardiac arrest. Unfortunately, the resus team were giving him one milligram of adrenaline as I arrived, but it was the best I could do for the patient.'

'Anything else?'

'Yes, there was a puncture wound on the patient's arm. I took a photograph of it.'

There was a pause. Projected onto the large screens was a close-up of Hamish's arm. Except it wasn't really Hamish's arm. It was a picture of his corpse. Prior to the car crash he was beautiful and perfect, almost entirely unblemished. But on this picture there was a red dot where someone had inserted a needle into the vein in the crook of his elbow.

A second picture appeared on the screen. This time, it was a zoomed-out picture, showing the whole of Hamish's arm, where the red dot was just visible.

'What is this?'

'That's the puncture wound,' said Dr Bleasdale.

'How did the resus team administer the adrenaline?'

'Through the cannula, which was already inserted.'

'And what did you find when you did an audit of the adrenaline on the arrest cart?'

'We found that the number of syringes of adrenaline didn't match up with what had been recorded as being administered that day. Also, no one could account for the empty syringe in the sharps bin. I put two and two together and...'

'And?'

'Left it to the police.'

'Thank you, Dr Bleasdale. Please wait there, as my learned friend may have some questions for you.'

Ferguson stood up. 'Dr Bleasdale, I want to take you back to something that you said at the very beginning of your evidence. You said, "There had been a few suspicious deaths recently."' Ferguson picked up a glass of water from the bench and took a leisurely sip. 'Do you stand by that?'

'Yes.'

'Let's look at the timeline in this case. We've got Zane Chan who died on the third of December in the year prior to Hamish Ryan's death, Gail Bridges who died on the fourth of January, a month later, and Andrew Chapman… So, what we've got there is a cluster. Would you agree?'

'Yes, there are certainly a few grouped together,' said Dr Bleasdale.

'And then we've got a case almost eight months later, in August.'

'Yes.'

'Do you stand by what you said earlier: "There had been a few suspicious deaths recently"?'

'Yes.'

'It's not recent, is it, when there is an eight-month gap between deaths three and four?'

Dr Bleasdale blinked, her bright eyes frustrated behind her glasses. 'My understanding of the evidence is that the police found a number of cases which they initially considered to be suspicious but then whittled it down to four. There were lots of deaths in that eight-month period where I was uncertain as to why the patient had gone into cardiac arrest. To put it into perspective, we had twenty deaths in a nine-month period on our ward. We normally have five or six. And Quinn was the common denominator for them all.'

'But the police haven't charged the accused with those twenty deaths, have they?'

'No, but that's an extraordinary statistic. We no longer have that level of death on the ward.'

'And why didn't you do something before the fifth of August? You're telling this jury that you thought patients were being killed. If that was true, surely you'd have done something sooner.'

'It's a very serious thing to accuse a colleague of something so heinous. Nurses work tirelessly for their patients, often at the expense of their own wellbeing. It's completely alien to everything we stand for to intentionally harm patients. So I had my suspicions, but I couldn't be sure.'

'Surely you wouldn't have waited to see if this person struck again if you really thought there could be any chance of foul play?'

Dr Bleasdale took a steadying breath. 'I thought—rightly or wrongly—that patients would be best served by this man being caught with proper evidence. If there was an allegation made against him, it might spook him, he might change his practices, or he may just go off to another hospital and set up again there. I didn't want him slipping the leash…'

Leonie felt a strange mix of admiration and horror for the straightforward way in which Dr Bleasdale described this awful calculation: do something to stop any more patients from being killed, or wait for him to strike again to catch him once and for all. Would things have panned out differently for Hamish had she said something sooner?

Ferguson kept trying to talk over Dr Bleasdale. His small, sharp vocalizations peppered her words, trying and failing to interrupt her. But Dr Bleasdale steamrollered through, giving her account slowly and carefully.

'…I knew that if he was a killer, he'd strike again. I wanted to catch him before any more patients were hurt, but the only way I could do so was to wait for him to do it again, and then I would take the necessary measures to preserve evidence, which is what I did in August last year.'

'I want to move on now to another part of your evidence. You say that you would check the arrest cart for adrenaline?'

'I ensured a more comprehensive checking system was put in place.'

'Did you have the authority to do that?'

'No, but it wasn't an official investigation. I did it under my own steam.'

'Some of the evidence given in this trial suggests that the system for monitoring the amount of adrenaline used and the amount of adrenaline on the cart was not watertight.'

'That's exactly why I asked the nurse to do extra checks.'

'But things could have slipped through the net while he wasn't on shift?'

'Of course they could. I didn't have an investigative budget; I just did the best I could with what I had. And anyway, that nurse's shift pattern fell during the week of the fifth of August, so they were definitely checked properly.'

'But you were only checking the carts on your ward, is that right?'

'Yes.'

'If someone was going to commit a murder, wouldn't they take their weapon of choice from a ward where they weren't working?'

'It wouldn't be normal to see nurses from another ward, so no, I don't think you'd go to another ward.'

Ferguson nodded, his clenched jaw visible even from the jury box. So far, he'd been unable to land any blows on this witness.

'Dr Bleasdale, there's just one last thing I wanted to ask you about. Could it have been someone else who injected Hamish Ryan with adrenaline? A stranger off the street, perhaps?'

'Who? Who is supposed to have done this?'

'I'm just asking if it's possible.'

'Preposterous. Who would do that?'

'You agree it's possible, though.'

'What do you mean by possible? Almost anything in the world is possible, as long as the laws of physics are obeyed. So yes, there is a technical possibility, but in reality? No, it couldn't have happened.'

'Couldn't or shouldn't?'

'Couldn't.'

'Thank you, Dr Bleasdale. No further questions.'

'I think someone needs to check it out,' said Anthony, who rarely volunteered to do anything. He tended to fade into the background with the likes of Jill. Small talk and vapid complaints about jury service tended to be the extent of his contribution. 'I think someone else should come with me.'

Tanbir raised a shaky hand.

'Two's enough,' said Diren. 'We don't want to lose any more than that.'

Leonie winced a little at the tactlessness of the remark. Anthony and Tanbir looked at each other uneasily. Then they left.

At least ten minutes went by in stiff silence, interrupted by the occasional banging.

After a while, Leonie noticed that the noise from the room above had stopped. She looked up at the ceiling.

Sim did the same. 'Maybe Anthony and Tanbir found whoever it was.'

'Maybe.'

Other people started to cotton on to the fact that it had gone quiet.

'Should someone go and look for them?'

'I can't emphasize enough how stupid that would be,' said Diren. 'If something has happened to them, it would almost certainly happen to anyone who went looking for them. Haven't you seen any horror films?'

Rob made a noise in the back of his throat that registered his displeasure at Diren's tone, but it was clear that Rob was not someone who tended to watch horror films.

Charlie stood up and started to pace.

Wynona said, 'Can't you just do whatever you normally do when we have to wait?'

'It's been *six hours*,' said Charlie. 'I can't look at my phone because the news is giving me anxiety.'

'Same here,' said Jade. 'I've used up all of my allotted screen time.'

'I honestly think I need to go for a walk or something,' said Charlie. 'I can't just sit around waiting any more.'

Diren shook his head in disbelief. 'Do some fucking push-ups in the corner or something.'

The resentment between the ten of them seemed to hum. The tension was dispersed by loud footsteps coming from the small corridor that led into the jury gallery.

Anthony and Tanbir returned, trailed by a large balding man in his fifties wearing a uniform. The logo on the left breast identified him as an employee of the private security company responsible for guarding the cells. Around the prison guard's wrists were red lacerations which revealed that he had been wearing the cuffs which now hung from his belt.

The prison guard's name was Geoff. They sat him in a chair and gathered round to hear what he had to say.

'Start with the visitor,' prompted Anthony.

Geoff looked reluctant to recount what had happened. He took a deep breath. 'This morning, Mr Quinn had a visitor. She was about this high'—he held up his hand, indicating a woman of around five foot three—'and had sort of purple hair. Reddish, purplish colour.'

'Did she give a name?' asked Leonie.

'All visitors have to put a name down in the logbook, but I can't remember it for the life of me. Number of visitors we get… I think it might have begun with A.'

'Not Susan, then,' said Lucas, sounding bored. 'If that's what we were supposed to think.'

'If it *was* her, she wouldn't have used her real name,' said Charlie. 'She could lose her job for visiting defendants.'

Jade nodded. 'Plus, I heard somewhere that when people are forced to come up with a fake name, they often choose one beginning with A.'

Lucas looked unconvinced. 'So, because she's got hair that is sort of similar to the usher's and had a name which may or may not begin with A, we're supposed to conclude that it was definitely Susan?'

'What else could you say about her?' Leonie asked Geoff, ignoring Lucas.

'Well, she was short and curvy. Not, you know, larger, but not stick thin either.'

'And had she visited him before, do you know?' Leonie asked.

'I didn't recognize her.'

'And you've worked shifts over the last ten weeks?'

'More than I could count.'

'Most days?'

'Yep. Mouths to feed, you know?'

Leonie nodded. 'Just to recap: a woman with red-purple hair, who is short and curvy, visited Quinn for what appears to be the first time on what in all likelihood would have been the last day of the trial had it not been for the chemical attack. This is also the same day that we get an usher we don't normally have who also fits that description. Does anyone else think that it could be the same woman?'

Almost everyone agreed with her. Lucas's jaw remained set.

Leonie added, 'Also, does anyone recall a woman of this description in the public gallery?' There was a general murmur to indicate that no one had. 'So, this is a friend so dear to Quinn that she visits him in the cells, but doesn't bother to turn up for moral support on a single day of a ten-week trial?'

'Okay, I see your point,' said Lucas.

'Was she wearing civvies?' asked Rob.

'Yes, a sort of black t-shirt and skinny jeans.'

Hence you noticing the curves, thought Leonie.

Rob said, 'I didn't get a look at her clothes because of those black robes the ushers have to wear. Can anyone remember?'

Leonie, who had handled Susan's dead body, didn't think she could forget. 'She wasn't wearing that,' she said in a small voice. 'She was wearing black work trousers, a lilac blouse and a navy cardigan.'

'She must have changed,' said Rob.

'Would anyone have spotted her on her way to the cells?'
Leonie asked Geoff.

'No one would question seeing her in the corridor where the cells are because there's lots of other things on that corridor. As long as none of her colleagues saw her coming in or out of the specific door leading to the cells…'

'Are the corridors busy?' asked Leonie.

'Search me. I'm below ground most of the day. But I don't think so.'

'Sorry, we cut you off from telling us what happened. This woman came to visit Quinn this morning?'

'Yes, we took him through to the visiting room. It's got three booths. Chair one side, visitor on the other side of a perspex screen. We're in the next room.'

'Could you hear what was being said?'

'Sometimes we can—if they don't keep their voices down—but both Quinn and this woman were softly spoken, so I couldn't.'

'Was this visit before or after we heard about the chemical attack?'

'Before. I was late hearing about the chemical attack. We only had one prisoner down with us in the cells, and that was Quinn.'

'No others?'

'Three came in the van, two were released on bail. So, just Quinn.'

'How many of you were in the cells?'

'Three prison guards, but only one person was needed to sit outside his cell, so we rotated between us. I was watching him when the chemical attack was announced. It's difficult to get reception down there, so I was the last one to hear what had happened. By the time I got up to speed on, most of the lads had gone off in the van, leaving me with Quinn.'

'Did you tell him what had happened?'

'Of course.'

'What happened after you told him?'

'To begin with, we just waited.'

'Waited for what?'

Geoff shrugged. 'More news?'

'And then what?'

'I called all of the people I love, made sure they were okay…'

'Did he overhear that?'

Geoff gulped. 'Yeah.'

'Did you mind him overhearing personal information?'

'Well… I didn't care. I was just thinking, "I hope my family are safe."'

Rob gave a brusque nod of agreement.

Leonie thought that she could see where Geoff's story was going. In her yearning for more information about what might await Quinn were he to be convicted of Hamish's murder, she had found herself googling prison conditions for lifers. She had been disgusted to find out that Rose West enjoyed privileges normal prisoners did not. Such was her talent for grooming prison guards, they had to rotate them every six weeks. Then there was Harold Shipman, who had been allowed to push a wheelchair-bound inmate around the health centre and take meals to others.

The evidence demonstrated that Quinn could charm people with alarming ease. If he was of the same ilk as the likes of Shipman and West, he would be more than capable of manip-ulating Geoff. After all, why wouldn't prison guards prefer the mild-mannered non-violent prisoner when they have so many foul-mouthed and terrifying inmates in their care?

'Okay, so what next?'

'We got chatting.'

Leonie didn't fill the silence with questions this time.

Geoff ran his fingers over his bald head nervously. 'He asked who I'd been calling, if they were okay. It just seemed like, I don't know, polite conversation?'

Classic, thought Leonie. *Ask them questions, show empathy, pretend you care.*

'So I told him, yeah, I'd called my kids, my wife, my brother, my parents. He asked whether my children were at school, I said they were. He asked if they were forced to stay inside and I told him that yeah they were, but luckily their school is outside of the city, it's on the outskirts, really, in a little village. Then he started telling me about how he'd grown up in a village and we, er, joked a bit, about village life. He said that where he came from, everyone knew everyone's business, but it was nice, even if people were nosy. He said that if someone fell down in the street, there would always be a neighbour on hand to help. I don't know how, but I got to telling him about the village Facebook group…'

Leonie wanted to put her face in her hands. Didn't they teach prison guards about this stuff? But it wouldn't have seemed like grooming to Geoff, because he was a bald middle-aged man with a tough-guy job, not a little girl on the internet. And Quinn's remarks wouldn't have been a come-on, they'd have been exactly how Geoff described, a polite enquiry. Quinn would have known to laugh in all the right places, but he'd have just been pretending to know what it was like to live in a small village where there was a Facebook group with weird hierarchies and passive-aggressive posts about bin placement.

'And so, yeah, we got chatting… About his loved ones. He just wanted to call them. To know they were okay. He cried. He said that his mum had Alzheimer's and wouldn't be able to follow the stay-inside order because she'd forget. He wanted to ring her, and then maybe her neighbour…' Geoff looked around, imploring them to understand.

'Don't worry about it, Geoff,' said Anthony, kindly. 'You thought you were doing a nice thing.'

'And, I just had to. I had to let him have a phone call. What kind of a bastard wouldn't? My mother-in-law has dementia, and I know what it's like… So I agreed to let him out of his cell to have a phone call.' Geoff took a deep breath. 'What I didn't anticipate was that the line would be cut.'

'Which is why the detail about the woman who came to visit Quinn is particularly important,' said Tanbir.

Leonie couldn't fault Tanbir's logic. Susan must have cut the line.

'And, well, once he was out of the cell… It was deserted. No one else around, no instructions, nothing from the higher-ups. Just… Empty building. So I agreed to take him up to the phone in the main atrium. You know where that is?'

'Some of us do,' said Diren. 'But most of the time jurors don't go over there.'

'Of course,' said Geoff. 'Anyway, before we left, there were two gas masks in the bit where the lockers are. It's where visitors have to put any electrical items. That's where the signing-in sheet is as well. And Quinn said, "We better put those on, don't you think?"'

Leonie's heart went out to Geoff as he rubbed his bald head again.

'So, I did as he suggested. It meant my vision was restricted.

I think that while I was putting my mask on, he got his mitts on the handcuffs, because when we came out into the atrium, he cuffed me. Hands behind my back. Nothing I could do. We cuff them in that position because it's impossible to attack the guard without taking yourself to the floor. The last place I wanted to be was on the floor, so I complied. He said, "Geoff, I'm so sorry about this, I really am. I like you, you're a nice guy, don't worry, someone will come and get you…" Then he said, "But the thing is, I'm an innocent man. I didn't do what they're accusing me of, but I know they're going to convict me anyway. So I've got to take you somewhere people won't find you for a while."'

'Why didn't he just lock you in the cells?' asked Diren. 'If he wanted you out of the way?'

Geoff made a 'search me' gesture, but then said, slowly, 'I sort of think he meant it. He didn't want to do me harm, he just felt there was no other way of escaping. Had to put me somewhere it would take people a while to find me, but didn't want to stick me in the cells where I'd get locked in and probably die of thirst before someone came in on Monday morning.'

A likely tale, thought Leonie. None of this was a coincidence. He must have worked out where in the building the jurors were likely to go once they'd decided to leave their room. If he had Susan's help in anything—cutting the phone lines, leaving the gas masks there—she'd also have helped him work out where the jurors were going to be. He left Geoff up there to mess with them.

'Then I saw that woman. I can't say for certain it was her because I couldn't see her face—she was wearing a mask too—but her hair was that purply, reddy colour. She was dressed differently this time. I realized she was an usher. I was sure she'd help me once she understood what had happened. I said to her, "Excuse me, but this is a prisoner and I'm a prison guard, can you help please?" She just ignored me. She looked at Quinn and then gestured for him to follow her.

'Anyway, so, as he was walking me up to the room where I've been since, he told me about why he had to do this. He said that he was innocent but he could tell that the jury were going to convict him. I said, "You don't know that. If you're innocent, won't there be evidence to prove it?" He laughed at me. Said he didn't know how I could be so naive. He asked me whether I had any prison-guard mates who'd done something they shouldn't have. Beat someone up when they thought they could get away with it, hit them a couple more times with a baton for good measure. Well, he wasn't wrong. Prisons are tough. Prisoners are horrible. They spit at you, they throw their shit at you. So, yeah, we get our own back when we can. He said, "That's the thing. The prison guards know they can get away with it. It's the same with the doctors who are lying about me." Then he looked at the woman and he said, "You believe me, don't you?"'

'What did she do?'

'She didn't say anything. Just pointed in the direction of the room I was left in and walked off. He took me to the room, all the while telling me that he was innocent and he knew he wouldn't be acquitted by the normal route, so he was taking his chances. Then he taped my mouth, cuffed me to the radiator, and left me there. I've, er, pissed my pants, to tell you the truth.' He looked down at himself, mildly disgusted.

'Do they have lost property?' asked Leonie, who'd registered the stench of ammonia.

'I could get my civvies from the locker downstairs,' he said.

'Okay, but I want to ask you a couple more things first if that's okay? Why did it take you so long to alert us to your presence after you heard us come in here?'

'That's how long it took me to hook my leg around the nearest chair. I tried banging with just my feet, but it wasn't enough, you can't have been able to hear me. So then I had to get something I could knock onto the floor with my feet. It was just out of reach. I had to bend and…' He looked down at his wrists, which were red raw and lacerated.

'Those need antiseptic,' said Viv.

Geoff winced at the thought of it.

'Any more questions for Geoff?' asked Viv, 'because I think he needs looking after now.' She smiled kindly at him. 'There must be a first-aid kit somewhere. Come on, Jill, let's take this young man to find some clean clothes and some bandages.'

The two women left, chaperoning Geoff as though he was a small child who'd fallen over in the playground.

'Will they be okay on their own?' asked Rob. 'No offence to Geoff, but he let Quinn get one over on him once…'

'I don't think Quinn is that sort of operator,' said Charlie. 'That was classic grooming.'

Leonie found herself reflecting again on how helpful the youngest jurors could be, with their true crime obsession and greater psychological awareness.

'There were some inconsistencies in the story,' said Charlie. 'I think he tried to make it sound like Quinn forced him more than he did.'

'Go on,' said Leonie.

'Well, firstly, why would Susan have known to leave the masks down there if she'd visited him *before* the chemical attack? She can't have done.'

'Good point,' said Tanbir. 'So, either there were no masks and he was making that up, so there was a valid reason why Quinn was able to cuff him, or she visited after the attack had been announced.'

'Exactly. Did you notice how he hesitated when Leonie asked whether she visited before or after?'

'Now you mention it…' said Tanbir. 'And all that stuff about Quinn talking to him as they were walking…'

'Bollocks,' agreed Charlie. 'I bet that was all being said while they were still in the cells. He probably believed him. It's been how many hours? Plenty of time for Quinn to work on Geoff. By the end of it, Geoff probably believed he was innocent. I bet he happily followed after him and was only cuffed at the very last minute,' said Charlie. 'If he really had been led against his will, he would have screamed the house down. He didn't, because Quinn had already convinced him he's innocent.'

Leonie wasn't the only one who thought that Charlie's argument was compelling. She noticed Tanbir nodding.

'These sorts of people are good at convincing others,' continued Charlie. 'You know, like—'

'What do you mean "these sorts of people"?' asked Lucas.

'Sociopaths, narcissists…'

'You're jumping to a lot of conclusions.'

'Did you not hear Geoff's story? It was textbook. Haven't you seen that documentary about—'

'Don't believe everything you watch on TV,' said Lucas.

'But this is verified,' said Charlie, frustrated by Lucas's intransigence.

Lucas shrugged, as though independent verification was unimportant to him. 'There's nothing in that story which made me think Quinn was a killer.'

'Pardon?' asked Leonie, unable to stay quiet. 'He *cuffed* a prison guard after convincing him to release him from his cell—'

'How does that make him guilty? Trying to escape doesn't make you guilty. I'd do it, if I was innocent and accused of a crime. If I had the chance, anyway.'

Some of the jurors seemed convinced by this argument.

Leonie realized that the ten of them had started arguing about Quinn's guilt or innocence when not all twelve of them were present.

It was the first time they'd properly broken one of the rules.

Leonie looked out of the window. The only available view was of the building on the other side of the narrow street. It was split in two, the shadow cast by the court building creating a diagonal line across the white brick glowing golden in the setting sun.

The expert gave his affirmation before turning to Ms Khan KC.

'Dr Goel. Please could you give your full name and occupation?'

'Dr Vivek Goel, Consultant in Clinical Pathology at the university hospital.' The witness spoke with a slight Dutch accent.

'You conducted the postmortem in relation to Hamish Ryan, is that right?'

Hearing Hamish reduced to a corpse, listening to details about how he'd been cut open, examined, tested, was torture. But Leonie endured. She needed to hear this, needed to understand the evidence the prosecution was levying against Quinn.

'Yes, that's right.'

'What were your conclusions as to the cause of death?'

'I concluded that he died as a result of an adrenaline overdose.'

'Can you take us through your findings?'

Dr Goel counted the points off on his fingers, going through the evidence of the mark on the arm, the missing syringe, the vial in the sharps bin. 'In the absence of any other cause of cardiac arrest, my conclusion was that it was adrenaline which was the cause of death. This is particularly so, given the resus team followed the Advanced Life Support Guidelines but to no effect.'

'What are the Advanced Life Support Guidelines?'

'They provide instructions for how to respond to a cardiac arrest. There are four planks of resuscitation: CPR, defibrillation, ventilation, and adrenaline.'

Khan flicked through the pages in front of her. 'There was also a blood test done at the hospital, is that right?'

'Yes, and it showed extremely high levels of adrenaline.'

'How is adrenaline quantified in the blood?'

'It's quantified by nanograms of the substance per litre of plasma. Plasma adrenaline concentrations in resting adults are usually less than ten nanograms per litre, but they may increase by ten times as much during exercise or sexual intercourse, and by up to fifty times or more when stressed. Intravenous administration of adrenaline to acute-care cardiac patients can produce plasma concentrations of between ten thousand and a hundred thousand nanograms per litre. Most cardiac patients receive intravenous adrenaline every three minutes, according to the ALS Guidelines.'

'What was the plasma concentration in Hamish Ryan's blood from Dr Bleasdale's sample?'

'The test came back with fifty thousand nanograms per litre. Normally, after one intravenous dose from the pre-filled syringes, you'd expect a plasma concentration of around thirty-five thousand nanograms per litre. There's an elimination half-life of about two and a half minutes. This means that he must have had more than one dose of adrenaline when the blood was taken.'

'Just to recap, you're saying the amount of adrenaline in his blood could not have been generated by a single one-milligram dose of IV adrenaline?'

'It could not.'

Khan ended her questioning there and handed over to Ferguson.

'You said in your evidence that the elimination half-life of adrenaline is two and a half minutes.'

'Yes, that's around right. Two to three minutes.'

'But what we don't know in this case is what time the alleged first dose of adrenaline was given, do we?' Ferguson seemed very pleased with this point, but Leonie was at a loss as to how it helped his case.

'We don't, no, but the amount of adrenaline in the plasma is only going to reduce, not increase.'

Ferguson pressed on. Leonie had spotted that this was a tactic of his. Whatever he said, he imbued it with supreme confidence, such that she noticed other members of the jury were more taken in by the way he said things rather than what he was saying. 'But you accept your calculation isn't an accurate one?'

'I can't be precise, but I can be sure that more adrenaline was given than the one milligram they knew about at the time the blood was taken.'

'There's no evidence you could point to in Hamish Ryan's postmortem which proves the cause of death was adrenaline, is there?'

'All postmortems rely upon external facts to some extent or another. The clinical picture lives in the context of the facts I'm given about the patient.'

'But there's nothing physical, like the state of the heart or dilation of blood vessels which says for definite it was adrenaline poisoning?'

'No, there's no silver bullet, but there is a clinical picture and a set of facts. Putting them together, I'm sure that Hamish Ryan was given an overdose of adrenaline.'

Again, Ferguson moved on without acknowledging what the witness had said. 'You say "overdose", but the height of the prosecution case is that Nurse Quinn only administered one dose of adrenaline.'

'Yes, and one milligram of adrenaline is enough to make a patient in Mr Ryan's condition go into cardiac arrest. It should only be given to patients who have already gone into cardiac arrest.'

Ferguson flicked through his pages, and, unable to find any inspiration there, ended his cross-examination.

Later that afternoon, they were presented with their first table. It was a table showing all of the staff on the ward for each of the deaths. Quinn was the only one on shift for all four.

*

As they left the court building that day, Sim was jittery with excitement.

'You'll never guess what I'm doing.' Before waiting for her answer he said, 'I'm going on a date with a rock star. Look.'

He showed her a picture. In the foreground, his arm outstretched in 'selfie mode', was a beautiful man, his face sweaty and his eye makeup disarranged. In the background were a range of different band members and a couple of people who looked like managers or roadies. They were backstage in the band's dressing room, clearly celebrating after a successful gig. There was someone in the background that Leonie recognized. She felt an uncomfortable jolt in her navel.

She handed the phone back to Sim, uneasy. He stared at it again and she had the impulse to snatch it from his hands. Luckily, he only had eyes for Amir, the man who had taken the picture.

After five minutes, Viv and Jill returned.

'How come you're back so soon?' asked Anthony.

'He didn't really want our help,' said Viv. 'We took him to the end of the corridor and he said he'd be fine on his own. He knew where his clothes were and where the first-aid kit is kept, so he didn't need our help.'

'Do you think he didn't trust you?'

'I'm not sure.' Viv shrugged. 'Maybe he just felt emasculated.'

There was an uneasy silence.

Rob asked, 'So, is he coming back here for safety in numbers or what?'

'He didn't say.'

'Sounds like he's trying to get out.'

'Who knows?'

Everyone went silent. Leonie felt like she could read what the others were thinking as though it was being broadcast: if Geoff managed to exit the building without coming to any harm, could they?'

'We should barricade the doors,' said Diren. 'Now you two are back. We need to stop Quinn from getting in.'

'What if Geoff wants to join us?' asked Jill.

'Geoff has decided to take his chances. We need to look after ourselves.'

They set about propping up chairs against the doors that led into the jury gallery, focusing on the double doors separating the corridor from the staircase. It was agreed that they should keep the access to the corridor open so they could still get to the toilets. A large group of them moved a heavy table to block access to their little enclave.

Leonie was part of a smaller group who set about securing the other side of the room.

'Hey, look in here.' Diren was pointing to a door in the corner of the canteen, which led to a tiny kitchen. In the kitchen was another door opening out into a corridor.

'I thought the only way into the jury gallery would be by the main staircase,' said Leonie. 'But there's this whole warren of other corridors back here.'

'Let's just seal off this door,' said Sim.

They propped one of the tables and a few chairs against the door which led to the kitchen before returning to the main room.

'That was a bit of an overreaction,' said Lucas. 'We might need to get out of this place fast and we've just put a load of obstacles in our way.'

'We're trapped in a building with a potential serial killer,' said Diren. 'I'd rather not take any chances.'

'I'd rather not take any chances when it comes to us getting out of here.'

Leonie said, 'How about we go back to discussing the case? That's the only way we'll know what we're dealing with. Do we have a serial killer on our hands, or an innocent man who happens to chain security guards to radiators?'

'I'd chain someone to a radiator to avoid going to prison for something I didn't do,' said Lucas.

'But you've just heard that he's a master manipulator. Classic psychopath,' said Leonie.

'You're relying on something that happened outside of the courtroom,' said Lucas. 'If we're deliberating properly, we shouldn't be taking that into account.'

'Agreed,' said Rob. 'If we're going to do it at all, let's do it properly.'

There were mixed feelings about returning to the topic of the trial, but Leonie knew that if Rob had decided they should deliberate, the others would fall into line soon enough. She pulled out her folder of notes and studied them while the discussion carried on around her. She had to nail down this adrenaline point. If she fell at the first hurdle, then it was all over. Quinn would be acquitted.

'Here!' said Leonie, pointing at a page. The evidence was from a month ago.

'Dr Goel's evidence,' she said. 'The prosecution expert. Earlier, Lucas said that all the blood test does is prove something we already know, which is that he was given adrenaline before the test was taken.'

'Yeah,' he said.

'Well, Dr Goel said that the test shows more than that. It shows that there was more adrenaline in his blood than if he'd just had the shot the resus team gave him. Where did the extra adrenaline come from?'

'It could be a margin of error.'

Leonie checked her notes. 'What, forty per cent?'

Lucas shrugged as though such a detail was beneath him.

'Let's have another show of hands,' said Rob. 'Hands up who thinks that the fourth victim died because of an adrenaline overdose?'

Everyone's hands went up apart from Lucas's.

Addressing Lucas, Diren said, 'Let me get this straight. You think that someone just went into cardiac arrest for no reason?'

'No, I'm just saying I'm not sure that an injection of adrenaline caused him to go into cardiac arrest.'

'What the fuck did, then?'

'Is it for me to say?'

'Well, if you're in doubt, then yeah. How is there doubt if there is literally no other explanation?'

'What if there is an explanation out there and we don't know it?'

'That's speculation,' said Leonie. 'The judge told us to decide the case only on the evidence.'

'Listen,' said Rob. 'We're getting too bogged down in the details of the blood test, but it's simple. People don't just spontaneously go into cardiac arrest.'

Lucas looked at Rob. 'Okay, so if you're not getting "bogged down" in the details of the blood test, then how do you know it was adrenaline that caused the cardiac arrest?'

Rob blew out his cheeks and spread his hands. 'I just said, didn't I? People's hearts don't stop working for no reason. No reason we've been given, anyway. Do you accept that?'

'I do,' said Lucas.

'If we all accept that people don't just spontaneously go into cardiac arrest for no reason,' said Tanbir, 'and if we accept that there is no other possible explanation as to why Hamish Ryan went into cardiac arrest, then the circumstantial evidence confirms that the cause was adrenaline.'

'Mmm,' said Lucas. 'Circumstantial.'

'Not this again,' said Leonie. 'Circumstantial evidence *is* evidence. It's a matter for us what weight we attach to it. I say it's very strong circumstantial evidence.'

Lucas was still prevaricating.

'It's like—'

'No more metaphors,' said Rob. 'I don't think they're helping. It's just straightforward common sense.'

All eyes were on Lucas. He let out a sigh. 'All right.'

Leonie sat up straighter. They had surpassed the first hurdle.

'But that's only step one,' said Lucas, clearly regretting having given into peer pressure. 'This doesn't prove Michael Quinn did it. In fact—'

'Let's just leave it at that for now,' said Rob.

'I need a slash anyway,' said Lucas, getting up.

A couple of others also voiced the need to use the toilet and went after him.

'I think we should turn the lights on,' said Viv. 'We're sitting in half darkness.'

Those who had gone to the toilet returned after a few minutes.

'Have you been discussing the case without us?' asked Lucas.

'No,' some of them replied.

'Yeah, right. You were discussing it when Viv and Jill were helping Geoff.'

'You were one of the ones discussing it!' Sim pointed out.

'I didn't start it.'

'It's not "who smelt it dealt it". It was an honest mistake. We can always recap our discussions for Jill and Viv.'

'That's not the point. We've already broken the rules. If you lot convict him, I'll tell the judge about it.'

So that was how he was going to play it. As soon as he thought that the case was going in a direction he didn't like, he was going to play dirty.

*

Leonie got up to walk away from the bickering. This is what she'd wanted, wasn't it? For them to deliberate?

No, you wanted them to agree with you.

There was a small flight of steps that led up to the out-of-use canteen. The view from the window in here was the same as in the main room: the blank facade of the building opposite. There were no lights on over the way. Leonie wondered what had happened to the people inside, the ones whose hands had pressed against the glass with such urgency.

She approached the window and leant forward so that her face was nearly touching the glass. To her right was the main road where the army vehicle had trundled along, telling them all to stay inside. To her left, in the narrow gap between buildings, she could see the park which lay on the other side of the dual carriageway. Trees guarded the wrought-iron entrance, their leaves gilded by the low-hanging sun.

She took in the view for as long as she could bear to be in this uncomfortable position, before turning her back and sitting on the windowsill.

What did she want from this? This could be the end of the world as they knew it and all she could think about was Quinn. How much negative energy had she harboured in her body thinking about one evil nurse? Wouldn't it have been healthier to look back on her time with Hamish, grieve him properly?

No, that's not possible. Those memories were too heavy.

Instead of dealing with her grief, she'd poured her energies into getting justice. She hadn't allowed herself to process his death. They'd always said that, if one of them died first, the other was allowed to grieve for a year, but then they had to move on and be happy. It had seemed like such a pragmatic solution, but one that would never be needed.

She tried to think of a memory that wasn't too painful to recall. However, her mind filled with their most intense moments, like the day they moved in together.

The first twelve months of her relationship with Hamish had been euphoric. Though Leonie was creative, she was also a realist. She knew that love was nothing more than hormones and neural networks, but it was wonderful. It was like she was floating on oxytocin, permanently tipsy.

She turned to poetry as an outlet for some of this intense feeling. There was so much nervous energy bubbling under the surface, she felt she needed to do something with it.

She wondered if she could explore her ideas about neuro-chemistry being the root of love. The resulting poems were romantic but scientifically accurate. The contrast between the scientific language and the emotional honesty gave them life. They were probably the best poems she'd ever written.

A tutor at university once told her class that simply saying 'I love you' was stylistically bereft. The tutor had forbidden them all from uttering such banalities. Leonie told Hamish she loved him most days.

But these poems were something else. They were artistically rich and experimental.

Often, people thought that reducing love down to the physi-ological reality was impersonal and boring, but Leonie's poems focused on how it was only Hamish who had ever made her feel that way. At twenty-five, never having fallen in love before, Leonie had finally alighted on someone who engendered this feverish response. And not only that—he felt the same way about her. She was plain and unsophisticated, but Hamish found her attractive.

After three months, they decided to move in together. When they pooled their mediocre salaries, they were able to rent a slightly nicer flat than they could have afforded separately.

When Leonie's parents had realized she'd be moving out, they jumped at the chance to offload her childhood crap. Boxes were filled with Leonie's reports from school and swimming certificates. She dreaded unpacking, and the laborious task of going through it all.

On moving day, she and Hamish eschewed their usual 'best selves' for comfortable clothes and practical hairstyles, Hamish using a bandana to pull his curls back from his face. By the time it got to three in the afternoon, Leonie's stomach cramped with hunger. They'd been so focused on moving, they hadn't stopped to eat. There was a Co-op down the road from them. Leonie offered to go and grab them some late lunch.

When she got back, she pressed the buzzer for their new flat. No one answered. She rested the oven pizzas awkwardly on her hip while she fished around for her key fob.

As she made her way up the stairs she said, 'We need to speak to the landlord about the buzzer, it's not work—'

Hamish was sitting, deep in the pile of boxes, reading some old notebooks from Leonie's parents' garage.

She dropped the pizzas and picked her way through the boxes as quickly as she could. 'Hey—stop it—STOP—*please*, Hamish—that's private.'

He was reading her cringeworthy poems from her teenage years, and probably her more recent ones too.

Barely looking up from the pages, he said, 'The buzzer's working. I was just distracted by these.'

She waited for him to laugh at them or tease her. Why didn't she have the sense to burn them straight after writing them?

He looked up, awestruck. 'These are amazing.'

'They're stupid. Embarrassing. I wrote them when I was young.'

'You said you wrote poetry, but I didn't imagine… This is some seriously deep stuff.'

Leonie couldn't help but scoff. It was juvenile trash.

'I mean it.' He stopped to read out a line. 'It's brilliant.'

Though she was irritated at him for breaching her privacy, it was like that first moment when she'd wheeled over to sit next to him and they'd struck up a conversation about Tool. This insanely beautiful man was looking at her like she was some sort of goddess, all because of poems she wrote as a teenager.

*

'Okay?' asked Diren. She'd been expecting Sim.

'Yeah, it's just so frustrating, arguing all the time.'

'It's what we signed up for,' he said.

'I suppose. I just want this to be over now. I want to go home.' She thought about the cat waiting at home for her. He must be starving.

Leonie always said that they called him Ollie after Oliver Twist because his meow sounded like 'more' when he was asking for food. Hamish always said that he was named after Oli Sykes, his favourite singer. It was one of the first fault lines, a divergence in the shared mythology of their relationship.

Diren stepped closer. 'We'll be okay, Leonie.' He put a hand on her shoulder.

'It'll be weird not seeing one another again, won't it?'

'There's a chance we'll bump into one another. Stranger things have happened.'

'We never bumped into one another before. How strange is that? We've all been circling the same few square miles but have never met before. We could have passed one another on the street but never stopped to notice.'

'I'd have noticed you,' he said.

Leonie blushed against her will. She tried to force her face into an expression which was nonchalant. 'That is *not* true. It's just proximity, isn't it? I'm sure on the outside you'd prefer someone, I don't know, slimmer, younger…'

'You must be joking,' he said. 'Proper women have curves.' His eyes swept her body with the appreciative glance of a connoisseur of the female form.

Hamish would never have fancied her looking like this. He hated all forms of plastic surgery, and definitely found Leonie sexiest when she was at her slimmest. She couldn't help but be flattered by Diren's attention.

Not knowing how to respond she said, 'Well, thank you.'

Leonie tried to avoid looking Diren in the eye, because she knew he would be staring brazenly into hers.

She was saved from having to invent an excuse to leave because there was a commotion coming from the next room.

Leonie rushed back into the main room, where several people were standing up, crowding around Tanbir's phone. Tanbir was saying 'shit' a lot.

'What is it?' Leonie asked Sim.

Sim looked back at her a little coolly. His eyes flicked from her to Diren with a hint of accusation.

'There's a video that's gone viral,' he said, his tone lacking warmth.

Leonie joined the scrum of people trying to get a look at Tanbir's phone.

She was looking at a block of university halls not too far away. The video was being taken from inside the building opposite.

An army vehicle not dissimilar to the one they had watched crawling down the street telling people to remain inside was doing the same thing, reiterating the same message.

From the double doors at the bottom of the building emerged a figure. It was a young woman. Her hair was long, but it didn't look healthy. It was tangled, matted. She had clear signs of injury to her face. A black eye. Scratches. Her arms also bore defensive marks. She approached the armed vehicle slowly, hands up. A soldier jumped out and pointed his gun at her. She lifted her hands higher but kept walking forwards.

Her voice was muffled, but the meaning of her words was clear. 'Help me. I can't stay here. Help.'

The loudspeaker could be heard. 'Get back inside. You must return to the building. Get back inside.'

The woman continued to walk towards the gun.

She was crying.

'Get back!'

She was less than a metre from the gun. The soldier didn't retreat at all. They held their position.

'Get back. Get back or we will shoot. Get back!'

A single shot was discharged. The woman dropped to the floor. Whoever was filming lost control of the camera.

'I told you,' said Lucas. 'I fucking told you. It's all about control.'

Leonie wanted to snap back, but the incident was still reverberating, her pulse thrumming, her mind not quite caught up with what her body was reacting to.

'She was told to get back,' said Rob. 'She didn't do as she was told. She was warned.'

'She'd been assaulted,' said Jade. 'It wasn't safe where she was. The attacker was clearly in the building.'

'She's a fool, isn't she? For putting herself and everyone else in that building in danger.'

Leonie felt like reminding Rob that he and Wynona had been the ones who had wanted to leave at the beginning and to hell with putting all of them in danger.

'Looks like the real threat is outside,' said Lucas. 'The fucking government. That was state-sanctioned murder.'

'This sort of stuff happens when order breaks down,' said Diren. Leonie couldn't help but notice the gleam in his eyes. It was like his dreams had come true and he was able to live out his *Mad Max* fantasies. 'People in authority start doing stuff they wouldn't normally do in times like these.'

'This is what they've been waiting for,' said Lucas. 'All they needed was a convenient excuse.'

'Have they given any rationale?' asked Leonie.

'Apparently the nerve agent is so transferable that if people leave the cordon, they could spread the poison around the city.'

'She wasn't leaving the cordon,' argued Jade. 'She just wanted to leave the building she was in.'

'Look,' said Leonie, trying to inject some reason into the discussion. 'It was fucking horrendous, it was a massive overreaction…'

There were lots of protests at this.

'…But this is an unprecedented public health disaster. Clearly the authorities are struggling to cope with it, but we will get evacuated eventually. They said to stay inside until we get further instructions. They'll let us out once it's safe. We need to just stay put. There's nothing we can do for now.'

To her surprise, this worked. They listened to her. It was a thrill, being able to persuade people. She understood how Ferguson and Khan could get a kick out of it. Slowly, the jurors returned to their circle.

It took a long time for people to digest what they'd seen. Leonie didn't think she'd forget seeing the woman's body drop in an instant. It seemed to replay over and over again in her mind, and she had the strange urge to watch the video again, almost as though repeated exposure to it might numb its effects, or perhaps she wanted to make sure she'd really seen that happen. Whatever the reason, it was like an itch that she couldn't scratch.

After what felt like an interminably long time, Charlie broke the silence.

'So,' he said. 'Are we discussing the case? Because there's some stuff I want to say.'

Rob, who had been staring out of the window as though waiting for rescuers, looked around at the others, who were bored and restless. 'Sure.'

The others reluctantly turned their attention to Charlie.

'Right, so we decided that Hamish Ryan was killed by adrenaline.'

'I still think that's faulty,' said Lucas.

'Too late now,' said Charlie. 'You agreed to it.'

'So, I can't change my mind?'

'Not if you're just being bloody-minded. You're not taking it seriously.'

'I'm taking it more seriously than all of you. The prosecution can't be trusted. We've got to have doubt. If we don't have doubt, we don't have anything.'

'Anyway,' said Charlie, 'if we agree Hamish Ryan was poisoned, the next question is whether Quinn did the poisoning.'

'The evidence on that is pretty patchy from where I'm standing,' said Rob.

'There's no real evidence at all,' agreed Lucas. 'This whole thing is a stitch-up.'

Leonie knew she needed to counter this immediately. 'The only explanation put forward by Quinn's team for the adrenaline getting into Hamish Ryan's bloodstream is that a stranger walked in off the street. On a busy ward where there are nurses at the nurse's station the whole time? It doesn't stand up.'

'He doesn't need to prove anything, though,' said Lucas.

'It comes back to there being no other explanation—'

The discussion was cut short by a sound coming over the Tannoy. A song. 'Adrenaline'.

Then someone started to speak. It was Quinn's voice, unmistakably.

'At least one of you is lying. There are two people in this building who knew each other from before. You can't trust either of them.' The song started playing again before cutting out.

Sixteen of the waiting jurors followed Susan down several corridors and into the courtroom. They were about to be empanelled; the archaic name given to the jury selection process.

They huddled in seats near to but not actually in the jury box.

A man in black robes sat in front of the judge's bench. In his hands was a deck of cards. So quaint and old-fashioned.

One by one he called out names and they took their seats in the two rows in the jury box. Leonie did the maths: a three-in-four chance of getting picked. Decent odds.

'Jade Harrison.' A young girl with silver-grey hair ambled over to the first seat, her sleeves tugged down over her hands.

'Tanbir Chatterjee.' A nervous-looking Asian man took up his seat.

'Wynona Davies.'

'Robert Wilson.'

That was four people now, and still Leonie's name hadn't been called. One third of the jury had been established and she wasn't on it. Two more names were called.

First was 'Diren Zorlu', an olive-skinned man somewhere between five and ten years younger than Leonie. He took up the first seat on the second row.

Next was, 'Lucas Woodward'. Before now, Leonie had thought of him as Hipster Dude. He took up a seat next to Diren.

They were into the second half now. Sweat was gathering in the small of her back.

Two other names were called. Neither of them were people Leonie had paid much attention to.

'Charlie Scott.' The youngest of the potential jurors—a pretty boy with a floppy blond mop—was called.

Come on, thought Leonie. *Me next.*

Two other names were called out: one young and the other elderly.

'Simbarashe Moyo.'

Just two names left to be called. The odds had plummeted to one-in-three.

'Leonie Vogt.'

Sweet relief. She was on the jury. On Michael Quinn's jury. She heard one more name called out and they were formed. She had made it.

*

'Ladies and gentlemen,' said the judge to the twelve people seated in the jury box. 'Shortly we are going to swear you in as members of the jury. This is going to be a very long trial, because it concerns multiple allegations of murder. The current time estimate is eight weeks. Please raise your hand if you have any holidays or surgeries due to take place in that period.'

The ears of the four leftover jurors pricked. Maybe this was their chance to get on a jury. They seemed much keener now that they knew it was a murder trial.

The lady to Leonie's right raised her hand. An usher approached her so that the lady could whisper in her ear. Leonie was just able to overhear her say that she was going to have an operation on her cataracts in two weeks.

This information was passed onto the judge, who duly discharged the juror, for her to be replaced with an elderly gentleman.

There seemed to be no other difficulties with jurors sitting for the next eight weeks, so the judge turned to his next topic. 'Now, the next part of the process is very important. Your role as a jury is to make judgements about people. Judgements about whether they've been truthful, about whether they are correct in what they're saying. It is of utmost importance that none of you know anyone involved in this trial to avoid your judgement being clouded by preconceptions or advance knowledge of any of the people who will come before you to give evidence.

'What I'm going to do now is ask Ms Khan KC, who prosecutes, to stand up and read out the list of names of the people and places involved in this case. If you know anyone, or know anything about them, please raise your hand.'

The beads of sweat which had been making steady progress down Leonie's back now collected in a pool above her waistband. This could be the moment where she would falter, or be found out. She'd wondered whether there would be some sort of investigation into their backgrounds to make sure they were suitable, but there was none of that. She'd seen courtroom dramas where private investigators had whole folders on potential jurors. It wasn't so in this case.

After the judge gave his spiel, Counsel for the prosecution got to her feet.

'Members of the jury, this case concerns the defendant, Michael Quinn, who was a nurse in the city hospital. Please consider him carefully. If you know him, or know of him, or have ever been treated by him, please raise your hand and inform us of your connection to him. Look closely. Just because you don't recognize the name doesn't mean you won't recognize the accused's face.'

Leonie forced herself to look over at Quinn. She met Quinn's eyes and for a moment she thought she saw recognition there. Perhaps that was just her guilty conscience, but she could have sworn he was about to raise a hand and point in her direction.

Once they had finished scrutinizing Quinn, they returned to Ms Khan. No one raised their hand.

Nor did anyone in the public gallery protest. Leonie was terrified that a police officer, or another member of staff at hospital might have spotted her, but it seemed that, so far, she was in the clear. She couldn't believe that the entire process was reliant on their honesty.

Ms Khan continued. 'The other people you need to be aware of are the victims in this case. Please, if you know or know of any of the names I'm about to read out, raise your hand.

'Zane Chan, Gail Bridges—'

One of the jurors raised her hand. An usher approached her, and she whispered something into his ear. This was then relayed to the judge, who waved his hand.

'Thank you very much for letting us know,' he said. He really did sound grateful.

Leonie realized that this unctuous tone was to encourage others with personal connections to anyone involved in the case to come forward.

The clerk who sat at the desk below the judge's bench retrieved her cards and read out a name. The juror who raised her hand was swiftly replaced by another middle-aged woman called Jill Churchill.

'Thank you,' he said to the departing juror, before turning to the new one. 'Welcome. Please continue, Ms Khan.'

Khan read out the remaining two victims' names. 'Andrew Chapman and Hamish Ryan.'

Leonie held her breath. Her hand remained firmly in her lap. She hadn't got this far to turn back now. If only she could stop the colour from rising in her cheeks. The courtroom was air conditioned, so it would have been incongruous to see a red, sweaty face, even on this baking hot summer's day.

This could be it. The moment where she was found out. The moment when a private investigator stood up at the back of court, pointed at her and said, 'It's you.' None of that happened. No one checked anything. They just asked the question and expected people to answer honestly. It seemed to be a hallmark of the constitution in the UK that people were expected to tell the truth. It had been one of the things which had made it so difficult to rein in the incumbent Prime Minister. His lies in the House of Commons often went unchecked because there was a chap's code of honour, and the system simply wasn't designed with someone breaking that code in mind. Nor did it appear that the justice system was prepared for someone who was willing to go to any length to get onto a jury.

Next, Khan read out the long list of witnesses. There were two more substitutions as a result of this process. First, a tall, balding man with a prematurely lined face called Anthony Jacobs took his seat. Then, a new juror filled the spot to Leonie's right. An eye-catching woman with an unusual dress sense called Viv Cohen. Leonie realized now why it was so important to have a panel of sixteen. She needn't have been as bothered about not getting onto the jury first time. This process had weeded out four of the original twelve, meaning they exhausted all four additional jurors from the panel.

Next, the defence barrister read out a smaller list of names of witnesses, and finally Quinn was given the opportunity to object to the members of his jury on the basis that he knew any of them, or that they knew him.

Leonie's heartbeat started thrumming in her ears. She was sure that he was going to point to her. He didn't know her name, but he might recognize her face, despite all of the fake tan and the weight gain and the new haircut and the cosmetic work. His eyes roved over the jury, cold and calculating, but he didn't single anyone out. Leonie wanted to breathe a sigh of relief, but she managed to let out a measured breath.

No one paid any attention to Leonie. Their focus was on the judge, who was telling them about lunch arrangements. No evidence will be heard today, he said. The prosecution would give their opening speech after the lunch adjournment.

Having successfully wormed her way onto the jury, Leonie walked away from the courtroom feeling lighter.

Rather than take them back to the large jury gallery, they were shown into a room very close to the courtroom with a long table and twelve chairs around the outside. There was a tea and coffee station, which Leonie approached for something to do. In front of her was the olive-skinned man, Diren. His gaze swept up and down her body and he muttered 'MILF' as he turned his back on her to make himself coffee.

'Pardon me,' said Leonie.

He turned back to her, smirking. 'What?'

'You heard me. You said something rude.'

'Did I?' He stirred his coffee and left, still sneering. Something about the bracing of his shoulders signalled some-one who was ready to dive into chaos or create some, if he found it lacking.

'I heard it,' said a voice behind her. It was Simbarashe Moyo. 'What a tosser.'

'Yeah, he is,' said Leonie.

'I'm Sim, by the way,' he said.

'Leonie.'

Whatever panic Quinn was hoping he would induce with his words was already catching.

'He's just trying to freak us out,' said Leonie.

'Who here knows someone else from before?' asked Rob, eyeing everyone.

'Is this why someone took my phone?' asked Sim. He turned to Jade. 'Was it you? Were you hoping you could get Amir's number or something?'

'Calm down,' said Leonie. 'You were accusing Viv a minute ago.'

Viv looked appalled. 'What? I would never…'

'Oh, thanks a bunch, Leonie,' said Sim.

'Was it you two?' Rob rounded on Leonie and Sim. 'You've been unusually chummy since day one.'

Sim laughed bitterly. 'Not any more.'

Leonie felt that like a slap.

'Does that mean you *were* friends before you met here?' pushed Rob.

'No, we'd never met,' said Leonie. 'And the same could be said of you and Wynona. You've always seen eye to eye.'

'What are you insinuating?' asked Wynona.

'Nothing, I'm just throwing Rob's logic back at him.'

Wynona's nose twitched with dissatisfaction. 'What about you two?' Her eyes flitted from Diren to Leonie. 'The pair of you have been getting cosy.'

Leonie knew that everyone would see how quickly she'd flushed. There was no point in denying it. 'You're giving him exactly what he wants. He wants us to panic. Let's just carry on discussing the case.'

'I want to know who stole my phone,' said Sim. 'How am I supposed to trust anyone here knowing that they stole from me?' He glared around at them all.

It took all of Leonie's resolve to keep her face free of guilt. She couldn't risk meeting Diren's eye.

'What was the song he was playing?' asked Charlie.

'It's called "Adrenaline",' said Jade, pointing at her hoodie. 'It's an Acid Rain song. We heard it being played while we were out getting food.'

Charlie looked puzzled. 'You never said.'

'I forgot. We found, you know, Susan, not long after.'

'Maybe he knows where we are,' said Rob, speaking in a whisper. 'We should have stayed in the other room.'

Diren looked exasperated. 'We'd have been trapped in there. There are more escape routes here. More places to hide.'

'More places for him to hide from us,' said Rob.

'Who says he's going to try to harm us?' asked Lucas. 'He hasn't done anything. We haven't found him guilty.'

'We haven't found him innocent either,' said Charlie. 'And he has done *something*. He's taunting us.'

'You're jumping to conclusions,' said Lucas.

Charlie ignored this and spoke to Jade. 'What are the rest of the lyrics to the song?'

Jade recited the verse with ease.

> Drag me down to your level
> At least it's warm
> In the eighth circle of hell

Well. Wouldn't you like that?

For me to be at your level?

They looked at one another, nonplussed. Charlie frowned, contemplating the lyrics but finding no meaning in them.

The only person to make any comment was Wynona. 'Sounds rubbish. They tried to make "level" rhyme with "hell", but it doesn't.'

Like she could do any better, thought Leonie.

'I'm only speaking the lyrics,' said Jade, frustrated. 'It sounds better sung.'

'Maybe we should have got Charlie to sing it,' Wynona said with a knowing smirk. 'Then we might "get it".'

Charlie's face dropped.

'Can he hear what we're saying?' Sim looked around as though looking for bugs. 'We'd just decided that adrenaline was the murder weapon and then he played that song. There's no way that's a coincidence.'

Other eyes darted to the corners of the room, just like Sim's had.

'Maybe we should move again,' suggested Jade.

Diren shook his head. 'It's what he'd want us to do.'

'I think we should carry on deliberating,' said Leonie. 'Doesn't it make all the difference? Whether we're trapped in a building with a serial killer or not?'

'I'm all in favour of treating him as though he's a dangerous murdering bastard before we decide on things by committee,' said Diren.

'Same here,' said Charlie. 'Who cares if he killed those four people? He tied up Geoff.'

'Let's carry on as we were,' said Leonie. 'Let's discuss the case.'

'I want to know who here knew one another before they were called onto this jury,' said Rob.

'How are you going to work that out?' asked Leonie.

'We should go round and get everyone to say who they are and what their background is.'

'It's a waste of time.' Leonie didn't think she could bear to hear Rob talk about his job in insurance again.

'We've got all the time in the world. No one knows when we're getting out of here.'

'I don't want to come back here ever again,' said Leonie. 'Let's at least make sure we leave with a verdict, then we don't ever have to.'

'We will reach a verdict, but first I want more information about everyone in this room. I'm going to start with you.' Rob looked straight at her.

She stared back defiantly, though the last thing she wanted was to be asked questions about her invented past.

They returned the chairs to their customary circle. This time, everyone was looking at Leonie. She felt an inkling of sympathy for the witnesses who'd given evidence. She hadn't appreciated how it would feel to have the collective attention of the whole room trained on you and your story.

'So, what do you do?' asked Rob.

'Do?' Leonie decided to play up to the image of someone who didn't need to work because of a divorce settlement.

'For money,' clarified Rob.

'Well, that's complicated,' said Leonie.

'As I thought.' Rob's smirk was nasty. 'You have plenty of money, but you didn't earn it?'

Leonie remained taciturn, neither confirming nor denying Rob's preconceived bias.

'What does your ex-husband do, then?' he asked.

'He was in tech.'

'Can you be more specific?'

'Not really. Went over my head.' She smiled benignly.

She tried to focus but couldn't stop thinking about the song lyrics from 'Adrenaline'. They kept swirling around her head. Her eye was drawn to Jade rolling up the baggy sleeves of her hoodie, revealing the tattooed lyrics on her arm. Alien Pandemic lyrics.

The truth about how Leonie and Hamish had earned their money was that Hamish had been a songwriter. It had been Josh who had got Hamish into 'the industry'. After their first time at Subculture, Leonie and Hamish continued to hang out with Josh and Amy.

'What do they do?' Leonie had asked not long after she first met the couple.

'Josh is a producer,' said Hamish. With much less interest, he added, 'Amy works in the Civil Service or something.'

'Are you going to see if Josh will sign Something Cool?'

Hamish grimaced on hearing the band name. 'No. I know I'm flogging a dead horse there. Josh told me as much.'

Leonie kept quiet. To agree would be mean, but she wanted him to take her opinions seriously, and no one who said Something Cool had a future in the music industry could be taken seriously.

'But the one thing I have some talent in is the writing. My riffs are great and so are my melodies.'

'You're thinking of going into songwriting?'

'Yeah. Josh said I could send him some demos.'

'Would you be okay with that? You know, not being centre stage?'

'Of course! I have no interest in fame. The most powerful and influential people in the music industry are the nameless, faceless people you wouldn't know if you saw them in the street. I think Josh could help me get in touch with a few people.'

'What will you write?'

'There's this new type of music around at the moment and it's right up my street. Listen to this.'

Hamish connected his mp3 player to the speakers. Leonie had got used to the primal screams and thrashing guitars by now. In fact, there were times when she loved them.

This music was unlike anything she'd heard before. The unclean vocals were kept to a minimum, peppering the music rather than dominating it. There was a heavy reliance on electronic sounds, and an almost pop sensibility. Leonie found herself wanting to sing the chorus after only one listen.

'Good, isn't it?' asked Hamish.

'It's really catchy.'

'They call it electronicore. It has the potential to go pretty mainstream.'

'What's this band called?'

'Alien Pandemic.'

'Good name.'

'It's great. Anyway, I really think this could be my niche.'

Leonie watched Jade. Cripplingly self-conscious, she contin-ued to play with her hair, pick her nails, fiddle with the silver pendant around her neck, anything that gave her an outlet for her nervousness.

Leonie would have loved to tell Jade that the lyrics tattooed on her arm had been written by her husband.

'Do you have a vocation at all?' asked Rob.

Leonie answered honestly. 'I'm a poet.'

'Anything we'd have heard of?'

Her answers were measured and unruffled. 'Read much poetry?'

'Er, no.'

'I expect not, then.'

'Any friends?'

'I have them, yes.'

'Anyone from this jury?'

'No, definitely not. Not from before, I mean.'

'Not your type of people, are we?'

'It's a city. Our paths have never crossed.'

'I'll bet they haven't.' Rob scratched his chin. 'Kids?'

'No.'

Rob looked around at the others. 'Anything anyone else wants to clarify?' Everyone shook their heads.

After that, Rob interrogated everyone one by one. Occupation, friendship circles, any potential for crossover in hobbies. Wynona worked in a bank and had the same group of friends she'd had at school. She made the mistake of pretending she was an investment banker, but really she was a member of administrative staff. Diren picked up on this in an instant. So much of her identity and self-belief seemed to derive from her role in middle management, and Diren was ripping it apart for no reason other than his perverse pleasure.

'Stop it,' Leonie murmured to Diren.

'What?'

'Stop taking the piss for once.'

Diren tilted his head as though he was disappointed in her. How did he always manage to see through her? He was right; she was a hypocrite. She'd been all too happy to sit in her ivory tower with Sim.

However much Wynona wanted to be seen as a big boss in the world of business, Tanbir and Sim had the most corporate jobs. Tanbir was a civil engineer working for a multinational consultancy, while Sim worked as an architect in a large firm whose sleek glass offices sat in glinting skyscrapers.

'Listen, Viv,' said Sim. 'I'm really sorry about earlier. It was muggy of me to suspect you. But when someone's betrayed you like that, it makes you paranoid.'

She smiled and waved away his apologies. 'No need. I have every sympathy.'

Viv was at the other end of the spectrum from Sim and Tanbir: a reiki healer whose friendship groups came from her church.

Diren was a security guard. He had a close-knit group of friends he referred to as 'the boys' and an active lifestyle involving regular gym sessions and playing football to a decent level.

As for the younger ones, Jade worked in an alternative clothing shop.

'I bet you meet lots of interesting people,' said Viv.

'Er, yeah. That's sort of the problem? I'm not much of a people person. I like my own company.'

She wanted to be a songwriter. The bands and hobbies she liked were pretty incomprehensible to the likes of Rob. Charlie worked in a supermarket. His history had been so thoroughly excavated earlier that his story wasn't picked over too much. Lucas said that his passion was crypto but, in the meantime, he worked as a data-entry clerk via a temping agency. Though he tried to make it sound more exciting than it was, it was clear to Leonie that his social life was confined to beers with a few mates who he didn't really like, live cam girls, and his right hand.

Anthony was an accountant for a small local outfit while Jill worked as a teaching assistant in a primary school. Both of their social lives revolved around the many after-school activities of their children in what seemed like a losing battle to tire them out so that they could get some peace post-8 p.m.

After he'd finished questioning others, Rob subjected himself to the same indignity, but no one cared too much for Rob's work in insurance and the sedate, middle-class life he and his family led. The only time Rob showed a little bit of humanity was when he described the battle that he and his wife had faced in securing the appropriate support for their disabled son. After that, Leonie felt she understood Rob a little better, especially his anxiety that his children were okay.

Once the interrogation was over, Rob continued to eyeball Leonie. He knew there was something off about her, he just didn't know what. If Rob had picked up on the fact Leonie was lying about something, it might only be a matter of time before someone else worked out what that thing was. They needed to come to a verdict as soon as possible.

'Hey, I've got an idea,' said Sim. 'You know he said that two people here know one another from before? What if it's something to do with Susan? What if she's the one someone knew from before?'

They all looked at each other, suspicions pinballing. Rob looked at Leonie. The intensity of his glare was interrupted when more noise came over the Tannoy.

People jumped and looked around, as though looking for the person speaking.

'For fuck's sake, not again,' said Rob.

I'll be by your side
In the morning light
When night draws in
I know your every sin
I'll haunt you for ever
Even when the lights go out

With that, they were plunged into darkness.

It took Leonie a couple of seconds for her eyes to adjust to the lack of light. There was still just enough pale blue light coming from the windows to be able to see everyone, but not clearly.

'I'm guessing that was more Acid Rain?' asked Charlie.

'Yeah,' said Jade. 'That song is called "Eclipse".'

'The prick's toying with us,' said Diren.

'It's definitely him,' agreed Leonie.

Leonie sensed Diren move closer to her. He then addressed the group. 'If we can find the plant room, we'll be able to turn the lights back on, but the problem with that is he could just turn them off again.'

'That would defeat the whole exercise,' agreed Rob. 'But I don't like the idea of being without light.'

'Nor me,' said Sim. 'How will anyone know we're in here if the lights are off? They might not look for us.'

This caused a great deal of unrest.

'Bottom line is we need to get the lights back on,' said Wynona.

'Agreed,' said Diren. 'But how do we stop him from turning them off again?'

'We could try and find him?' suggested Jade.

Diren shook his head. 'There's no way. This place is massive.'

'Well, we know where he was thirty seconds ago.'

'And in thirty seconds he could have gone in one of eight directions. It'll take us ten minutes to get down there, by which time he could be anywhere in the building.'

'But we can't just sit in the dark,' said Rob.

'What if he wants us to go and turn the lights off?' said Leonie in a quiet voice. 'It's like he's been trying to draw us out this whole time. Maybe his intention is for us to go and find the plant room.'

'Why would he do that?' asked Rob.

'Maybe it's a trap?'

'I can't see it. He's not physically dangerous.'

'He's a murderer,' said Leonie. 'That's the definition of physically dangerous.' A small part of Leonie acknowledged that Rob was right. Quinn wasn't an immediate danger; he was insidious. He took his time. 'All that's stopping all of us from killing each other are societal rules and empathy. He doesn't care about those things. The filter isn't there for him. That's what makes him dangerous.'

'We still haven't decided whether or not he's guilty,' said Rob.

'Then let's carry on discussing it,' said Leonie, but there was no enthusiasm for the proposition.

'We've got to do something,' said Charlie. 'How about if a group of us goes down to find the plant room and then there'll be safety in numbers?'

'That doesn't stop the problem of him coming to find the people left behind,' said Leonie.

'Okay, so let's make sure that we leave some strong, fit people behind in case he does come up here,' said Diren.

'And how do we stop him turning the lights off again?' asked Jade.

'It's like standing up to a bully,' said Rob. 'He's just testing us.'

'Unless we relocate?' suggested Sim. 'The plant room is bound to be downstairs in the basement somewhere. It is in almost all buildings. So if we stay in the atrium, or the canteen, or somewhere which is close to the plant room, then we control the lights, not him. And we'd still have creature comforts. There's the canteen. There are the loos. Okay, the seats aren't as comfortable, but…'

Leonie could see the others mulling over Sim's suggestion. It was the most logical answer to their problems, but she could also tell that they were comfortable in this room. It was familiar, there was plenty of space for them, but it was also self-contained with its own toilets and mini, albeit out-of-use, canteen.

'He's got a point,' said Diren.

Viv, Wynona, Jill and Anthony all looked sceptical.

'How about a group go and find the plant room first?' suggested Rob. 'If the lights go off again, we can do what he says as Plan B.'

Several people nodded in agreement. Lucas was desperate to be one of the people to leave the jury gallery and Leonie wondered whether he was going to make a run for it. As much as she would have liked to see the back of him, all twelve of them would be needed to deliver a verdict. In the end it was decided that Leonie, Diren, Jade and Wynona would go down to the plant room.

They made their way along the same route as they took to get to the canteen a few hours previously, using the torches on their phones to navigate. There were many windowless corridors. Perhaps Leonie was just being dramatic, giving in to that primal fear of the dark, but the contours of every piece of furniture were invisible, so each shadow whispered with menace.

There was a strand of melody, muffled. She strained to listen.

'He's playing it again,' she whispered.

This time it wasn't blaring through the Tannoy, but seemed to be coming from a smaller device, like a phone. She wondered how Quinn had managed to get his hands on one.

Diren's voice was stern. 'Ignore it. Let's just focus on getting the lights back on.'

Leonie nodded and carried on walking, haunted by the Acid Rain music.

Once down on the ground floor, they systematically searched each of the corridors leading away from the pentagon-shaped atrium, looking for the plant room. It didn't take them long to find the right door.

They used Susan's pass to gain access. A small flight of concrete steps led them down into the basement room. The floor was stained with damp. In the corner was a series of pipes and large aluminium-covered vents. On the wall adjacent to the door were fifty or so grey panels, each labelled with a yellow sticker.

Leonie hovered at Diren's shoulder, shining the torch in the direction he indicated. He flicked some switches on the switchboard and the light for the plant room came on.

'Done,' he said. 'Let's get out of here.'

They emerged into the atrium.

'Adrenaline' started playing again.

> It's time we said our goodbyes
> Why is it always fight or flight?…

Still from a phone, but it was louder this time. That meant he was closer than before.

Leonie stopped walking. Diren did the same. He took on the bearing of an animal that sensed danger.

The sound was coming from the corridor opposite.

'Oi, you two,' Diren whispered to Jade and Wynona. 'Wait here,' he said. 'We'll go and check it out first and then come back for you.'

Wynona shifted her weight impatiently and Leonie wondered for a fleeting moment whether she was considering making a run for it. It would be madness to do that, but people made irrational decisions where their children were concerned. Leonie only hoped Jade would talk some sense into her if she tried.

Leonie stayed close behind Diren as they crept towards the sound of tinny music.

It seemed to be coming from an office with a wired-glass door, a blind covering the window. A plaque on the wall next to the door said *Probation*. Below that was a black box. Diren held the lanyard in front of it. A loud click signalled that the door had unlocked. They waited a couple of seconds before Diren pushed it open. He scanned the room and checked behind the door before entering.

Leonie followed suit, shutting the door behind her.

The room was empty, but they were definitely in the right place, because the music was so loud. While Diren was checking under the desk and behind the cabinets to make sure no one was hiding, Leonie walked over to the desk, on which an old-fashioned computer stood, with a grubby keyboard. Propped against a mug of half-finished coffee was a mobile phone playing 'Adrenaline'. Leonie pressed pause. The home screen showed a picture taken of Leonie, Diren and Susan as they'd walked through the court building eight hours previously.

Diren was still checking to make sure the small office was empty.

'Look at this,' Leonie showed him the phone's lock screen. 'What's he playing at?'

'Mind games.'

Diren peered around at the room, no doubt wondering if there was anything useful in here.

Leonie flicked the light switch. The tired grey carpet came into sharper focus, the monitor with fingerprint smudges, the cluttered desk and stained walls. Everything looked so ordinary. There were only a few clues as to the disaster that had taken hold of the building. An apple with one bite taken out of it. A half-finished yoghurt, the spoon erect.

Diren picked up the apple and took a bite. His eyes closed as he savoured the taste.

He was still chomping on the apple as they walked back to the atrium. When they got there, Jade stood alone, looking nervous.

'Where's Wynona?' asked Leonie. 'She hasn't made a run for it?'

'She said she needed the toilet.'

'For fuck's sake, we were only gone for five minutes,' said Diren through a mouthful of apple.

'Look, when you've had kids, your pelvic floor isn't what it used to be, okay? Give the woman a break.' Jade looked to Leonie as if to say, 'Am I right?' but Leonie didn't back her up. She was more worried about what might have happened to Wynona.

'She can't have gone far,' said Leonie. 'Where are the nearest loos?'

Jade pointed down one of the corridors shooting away from the atrium.

All three of them entered the toilet. After a quick search it became clear that Wynona wasn't there.

'Where the hell is she?' asked Leonie.

'This happened before. Rob and Wynona got lost.'

'That was different,' said Leonie. 'He hadn't made his presence known then.'

'She's right,' said Diren. 'Why the hell would she leave the bathroom and not find you?'

'I knew this would happen,' said Leonie. 'I knew he was intending on separating us somehow. He managed to lure her away.'

Diren shot a look at Leonie, and she could tell he was a little wounded by the implied criticism.

'I'm not having a go, I'm just saying from now on we really need to stick together.'

He nodded in an uncharacteristic show of humility. 'Fair enough. Right, let's make sure we get back to the others. I wonder if we should be searching for weapons or something.'

'Where are we going to get those from?'

'Exhibits? Police sometimes bring knives and guns to court for evidence. Maybe there's some lying around.'

Leonie shook her head. 'Let's just find the others. Safety in numbers.'

Diren nodded and took one final chunk out of the apple before leaving the core in one of the sinks.

In the distance, Leonie thought that she could hear raised voices.

Diren and Leonie looked at each other. Wynona's name passed between them, unspoken.

A loud bang came from the direction of the atrium.

They rushed out to see what the source of the noise was.

When they emerged into the atrium, they were greeted with a broken body lying in the centre of the floor.

Ollie's wet, cold nose tickled Leonie's cheek. He patted her cheek with his paw.

'Yes, I'm alive.'

He came up close and sniffed her face.

'All right. I'm up. I'm getting up.'

She kicked back the covers. It was stiflingly hot in her bedroom. The sun had already been up for a few hours, though it wasn't yet 7 a.m.

As she stepped on the scales, she had to shield her eyes from the sun.

Another kilo since last week.

Ollie croaked at her from behind the bathroom door.

'I'm coming,' she told him.

Downstairs, the house was a mess. She had the feeling of a life derailed. There was no routine, no structure.

After squeezing half a pouch of wet food into Ollie's bowl, Leonie sat at the breakfast bar. The jury summons was in her peripheral vision, lurking at the edges.

After making herself a flat white, she sat on the sofa in the snug. She pulled out her phone and looked at the maps app, going over the journey to the Crown Court for the umpteenth time. She returned to it in those quiet moments where there wasn't much else to think about. Before Hamish's death, she'd filled those silent moments with music or podcasts. Now she left those blank spaces alone, allowing her thoughts to coalesce around certain obsessions, like what does one wear to jury service? Gone were the days when everyone was expected to wear suits. Leonie had one for funerals and that was it.

Unbidden, a memory of Hamish's funeral washed up on the shores of her mind. Beached there. She closed her eyes quickly to stem the flow of tears. She got up and dressed herself. Her first time leaving the house in months save for essential trips to the doctor or supermarket.

*

So far, the first day of jury service was not proceeding along the lines she'd imagined. It was like watching a poor adaptation of a favourite book. She'd imagined strolling into the building and immediately making friends. She'd imagined others laughing at her jokes.

Instead, she alighted from the bus into a muggy, pollution-thick day.

In the alternate dreamworld, the day had been bright and breezy and her hair had shone like silk while her skin glowed with youthful energy. In reality, the bus's exhaust fumes gathered in her throat, making her want to choke.

The court building didn't look the same as it had on her maps app. It looked flat in pictures, but in person, the scale impressed her.

Once inside, she was greeted by security. After being given the once-over by the security guards, Leonie pulled at the elasticated sleeves on her black dress, trying to coax some air into her armpit region to avoid unsightly sweat patches.

Clutching her jury summons in her hand, she followed the signs to the jury gallery. After giving her name and juror number to one of the ushers, she went through to a large room where over 100 people sat, waiting for instructions. As she'd anticipated, no one was wearing a suit. Even the most formally dressed men had opted for slacks and a shirt. No one approached her or returned her smile. There was a sweaty fug in the room, not relieved by the open windows.

She looked around for a vacant seat. There was a vast array of different people here of varying ages. The majority were glued to their phones, but others had their noses in books. Leonie would have loved to read on a day like today. But there was no way she'd have been able to lose herself in another narrative when her own life was proving so dramatic.

There was a spare seat in the corner, so Leonie picked through the occupied chairs to get to it. The space had the feeling of a doctor's waiting room. No one was talking, but they were all here for the same thing. Leonie was still feverish with nerves and saw the waiting potential jurors as competitors.

After what seemed like an age—she was sure it was nearly lunchtime now—a woman came into the waiting room. She had plum-coloured hair and a lanyard, which picked her out as one of the court staff. She wore a black gown over smart casual clothes.

Later, Leonie would find out that these black gowns were worn by ushers.

Even later than that, when geopolitical events in the outside world locked them inside this building, Leonie would discover that this woman's name was Susan. That's the name the usher would give to her, anyway.

Susan looked around the room. She called out around fifty names. Leonie was one of them. They were all told to go home for the day.

Leonie felt a surge of panic.

Diren walked straight over to Geoff's body and pressed the pulse point on his throat. Leonie struggled to see how Geoff could be anything other than dead. His head was twisted at an unnatural angle. The neck had to be broken.

She circled the body, looking around for any clues. When she couldn't see any, she tilted her head to look up. She saw the balustrade which ran around the mezzanine floor above.

Diren was also looking up at the mezzanine. Without having to say it aloud, they were thinking along the same lines: there was no way Geoff could have fallen accidentally. Nor was it likely that the fall had killed him—it was only one storey. Neither insulted the other by saying aloud what had so clearly happened.

Jade asked, 'What the fuck?'

Leonie held a finger to her lips and shook her head. Then she was distracted by something. A light flashed in the corner of her vision, forcing her to blink. She looked towards the front of the building, where the glass windows took up a large proportion of the building's facade. The light pierced the darkness. With a quick glance at Diren, she moved towards the flight of steps which led down to the main entrance. To her right was the security hut; to her left was the table and metal detector.

Mostly, Leonie saw her reflection in the panes of glass. As she got closer, she was better able to see what was happening beyond the tree-lined car park, which lay a whole storey below. In the next street over were people in white hazmat suits carrying torches and what looked like jet washers. They seemed to be spraying some chemical from the pipe, which must neutralize or otherwise wash away any nerve agent that coated the city.

Diren arrived at her side. She gripped his hand. He squeezed back.

'It's nearly over,' whispered Jade from behind them. 'We'll be allowed out soon.'

'Let's tell the others,' said Diren.

'That it's nearly safe to leave, or that we've got a murderer on the loose who might kill us all given half the chance?' asked Leonie, trying to keep her voice light.

'Definitely the former. We'll have to think carefully about how we approach the latter.'

'Geoff's death cements it. Susan's was enough—'

Diren tensed and dropped her hand. His face was rigid and he had the same unhealthy pallor as when they'd found Susan's body.

'What's the matter?'

'It's nothing.'

'You don't have to—'

'I'll tell you later. We need to get back to the jury gallery, tell the others.'

Before leaving the atrium, they went over Geoff's body and checked for anything that might be useful. Diren was less concerned about searching the dead body this time. The only thing of any use was the set of handcuffs, which Diren tucked into the inside pocket of his jacket. The walkie-talkie was useless with only one handset, so they left that behind.

They agreed to head back to the others.

Leonie let Jade walk on ahead. She hovered behind and spoke to Diren in an undertone. 'You can tell me. I won't judge.'

'I walked in on him.' Diren said this quickly, as though throwing the words out there would make it easier.

Leonie let him tell her in his own time.

'My stepdad. Well, one of my stepdads. My mum had a lot of boyfriends when I was growing up, but this one was my favourite. All of the others were shitheads. But Nigel was a good bloke. He looked after me and my sister properly. I felt safe around him. And then one day I walked into the downstairs toilet and found him.'

'Fucking hell, Diren, I'm so sorry.'

'I was ten.'

'Did you ever get therapy, or—'

'No. Therapy wasn't a thing then, was it?'

Leonie didn't want to contradict him because she knew what he meant. It certainly wasn't as ubiquitous or as accepted.

'I'm so sorry you had to go through that.'

He shrugged. 'His family blamed my mum. But it wasn't just the shock of finding him, I… I loved Nigel. He was the first one who really felt like he could be my dad.'

Leonie tried to give Diren a one-armed hug, but he remained stiff.

'Sorry,' he said.

'You have nothing to apologize for. Thank you for telling me.'

'Let's catch up with Jade. We'll decide between the three of us what to say to them as we're heading back.'

*

The conversation was fraught and whispered. Diren was on alert, constantly looking over his shoulder, stopping at regular intervals to listen out for noises.

'We've just got to tell them straight,' said Leonie.

'I agree,' said Jade. 'What's the problem?'

Diren leant in to speak in an undertone. 'We could end up having the heat on us.'

'How?' asked Leonie.

'We're always the ones finding the bodies. It's always us telling the others what's going on.'

'Because we've been down here before. Anyway, we mixed it up this time. It's us three and Wynona rather than us three and Sim.'

'And she's the one who didn't come back.'

'They can't be suspicious of us.'

'They're already suspicious.'

'Okay,' said Leonie. 'You can take the lead on telling them.'

'No,' said Diren. 'They'll trust Jade more. They're more wary about the two of us.'

Jade raised her eyebrows. Leonie knew she'd seen the hand-holding earlier. She didn't care. It was a crisis. It was natural that people would seek comfort from people they've been through trauma with. Why was she justifying this to an imaginary Jade? It wouldn't be Jade she'd have to explain herself to, but Sim.

'Okay, I'll do it,' said Jade. 'I'll just tell it to them straight.'

Leonie felt that Jade's characteristic bluntness would be helpful. People would be more likely to believe her.

When they returned to the jury gallery, heads swivelled in their direction. Rob was the first to ask, 'Where's Wynona?'

'Listen,' said Jade. 'A lot of shit went down.'

As Diren predicted, sceptical glances were shared.

'What kind of shit?' asked Charlie.

'I'm telling you now.'

Jade went on to describe everything that had happened, from Leonie and Diren finding the phone—Leonie held up the phone and showed them the lock screen—to Wynona asking to go to the toilet and never coming back, to them finding Geoff spreadeagled on the atrium floor. There were a lot of questions.

Finally, Diren stepped in to tell them that they'd seen people in hazmat suits cleaning up the city.

'Maybe we'll be able to leave soon?' asked Anthony.

'Maybe,' said Leonie. 'But shouldn't we focus on the fact that there have now been two deaths and one disappearance? I always said that going to turn the lights on was a trap. I think Quinn got her.'

'Would there have been time?' asked Tanbir. 'Between Wynona going missing and you finding Geoff? For Quinn to hide Wynona somewhere and then kill Geoff?'

Leonie did some quick calculations in her head. How long were they in the toilet for? She settled on, 'There would have been just enough time. But it would have been close.'

'Why didn't you look for her?' asked Rob.

'Hey,' said Diren, temper rising. 'There's someone out there pushing people over balustrades and plucking middle-aged women out of toilets. We weren't going to put ourselves in danger. We saw what we saw, and we came back here to tell you.'

'We should look for her,' said Rob.

'Too dangerous,' countered Leonie. 'He wanted us to turn the lights back on. He wanted us to find this phone. All so we'd come out into the open, and then he took one of us.'

'We're sitting bloody ducks,' said Anthony.

'We're better off staying here,' said Leonie. 'We've got the advantage.'

'Someone here isn't telling the truth,' said Lucas. 'And I think it's one of you three. You've got it in for Quinn.'

'I haven't got it in for Quinn. I just think that serial killers should go to prison. I don't understand why you defend him so much.'

'Because he's innocent until proven guilty and all you do is say "no smoke without fire" and expect the rest of us to agree with you. It might not be Quinn. Let's stop making assumptions.'

'Why is he playing a song called "Adrenaline"?' asked Leonie.

'Listen,' said Jade. 'About the music. I've got something I wanted to say about that.'

Leonie looked to Jade, feeling hopeful. Had she found some link that would prove Quinn's guilt?

'I did some googling earlier, and I found something out. I looked on the Wikipedia page for "Adrenaline" and listed as having songwriting credits is a man called Hamish Ryan.'

'We're celebrating,' Hamish said one day after work.

Leonie was still working in the office, while Hamish had managed to get a slightly better job in another insurance company.

She consulted her phone to check the date. It wasn't an anniversary. 'Celebrating what?'

'We're going to meet up with Josh and Amy. Proper champagne moment. This is mega.'

'The suspense is killing me.'

'I sold a song. No, not just one song, several songs.'

'Wow, who to?'

'Alien Pandemic. It's for their sophomore album. They're expected to go stratospheric.'

Leonie could barely believe it. This is what he'd wanted for so long. She did the only thing that was befitting of the occasion and grabbed his elbows. Together they jumped up and down in the customary celebration dance of two people who can't believe their luck.

They stopped, panting, beaming.

'No more office work. No more insurance. Fucking hell, it's bliss. Fucking hellll…'

Leonie dressed up for the occasion. She'd recently bought a skin-tight black dress with lace panels and a pair of New Rocks which had chunky platforms. It was the first time she'd get to wear the new outfit.

They went to a fancy restaurant, followed by Subculture, followed by Josh and Amy's suburban kitchen that smelled like dogs. Josh passed a bong around. The dog smell was soon overpowered by the smell of weed.

They were merrily stoned.

'When did life get this fucking good?' asked Hamish, even though life had not yet changed. They were still in the same place, on the same bean bags, doing slightly different drugs.

'Have you played it to her yet?' asked Josh.

Hamish shook his head. 'Your speakers are better, mate.'

'You *haven't* played it to her?'

Hamish shook his head, grinning.

Josh was astonished. He looked down at the bong, disappointed. 'But this is totally the wrong drug to go with Alien Pandemic.'

Leonie sniggered in the stupid way stoned people did. Josh was talking about music-and-drug pairings like some people talked about food-and-wine pairings.

'Fuck it, she's gotta listen to it. It's *sooo* good.' Josh went and got a CD from another room and fed it into the player.

The beginning of the album was haunting.

'It's a concept album,' said Josh.

There was a weird, alien sound which gave way to a catchy riff. Soon the lead singer was screaming his lungs out before moving seamlessly into the clean vocals.

Leonie nodded her head appreciatively until something started to bother her.

The lyrics were familiar. As with all the best albums, the songs were about love. But Leonie noticed other things, turns of phrase. There were images interspersed which gave her déjà vu. There were also an unusual number of references to things she had liked at secondary school.

She turned to Hamish, stricken. He looked nervous.

'I can't believe you.'

Feeling a bit sick, she managed to roll unceremoniously off the bean bag. Soon, she was tottering on her clunky new boots out of the kitchen, into the hallway, and out onto the street. Faint sounds of guitars and drums followed her out. As did Hamish.

'Leonie, don't be angry. You've done something amazing.'

'I've done something, *I've* done something?'

She tried to walk away from him, but she was unsteady on her feet, surely about to vomit any moment now. What would the neighbours think? She laughed in that lazy, stupid way again.

'Leonie, please,' he grabbed her arm and tried to get her to turn around to look at him.

'Get off me.'

Had she not taken a hit on the bong, she might not have had the courage to speak to Hamish like this, might have realized what she was doing. She was breaking up with him. Her perfect man. The jigsaw that slotted perfectly into place and triggered all of those happy chemicals in her brain. She'd have thought that no one else would ever make her feel like this again.

He continued to chase after her.

'Am I going to get a credit?' she asked.

'Is that what you want? If that's what's upsetting you, I could get you a credit.'

'I don't need a credit. It's the last thing I want because I don't want my name to be associated with the poetry I wrote when I was still a sixteen-year-old virgin.'

'But it's brilliant. You heard Josh.'

'Fuck Josh. And fuck you. I can't believe you just stole my words without asking me.'

'I can make sure you get money for them.'

'It's not about the money!'

'What is it about, then?'

'It's about a total breach of trust. Those were pieces of my soul and you just took them and put them to a fucking guitar.'

'I thought they were brilliant. The world will see that now. Your stuff is amazing.'

'I don't know where to begin. You just took it for yourself. Didn't ask. No consent. And, yeah, how am I supposed to get any compensation for this?'

'I thought you said it wasn't about money?'

'It's about our relationship, Hamish. You took something from me without even thinking about how I might feel. You don't even think that I deserve money. Finders keepers.'

'Leonie, what's mine is yours.'

'No, it's not.'

'Well, it was going to be. I was going to propose.'

'Fat chance of me accepting that.'

'Please.'

Pathetically, he got down on one knee.

'This is not the way to propose. We're both wasted as hell. I don't trust you any more. Goodbye, Hamish.'

She moved back in with her parents. Hamish no longer needed her rent. Alien Pandemic's second album went platinum in three countries and gold in four others. It hit number one in the anglophone world and received radio plays for years to come.

Alien Pandemic went from playing venues that could seat hundreds to selling out arenas three nights on the trot. It was a British rock success story that hadn't been seen since Oasis's second album dropped.

Hamish made more money out of that album than he had any business to. And Leonie carried on working in the office, writing poetry about her feelings. She sure as hell had a lot of feelings about what Hamish had done.

'So, what if like, he's playing the song, not to intimidate us or anything, but to tell us that he didn't kill Hamish Ryan, that maybe someone else did?' asked Jade.

Lucas's eyes widened and he started enumerating all the different reasons why this was a significant piece of information.

Jade joined in. 'Because he must have made a load of money out of that song. And I looked into his other songwriting credentials. He wrote "Cosmic" for Alien Pandemic, which was a massive hit.'

For Leonie, the song 'Cosmic' was reminiscent of an unruly gaggle of life experiences. Songs like that often were. Those one-hit wonders that seem to follow you throughout your life. It was the soundtrack to her and Hamish breaking up for the first time. Then it was played every week at Subculture. It was on Kerrang! Radio when Kerrang! was a thing. It had even been played at her wedding reception, for she and Hamish had reconciled less than a year after their argument. He had proposed almost the instant they were back together, and Leonie had accepted because she was young and foolish and there was something ten times sweeter about the second time around; no one fell in love as deeply as those with a recently mended heart.

She hated the song and always would. Not just because it was symbolic of Hamish's betrayal, but because she couldn't stand to hear her own words.

'We're not supposed to do our own research about the case,' said Leonie. 'We're not supposed to know anything about the case other than what we hear in the courtroom.' She acknowledged privately that she knew more about Hamish than any juror should ever know about a murder victim.

'We've heard it now,' said Lucas. 'What are we supposed to do?'

'Put it out of your mind,' said Leonie. 'If the defence barrister thought it was relevant, he'd have made sure the evidence was put before us, but they clearly haven't found a link between the songwriting and the murder—'

'So, what are we saying?' Lucas spoke to the rest of the group, ignoring Leonie. 'That thing that was said over the Tannoy? That one of us knows one another from before? Maybe it has something to do with this Acid Rain connection.'

Jade looked to Sim.

'What? It has nothing to do with me. I don't know this Hamish guy.'

'But you dated Amir Bernard, right?' asked Jade.

'Yeah, but it's not like I met the rest of the band or anything, let alone the guy who wrote some songs for them. It was kind of a one-on-one situation, if you get me?'

'We "get you",' said Rob, not bothering to keep a note of distaste from his voice.

'Sim doesn't have anything to do with the murder,' said Leonie.

'How would you know?' asked Rob. 'You said earlier that you two didn't know one another from before.'

'We don't. We first met on the day we got selected. I just know because obviously it was Quinn who murdered Hamish, and Sim has no connection to the hospital. This whole thing is a red herring.'

Lucas wore a pensive expression which may have been calculated to make him look intelligent but only succeeded in making him look dense. 'If this Hamish guy was rich, then it makes a lot of sense that other people might want to kill him. People who would benefit from his life-insurance policy or his will. That's way more motive than Quinn has.'

Leonie bit back, 'So just because someone's rich means they can't be a victim of their nurse or doctor? That's crazy. Benefiting from his client's will was what did it for Shipman in the end, yet he murdered hundreds of people before that.'

Lucas continued to wear that stupid frown. 'We haven't heard anything about the other potential suspects. Nothing at all. All of the evidence has been focused on Quinn.'

'Because there is no evidence of other suspects. The only evidence points towards him.'

'They didn't look hard enough. The police had tunnel vision from day one.'

'This is ridiculous,' said Leonie. 'He's totally playing you. He's doing all of this to make you think like this and you're going along with it because the idea of a complicated con-spiracy appeals to you more than a straightforward solution. It's Occam's razor.'

'Occam's razor is a general rule, not a principle we should be using when determining a man's guilt.'

'Hold on,' said Diren. 'We're way off track. What are we going to do about the fact that Geoff has been killed and Wynona has gone missing?'

'I think we should look for Wynona,' said Rob.

'Same here,' said Viv.

Rob looked accusingly at Diren and Leonie. 'I can't believe you didn't look for her.'

Diren bristled and looked for a moment as though he was going to snap back at Rob. Leonie put a hand on his shoulder and he eased off. She sensed that Sim had witnessed this. He looked away when she checked to see if he had been watching.

'Why are we thinking about looking for Wynona when the threat is in here?' asked Lucas. 'Someone here is lying to all of us. Someone here knows someone from before.'

'Why are you dancing to his tune the whole time?' asked Leonie. 'All he has to do is suggest something and you're convinced.'

'We need to discuss what we're going to do next,' said Diren, ignoring Leonie and speaking to the others.

Rob was the first to answer. 'Find Wynona, obviously. We need to make sure she's okay.'

Leonie fought the urge to suggest they deliberate. She still wanted them to convict Quinn. But with Wynona gone, she didn't know whether their verdict would mean anything. The only thing that had kept her going for the last ten hours was finally finding Quinn guilty, ensuring that she at least came away from this nightmare with a verdict. The only way to do that would be to make sure there were twelve of them. While Diren might say they should stay safe, Leonie wanted to search for Wynona.

Anthony appeared at Rob's side, backing him up. 'Well?' he asked. 'Don't you agree we should be looking for her?'

Tanbir's large eyes were fixed on Anthony. 'We're so close to leaving this place,' he said. 'Let's not take any risks.'

Anthony rounded on him. 'How would you feel if you were in Wynona's shoes and someone was saying the same about you?'

Tanbir shrank into himself. 'Okay, I'm sorry. You're right.'

Leonie was intrigued by the volte-face. 'I'll help look for her.'

'Anyone else?' asked Rob.

'No,' said Lucas. 'We need to work out who the viper in the nest is. Hamish Ryan wrote for Acid Rain and that seems like a weird coincidence.' He looked at Leonie. 'Someone isn't telling the truth.'

How much could he find out about Leonie's connection to Hamish? Over the years, there had been plenty of photos posted online of the pair of them. Though Leonie had done her best to scrub the evidence, there was always a risk that Lucas might discover the connection. Anything posted on the internet left a trace.

Hamish and Josh had made good money from writing and producing Alien Pandemic's sophomore album—extremely good money—but after that, the creative side no longer interested Hamish. He'd always said that the most powerful people in music were the ones you wouldn't recognize if you saw them on the street. As a result, Hamish wasn't famous. After his one foray into songwriting, Hamish got a top job at a streaming giant and happily faded into obscurity. It was around the time that all creativity went out of Hamish's work life that their relationship began to go stale. Leonie had never wanted to admit it, but a big part of what made their relationship work was their shared love for a type of music Leonie was only pretending to like, at least at first. Sure, she'd gone on to develop an ear for heavy metal, but in all honesty, she would always prefer to listen to pop songs from her youth than anything Hamish liked.

After he made so much money out of her poems, he had over-compensated by encouraging her to write more poetry.

'You could do something amazing. It's such high-quality stuff.'

'I told you. It's not about the money.'

He looked confused. 'Then what is it about?'

'It's about the feeling I get when I create something, express myself.'

'But who are you expressing yourself to if it never gets published?'

'I thought this was something we had in common,' she said. 'My poetry doesn't need material value; its worth is in the satisfaction of creating something.'

She realized that Hamish no longer cared about art for art's sake. He had become so corporate that for him music was only as good as the number of downloads it generated.

But, in all honesty, she hadn't written a poem she liked since Hamish had stolen her words, and they'd gone on to be adored by millions of people around the world.

The group was split almost evenly down the middle, between those who believed the only sensible thing to do was stay put, and those who considered the only moral thing to do was to look for Wynona.

Lucas and Rob were at loggerheads in this regard.

Leonie was conflicted. They needed to find out what had happened to Wynona. If they could return Wynona to safety, or confirm that something bad had happened to her, Leonie's plan to convict Quinn would remain on course. Either they would be reunited as a jury of twelve, or there would be some legitimacy to carrying on as a group of eleven. She didn't want anything bad to have happened to Wynona, and very much hoped she returned unharmed, but she had been clear from the outset that the threat in the building came from Quinn. It was the others who hadn't listened.

She did not feel safe leaving the jury gallery now that she knew Quinn had been taking photographs of her without her realizing. If someone could skulk around unnoticed like that, there was no way she could guarantee her own safety. The fact that Quinn had now turned his sights on the jurors made things even more precarious. She wondered if there was a way around this obstacle. They needed to come to a verdict. She felt that there was added pressure now. Not only was Rob on to her, but the Acid Rain connection had been discovered. It might only be a matter of time before more secrets were revealed. Sure, any deliberation would be without all of them present, but they had already breached that taboo, as Lucas had so helpfully pointed out.

How serious had he been about his threat to tell the judge they'd broken the rules? If only she could find a way of getting something on him…

It was clear that neither he nor Rob was going to back down.

A schism had formed.

Rob and a group of younger jurors agreed to go and find Wynona. 'We owe it to Wynona to look for her. If all of us get out of here alive, she deserves to as well. She's got children.'

Leonie bristled. She couldn't help but feel bitter when people with kids used it as the ultimate trump card. It made sense; their lives had more responsibilities, but she couldn't help feeling it cemented her place in society as a middle-aged cat lady.

'You coming, Leonie?' asked Sim. They were sitting in what Leonie saw as their corner of the room.

'Er,' Leonie hesitated. She looked over at Diren. His expression was stern.

Sim registered who she was looking at. His face betrayed the realization that he was no longer her closest friend in the room. Diren, of all people, had usurped him. 'Fine,' he said, voice tight. 'It's clear where your priorities lie.'

'What? With staying alive?' She kept her voice low. No one had spotted that they were having a mumbled argument. She didn't want to draw attention to it.

'You were happy to roam around the building when you were with *him*.' Sim jerked his head in Diren's direction.

'That was different.'

'How? Because I'm not an alpha male?'

'I don't think about men in terms of the Greek alphabet. Plus, you're not exactly weedy.'

It was true. Sim had a gym-honed body; he'd shown Leonie his dating-app pictures. Nevertheless, she had always sensed that his muscular frame was more form than function.

'Don't try to flatter me. I can see what's happening here.'

Leonie took a deep breath. She did not want to fall out with Sim. Not only was he a great balm to her, but she needed to retain as many allies as she could. 'I'm going to pretend I didn't hear that.'

'Is something going on between you two?'

She struggled to put it into words. 'Please don't judge me.'

He looked haughty. How dare he? Amir was good looks and inappropriate behaviour personified.

Leonie tried to justify herself. 'I just think that the risk assessment has changed. Sure, we knew Quinn was out there, but now we know he's taken secret pictures of us, killed Geoff, and taken Wynona. It's a totally different proposition than when we were going to the canteen for food or to the plant room to turn the lights back on. We know we're his target now.'

'So if it benefits you, you'll put yourself in danger, but when it's just about helping someone else you won't? I didn't realize you were so selfish, Leonie.'

She noted the switch from nickname to full name. 'That's a bit unfair.'

'Is it? Where has the woman from this morning gone? The one who was banging on a water jug and keeping everyone safe?'

'She—I—I'm just scared, okay?'

Sim raised a sceptical eyebrow. The discussion was at an end. Anthony and the group of younger jurors, which included

Jade, Charlie, Tanbir and Lucas, was already starting to move the table to allow them to open the doors to the staircase.

'I'm going,' said Sim with a note of self-righteousness.

Leonie watched as he went to help dismantle the barricade so he could join the others in search of Wynona. She knew she should go after him, but pride wouldn't let her.

*

Once the search party had left, Leonie helped Diren and a couple of others to move the table back in front of the double doors. She felt wretched about locking Sim out. She took herself off into the corner and sat down to stew for a while.

Diren approached her. 'Are you feeling bad about blocking them out?'

She nodded.

'Don't. They've put us at risk by splitting up the group.'

He always saw things in such black-and-white terms. It was survival or else.

'Everything feels unmoored,' said Leonie. 'People are starting to behave strangely.'

'This is how it goes. Without structure, we descend into chaos. Like you said earlier, the only thing stopping us from murdering one another is societal norms.'

She didn't know how to respond, other than to nod vacantly.

They were sitting apart from the other jurors, on the other side of the room. The three remaining jurors watched them closely.

'They suspect us,' whispered Leonie. 'They're starting to wonder if we know one another from before.'

'Fuck 'em.'

'They feel intimidated by alliances.'

Diren moved closer to her and dropped his voice. 'We need to stick together.'

The sky was now void of natural light. Instead, the room was flooded with the harsh electric beams from a nearby lamp post.

Diren continued to keep his voice to a murmur. 'Look, the others—'

'Even Sim?'

'Especially Sim. The herd mentality has set in, I can feel it. They're looking for someone to pin stuff on and I can tell they're starting to target you.'

Leonie dropped her chin to her chest. 'Rob keeps looking at me. I think he knows something.'

'What?'

Leonie stared at Diren for a long time. 'It could be the phone thing.'

He searched her face. 'Is there something else?'

She nodded.

'Are you going to tell me?'

She shook her head.

'Is it relevant to what's going on?'

Of course it was. But she couldn't tell him. She'd lose his trust. 'Er, maybe.' After all, she couldn't know for certain that Quinn had worked out who she was. 'You've just got to trust me.'

'But you're not telling me the whole truth. We need to rely on each other. That lot aren't on our side.' He jerked his head in the direction of three jurors sitting on the other side of the room.

'It's not about sides.'

'It is now. The situation is starting to do strange things to people. It's obvious, isn't it? They know they're being hunted but don't want to acknowledge it. At least we've accepted it. We know the danger we're in.'

Leonie took a deep breath. 'Okay.'

'Tell me what's going on, Leonie.'

'I can't. Not now. I will, I promise, but let's get out of here first. Just know it isn't going to change anything right now.' Diren remained unconvinced. 'Please, trust me.'

The deep furrow between Diren's eyebrows made Leonie doubt that he was going to accept her silence. Eventually, he said, 'Okay. For now. But we stick together, yeah?'

'Yes.' Their fingers interlocked.

He didn't do anything but stare at her with uncomfortable intensity.

*

The quietness had an uncomfortable quality to it. She strained to hear what was happening outside, to see if there were any more men in army trucks shouting from loudspeakers, listened out for the sound of the people coming to save them.

There was nothing.

She stopped to think about that. Nothing. Something was missing.

'The helicopters have stopped,' she said.

She approached the window and looked up at the night sky. The sky hinted at a darkness which she might have been able to discern, if only she could see through the glare of the street lights.

There were no flashing red pinpricks, no searchlights. The helicopters had gone.

'There are no more helicopters,' she said slowly, with the dawning realization that it had been this way for a while. 'What does that mean?'

She knew that the others were reluctant to humour her. Nevertheless, they looked worried.

Diren got up to look out of the window. 'You're right. It's probably a good sign.'

'Is it?' asked Jill. 'Or does it mean that they're abandoning us? We haven't heard anything about being evacuated. We haven't seen any army trucks.' She was working herself up.

'We saw them cleaning the city a short while ago,' said Diren calmly. 'It's not going to take five minutes. We just have to be patient.'

'They're leaving us to rot in here. We need to get out.'

'Sorry I mentioned it,' said Leonie. 'Diren's right. It probably doesn't mean anything.'

Jill and Viv exchanged knowing looks.

Diren pushed on anyway. 'Those helicopters were probably press. There's nothing for them to see now, is there? It's dark.'

Only Viv seemed convinced. The others remained on edge.

The five of them sat like this, no one daring to break the uneasy armistice, for the best part of an hour.

The first thing that alerted them to the fact that the others had returned was the sound of feet on the staircase. Then there was the banging on the doors and calls to let them in. They didn't sound fearful, like there was a killer at their back. They were jubilant.

They all looked at one another hopefully. The others must have found Wynona.

Leonie and Diren were the first to start dismantling the barricade. The others joined in not long after. It only took a minute to clear the way for the others to get in.

Sim bounded in first, beaming at them. Close behind was Rob, who came in holding Wynona's hand. He raised her arm as though she was the winner of a boxing match. Jill and Viv crowded around her, pleased that she had been found, and that she was unharmed. Leonie watched as the rest of them trickled in, looking pleased with themselves. There was a note of 'told you so' in their expressions. They had been right to take the risk.

Trailing in behind them was the last person Leonie expected to see.

Michael Quinn entered the corridor, apparently at the invitation of those who had found Wynona.

He locked eyes with Leonie and his lips parted in a toothy smile.

FIVE MONTHS BEFORE

On Saturday mornings, Leonie performed her rituals. She'd been doing these for ages now, and since Hamish died, it was nice to have something to fall back on. Some structure to her week.

She'd been attending this particular beauty therapist on a regular basis for long enough that she had achieved the coveted prize of a regular Saturday-morning slot. Every week, she would get a full-body scrub and a fake tan top-up. All other beauty treatments were on a four-week cycle: nails, waxing, eyebrows, lashes. She went elsewhere for the more hardcore treatments. The Botox, the fillers. Each bit of her beauty routine was constantly topped up the moment things started to slip so that she always looked polished.

The phone rang. Leonie saw the name that flashed up and knew she'd have to take the call. However, her nails were still curing, so she couldn't touch the phone.

The beauty therapist asked, 'Do you want me to?'

'Yes please.'

The therapist swiped the green phone symbol and placed the handset on a little stand so that Leonie could take the call without having to put it on speakerphone.

'Thank you,' Leonie mouthed to the therapist, then, 'Hello Rachel.' Rachel was Leonie's family liaison officer.

'Hi,' came an earnest voice. The 'Hi' lasted for much longer than any normal 'Hi'.

'Oh, hi,' said Leonie, mimicking the caller. 'Nice to hear from you. Erm, I mean. Well, you know, not *nice*…'

'I get it, don't worry. You're not the first and you won't be the last.' Rachel's voice went all singsong and cheery. 'Look, it's not good news as such, but it might be welcome news.' Her voice switched from cheerful to serious. 'We've got a date. For Quinn's trial, that is.'

'Oh yeah?' Leonie strained to keep her voice light.

'First week of July.'

'Really?'

'Really.'

'So…'

'Don't worry, you've got some time to think about this. A lot of time. Because the trial itself will probably last for two months at least.'

'That's… quite a stretch.' She'd put her foot in it again. 'Sorry, I didn't mean—that wasn't a pun. I meant a stretch of time for me to wait, not a stretch of time in, you know…'

'Leonie, don't sweat it. It's what I'm here for. Bereaved people always feel like they've got to be on their best behaviour, but that's not the point. I just wanted to give you some pre-warning.'

'Two months…'

'That's what they tell me.'

'Will you be watching the trial?'

'Er, no. Not unless…'

'Oh, no, I'll be staying well away.'

'Understandable.' Leonie could detect a distinct note of relief in Rachel's voice. Her caseload was clearly too heavy. 'Want me to pop round?'

'Oh, no thank you… Place is a tip…'

'Fantastic.' Rachel sounded too grateful for the reprieve. Clearly aware of her slip-up, in a more tentative tone of voice she asked, 'Don't worry if you change your mind about the trial. I can support you if you need.'

'No, no, it will be too traumatic.'

'I totally understand. Feel free to give me a call at any time. I'm only a phone call away.' Her voice went cheery and sing-song again.

'Will do,' said Leonie.

Rachel hung up.

The beauty therapist didn't ask who had called. She was discreet, which was what you wanted from someone who pulled hot wax inches from your nether regions.

Later, when Leonie got home, she looked again at the jury summons, even though its contents were imprinted on her mind.

You have been selected for jury service.

Your name was randomly selected from the electoral register.

Her summons was for the first week of July.

'I'm sorry, but what the fuck is going on?'

Leonie was staring at the group who had brought Quinn back.

Jade, Sim, and Charlie were avoiding her eye, while Wynona was looking straight back at Leonie, defiant.

'He explained everything to me,' she said. 'He's innocent.'

Quinn was standing not far away, awkwardly listening in. Diren was standing guard, watching his every move.

Leonie couldn't believe what Wynona was saying. Quinn had taken her, hadn't he? Surely he had done so by force?

'This is the maddest, most inappropriate… He's the fucking defendant. We shouldn't be speaking to him at all.'

'I believe him, Leonie. He told me—'

'He shouldn't be telling you anything! This isn't how it works. He had his chance to give evidence. That's it, evidence over. We're not supposed to hear any more. And to make it worse, you've heard something the rest of us haven't.'

'But we have the chance to right a wrong, prevent a mis-carriage of just—'

'I don't trust him. I don't believe him. I think he's a murderer. What on earth made you think you had the right to bring him back here and expose us all to that level of risk?'

Anthony stepped in. 'Hey, come on now, that's a bit strong.'

'A bit strong? Are you all out of your minds? He might be a serial killer.'

To her surprise, Rob was with Leonie on this. 'Leonie's right. This is bizarre.'

Leonie was grateful for the support but couldn't work out why Rob had allowed Quinn back in the first place. However, the presence of Quinn seemed to have momentarily distracted him from whatever it was he suspected about her.

'He has escaped lawful custody,' said Leonie. 'Technically, he's a fugitive and we should be subjecting him to citizen's arrest until the authorities arrive.'

Rob nodded. 'We're going to have to find a way to detain him—at least until we've deliberated.'

Leonie didn't like the sound of that. Guilty or not, Quinn was still at large. The chemical attack hadn't changed that.

Wynona tried to intervene, but Rob raised his hand.

'I'm sorry but we've got to do this properly. In a bit, you can tell us why you think he's innocent.'

Wynona opened her mouth to respond.

'Save it, Wyn,' he said.

The next task was to find a way to detain Quinn. It was agreed that the best place to put him was in the canteen, and to handcuff him using the cuffs Diren had taken from Geoff's body. They agreed to check in on him at regular intervals.

Leonie felt it was far from ideal that the subject of their deliberations would be next door, able to hear every word, but she was glad that they'd all seen sense and agreed to detain him, at least for now.

While Diren and some others were working out the finer details of how to handcuff Quinn and where to put him, Leonie went over to speak to Sim.

'What the hell were you doing?' she asked.

'It was the only way she'd come back with us.' Sim addressed a point beyond her right shoulder.

'He must have got to her. Couldn't you at least have put him in an arm lock or something? He's dangerous.'

'He didn't hurt Wynona, did he?'

'Maybe not, but he's clearly worked on her. Psychopaths are perfectly capable of inflicting harm without physical violence.'

Sim rolled his eyes. 'Look, I don't know why you're so bothered. Who's going to care about the verdict with all the crap that's going on outside?'

Leonie was struggling to formulate her arguments.

Before she could say anything, Sim added, 'And anyway, I guess we have put him under citizen's arrest or whatever—how do you know this stuff?—so no harm done.'

Leonie felt betrayed by his indifference. Didn't he see what had happened to Susan? Didn't he hear about Geoff? Had Quinn got to him too?

'I don't understand why people are forgetting that we're the jury and he's the defendant and this whole thing is so fucked up.'

'Wake up, no one cares about stuff like rules and juries and the law any more. The world is going to shit. Haven't you seen what happened at the Viva building?'

The Viva building was a large skyscraper the other side of the city's civic centre.

'No?'

Sim pulled out his phone and read from an online post. 'There's been a standoff between civilians and the army at the Viva centre. When a diabetic ran out of their insulin, people inside the building tried to leave to get help or medicine. Some of those who refused to surrender were shot.'

'Oh my God.' Then Leonie wondered about the source of

the information. Why hadn't this been on the official news? 'Is that from Facebook?'

'Yeah.'

'Well, maybe someone's making it up.'

Sim groaned with frustration. 'Do you not get it? The government isn't going to allow this sort of stuff to be reported on until the situation is under control.'

It sounded like a conspiracy theory to Leonie. She couldn't help but look sceptical.

'You really care more about making sure one man goes to prison than what the jackboot thugs out there are doing?'

'Of course I care about state overreach. But I'm also concerned that there's a murderer literally next door.'

'I really don't think you've worked out how crazy things have gone. It's basically martial law out there now. The PM's lost control. Why are you so obsessed with one man?'

'Because if we don't have rules and laws and systems in place that people obey, we may as well give in to anarchy.'

'Anarchy might not be too far away. What about that woman we saw shot by the authorities? Think there's going to be an investigation into her death? Or a trial?'

'Er, yes?'

'I don't think so. I think she'll be seen as collateral. None of this small stuff is going to matter any more.' With that, Sim left to go and sit with the younger ones.

Leonie looked after him but didn't follow. Instead, she waited for Diren to come out of the canteen. He had a clutch of objects in his hands, including the skeleton key that had been missing when they searched Susan's body.

He answered her quizzical look. 'Got it all from Quinn. Made him empty his pockets.'

'Good.' She leaned closer and whispered in his ear, 'They've all been taken in by him. None of them care any more. Sim says everything is anarchy.'

Diren gave her a bitter grin. He didn't say 'I told you so' in so many words, but Leonie got the hint.

Once Quinn was securely handcuffed in the next room, they sat in a circle and looked to Wynona. Not everyone was focusing on Wynona. Leonie had the burning sensation of being watched. She looked over at Rob, who had been staring at her.

What does he know?

'How did he take you?' asked Diren. 'One minute you were there, and the next you weren't.'

'Well, he did put his hand over my mouth and told me not to scream.'

'When?' asked Jade.

'Just as I came out of the toilet.'

'So, he'd been waiting for you?' asked Leonie.

Wynona looked a little defensive. 'Yes.'

'Did you scream?' asked Jade.

'No, I was too frightened. After that, he pulled me into a side room and he just sort of… waited. Didn't say anything for, ooh, I don't know, half an hour? It was difficult to tell, but it was a long time. But once he was sure you three had gone, he started to talk. He explained that the whole thing is a complete set-up. He said that the staff in the hospital had always had it in for him, that they didn't like him. And he said that they were all lying. He said that there are other experts out there willing to give evidence to prove he was innocent, but they wouldn't come forward because they didn't want to disagree with colleagues…'

Wynona continued to witter on, repeating verbatim all of Quinn's conspiracy theories and other nonsense. How could she have been so easily persuaded? Hearing her repeat it back, it sounded totally implausible. But somehow, when Quinn had explained it all to her, she'd swallowed it whole. It was the same story that had convinced Geoff.

Geoff. How had Quinn pushed Geoff over the balustrade if he was watching over Wynona?

'…Then he said something that really interested me. He said that it wasn't him who had killed Hamish Ryan. He said that the person who did that was the usher, Susan.'

'Pardon?' asked Rob.

'Oh yes, he laid it all out for me. Except her name isn't actually Susan. It's Amy.'

Jade's mouth was wide open. 'So, she wasn't giving Geoff a fake name. Her name really did start with an A.'

Leonie was struggling to keep up with the change of pace. 'Hang on, hang on. If he knew who killed Hamish, why didn't he say so during the trial?'

'Because she only admitted it this morning,' said Wynona.

Leonie felt like the ground was moving beneath her. 'What about the other three patients, did he have anything to say about them?'

'He said that there was no evidence of those, and he's right, isn't he? It's only because of the Hamish Ryan murder that anyone suspected him.'

Leonie looked to Rob. He was staring at her, a mixture of fear and revulsion. She had the feeling that, pretty soon, Rob was going to drop whatever bombshell he'd been keeping to himself. To her surprise, he didn't say anything to or about Leonie. He just said, 'I think maybe we should discuss the case first and decide just on the evidence that we heard during the trial.' He spoke slowly, as though carefully choosing each word. 'Depending on the outcome, we can hear more from Wynona.'

Lucas was the first to speak. 'I believed him when he gave evidence.'

'He told clear lies in his evidence,' said Leonie.

'Like what?' asked Viv.

Leonie was ready. 'He lied about Dr Bleasdale, remember? He said that she was there before anyone else. We know that's a lie because he'd never said it before.'

Viv looked unconvinced. 'He could have been mistaken.'

'He was making it up on the spot because he thought it would cast doubt on Dr Bleasdale's evidence.'

'I agree with Leonie,' said Diren. 'It's obvious he made it up and the prosecution barrister caught him out in a lie.'

After Diren's intervention, more people started to agree with her.

'Does anyone else have anything to say?' asked Rob. 'Ideally someone who hasn't spoken yet.' He looked pointedly at Leonie.

'Yeah, I've got something to say about this Dr Bleasdale,' said Wynona. 'If she truly believed that he was murdering patients, why did it take her so long to speak up about it? She should have gone to the police.'

Quite a few jurors nodded in agreement.

Leonie knew she had to bite her tongue. Rob would only interrupt her and say it was someone else's turn. She looked to Sim, who was sitting next to her. He shrugged as though to say, 'I don't have an answer for that.' Leonie handed him her folder full of the jottings she'd made throughout the trial. She pointed at the note she'd taken of Dr Bleasdale's evidence which had addressed this exact point.

Sim, taking her cue, answered. 'I think she answered that question.' He started to read from her notes. 'She said that she… had a suspicion rather than evidence and she needed to gather proof before she could go to the police.' He did not sound at all convincing.

'The fact that there was no solid evidence until the Hamish Ryan collapse is worrying,' said Tanbir.

'Agreed,' said Jill.

'What about all that personality stuff?' asked Jade. 'He said horrible things about patients and had a God complex…'

'That's true,' Tanbir acknowledged. 'It's all part of the picture.'

'He talked about patients as though they were slabs of meat to be reanimated,' said Leonie.

Lucas shook his head and said, 'That's just gallows humour.'

'It's a bit more than that,' said Leonie.

'You can't convict someone of murder for an off-colour joke.' Lucas rolled his eyes.

'What about Caroline Harris?' asked Jade. 'She said what a bastard Quinn was to her while she was pregnant. That seemed super off to me.'

'The key piece of evidence,' said Charlie dramatically, 'is this.'

He held up the table of shift patterns demonstrating how Quinn was the only one on shift for every murder.

The table was passed around, even though most of the jurors should have had a copy in their files.

'This is very important evidence,' said Rob. 'If someone did kill all four patients, it had to be him.'

Lucas shook his head. 'You're all blind, honestly. This bloke's being stitched up and you're believing the prosecution witnesses just because they're for the prosecution. No other reason.'

'Are you calling us stupid?' asked Leonie.

'No, I'm not—'

'Sounded like it, to be honest, mate,' said Diren. His tone and posture were relaxed but still managed to communicate a degree of threat.

'It's not your fault. You're just… you know. We've been conditioned, haven't we, to believe this narrative?'

'What narrative?' asked Sim.

'That stuff like this matters.' Lucas brandished the table showing that Quinn was on shift for all of the murders. 'Let me explain why this is a load of bullshit. Number one, it shows that several nurses had the means and opportunity to murder patient number four. That's the only case we're supposed to be discussing at this stage. Remember we agreed to look at this case in isolation?'

They nodded.

'Secondly, you're only looking at this table.' Lucas stopped to flick through the pages in his file until he found the table which had been produced by the defence. 'When in fact this one is more telling. Here are all of the cardiac arrests which happened on the ward during the twelve-month period prior to patient number four's death. He wasn't on shift for half of them.'

'But those were all explainable deaths. There was a medical reason for them,' said Charlie. 'The table I showed you only showed the four suspicious deaths.'

Lucas spoke. 'Remember what Dr Bleasdale said. Her first thought was "not another one". So that just goes to show that there had been more unexpected deaths or cardiac arrests that we don't know about.'

'Did she say that?' asked Rob.

Leonie checked her notes. She had.

'The only reason the first three deaths were considered suspicious is because they're part of this so-called cluster,' said Lucas. 'Do you not realize what bullshit that is?'

'How is it bullshit that there were fewer deaths after he left?' asked Jade.

'I know about this stuff, yeah, because of, like, my interest in, like, crypto and statistics and stuff. The change in death rates on the ward could be within the range of expected statistical variance. Also, the change in death rate on the ward could be due to any number of factors. Random fluctuation, insufficient staff, crappy broken-down hospitals, human error, a load of sick patients, particularly in winter months, which is when the first three so-called murders took place.'

Leonie realized quickly that she had underestimated Lucas. She thought he was just some dude who didn't like mainstream narratives, but if that was the case, he'd put an unnerving amount of thought into this argument.

'Shall we have another vote?' said Rob. 'Hands up for guilty.'

Only Leonie, Sim, Diren, Jade and Charlie raised their hands.

'And not guilty?'

Lucas, Wynona, Viv, Rob, Anthony and Jill raised their hands.

'Undecided?'

Only Tanbir raised his hand.

'Okay, so it's down to those of you who think he's guilty to persuade the rest of us,' said Rob.

Leonie went first. 'He pulled the alarm. He was the one who noted the cardiac arrest.'

'But what does that prove? Where's the evidence that he was the one who actually gave Hamish Ryan adrenaline?'

Wynona nodded sanctimoniously. 'If he pulled the alarm, doesn't that sort of indicate that he wanted to save the patient?'

'No,' said Leonie. 'He's a murderer, but he's not stupid. If he hadn't pulled the alarm, the resuscitation team wouldn't have injected Hamish with adrenaline, which wouldn't have screwed up the blood results—'

'Hamish?' asked Lucas, now looking at her. 'That's a bit… familiar.'

'I'm tired of using formalities all the time. Or euphemisms like "the patient" or "the fourth victim". He's a human being, isn't he? Isn't it time we started to consider these people as just that, people? There are four of them who should be alive today. Alive with their loved ones—'

'There are loads of people who've lost loved ones today,' said Lucas. 'These four could have been one of the ones who died in the attack anyway.'

'How dare you,' said Leonie. 'How dare you think that twelve or eighteen months aren't worth living for? What if those were the months where their child graduated from university, or got married? What if there was a lottery win in those few months and they missed out on the trip of a lifetime? What if there was just one more lazy Sunday morning with the person they loved?' Leonie had to stop talking because there was a dangerous lump in the back of her throat.

'Come on,' said Rob. 'We're not supposed to be getting emotional about it.'

'Who said that?' shouted Leonie back at him. She could feel her credibility slipping through her fingers. 'At what point did the judge tell us to shut off all human emotion? This matters. They were people. So, yeah, I think we should be calling them Hamish and Zane and so on.'

'For what it's worth,' said Viv. 'Leonie's right. I don't think Quinn's guilty, but we should remember that the four victims are people too.'

Great, thought Leonie. *The only person on my side is the crystal-healing, chakra-aligning weirdo who everyone laughs at when her back is turned.*

'Fine,' said Rob in a tight voice.

'Every single victim died on his shift,' said Charlie. 'Same cause: cardiac arrest with no explan—'

'There were other deaths with the same cause that weren't considered suspicious,' countered Tanbir.

'Because they couldn't prove that they were also murders beyond reasonable doubt,' said Leonie. 'I bet there are loads of others they couldn't include, even though Quinn probably did them.'

'It's often the way,' agreed Charlie. 'Most prolific serial offenders are only convicted of a handful of their offences.'

'Exactly. That's why it's so important to note that the mortality rate decreased when he left. Let's just take a step back. We have the cluster of three deaths in December and January.'

'Exactly,' said Lucas. 'It was winter.'

'It's still a statistically significant cluster,' said Leonie. 'What do we know that happens after the third death? Shelley Roberts takes her own life. Are you telling me that Quinn had no part in her death? He pushed her to suicide.'

'Not this again,' said Rob. 'You can't blame others for stuff like that.'

'Can't you? What if you mentally torture someone for months?'

'Like a controlling and coercive relationship?' asked Viv.

'Precisely,' said Leonie.

'But this wasn't a relationship. It was a friendship,' said Viv reasonably.

'Haven't you ever had a friendship that's as intense and meaningful as a romantic relationship? When, if that relationship was over, you would feel the same type of grief as if you'd broken up with a boyfriend or girlfriend?'

Viv pondered this. 'I can't say I have.'

'I have,' said Jade. 'Definitely. My best friend from when we were kids. When we fall out and have arguments I feel miserable for days. Platonic love can definitely be powerful like that.'

'But they were work colleagues,' said Wynona. 'Not lifelong friends from childhood.'

'Not everyone stays in touch with childhood friends,' reasoned Leonie. She had not had particularly powerful friendships as an adult. She had put all of her eggs in Hamish's basket, with most of her friends being people she knew through him.

'And work friendships can be really strong,' said Charlie. 'There are people at my work who call each other'—his face wrinkled in disgust at the phrase—'work wives and work husbands. We spend like eight hours a day with these people.'

Leonie reflected on the intensity of her friendship with Sim which had formed in such a short period of time. The potent combination of proximity and stress had caused them to bond. That, and their slightly aloof regard for the other jurors.

Leonie picked up on Charlie's argument, 'Nurses are on shift for twelve hours. They're together in the most stressful situations. It could definitely be the case that Shelley and Quinn's relationship was close enough to be controlling and coercive.'

'We're getting off track,' said Rob.

'Sorry,' said Leonie. 'What I meant to say was that the eight-month gap could be down to the fact that Quinn only felt safe committing murder when Shelley Roberts was around.'

'Earlier you were saying that he was still committing murders in those eight months but that the doctors didn't have enough evidence for them.'

'Oh, couldn't it be either?' asked Leonie, frustrated. 'Both are equally plausible.'

Lucas shook his head. 'You're just willing to come up with anything that proves he's guilty.'

'Because he is,' said Leonie. 'He is guilty. That's just the overwhelming reality from all the evidence we've heard. His personality, how he speaks to patients, how manipulative he is…'

'What about the hard facts?'

'We've been over them a million times. He was on shift for all four murders. He's the only one who could have done it.'

'Let's get this straight,' said Rob. 'We need to look at the Hamish Ryan murder in isolation. It's the only one where there's proof that the victim was poisoned with adrenaline. The other murders only come into play if we think there's enough evidence on the Hamish Ryan case.'

'Okay,' said Leonie. 'Okay.' She struggled to think. She'd made so many notes, been over them so many times. But when it came down to it, what was the proof that Quinn had murdered Hamish?

'It's just speculation, isn't it?' asked Tanbir. 'We know someone killed Hamish Ryan, but the only reason we think it's Quinn is because of the presence of the other three cases. But the only reason the other three cases are relevant is because of Hamish Ryan's murder. It's circular. Rob's right, we need to separate them out.'

Leonie panicked. 'Dr Bleasdale is sure it's Quinn. I trust her judgement.'

'That's all very well and good,' said Tanbir. 'But it's our judgement that matters, not hers. And I have to confess that the evidence proving Quinn killed Hamish Ryan is shaky.'

'What about the lies?' asked Leonie.

'Lying in court doesn't prove guilt. The judge said as much.'

There must be something else.

'But his only explanation is that someone came off the street and onto the ward. Isn't that completely bonkers?'

'How many times do I have to repeat this?' asked Lucas. 'He doesn't have to come up with a plausible story. He didn't have to give evidence. It all comes down to the prosecution evidence. It was not enough.'

'I think we should have another vote,' said Rob.

Everyone but Leonie and Diren thought that Quinn was not guilty. Charlie and Jade both said that, although they thought it was likely that Quinn was the killer, they weren't sure. It was Sim's betrayal that hit her the hardest.

'That settles it,' said Rob. 'Not guilty.'

'But not all twelve of us agree,' said Leonie. 'The judge hasn't given us the direction which allows us to reach a majority verdict,' said Leonie, knowing it was a lost cause.

'And he's never going to,' said Rob.

Leonie could feel her eyes brimming with hot tears. She fought to keep them back.

Sim tried to put a friendly arm around her shoulder, but she pushed it away.

'I had to,' he said. 'The evidence just wasn't there.'

'We've just let a murderer walk free.'

She became aware that the other jurors were looking at her because she was making a scene, so she left the room, heading for the toilets.

As people called after her, all she said was, 'I need a minute.'

She knew that everyone else would be exchanging awkward glances in her absence.

In the bathroom, she felt at a loss. She thought that, once in here, her next move would become clear, but she just paced around aimlessly, tears running down her face. The absence of anything in which she could find comfort was stark. She craved a cuddle with Ollie.

Her previous heartbreaks had been dealt with by watching Anne Hathaway films while eating Ben & Jerry's, but all she had now was this grey bathroom, with its MDF cubicles and anti-slip flooring.

The reality of what had just happened hadn't entirely sunk in. For over a year now her sole focus had been ensuring that Michael Quinn ended up behind bars. And now it had all fallen apart.

The door opened. 'All okay?'

She'd expected to hear Sim's voice but instead she heard Diren's.

'I'm sure he's guilty.'

'Me too,' he said. 'I can totally understand why you're upset.'

'It's just… I need a minute.'

'You can take as long as you need,' he said as he rubbed her back with his hand.

She buried her face in Diren's shoulder and wept.

'Thank you. Sorry. I just…'

'They're idiots,' he said. 'Ignore them.'

She tried to regain some control over her breathing. Her reflection in the mirror told her that her eyes were puffy and some of her makeup had started to run. Grabbing toilet roll from one of the cubicles, she used it to dab at her face and clear away some of the errant mascara.

'I should warn you before we go back in there, they've decided that Quinn can stay up here, with us.'

'What? But… just because they don't believe he murdered those people doesn't mean he isn't dangerous. Have they… given him back his stuff?'

'No, I've still got it.'

'Okay. That's something. But seriously, why does he even want to be up here with us?'

'Beats me. He just asked politely if he could stay here. Said he's been really lonely all day…'

Leonie scoffed. 'But he's been playing with us, turning the lights out… the song?'

'Let's go hear what he has to say for himself.'

Leonie emerged from the bathroom to bashful looks from the others.

Quinn smiled magnanimously, as though generously bestowing his forgiveness.

'Listen,' she said. 'I've got some questions for, er, Michael.'

'Go ahead,' he said, grinning broadly.

'Was it you who's been playing that "Adrenaline" song?'

Quinn paused for a moment. 'Listen, I needed you to understand that it wasn't *me* who killed Hamish Ryan. Someone else had a motive.'

'Yeah, Wynona said. Amy or Susan, or whatever… Why did you take her stuff when you found her body?'

'Put yourself in my shoes. Imagine you've spent a year in prison for a crime you didn't commit. Wouldn't you do just about anything to free yourself? I took only what I needed and that was the skeleton key.'

'And Geoff? Did you kill him?'

Quinn did that same faux-shocked face she'd seen him do during the trial. 'I would never. I'm a nurse.'

She suppressed the shiver she felt on hearing him say that.

'Okay, why did you decide to handcuff him to a radiator and leave him upstairs?'

'I told you. I'm innocent. I really didn't think anyone would see it. Because that's the way it works. Whenever there's an institution versus the individual, the institution wins. The cards were always stacked against me.'

Lucas nodded sagely.

'Did you turn off the lights?'

'Yes.'

'Why?'

'I wanted to get your attention. I thought you'd have food and access to the internet. I wanted to know what was going on.' He held up the bag of salted cashews he'd been eating.

Leonie knew this was nonsense. He had access to both the canteen and a smartphone. If he wanted their attention, he could have put a polite message out over the Tannoy rather than his cryptic clues and creepy music. He had done it to split the jury up, so he could appeal to a smaller number of people.

'And the phone in the probation office? Was that connected to the internet?'

'The phone's owner was out of data. I didn't want them to incur charges.'

'Why leave it in the probation office playing that song?'

'You hadn't been listening to the Tannoy, so I knew I needed to get your attention. I needed to show you which two people knew each other from before.'

'Finished?' Rob asked her, testily.

A series of notifications pinged. They all pulled their phones out to check the news. Others chimed a few seconds later.

In the commotion, Rob moved closer to Leonie.

'I know it was you,' he said.

Leonie looked around to see if anyone had overheard. It seemed that no one had. Even if they were within earshot, no one was paying attention. Everyone was too absorbed in the news that flashed up on their screens.

First Parts of City Struck by Chemical Attack Vacated.

A cheer went up around the room.

Leonie read the push notification on her home screen. Apparently, there were some parts of the city within the cordon that were being securely evacuated by the army.

There was no information about how long it would take for everyone inside the cordon to be rescued. Still, it meant there was an end in sight, as long as the twelve of them could stay alive until the army came.

Around her, jurors were hugging. Others had tears in their eyes. Leonie felt detached from their jubilation.

After the first burst of happiness, they all sat down again, looking at one another awkwardly.

'Are we just going to sit and wait, then?' asked Charlie.

'Let's get pissed,' said Jade. 'There's got to be some booze in this place.'

'It's annoying we can't bring drugs in here,' said Lucas, trying too hard to sound cool.

'Er, well, I managed to smuggle some in. I needed them for the gig later. But… maybe there are other drugs!' said Jade, excited. 'Maybe the police bring them in as evidence. We could go find them. It would be like minesweeping but with police exhibits rather than unfinished drinks.'

'That's a bit fucked up,' said Charlie.

'Sorry, yeah. I forgot you had your…'

Charlie looked embarrassed. 'You guys can still drink if you want.'

'Where are we going to find booze?' asked Anthony.

'I bet you the judges will have whisky or something in their private rooms,' said Jade.

'But we don't have a key.'

Leonie knew Diren was the one who had the skeleton key, but she wasn't going to volunteer this information.

'We should celebrate, though,' said Viv. 'This is good news.'

Several pairs of eyes flitted to the Ikea bags by the door which held the remaining food.

'No,' said Diren. 'We should ration it. If we've got to stay here for another forty-eight hours while they clean up the city, I don't want to be stuck with a bunch of grouchy people who stuffed their faces in the first twelve hours.'

They ignored him, instead descending on the Ikea bags in the spirit of every man for themselves.

TWELVE MONTHS BEFORE

There was a beeping sound, which alerted Leonie to the arrival of a new message.

Let's meet. Usual place. 10 a.m.

She read the message and checked the time. It was 9 a.m. She had just enough time to get ready. She typed out,

Okay, see you then.

Leonie pressed *send* on the message before locking the burner phone away in the drawer under her desk.

She drove over to the park. There was a car park on the outskirts, but the 'usual place' was the coffee stand in the middle. It was a ten-minute walk and it had just gone 10 a.m. She walked towards the centre of the park and found the coffee stand. Sitting on a bench nearby was Amy.

Leonie bought herself a flat white before going over to sit next to Amy. Her face was gaunt and her skin was tinged grey. The clothes she wore hung loosely from her petite frame. Two inches of mousy-brown with some grey showed at the roots of her normally vampiric hair. She had always dyed it dark brown with just a hint of purple.

Amy didn't smile. There were no pleasantries exchanged between them that would mark them out as friends. Her demeanour was all business.

'Have you got it booked yet?' she asked, referring to the plastic surgery Leonie was planning on getting.

'Yeah. First operation is next week.'

'Are you nervous?'

'Yes. Going under a general is always a risk, isn't it?'

Amy took a moment to consider before nodding. 'What about your new name? Have you decided yet?'

'I'm going to go with Leonie because it's similar enough to Leonora that I'll answer to it.'

Amy played with the paper cup in her hands, picking at the rim. 'Well, I've found a way into the system. I can get you onto the jury.'

Leonie's legs went leaden. 'Right.' She tried to sound more grateful. 'Good.'

Amy's tone remained brusque. 'Just give me a date, name, and address and I'll do it.'

'Best send it to the new address,' said Leonie.

'Have you sold your old house yet?'

'No, I'm renting it. That's where Rachel—my family liaison officer—visits me.'

'Yeah, you need to keep the old house for as long as you need to be Leonora.'

'Agreed.'

'Okay, so give me the details and I'll get this jury summons to you. I'll make sure you're on that jury.'

'Thanks Amy, I—'

'Don't thank me.' Her face was stony. Their friendship had never recovered from what had happened. While Hamish had survived the car crash that landed them both in hospital, Josh had not.

Leonie hadn't been certain that Amy's job would allow her access to the roll of potential jurors but wasn't surprised that Amy had found a way. Amy was an usher in the local Crown Court; a boring civil servant, Hamish had said. He had never appreciated jobs that involved unglamorous public service.

'I'll be there on the first day of your jury service,' said Amy. 'I'll swap with an usher from another court and do everything I can to make sure you're picked for Quinn's trial. It's important we're not seen together after you get your surgery. Contact via the burners only from now on. After it's all over, break it up with a hammer, because that's the only surefire way to ensure the data is destroyed. Don't just take it to the tip.'

Amy got up and walked away from the bench without a hug, without a goodbye. Leonie watched her leave, the autumn sunshine picking out the purplish colour in her hair.

Leonie then commenced the process of getting plastic surgery to change her appearance. Money was no object. Leonie had inherited all of Hamish's money, and his life insurance would pay out in future. No one was checking up on what Leonie was buying in the wake of his death because the police had already arrested their prime suspect: Hamish's nurse.

The most drastic change to her appearance would come from the cheek fillers, which would change the contours of her face. Leonie had always had flat cheeks, and so was looking forward to seeing her face fill out into a heart shape. Her nose had always been upturned and narrow, with a defined ridge, and she was hoping that rhinoplasty would change her profile so that it looked less angular.

Hamish had liked the elfin look: thin and pale with short dark hair. That's how Leonie had looked when they first got together. A pixie bob, slender limbs, and an ordinary face made to look extraordinary by dint of her daring haircut and hollow cheeks.

'I don't want you to look like other girls,' Hamish would say, whenever Leonie expressed dissatisfaction with her androgynous appearance.

Now, all of that could change. Her appearance would soften. She'd have a new haircut, something lighter. In the past, they'd have called it highlights, but now it was something more sophisticated: a balayage.

She was already changing in ways she hadn't intended to. The way she held herself. She was more confident now. She was putting on weight.

With Hamish, she'd always been careful to watch what she ate. She knew his preferences. He liked them thin. And that meant 'them' in the plural sense of the word. She wasn't the only one. They were all thin.

The sugar rush wore off and they slumped back down into their seats, the world a little blunted after the ingestion of food.

Rob sat in the corner, video-calling his family. He was doing exaggerated faces and a strange voice—the sort of voice one reserves for children and pets.

The others talked about the impending evacuation. The reality was that they had no idea how long it would take, whether it would be in phases, or which parts of the city would be helped first. They traded scraps of information like half-smoked cigarette. Anthony knew a guy who knew a guy whose building had been evacuated. Most of them only knew people outside of the cordon. Had most of the people inside the cordon even survived? The unanswered questions mounted.

Leonie and Diren sat slightly apart from the others. She eyed Quinn, who was wearing the oversized grey suit he'd had on most days at court.

She leant to speak into Diren's ear. 'Having him just sit here, hanging around is just… wrong. It's too risky.'

'Look at me,' he said. 'It's going to be okay. I'm going to make sure we get through this.'

Jesus, she wanted him. He was everything Leonie had told herself she hated: apolitical, sexist, mean… But the intensity with which he looked at her was intoxicating. She wanted to be alone with him.

'I don't feel safe in here any more,' she said.

'We should stick with the group. There's safety in numbers.'

She squeezed his hand, her body shielding this gesture from the rest of the group.

Sim, Jade and Lucas went off in search of booze and drugs. They returned twenty minutes later with a handful of pills, a bottle of whisky, and a bottle of gin.

Having had minimal food and water, they got drunk quickly. They hadn't managed to find any drugs, so all they had was the handful of pills from Jade's bag. A couple of ecstasy tablets were handed around. Sim took one, as did Lucas.

'I can't,' said Charlie, though the look in his eyes said he desperately wanted to.

'Go on, Tanbir,' said Sim. 'I think you need it. Honestly.'

Tanbir took the little tablet and popped it in his mouth. Leonie worried for him. She was sure he'd never taken drugs and was only doing so because he fancied Sim and wanted to impress him.

Charlie received a ping on his phone. 'Oh my God, oh my God!' He looked around, beaming. 'My friend is being evacuated from a building a couple of streets from here. We'll be next. This is nearly over!'

A cheer went around. Spirits were rising but there was a volatility to the festivities. Leonie had the sense that things were careering off course.

Jade put her phone in a glass to amplify its sound. 'If I can't go to the gig, I'm bringing the gig to me!'

After turning the lights off, she blasted Acid Rain from her phone and danced with the wild energy of the intoxicated. The gin was passed around and most people took a hearty swig. She noticed Quinn declining politely but still gossiping and giggling away with Wynona and Viv. She could imagine him holding court at the nurse's station while he regaled his colleagues with amusing anecdotes and titbits he'd gleaned from others.

Someone had a 'disco lights' effect on their phone. They laid it on the table and different coloured lights swirled around the dark ceiling.

Charlie sat at the edge of the festivities, looking on with a mix of longing and mild terror at what was unfolding. Leonie decided to go over to him. She squeezed Diren's hand to indicate that she would be back soon.

'Charlie, are you okay?'

He looked uncomfortable at her approach. 'Yeah, it's just difficult for me. I have to try really hard not to, you know.'

'I get it. I had a friend who recovered from addiction. These situations are always the hardest, but I'm here if you need to talk to someone about it.'

The drug-addict friend Leonie was referring to was Josh. What had started off as a bit of a joke—Josh was the life of the party, Josh was always on hand to get the good drugs—had become something deeply unfunny.

After the success of Alien Pandemic, Josh had risen to new heights as a music producer, but he and Amy never moved out of the three-bed semi. They made improvements to the house; the furniture became more expensive, the kitchen had a refurb, and they exchanged their wooden banister on the staircase for a glass-panelled one, but the money they might have spent on a new house was being sunk into Josh's habit.

Leonie had noticed the purple bags under his eyes on their first meeting, but his face had taken on the gaunt, haunted look of a man in thrall to opiates.

She remembered walking into Josh and Amy's bathroom at one party, expecting to be able to use the toilet, but Josh was in there, completely wasted, sweating, trying desperately to get the needle in his arm, but his hand was shaking too much.

'What are you doing?' came a voice from behind Leonie.

Next thing Leonie knew, Amy was barging past her, rushing into the toilet. She took the needle from Josh's hand and instead of discarding it or taking it away, bent over him, tightened the tourniquet and inserted the needle carefully into his vein.

Amy turned around to see Leonie standing in the bathroom door. She looked ashamed.

'Sorry, I—' said Leonie.

Once the needle was safely out of Josh's arm, Amy ushered Leonie out of the toilet, leaving Josh splayed on the floor. 'Let me show you to our en suite. We don't like people using it for parties, but…'

'I'm sorry, Amy, I didn't mean to intrude.' Leonie followed her friend across the landing to the main bedroom.

'It's not your fault. I hate doing it for him, but I figure it's better I do it safely than he kill himself with an accidental OD.'

'Is he getting help?'

'I'm going to get him help, but he can't go cold turkey. It'll be too dangerous.' Amy opened the door in the corner of her bedroom. 'Anyway, there's the loo. I need to get him out of the bathroom before someone else walks in on him.'

Amy had been good to her word. She had checked Josh into rehab. It took four attempts, but eventually he got clean and was prescribed methadone, which he weaned himself off until he was able to stay off drugs for years. Getting clean was the end of his producing career, and Amy became the sole breadwinner.

Leonie had always admired Amy's stoic and pragmatic approach, not to mention her devotion to her husband during a time when most people would have left.

Charlie's eyes tracked Jade dancing with abandon, unadulterated longing in his eyes. It wasn't lecherous, merely sad. Leonie remembered something she'd meant to speak to Charlie about.

'Hey, can I ask you something?'

He remained taciturn.

'A while back, I saw you give a green plec to Jade.'

His head turned sharply to look at her. 'You saw?'

She nodded. 'Would you mind me telling where you got it from?'

'At a gig.'

Leonie cocked her head to one side. 'Charlie. Come on. You can be honest with me.'

His shoulders slumped. 'No, not at a gig. This second-hand shop. I just saw it.'

'After hearing that she liked the band?'

He nodded. 'Please don't say anything to her.'

'I won't.' She patted his shoulder. 'Listen, stay strong, and come and ask me if you need any help.'

'Thanks, but I'll be fine.'

Leonie sat back down next to Diren.

The effects of the ecstasy started to kick in for those who had taken it.

Tanbir could be seen dancing in the middle of the room. He had a strange look in his eyes which was a mixture of sheepish and 'come get me'.

Leonie felt only foreboding. She had the sense that they were racing into delirium. A cocktail of stress followed by their relief at the upcoming evacuation, mixed with all the alcohol and drugs, was a potent mix.

Rob was swigging the gin with relish, getting more and more inebriated. Leonie was worried about how much this would loosen his tongue.

She looked across to see what Quinn was doing. Like her, he was watching the festivities with something like anthropological interest, no doubt sober as a judge. But soon he made his way over to a group who were standing chatting and appeared to worm his way into their conversation with ease. He seemed to be nursing a drink of some description, but Leonie very much doubted that he was drinking alcohol.

People had reverted to their old clusters. Jade, Lucas, Tanbir and Sim were dancing, eyes glazed, the sweaty sheen of their foreheads glowing in the disco lights. Lucas was dancing along with the others, but his eyes darted around, paranoid. Charlie sat on the edge of the clique looking put out.

Meanwhile, Rob, Wynona and Anthony were discussing what they would do once released.

In the middle of the two groups, an uneasy bridge between them, Viv and Jill chatted awkwardly with Quinn.

'So tell me, Viv,' asked Quinn. 'What is reiki healing? I'm so interested in alternative forms of medicine.'

Viv looked politely confused. 'Really? But you're a nurse.'

'Exactly. That's where my interest lies—in healing patients.'

'The NHS don't tend to take too kindly to alternative remedies.'

'That's part of the problem, isn't it? We're holistic beings, not component parts to be disassembled and put back together again.'

Viv smiled. 'Exactly. Healing the body is one thing, but what about the soul?'

Leonie was distracted by Tanbir picking up empty water bottles and shaking them, searching for something to quench his thirst. 'I'm going to get some from the tap,' he said to the younger group.

'Are you sure you should be doing that?' asked Leonie. 'I don't think we've had the all-clear that we can drink anything other than bottled water.'

'Thirsty,' said Tanbir.

Quinn appeared at Tanbir's side with disconcerting speed. 'Are you thirsty? I'll go and find you something from downstairs.'

Leonie wondered if he was on the lookout for opportunities to get the jurors on their own. She sat back down and waited for Quinn to return.

After five minutes, he came back carrying bottled pre-mixed Ribena. Leonie felt the urge to warn Tanbir not to drink anything offered by Quinn, but she was reassured when the plastic seal clicked open.

Tanbir took a sip. 'Thank you.'

Leonie didn't see how he initiated it, but Quinn managed to detain Tanbir in a whispered conversation. He was muttering in his ear. What was he saying?

The next thing Leonie knew, Tanbir was marching—slightly unsteady on his feet—towards the older group. His unusually round eyes appeared even more disc-like now that his pupils were dilated, eclipsing his irises.

A dreamy smile came over his face as he walked. Leonie got the sense of foreboding people are said to have before a natural disaster strikes.

'Anthony,' said Tanbir, his voice the loudest Leonie had ever heard it. 'I've got something to say to you.'

Anthony, greying and balding, with his office-worker posture and dad bod, turned to Tanbir, perplexed.

'I'm in love with you.'

Anthony stared at Tanbir, but slowly his face turned to disgust. 'Is this a joke?'

Tanbir's smile faltered. 'No.'

'Did one of you pricks put him up to this?' he demanded of those who had taken drugs. They didn't help themselves by giggling.

Leonie got up and rushed over. 'They didn't put him up to it.' She had just seen Quinn manipulating Tanbir in real time. Before she could say any more, Anthony said, 'I've got a wife and kids. What the fuck is wrong with you?'

Tanbir's face went from vacant smile to terror. He bolted for the corridor.

Only Leonie ran after him. She found him sat on the staircase.

Leonie got down next to him and pulled him into a one-armed hug. She expected him to resist but he didn't. 'Hey, hey.' She tried to sound comforting. 'Are you okay?'

'I thought he loved me back.'

Leonie paused for a second. 'Look, Tanbir, don't take this the wrong way, but did you mean to say that to *Anthony*?'

'Yes.' He sounded utterly miserable.

'You love him?'

'Yes.'

'I thought you fancied Sim.'

'Anthony may not be what you consider beautiful, but I find him… incredible. He's hard-working. He loves his family. He's a decent stand-up bloke and I can't help it. I think he's wonderful.'

This was said so sincerely that Leonie had to conclude it was true.

It unnerved her that in under an hour, Quinn had managed to observe something in Tanbir that Leonie had been blind to for ten weeks. Already he had put it to use in an attempt to sow disquiet among the group.

'But he's married. And as you said, he has a family.'

'I know.'

'Then, why say it if you knew nothing was ever going to happen between you?'

'It seemed like a good idea at the time. Life's short. Today proves that. We could have died and I might never have told Anthony how I really feel.'

Of all the things Leonie thought she'd end up doing today, this wasn't it. Luckily, she had decades' worth of experience of sitting on bathroom floors and consoling drunken people who had been rejected by the object of their affections. Mostly Hamish's friends. She didn't have any of her own.

'Tanbir, listen to me. Who cares? You're never going to see him again. There's no need to be embarrassed. You can move on from this and no one will ever know. Just say it was the drugs talking and you hallucinated that Anthony was Ryan Gosling. Or, I don't know, Antonio Banderas. At least that one sounds like Anthony. And just say it was a moment of madness.'

'But what if I never love anyone like I love Anthony?'

'How old are you, if you don't mind my asking?'

'Twenty-five.'

'Guess what? I was around your age when I fell in love for the first time. I promise you; lightning will strike twice. It will strike multiple times. And next time, it might just be someone who feels the same way about you. Let's get back inside to join the others.'

Tanbir nodded his agreement. He stood up, unsteady on his feet, and followed Leonie back into the main room.

When they turned the corner into the jury gallery, Leonie had her speech prepared. *Yes, Antonio Banderas? Who would have known?*

However, no one was concentrating on Tanbir's ill-judged declaration of love.

Rob had got to his feet and was banging the empty gin bottle on the table. He was attempting to get up onto a chair, but Wynona was dissuading him.

'Listen, I've got something to say,' he said, his words slurred from drink.

Oh shit.

'There's someone here who isn't being honest.' He looked over at Leonie. 'Listen, Sim. It wasn't Diren who stole your phone. It was Leonie.'

'What?' It took Sim much longer than it would a sober person to piece together what had just been said.

His spaced-out eyes swivelled around and landed on Leonie. Her stomach dropped.

'*You* stole my phone? *You*?'

Leonie looked at Rob, desperate to find out how he knew.

He answered her look with a drunken leer. 'Viv tol'me.' The three words blended into one.

'I saw it happen,' said Viv. 'I saw her pick it up from the plastic tray.'

'Why, why didn't you tell me?' asked Sim.

'Not my place,' said Viv.

'But you told *him*?' Sim gestured at Rob. He took a moment to steady himself. 'So, you knew, but you didn't tell me?'

Rob shrugged. 'It's between you and Leonie. Not our business.'

Leonie's eyes slid towards Quinn. He looked jubilant.

'Listen, Sim, I'm sorry—'

'How fucking dare you?'

From behind Sim, Jade said, 'That was a really low thing to do, Leonie.'

Sim pointed at Jade. 'See!'

'I thought I was doing you a favour. You were heartbroken because of Amir and I was sick of having to console you every time he broke your heart.'

'You were sick of me?'

'Yes. All you talk about is men. It's boring. You never asked what was going on with me; it was always about you and your heartbreak and your interesting dating life. Just because I'm, you know, a divorcee, doesn't mean I don't have stuff going on.' Leonie had hoped that getting all of this off her chest would feel like purging the poisonous resentment that had built up inside her, but instead it felt like she was just heaping on more toxicity.

'Yeah, well none of that excuses you stealing a phone,' said Lucas, coming to Sim's aid.

'I know that,' Leonie snapped at Lucas. 'This is none of your business.'

'If you're stealing others' property, that's all of our business.'

'Unless you're stuck in a loop of getting with and being dumped by a rock star called Amir Bernard, I think your phone is safe,' said Leonie.

She knew she was on her own in this argument. Though she sensed that Diren had long ago forgiven or at least understood this particularly idiotic thing she'd done, she knew it was ultimately indefensible.

'I can't believe you,' said Sim. 'I feel violated. My privacy has been violated.'

'I'm sorry, I really am. I know it was wrong. But your relationship was toxic and I just—'

'Why didn't you give it back if you were so sorry?' asked Rob.

Leonie ignored Rob and addressed Sim. 'Because it became impossible to say anything once I started lying. I meant to find a way of returning it to you, I really did.'

'You're a lying whore.'

The use of the 'w' word shook Leonie to her core. She retaliated without thinking. 'And you're a vacuous husk of a human being. When was the last time you took anything more seriously than your highly filtered Instagram photos or your dating app bio?'

'The idea,' said Sim quietly, 'that you can call me vacuous, when you're an empty sack filled with nothing but silicone and CK Euphoria is pretty rich if you ask me. Also, Euphoria? Why is it still 2008 in your head?'

'2008 was a pretty good fucking year, thank you!' shouted Leonie.

'Characterless slug.'

'Why were you friends with me throughout the entire trial if you thought I was so awful?' asked Leonie.

They were spitting insults at one another like fighting alley cats.

'I wasn't your friend!' shouted Sim. 'How shallow are you to think that I was your friend? You were just better to talk to than these other cunts.'

'Charming,' said Viv.

Sim's defiant expression faltered.

'We didn't manage to bring any popcorn back from the kitchens, did we?' asked Diren.

'Fuck you,' said Leonie, rounding on Diren. 'Why do you enjoy seeing other people upset so much? That's pretty screwed-up, you know?'

Diren gave her a grin of even white teeth. 'At least no one gets upset when I tell them they're a—' Diren looked to Sim. 'What was it? Characterless slug? Something else about silicone? I think you look fucking cracking, by the way, always have. But yeah, if you're a cunt from day one, no one's upset when you're a cunt on day sixty.'

'Right!' shouted Rob. 'That really is enough use of *that* word.'

Over Rob's head, Sim said, 'People still get pissed off with you on day whatever.'

They went quiet for a moment. Everyone was looking at Leonie. The music from Jade's phone filled the space while the incongruous disco lights continued to swirl across the ceiling and light up people's features at random.

'Listen,' said Rob, addressing Leonie. He was still drunk, but he was fighting hard to keep his words under control. 'Apologize for stealing Sim's phone.'

'I have!'

'Apologize again.'

'Sim, I'm sorry. I truly am. It was a fucking stupid thing to do but I did it in the heat of the moment and then I didn't know how to come back from it. I'm so, so sorry.'

Sim shrugged. Then he went to sit in the corner and scroll through his phone with clumsy fingers.

The party atmosphere had been sucked from the room. Only Jade was still interested in the music. Everyone else was on something of a come-down.

When 'Adrenaline' came on, Leonie couldn't stand to hear it. She absented herself by going up into the canteen where the song wasn't so loud. It was dark. She looked out of the window at the blue night drawing in. Would they have to sleep here? She didn't think she'd be able to go to sleep with Quinn so close by.

'Want some of this?'

It was Diren. She turned around to see him on the other side of the room holding up the bottle of whisky.

'What is it?' she asked, unable to see the label in the gloom.

Diren looked down at the bottle. 'It's Japanese.' He joined her next to the window.

Leonie took the whisky from him and squinted at the label. 'Single malt.' She took a hearty swig, felt the heat in her throat. From there it spread to the rest of her body, enveloping her in a sense of calm and warmth.

She held out the bottle to Diren but he declined. 'I need to stay sharp. I meant what I said about keeping you safe.'

Leonie took another swig, maintaining eye contact with him. The others were wasted next door, and Sim had already decided to judge her for whatever was going on between her and Diren. Perhaps she should just throw caution to the wind.

Diren moved towards her and reached for the tie belt on her coat, which had been maintaining her dignity since she'd had to change out of her shirt dress.

Leonie hesitated, wondering whether this was a good idea. Diren put his fingers to her chin and tilted her head up. He planted a kiss on her lips.

They broke apart and she looked into his eyes, which were black in the dim light.

She wanted to be close to every part of him. Even more intoxicating was the way he repaid her gaze with equal intensity. She knew he found her hot. She couldn't wait to have sex with someone who was enthusiastic about being with her. Hamish never made her feel that way; she'd always been led to believe she was the lucky one.

A warm hand cupped the side of her hip. She grabbed the sides of Diren's face and kissed him back with fervour. He repaid her by kissing her back and running his hands over her body.

They broke apart again. 'Not here,' he said.

They left by the door in the corner of the canteen. They had to silently pick apart the barricade to do that. Every time one of the chairs clinked a little, they giggled. Once they were through, Diren locked the door behind them. They opened a random office. Diren swiped everything off the table and lay Leonie down on it.

EIGHTEEN MONTHS BEFORE

One day Hamish came into the kitchen while Leonie was loading the dishwasher. His wide smile irritated her: it was mostly *his* dishes that had been left on the side.

'Is it wind or am I going to have to ask what you're so pleased about?'

His expression betrayed fleeting irritation. 'Don't be gross. It's good news.'

She carried on loading the dishes, wondering if there was a way to do it so that he'd get the message that she didn't want to be cleaning up his mess.

'There's this amazing new band playing tonight. Called Acid Rain.'

'What kind of music?'

'My kind of music.' He sounded exasperated. 'Metalcore.'

'Pretty heavy?'

'Yes, but they're doing some really cool stuff. The vocals are insane and they mix it all live on stage.'

'Sounds… cool.'

Too cool for me.

'Yeah. They're going to be supporting Alien Pandemic. How special is that? It'll be Acid Rain's first ever arena gig.'

'Good for them.'

'I've got two backstage passes through work. Would you like to come?'

'Do you want me to?'

He came and hugged her from behind so she couldn't move. She was stranded in the middle of the kitchen holding his dirty plate, unable to reach to put it back on the side, unable to bend down to the dishwasher. She'd rather he forwent the romantic gesture and put his fucking dishes in the washer.

'Of course I want you to come,' he whispered in her ear. His breath warmed her neck. 'It'll be like when we first started going out.'

Was that what this was about? He wanted to relive the first few years of their relationship? That wasn't going to happen. Back then they were young and cool enough to feel at home in a grungy club thrashing away to some obscure band. Now they would look like weird older people who couldn't let go of their youth.

Still, she relented. Maybe it would help rekindle the spark.

Something needed to change. Cleaning up after someone else was not an aphrodisiac, yet Hamish always expected her to be ready and primed for sex. A couple of days ago she'd seen some messages pop up on his phone. She used the dropdown to work out what had happened. Hamish had been complaining to a friend that she wasn't as fun as she'd been when she was twenty-five. It hurt to know that her husband wanted to go out with an eternally preserved version of her, encased in time so that she could be 'fun'.

She allowed herself a flight of fancy. Perhaps if she was still writing poetry, she could have found a way to preserve her youth in the poems; enter into a Faustian pact where she remained beautiful as long as she kept feeding verses to the devil.

Sometimes she thought she hated her husband, but she would still do almost anything to keep him.

Hamish's comment about wishing she was still as fun as when they first met played on her mind as she was getting ready. She tried spiking her short hair with gel to avoid look-ing mumsy. Instead she looked like Sonic the Hedgehog. After smoothing it back down, she threw on an old choker in an attempt to look edgy.

The band were already playing when they got there. Leonie and Hamish hung in the wings, getting a close-up view of the set. Twenty-something Leonie would have been immensely jealous of thirty-nine-year-old Leonie.

Acid Rain were a seven-piece. In addition to the usual drums, lead guitar, bass guitar, and rhythm guitar, they had a keyboardist and someone on a turntable. The guitarists shredded their guitars at regular intervals, interspersed with catchy riffs. But the whole thing had a jerky, electronic feel.

The lead singer was an elfin woman with a blonde pixie cut so bleached that her hair was practically white. Her eyebrows had also been bleached until they disappeared into her forehead, making her kohl-lined eyes stand out even more.

Leonie found herself mesmerized by her. She danced around the stage with such manic energy, her whole body thrashing to the rhythm of the bass. When she sang, her voice was throaty like that of a forty-a-day smoker.

She couldn't have been more than twenty-two. She was skinny and flat-chested, wearing a checked shirt around her hips in lieu of a skirt, while on top all she wore was a bralette. Her sternum protruded out almost as far as her nipples. Just how Hamish liked his women.

Leonie could tell that the song was reaching its climax. The lead singer dropped her head and howled into the micro-phone. Her primal scream was seriously impressive. It was difficult for most men to make such a throaty sound, but hers was full-bodied while imparting immense pain. The crowd fed off it.

The band played a couple more songs. Leonie thought they were talented musically, but lyrically they were limited. The melody was well constructed, but the song rang hollow in the absence of any story to tell.

Leonie looked across at Hamish. He was enraptured and made no attempt to hide it. His head barely bobbed. He was transfixed, his eyes following the lead singer around the stage.

Some wives would have admonished him, told him to pick his jaw up off the floor. Leonie and Hamish were well past that sort of pretence.

When the band finished playing, Leonie and Hamish followed them into the backstage area. The band opened up bottles of beer and chugged them down. Most of them were dripping with sweat, makeup running down their faces. Their scant clothes stuck to their bodies. Leonie noticed a barrel-chested Asian man who had played bass with nothing but his body hair to cover his muscular upper body. He wore copious amounts of eyeliner and was undeniably beautiful.

Hamish walked straight over to the lead singer.

'Hey, my name's Hamish.'

She looked puzzled until he gave the name of the streaming giant he worked for. Then her face brightened right up.

'Oh, nice to meet you.' Her speaking voice was surprisingly high-pitched.

'This is my wife.' He put a cursory arm around Leonie's shoulder. 'We're big fans.'

Leonie realized why he'd brought her here. It wasn't so that they could rekindle the essence of their youth. It was so she could provide cover. If his wife was there, Hamish could introduce himself without seeming creepy. Then, once he'd established himself as a safe man—one she didn't have to watch out for—Hamish would turn on the charm.

Leonie felt sick. She knew he was often unfaithful, but to make her a part of the pick-up was just too humiliating.

A camera flash went off, momentarily blinding her.

It was the player with the heavy eyeliner and the rug of thick, dark hair coating his barrel chest. He was taking a selfie. Leonie didn't want this ultimate humiliation to be captured in any form, especially not photographic.

She turned on her heel and walked away from Hamish's side, leaving him there to gawp at the lead singer of Acid Rain.

As she walked, she strained her ears, hoping to hear him call after her. Even outside of the venue, she continued to listen out for footsteps, expecting to feel Hamish's hand around her arm, entreating her to return.

He didn't bother.

She got a taxi back to their house.

Hamish's car didn't appear on the drive for another twenty-four hours.

*

The morning after Hamish returned, Leonie went down to the kitchen to find a lime-green guitar pick in the corner of the kitchen island. It bore a symbol: 🌧. She picked up the plectrum and examined it.

Hamish walked in just as she turned it over.

'Oh yeah, Cassie gave me one of their plecs.'

'Cassie?'

'You know, the singer.'

Leonie left a beat. 'She doesn't play an instrument, let alone guitar.'

Hamish took a breath as though to say something but seemed to think better of it.

On the underside of the plectrum someone had inked an X in Sharpie. A kiss?

'One of a kind,' said Leonie.

'Yeah, it's kind of her symbol.'

'The band's logo isn't enough for her?'

'Don't be like that, Lee.'

'Sorry. You're right. I should be more like I was when we were in our twenties. When I was young and naive and willing to put up with your bullshit.'

'I'm not talking about this right now.' Hamish left the kitchen.

Leonie rested the plectrum back on the kitchen table. She stared at it for a long time, working out what to do.

Next thing Leonie knew, Hamish was taking a sabbatical from work. She didn't know whether his yearning to write songs was born from a belief that it would make Cassie fall in love with him, or if it was an excuse to spend more time with her, or a straightforward midlife crisis, but for the first time in fifteen years, music ceased to be mere numbers on a screen for him.

Little did she know that he had approached Josh—the guy who for Hamish would forever be the one that had spun gold—and suggested they get the band back together.

For months, Hamish and Josh seemed to be in something of a rut. Writer's block, some people would call it.

Leonie would routinely come home to find Hamish depressed. She soon learned not to ask him how his day had gone.

Then Hamish had realized there was something missing. The magic ingredient that had helped them craft musical genius fifteen years previously. Drugs.

Without any care for Josh's welfare, or respect for the mammoth task he'd achieved in getting sober, or thought for the wellbeing of Amy and Josh's young family, Hamish managed to persuade Josh to use again.

They would meet in Josh's garage—Josh always matching the right drug to the appropriate piece of music—and write. Hamish was sure to take the paraphernalia away before Amy returned home from work. Leonie never knew whether Amy suspected Josh was using again, or whether Josh and Hamish's attempt to gaslight her about it had been successful.

Then one night Hamish had let Josh get behind the wheel while under the influence of a cocktail of drink and drugs befitting only the most serious addicts.

It was dark. The sulphuric glow of the street light outside bathed Leonie's dark living room in yellow light. Leonie sat, reading under the glow of the floor lamp, Ollie curled up on her lap. She stroked him absent-mindedly.

Feet on the gravel drive. The key in the lock. He was back.

Footsteps. Shoes shrugged off. Coat hung up.

Her eyes were assaulted as Hamish flicked on the main light. 'Sat in the dark?'

'It wasn't dark,' said Leonie. 'I had the lamp on. It was cosy.'

'Seemed pretty dark to me. And you've got the curtains open. For fuck's sake, you know I don't like that. I like to shut the night out.'

I like to let the darkness in, thought Leonie. She'd allowed tendrils of it to creep into the house. It was a Japanese knotweed working its way through the masonry, holding their marriage in a vice-like grip.

Hamish didn't stay in the living room. Why did he need to disturb her equilibrium if he wasn't even intending on staying? She turned the main light off and sat under the small pool of orangey light left by the floor lamp with the peach lampshade.

In the other room, the fridge door opened. Food was pulled out. Eaten without grabbing a plate. Leonie certainly didn't hear the cupboard doors open, or the ceramic plates chink as one was retrieved. She heard soft padding as he climbed the stairs. The odd creak of the old floorboards.

Water jets hit the bottom of the shower tray. After half an hour, Hamish came downstairs, smelling fresh. Well, fresh-ish.

He still wore Old Spice. It was the rugged Scot in him. Not one to be taken in by fancy brands or more sophisticated smells, ten years of nice aftershave bought by Leonie at Christmas were left on the shelf to collect dust. Hamish stuck with what he knew best. What his father had worn. He was an 'if it ain't broke, don't fix it' kind of guy.

He was no longer wearing a suit, but an outfit more suitable for a wine or cocktail bar.

'For me?' she said, sounding pathetic even to her own ears. It's what he'd expect her to say.

'Josh and I are meeting the band.' He meant Acid Rain. He meant Cassie. 'Show them what we've been working on. I'm going over to his first.'

She knew not to ask if the writing was going well. She just said, 'Have fun,' and went back to reading.

The key turning in the ignition. Tyres crunching, car pulling off the drive and then away. Down their street and off to whatever bitch he was fucking, or so Leonie thought.

In fact, he did go to Josh's first. They were on their way to 'see the band' when the crash happened.

Later, she had still not moved from her spot on the sofa. She was no longer reading but watching television. The curtains were still open. Ollie was curled at her feet like a hot-water bottle.

Just over an hour after Hamish left, headlights bleached her living room.

She closed her eyes against them. More footsteps on the gravel. Her heart began to pound.

A knock at the door. It was a specific type of knock. She wondered if it was practised.

She opened the green front door of their crooked little cottage to find a policeman standing there.

'Can I come in?'

Everyone knows that when a police officer asks to come in without telling you why, the news is not good. Her legs were the first things to go weak. Then there was a plummeting feeling in her stomach. She could barely remember what happened next, what words were being said.

He was just here, she kept thinking. She touched her cheek. A trace of his saliva would still be there from when he'd given her that token kiss.

She was guided into the living room, where the police officer told her what had happened.

He wasn't dead. He was just injured, had been taken to the local hospital and was going to undergo life-saving surgery.

Her grief was split in two. In one direction was the fact that she and Hamish had been very happy, once. She grieved for that. On the other hand was the split second of relief she'd felt when she'd first seen the police car pull up outside her house.

I'm free, she thought. *I'm free to meet other people and really live my own life. Starfish in bed, fart on the sofa, wear no makeup, eat what I want, do what I want.*

She'd only tasted freedom—not even freedom, the promise of freedom—for less than a second, but it had already intoxicated her.

Was that really what she wanted? To be free of Hamish? She couldn't allow herself to acknowledge it.

'Look,' said the officer, shifting uncomfortably. 'There's something else.'

'Yes?'

'The person who was in the car with him. The driver. He's dead.'

'Josh?'

The officer nodded.

This news hit Leonie like a freight train. All she could think about was Amy and the kids.

'Was he… drunk?'

'We haven't had the results back yet.'

'Make sure to check,' was all Leonie could think to say.

She rushed to hospital to visit Hamish.

On her way in, she saw Amy coming out of ITU.

'Amy, I'm so sorry,' she said.

Her wet eyes fixed Leonie with a look of venom. 'Fuck you.'

Leonie couldn't believe this. The accident was Josh's fault. He was the one who'd been driving.

'Amy, wait—'

Amy rounded on her. 'It's *his* fault he's dead.'

Leonie was rendered speechless. How could it have been Hamish's fault when it was Josh who'd been driving?

The conversation had unnerved her, but she shook off the confrontation and went through to see Hamish.

She spent several hours waiting for him to come out of surgery. When he finally did, he was still unconscious, so she sat at his bedside, stroking his head, every bit the doting wife.

You stupid fucker, she thought. *You were trying to get your end away and look where it's got you.*

Hamish's phone was on the bedside table. The home screen lit up with a new email. Leonie took the phone off charge and held it in front of Hamish's face, using Face ID to unlock it. She opened the email. It was from Cassie.

We love the new track! Listen to the demo with my vocals x

There was an attachment titled 'adrenaline.mp4'. A cold sinking sensation spread through her. She scrolled back through the emails to find the document Hamish had attached at the beginning of the trail, which contained the lyrics. She opened it up and read them. They looked horribly familiar. All of those poems she'd written when they were first together. The pseudo-scientific ones about love. The bastard had done it again. She wanted to throw the phone across the room, wake him up, hit him, do anything to hurt him. It was one thing to take the piss out of their marriage by screwing women twenty years younger; it was another to take the piss out of her.

Because this wasn't her body, or her possessions, or anything material. This was her art. Her soul splayed on the page, for her eyes only. And he had taken that and done the equivalent of putting it in a sex-shop window for all to see.

He had learned nothing. He was still willing to degrade her poetry for money or sex, or both.

In the bed next to Hamish's, the patient's ECG flatlined. There was no need for Leonie to raise the alarm; nurses rushed over immediately and began to resuscitate the patient. Leonie watched carefully. They wheeled over the cart which had been resting against the wall for the entire time Leonie had been next to Hamish's bed. She hadn't noticed it until now.

One of the doctors or nurses asked for adrenaline and someone pulled a syringe from the cart. She watched a nurse administer a dose from a pre-filled syringe.

Leonie had to get off the ward. She was starting to find the atmosphere stifling.

Still, visiting hours weren't over yet, so it didn't feel right to leave. She decided to go down to the canteen. She'd lost count of the number of hours she'd gone without sleep.

Leonie got herself a coffee from the machine but wanted to find somewhere a bit more secluded to drink it. There was nowhere like that in the hospital, but the canteen was relatively quiet at this time of the evening.

There was a large area with the usual wooden tables and chairs upholstered with multi-coloured plastic seat cushions. Along one line of the wall were booths with banquettes in the same plastic material.

She slid into one of the booths for a bit of peace and quiet.

It wasn't long before two women in scrubs slid into the booth behind her, not realizing she was there.

It was only later that Leonie realized that one of the women was Dr Bleasdale.

Later, during the trial, she would suspect that she recognized some of the witnesses, but that could have been a retcon, something her memory concocted to suit her narrative. There might have only been agency staff in on the nights she visited.

But she remembered Dr Bleasdale.

Her voice was tense when she spoke, 'I'm becoming increasingly concerned about Michael.'

'There's no evidence, Helen.'

'What about the mortality rate on that ward? It's so much higher than all the others. The patients are no more sick. What other explanation is there?'

'Maybe there's something wrong on that ward, but it doesn't prove that he's the cause.'

'We should rotate the nurses, make sure by process of elimination.'

'Sorry, Helen, there's nothing I can do.'

Leonie sat stock still. She didn't want them to know she was there, that she'd overheard.

There was an uncomfortable silence during which neither of the two women spoke.

Eventually, the woman whose name wasn't Helen steered the conversation onto less controversial topics. Leonie had to wait twenty minutes for them to finish their food, by which time visiting hours were over.

As she walked down the long corridor towards the car park, she passed a nurse she thought she'd seen before on Hamish's ward. He was a slight man of just less than average height. His head was coated with even grey stubble. Something about him gave her an uneasy sense she couldn't put her finger on. She checked his badge. His name was Michael.

As she wandered out into the dark car park, an idea was forming in her mind. She pulled out her phone and dialled Amy's number.

Don't hang up, don't hang up.

'What?'

'Don't hang up on me! I've got something I want to discuss with you. Meet me in the park tomorrow by Brodie's coffee stand. I need to talk to you. Please.'

Amy gave a weary sigh at the other end of the line but agreed.

Leonie was taken aback when she laid eyes on Amy. In a few short days she appeared to have lost a significant amount of weight. There were large bags under her puffy, bloodshot eyes.

'Amy,' said Leonie on seeing her. 'I'm so sorry. What can I get you to drink?'

'Tea, please.' Her voice trembled.

Leonie ordered Amy's drink and returned to sit with her. She tried to hold Amy's hand, but she pulled it away. After that, Leonie decided it was better to take things at Amy's pace. She'd let her go first.

Once Amy had taken a few sips of her sugary tea she said, 'Did you know what they were doing?'

'I knew that they were writing again. Not to begin with, but eventually Hamish admitted that he was going to your house to write.'

'Not just that,' said Amy. 'Did you know that Hamish had persuaded Josh to use again?'

Leonie hesitated. 'No, I had no idea.' She really didn't. But in hindsight, it was the sort of thing that Hamish would do. Her poetry, his friend's sobriety, their marriage. They were all collateral as far as Hamish was concerned. He only ever cared about himself.

Amy didn't look convinced. 'He'd been using when he got behind the wheel.' The end of the sentence was almost incomprehensible, a wail of grief forcing the pitch of her voice to increase.

Leonie tried to physically comfort Amy again, but her attempts were shunned once more. 'I'm sorry. I really didn't know.'

The difference between Josh and Hamish wasn't that Josh was a drug addict and Hamish wasn't. The difference was that Josh couldn't live with not being a rock star, but Hamish was happier that way. Hamish was a rock star wherever he went. He didn't need to be the lead singer of a famous band to make people fawn over him. He'd only ever wanted to be a nameless, faceless suit making money out of damaged artists. Who cared who was credited for the songs, as long as he got his cut? Josh had dreamt of being a rock star from the first time he'd heard the opening riff of 'Sweet Child O' Mine'. The only time he felt truly happy was when there was a crowd of people singing his songs back to him. Instead, he'd spent his life watching sold-out stadiums screaming his songs at other people. Like many others before him, he'd used drugs to bridge the gap between the life he had and the life he wanted. But then the chemical addiction set in and held him in its grip.

'Why weren't they writing at your house?' asked Amy.

'I… I'm not sure,' she said honestly.

'Don't you know what he gets up to behind your back?'

'Of course I do.'

Landing this blow on Leonie seemed to give Amy some comfort. 'It's Hamish who should be dead, not Josh,' she said.

Leonie said nothing in response. She'd let Amy brood on this some more before she shared her idea.

'Hamish let him get behind the wheel when he was off his face,' said Amy. 'I hope he never comes out of that coma.' She got up as though to leave.

'Wait.' Leonie reached out and grabbed her arm. 'I need to talk to you about something.'

Amy seemed reluctant to hear her out, but then Leonie set about explaining the idea that had come to her last night.

'I know you think Hamish should be dead, not Josh. And there's nothing that can be done to bring Josh back, I get that, but there might be a way of making things fairer. I've checked with our financial adviser, and the royalties Josh would have earned are held on trust. That means you only have a life interest. The only way you or your family can get any of the money from Josh's earnings would be for Hamish to die too. I think there's a way of doing it without being caught.'

Amy listened intently. As soon as the prospect of murdering Hamish and avenging Josh's death was presented to her, Leonie saw the flicker in her eyes. The grief was raw. As far as she was concerned, Hamish had murdered Josh. He'd allowed him to take drugs again without any thought to the consequences of this for Amy and her children.

'Why? Why would you suggest this?'

Leonie thought for a long time how she was going to approach this. 'I know what Hamish did was awful. He got Josh back onto drugs just because he wanted to write songs the way they used to. It's pretty up there on the list of most morally depraved things you can do. Hamish may as well have left his car at the top of a hill with the handbrake off and watched as it rolled down to where Josh had been sleeping.'

'He's still your husband, though.'

'True. It's not just what he did to Josh. There's also something he's done to me and I can never forgive him for it.'

'What, shagging that Cassie behind your back?'

Leonie scoffed. 'No. Much worse than that.'

Leonie confessed to being the true author of the lyrics of Alien Pandemic's sophomore album and in, all likelihood, those of Acid Rain's next album.

'Woah. I never knew that.'

She knew Amy would understand.

'The idea came to me because…' She explained how she had seen the cardiac arrest on the bed next to Hamish's.

'I can do it,' said Amy.

'You're sure?'

'I'm the one with the experience of sticking needles in veins. We don't want anything being fucked up at the last minute. Whoever does this will need to be quick. I've got a steady hand.'

Leonie nodded.

Cautiously, carefully, they hatched their plan. Amy would attend the ward during visiting hours, which finished at 7 p.m. Thereafter, she would find a way to sequester herself on the ward. Perhaps in the toilet, or in the cupboard where they kept the towels and bed sheets. There, she would change into a uniform, perhaps wear a medical mask to stop Hamish from recognizing her if he woke. When everyone was asleep, she'd approach Hamish's bed and, as she had done time and time again for Josh, find Hamish's vein and insert the syringe. She would inject him with enough adrenaline to kill him.

If anyone asked, they were each other's alibi.

'There's something else,' said Leonie. 'That I think will give us cover. There's a nurse in the hospital who's suspected of killing patients. I heard the doctors talking about it. They're waiting for another suspicious death and then they're going to get him convicted.'

'How do you know?'

She recounted the conversation she'd overheard in the hospital canteen and then described how she saw Michael Quinn on Hamish's ward.

'So you've got to do it when he's on shift. If you don't see him on the ward, back out and go another day.'

'That seems even riskier.'

'I saw him on a night shift yesterday. They do four days on, four days off. It's a three in four chance that he'll be on shift again tonight.'

'So, it's tonight,' said Amy.

'If he's charged with Hamish's murder, we've got to make sure he's convicted. If he's not convicted, there's a risk the police will keep the investigation open.'

'How are we going to ensure he's convicted?'

'You can get me onto the jury.'

Amy mulled this over. 'It would make sense,' she said. 'But it puts you at risk.'

Leonie shook her head. 'I've looked into it. It's a contempt of court to publish details about jurors in the UK. People won't be looking into me at all.'

'Only if you're sure.'

'I'm sure. It's an extra layer of protection for you. If someone else goes down for Hamish's murder, the case will be closed. No cold-case-review team picking over the facts.'

Amy furrowed her brow. 'But what if he's not a murderer?'

'He is. Honestly, the doctor I overheard was sure of it. If any-thing, we're stopping a murderer from continuing his spree.'

Amy thought for a long time before speaking. 'Okay. I'll do it.'

*

Later that evening there was another knock on the door. A different police officer asked to come in.

Leonie's heart started to hit her rib cage. It felt like her heart had grown bigger, more alien.

'We're very sorry, Mrs Ryan. Your husband passed away this evening…' His words faded as though broadcast through a radio dipping out of signal. '…Circumstances… suspicious… adrenaline… arrest.'

This time she descended into a catatonic state. She felt hands on her arms, her back, sitting her down, supposedly soothing her. Something about a family liaison officer.

Boots trampled all over her house, fingers picked through private possessions, while prying eyes looked in wardrobes and corners normally kept from view. The invasion felt like a violation.

'We'll be in touch.'

And then they were gone.

The feelings of elation and freedom she'd had when she heard he was in hospital dissipated.

What have I done?

Leonie and Diren lay there for a while, using Leonie's coat as a blanket. She cuddled up to his body, stealing his warmth.

Where Diren was sleepy, Leonie was alert. She lay awake, thinking.

Her mind turned to the evacuation. It felt within touching distance now. But if the rescue didn't happen within the next few hours, she'd have to think of a way to convince the others about the danger posed by Quinn. The easiest method would be to prove that he'd killed Geoff. But on Wynona's account, Quinn can't have been the one who pushed Geoff over the balustrade. Either Wynona was lying—why would she—or someone else pushed him, but who?

'Listen,' said Leonie. 'I've been thinking. There must be someone else in the building.'

Diren rolled over and yawned.

'Wynona said that Quinn watched over her for thirty minutes, or however long it took for us to leave the atrium.'

'I'm not sure I believe her,' said Diren. 'Why didn't she cry out if she knew we were not far away?'

'She was scared? Some people think it's better to comply with their captor than to call out.'

'Then they're stupid.'

'Wynona isn't going to think the same way as you.' Leonie sat down on one of the office chairs. 'What if she was telling the truth? It means Quinn must have had another accomplice.'

'Another?'

Leonie hesitated. 'Yes.'

Diren sat on the table in front of her, still topless. He placed his hands on the arm rests either side of her. It wasn't intimidating, but it was intimate. 'Tell me. You know something. I need to know what it is.'

Leonie put her face in her hands. The secret felt too heavy. She would never tell him. She would never tell anyone what she had done. It was in that moment that she realized it would be something she'd carry for ever, and now she didn't even have Amy—the only other soul who knew her secret—to share the burden.

But she had to say something. He had to know at least part of the truth. She took a shuddering breath. 'I'm the one who knows someone from before. I was married to Hamish Ryan.'

*

Diren listened in silence as Leonie explained. When it came to justifying her presence on the jury, she made it sound as though she wanted justice for Hamish, and made no mention of her real motive, which was to cover up the crime committed by her and Amy.

Diren didn't say anything, he just listened. The unasked question—how could you be so sure it was Quinn?—hung in the air between them. Leonie decided to answer it, even though it hadn't been asked.

'I was in the hospital canteen. I overheard Dr Bleasdale telling a colleague all about him. She told her colleague loads more than came out in the trial. Those details we never heard, probably because they weren't admissible. We only had half of the story. All of those times when we were sent out of court, they were arguing over whether we could hear details like that.

In the end, the jury had the equivalent of a book which was missing chapters.'

'The number of deaths in the hospital always played on my mind. And how they dropped after he left.'

'Exactly,' said Leonie. 'And now he's going to walk free. I thought the chemical attack was a sort of punishment for what I'd done.'

Diren cocked his head. 'That's a bit self-centred, isn't it? I don't think the universe arranged the attack just for you.' His smile was playful, teasing. He didn't hate her. But then he didn't know the full story.

'You know what I mean. It's been horrendous for all of us but great for him. He might break free in all the chaos.'

'He'll never be able to work as a nurse again, though.' The look Diren gave her laid her bare. 'How did you manage to get on the jury of the man who killed your husband?'

Leonie paused. Had Amy still been alive, she would never have given away her secret.

'I had help,' she said. 'You know "Susan"? Her real name was Amy, and she was a close friend of mine. She pulled a few strings and…' Leonie spread her hands.

'Is the contact between you traceable?'

'No, we used burner phones.'

Once searched by security, Leonie made her way up to her locker.

As she was running a little late, this was the first time that no one had followed her from security in a week. She was completely alone when she opened her locker, so she took the opportunity to finally do what she had been meaning to ever since she'd stolen Sim's phone. Sim was someone whose phone was set to automatically download images he received via WhatsApp. Leonie had seen him type in the passcode to check for messages from Amir, or else to show her pictures of the two of them together, on countless occasions and she had come to know it almost as well as her own.

She went into the phone and deleted the photo Amir had taken backstage, the one where Leonie and Hamish were just visible. It was grainy and poorly lit, but you could see how mesmerized Hamish looked. What a pathetic idiot he was. She deleted the image from the gallery and from the app. There. No more evidence of her connection to Hamish. Now all she had to do was find a way of getting Sim's phone back to him.

Next stop: the retiring room. She was walking along the corridor when a door opened to her right and she heard someone say,

'Leonora.'

She stopped dead. Amy's face seemed to hover in the gap between the door and the frame as though disembodied.

Without missing a beat, Leonie went inside the room. Amy shut the door and locked it using a skeleton key she pulled from her hip.

'What are you doing?' asked Leonie. 'We're not supposed to talk to one another.'

She took a closer look at Amy. Her hair was a more vibrant shade of purple. It was shorter and coarser than it had been before.

'I needed to talk to you. Don't do this.' Her voice was desperate. 'Please, make sure he's acquitted.'

'You're kidding.'

'I'm not. Please, I can't live with this on my conscience.'

'He's guilty. I'm convicting him.'

'He's not. You know he didn't kill Hamish.'

'No, but he killed the other three. I can't just vote guilty for them—it would look suspicious. There's more evidence against him for Hamish.'

'Yes, because I planted it.' Her response came out in a hiss.

'You're not going to sabotage this, are you?' asked Leonie. 'After everything? This is the final hurdle. Once he goes to prison, you're free.'

'I'm not, though, am I?'

Leonie took a moment, choosing her words. 'Is it just the Hamish thing that you're worried about—'

'No. He deserved to die.'

'There's no need to feel guilty about Quinn. He's a serial killer.'

'How do you know?'

'The doctor in the hospital—Dr Bleasdale—she was so sure.'

'She's not psychic, though. Feeling certain about something doesn't make you right. I've seen it happen time and time again. Witnesses who swear blind that they're telling the truth get contradicted by CCTV.'

'It's not just Dr Bleasdale. I've heard all the evidence now. Not only did he kill those three people—and probably many more—he's a psychopath. He's very dangerous.'

'Please don't let this hang over my conscience.'

'It will hang over mine if we don't send someone to prison who deserves to go. Murderers should pay for what they've done.'

'If you believe that, why don't the both of us walk into a police station now and turn ourselves in?'

Leonie didn't have an answer to that.

'Yeah, I thought so. I'm not going to be responsible for ruining a man's life.'

'What about the lives of your children? How are they going to cope if you go to prison?'

'I've got a sister…' She didn't finish the end of the sentence.

Leonie looked again into her haunted eyes. She had given up.

'I've risked going to prison so that your kids would still have one parent. Every day of this trial I've been wondering when my time is up. You can't back out now. We're so close.'

Amy raked her fingers through her split ends. 'It doesn't need to go this far. No one suspects me. As long as the police think they've got their man, who cares if he's convicted? They won't carry on looking.'

'You've got to trust me. The evidence is clear. This man is a serial killer. Let's at least make sure a guilty man gets punished for what he's done.'

They stared at each other, neither one backing down.

Amy asked, 'You're determined to go through with this?'

'I am.'

'Fine.'

Leonie took that as Amy's blessing. Later, she came to wonder whether Amy had been sincere at all.

TWELVE AND A HALF HOURS
AFTER THE ATTACK

Leonie pressed her fingertips over her closed eyes. 'And we still haven't answered the question: how was Geoff pushed? Quinn can't be in two places at once.'

Diren scratched at the stubble on his neck. 'Which brings us back to what you said about him having an accomplice. It can't have been Amy because she's dead.' He frowned. 'But he must have had help.'

'Who said he was pushed? Maybe he just fell?'

Diren frowned. 'How? And at that exact moment? It's too much of a coincidence.'

'We need to go back that way anyway. I'm thirsty. I want to get a drink from the canteen.'

They left the room and found themselves in one of the many identical corridors in the green-and-white labyrinth.

Not long after, they were at the balustrade from which Geoff had fallen. Geoff's body lay spreadeagled one storey below.

There was nothing immediately apparent as to how it had been done. Leonie half expected to find a piece of burnt rope and a bit of candle wax on the floor. Like in a Golden Age detective novel.

The two of them inspected the area.

'Maybe he just left him hanging over the balustrade,' said Leonie. 'You can suffocate someone if you leave them in a certain position for long enough.'

'How could he be certain he'd fall at just the right time?'

'Quinn's a risk-taker. All of his murders involved an element of luck.'

'There's got to be another explanation.'

'We're back at him having an accomplice.'

'Was Amy definitely dead?'

Leonie was taken aback. 'Of course she was. I held her. She was hanging from her neck…'

Diren flexed his palms. 'All right, all right. It's just, you know, I didn't look too closely.'

Leonie softened her voice. 'I know.' She looked again over the balustrade. 'Well, we're not going to work it out from here. Let's get what we came for.'

They made their trip to the canteen and came away with two cans of pop and three bags of crisps. As she emerged from the corridor into the atrium, she saw something reflected in the glass walls of the security cabin. Lights, flashing. She ran to the front windows and saw an army truck driving past. She realized that they weren't flashing, just intermittently obscured by the large hornbeams which lined the car park and pavement. Leonie dropped the food and drink and pressed her body up against the glass. She shouted, banged on the window, pleaded with the soldiers to come and get them. But it was too late. The vehicle was already turning the corner.

Even if they'd seen her, would it have made a difference?

She turned her back to the glass and slid down, letting out a sigh of defeat, almost a whimper.

'Good try,' said Diren. He crouched down to pick up the things she'd dropped. Then his whole posture changed. She'd only seen him do this when he sensed danger. But this time, it wasn't danger he'd sensed, but an opportunity.

He stared into the glass security cabin. 'CCTV.'

'What?'

'There are CCTV monitors in here.' He had already pulled the skeleton key from his pocket and was unlocking the security cabin.

'Do you know how to work them?'

'I'm a security guard in a shopping centre. Watching CCTV is about ninety per cent of my job.'

Leonie found his self-deprecation endearing. He could have told her he wrestled machete-wielding criminals or returned lost children to fraught parents, but right now, his ability to find relevant footage was more valuable.

The screens flickered on. There were only six cameras: one covering the atrium, three covering the mezzanine waiting area, one in the corridor where the canteen was, and one for the steps at the front of the building which led down to the car park. There was nothing showing the private half of the court building. Only the public areas were monitored.

Diren rewound the footage from the camera which covered the mezzanine waiting area and balustrade.

'Can you go back to when Geoff was pushed?'

'That's what I'm doing.'

She waited patiently.

'Damn.' He'd gone too far. A few clicks later and, 'Here.'

Leonie peered at the tiny screen.

Quinn, Wynona and Geoff were standing on the mezzanine. Geoff had his back to the balustrade. Wynona was poking him in the chest. Though she was much smaller in stature, Geoff was cowering. Everything about her posture and manner indicated someone who had taken leave of their senses. Quinn, if anything, was trying to calm her down. He tried to hold onto her wrists, but she threw him off.

Geoff took the opportunity to try and walk away but Wynona renewed her attack, shoving him. Again, Quinn, held her back. They struggled. Wynona finally pulled herself free, but the force of it was like a rubber band being released. She collided into Geoff, who was caught off balance. Top heavy as he was, when his backside hit the edge of the balustrade, he tipped backwards over it.

Leonie stared at the footage. Had her face allowed, her eyebrows would have been up near her hairline. 'What on earth?'

'I don't get it,' said Diren. 'What were they arguing about?'

'I don't know. But I remember hearing raised voices.' Leonie paced around the tiny security cabin. 'This raises more questions than it answers. What was Wynona doing with Quinn and Geoff in the first place?'

'Let me look at some other cameras from around that time.' He switched to the footage of the atrium and rewound the tape.

It was uncanny watching it back. Diren, Leonie, Jade and Wynona came down the stairs, disappeared into the plant room and emerged a few minutes later. They stopped. That must have been when they heard the music playing. A couple of words passed between them, then they split up. Not long after, Wynona went in the direction of the toilet, just like Jade had said.

Diren turned to the CCTV of the corridor where the canteen and toilets were. Wynona never entered the toilet cubicle. She just waited. Waiting for what? Or whom?

'What the hell?' asked Diren. 'What's she doing?'

Leonie pondered this for a long time, still watching the footage. As soon as Wynona saw the three of them coming to look for her—probably spotted them through the porthole windows—she turned and ran away.

'She was waiting for him,' said Leonie.

Diren searched through more footage. Eventually he came across a section where Wynona and Quinn were walking along the mezzanine together, deep in conversation. Leonie checked the time stamp. It was not long after they'd returned to the jury gallery to tell the others that Wynona had been taken.

What was going on here? Wynona worked in a bank. There wasn't anything obvious connecting her to Quinn. But nor was there anything obvious connecting Leonie to Amy or Hamish. Leonie remembered something from earlier. Something which had never been properly explained.

'Remember all that time when Rob and Wynona were missing?' asked Leonie. 'What if they came across Quinn? He must have got to them somehow.'

'How?'

'I don't know. He managed to persuade Geoff he's innocent, and we've just seen him do a number on Tanbir. He could talk a fish into buying a bicycle, that one.'

Diren let out a heavy sigh. 'We'll never be able to prove it.'

Leonie thought so too. They wouldn't be able to confirm it by watching the CCTV because it would have happened in the part of the building not covered by cameras.

'Rob's been pretending he wanted us to deliberate. If anything, it played into Quinn's hands because it got people to question whether he was guilty…' Leonie realized that Quinn had been playing her all along, pulling strings from afar, making his marionettes do all the work. He was going to find a way to ensure she went down for what she'd done. It felt like the pressure valve in her brain had finally reached its limit. 'They know. I think they know what I did. He's going to make me pay for it.'

'Look at what's going on outside. It's the end times. No one's going to care about you trying to avenge your husband's death.'

'You don't know that. Things could go back to normal and then they'll definitely care about me perverting the course of justice.'

'Let's get out of here. We could run away, just the two of us.'

'And let this hang over me for the rest of my life?'

'I don't think we should go back to the jury gallery. I don't want to be anywhere near that guy. He could slit everyone's throats in our sleep.'

Leonie's mouth had gone dry from fear. She picked up one of the cans of pop and cracked the seal before taking a sip. A bit of rubble shifted in her mind, revealing a memory. 'The Ribena. He went to get Tanbir a Ribena. Why? What was he doing? I don't believe he was just doing it to be nice. He must have had a reason.'

'Let me have a look through the footage,' said Diren. 'What time did he get the Ribena?'

'An hour ago?'

Diren scrolled back through each of the cameras. Finally, he found a video of Quinn entering courtroom 8.

When Leonie and Diren entered courtroom 8, it had the same eerie feel as the rest of the building. Something only half finished. Paperwork littered the benches where the legal teams sat. Leonie picked over the documents from the prosecution side and found a case summary. She read it in silence while Diren also rifled through papers on the defence side.

'Looks like Jade was right. There has been a drugs case going on this week. In this courtroom.' Leonie began to read the case summary aloud. '"Police executed a warrant on a suspected drug 'cutting house', where powder was being packaged for street supply. Among the seized items was a small amber glass jar containing a few grams of a pale powder. Field test strips came back positive for a fentanyl analogue—later confirmed by lab analysis to be carfentanil."'

'Isn't that like a synthetic opioid?'

'If you say so. I'm going to try and find the list of exhibits.'

She searched the desk but there wasn't anything immediately apparent. Stopping for a second to look around, she spotted a cupboard next to the clerk's desk. The cupboard door was open. Inside was an empty plastic tube. It was damaged. She held it up for Diren to see.

He inspected it. 'There's an exhibit number here. Did you find the list?'

'No. Let's have another look.'

Diren was first to find the Premises Search Booklet. They read it together, arms touching. Diren put a protective hand on Leonie's back.

EXHIBIT: RH/01 – *black Samsung mobile phone*
EXHIBIT: RH/02 – *heat-sealed clear plastic bag containing 2 kg white powder (suspected bulking agent)*
EXHIBIT: RH/03 – *notebook containing handwritten entries of quantities, dates and initials*
EXHIBIT: RH/04 – *cardboard box containing 500 unused clear self-seal plastic bags*
EXHIBIT: RH/05 – *amber glass jar containing pale powder*

Leonie inspected the plastic tube which had housed exhibit RH/05. She carried on reading the evidence booklet. 'It says, "…because carfentanil is active at microgram quantities, the jar was sealed inside a clear polycarbonate evidence tube with a red tamper tag. Can only be observed from a safe distance." What does that mean?'

Diren pulled out his phone and typed away. His eyes shot back and forth as he read the results. 'Oh no. Look up "Moscow theatre hostage crisis".'

Leonie pulled out her own phone and found an article on Wikipedia:

Moscow Theatre Hostage Crisis

In 2012, a team of researchers at Porton Down found carfentanil in clothing from two British survivors of the 2002 Moscow theatre hostage crisis. The team concluded that the Russian military had used an aerosol mist of carfentanil to subdue Chechen hostage takers.

'Oh my God.'

He read over her shoulder. 'Looks like Quinn's got his hands on a whole new kind of poison.'

Leonie's heart started to pound painfully. It would be just like all of his other murders: it would look like an accident. He would find a way to get this drug into their systems. Into their food, or into the air perhaps. If anyone found a bunch of jurors dead from symptoms consistent with a chemical attack, they'd jump to the obvious conclusion. No one would check to see if the bodies were contaminated with a different substance entirely. And Quinn would escape into the chaos and terror and get lost in it.

They would all die. Every one of them. Just like those painful, twisted bodies on the street. Rob, never able to hug his son again. Anthony, never able to feel exhausted while walking his dog at 5 a.m. before getting his many children ready for school. Wynona, never to bark awful orders at her underlings. Tanbir, never to experience love for the first time and have it reciprocated.

And Sim. For everything that had happened between them, Sim was still Leonie's friend.

'We need to warn the others,' said Leonie.

'Are you fucking insane?' Diren's splayed his hands in frustration. 'The danger isn't out there any more. It's in here. That stuff is basically like a chemical weapon.'

'He can't make it airborne. That's too complicated. But he could convince them it's cocaine or something. You saw the atmosphere up there. They're delirious.'

Diren shook his head. 'Which is exactly why we can't go back. We need to get out of this place. What if he tries to put it in the ventilation or something?'

'The aircon's off,' said Leonie.

'So? Did you not read the article? It's almost as potent as the nerve agent outside. Fuck, I can't believe they would be so idiotic, bringing it to court… We need to leave. Now. No one can help us with this. Cavalry aren't coming. We've got to look after ourselves.'

'And leave them all to die? What if we hunt down a pair of gas masks? I don't think we took all of them to the jury gallery. There might still be a pair in the deliberation room.'

'You're crazy. This is a suicide mission. And for what? Those twats? Rob and Wynona have been lying to us for hours.'

'They're still good people,' said Leonie, her tone pleading. 'On the whole. It's not their fault they've been taken in by a psychopath.'

'What about you? You deserve to live, if only because you were the only one not stupid enough to be taken in by his act.'

'I've got a cat. That's it. That's the only living creature who would be sad if I don't come home tonight. And, let's face it, he'd get over it if someone else started feeding him.'

'I'd care, for fuck's sake!'

They had reached an impasse.

'Please. We can find gas masks.'

'I told you I'd look after you and I meant it.' He rested his hands on her hips.

'We're not even allowed out yet.'

'Parts of the city have already been evacuated. As long as we stay under the radar, we'll be fine. My car is in a multi-storey just around the corner. As soon as we get to that, it'll all be okay.'

Leonie was in turmoil. Of course, she wanted to go with Diren. Of course, she wanted to keep him happy and ensure the both of them were safe. She wanted to be back in her comfortable home right now, eating nice food and fussing

Ollie. But she couldn't just abandon the others to their fate.

She felt like the decision would split her in two.

'I'm making the decision for you,' said Diren. 'We're getting the fuck out of here.'

They agreed that leaving through the front door would be too risky. Though Leonie had never entered through the front (that was for defendants, lawyers, and other ne'er-do-wells), she knew what it looked like. The court building was such an eyesore, a dominating presence, up high on the hill with thirty steps leading up to its glass frontage. It was exposed by design. They would have to find a side entrance. The back one was inaccessible to them; that would require going near the jury gallery. They managed to find a lift which took them down to the underground car park. The shutter wouldn't open on their approach, but it was as easy as pressing a button and they were outside on the street.

After so long inside the stuffy, unventilated court building, just the smell of petrichor and the rustle of leaves was unspeakably beautiful. But it seemed wrong to be out here. They could have been in the midst of a zombie apocalypse. No sounds, no passing cars. Total desertion. They were standing directly under the streetlamp, bleached and picked out as though by a searchlight.

Diren grabbed her arm and pulled her into a crouch behind some bushes.

'We'll need to make sure we don't break cover. I can get us to the car park. Just stay close behind me at all times.'

This is nuts, thought Leonie. It was like being in a war zone.

A sound cut through the empty street. Tyres on tarmac.

Fuck, fuck, fuck.

'Stay inside until we give the order. I repeat, stay inside until we give the order. No one is allowed out before the evacuation order.'

Leonie felt sick to her stomach and her heart was now hammering so painfully that she thought a cardiac arrest might kill her before any chemical attack. What was she doing hiding in a bush with Diren? She was not cut out for this. No way was she going to be able to run and duck and hide behind lamp posts or in alcoves until they got to the multi-storey. And what right did she have, when the others were cooped up inside with Quinn and enough carfentanil to kill them all? This wasn't right. She could feel it in her bones.

'We've got to go back.'

'We can't now.'

'We literally can. We've only gone about ten metres.'

'I thought you trusted me.'

'I don't trust myself out here. Look at me. I'm wearing a trench coat with nothing underneath. I'll get us both killed.'

'Leonie, don't be ridiculous.'

'I'm sorry. I know you don't want me to, but I've got to go back.'

Leonie lifted her head up and looked around. No sign of anyone. She kept low and crept back to the car park. The shutter was still raised. The whole time, Diren was hissing in a coarse whisper, telling her to come back. She could hear him saying her name over and over again, pleading with her. She should never have agreed to this.

Once inside the car park, she relaxed. It was going to be okay. No one could see her in here, and Diren could find his car and stay safe in there and it would all be okay.

She turned around. Diren was running towards the car park.

He didn't pay heed to his surroundings. He was too intent on Leonie, making sure she was okay. Which is why he didn't see the army vehicle loop back around.

'I said stay inside!' shouted the person with the loudspeaker, their voice distorted and robotic-sounding.

Diren turned and put his hands up. 'I'm getting back inside. I promise. I'm literally metres away.'

'Where have you come from?'

'Just in there.' He gestured back. 'I only came out for a second. We've been inside the whole time.'

'You're not supposed to leave. You'll spread it.'

'But this area has been cleaned. We saw them earlier.'

Silence. It lasted for so long. Every fibre of Leonie's being was on fire. Fear and adrenaline coursed through her until she shivered.

The shot was fired with no further warning. Diren dropped to the floor.

She had to wait for the truck to complete its loop. The whole time she felt frozen by fear and shock. Diren was still alive, she could hear him groaning. They hadn't shot to kill, just to stop him from moving. What was that all about? Plausible deniability. The whole situation was insane beyond measure.

'No, no, no, no…' Leonie crouched in the foetal position, watching as Diren writhed in agony.

When the truck was definitely gone, she dashed out and tried to pull him back inside.

'No,' he protested. 'No. Leave me.'

'Shut up.'

'My fault.'

'It was not. And be quiet.'

Reluctantly, he agreed to lean on her as he hobbled back to the car park. Once back underneath the shutter, he collapsed.

She had to think fast. She found the wound in his leg and pressed down on it hard. She pulled off his t-shirt and wrapped it around his leg in a makeshift tourniquet. It was the best she could do, but it still wasn't good enough. She couldn't comprehend that the human body could contain so much blood. She worried that they'd hit an artery.

He was heavy. Much too heavy for her. She looked around. Was there anything she could use to take him back upstairs? In the corner of the car park there was a small pallet trolley. She could just about lift him onto there. What she did next didn't even require thought. It was like her whole existence narrowed to the next decision, which was to call the lift and take Diren back to the atrium. Then she was in the security hut, not entirely conscious of how she got there, or what had made her think of this idea. She used the Tannoy, pressed the button.

'Please help us, please. Diren's been shot. Please come and help me.'

Then she returned to Diren, who was losing so much blood. His beautiful face had gone grey.

Pressure on the wound, put pressure on the wound. It was all she could think. It was all she knew.

Moments later she heard a thunder of footsteps. Quinn was leading the charge. Once he got there, he took over entirely. He ordered people around, told them what to do.

Oh my God, she thought. *He's going to save him. He's actually going to help.*

Leonie stood back and watched him at work. He located the wound, complimented her on the tourniquet and the pressure. Then, when someone came back with the first-aid kit, he managed to bandage him up as best he could.

'Is he going to be okay?'

'He needs a hospital.'

'They won't take him, will they?'

He shrugged.

'What were you doing?' asked Rob.

'Trying to leave.'

He huffed. 'After all that song and dance the two of you made about us not leaving.'

'Yeah, well I think you've got your poetic justice,' said Leonie.

Diren croaked. Leonie dropped to his side. He was fading. She tried to find his pulse point but couldn't.

Quinn knelt down and found it straightaway. 'It's weak. I'll try ringing nine-nine-nine but I'm not sure what good it will do.' There was an old-fashioned payphone on the wall. After a few minutes, Quinn said, 'It's engaged.'

'No, you're okay, Diren. You're okay.'

He's strong. He'll be fine. He's the healthiest and fittest one here. If anyone can pull through…

Everyone's phones pinged. The noises went off like disjointed dominoes.

They all scrambled to read the message delivered by the Government's Emergency Alerts system.

Wynona read hers aloud. Normally, Leonie found this habit to be irritating, but right now she was too focused on Diren to care.

'"Our emergency responders have been working hard to sanitize the city and make it safe. The emergency cordon is being lifted for most of the city."'

It appeared that at last they had worked out how to send messages to those in a certain geographical location.

Wynona carried on reading from her phone. '"Check this map to see which parts of the city will remain in lockdown." There's a map. Oh my God. We can leave. We can go.'

They all pelted for the door.

What about Diren? Aren't they going to try to save Diren?

'Leonie.' It was Sim. He placed a hand gently on her shoulder. 'There's nothing you can do for him.'

'There is. We can get him to a hospital. It'll be fine.'

'No, it won't.' He looked around wretchedly. Everyone else had gone. Everyone except Quinn.

Sim hovered for a moment, not sure what to say, but then he left.

And it was just Leonie, trying to speak to Diren, to get him to hear that it was okay now, they could leave. They were being evacuated.

But Diren had stopped breathing. What had been the weak rise and fall of his chest had now slowed to nothing. She put her ear over his mouth, hoping to feel the warm curl of his breath, but none came. She performed mouth-to-mouth, tried chest compressions.

'Aren't you supposed to be helping me?' she shouted at Quinn. *Why is he here? Why is he watching this?*

'I'm really sorry,' he said. 'But I can't do anything.'

'This is all your fault,' said Leonie. 'You were going to poison everyone.'

'I really wasn't.'

'What about Geoff, you killed Geoff.'

'No, I didn't.'

'But I saw you on the CCTV. You threw his body over the thing.'

'It was an accident.'

'Why move him, then? Why not just leave him like you did with Amy?'

'To distract you. So I could go and get Wynona.'

'You took her in, all right. Hook, line, and sinker. Her and Rob.' She tore her eyes away from Diren and looked at Quinn.

He looked slightly bewildered, looking out at the night sky and all the possibilities it might bring. Lost, almost, like he didn't know what to do with all this freedom.

It's an act, she told herself. *It's all an act.*

'I really didn't kill anyone,' he said. 'And I think you know that, deep down. I think you need to believe I'm a bad person to make what you've done okay.'

There was nothing she could do. She couldn't force him to tell the truth, but she could try to catch him off-guard. 'Why did you go into courtroom eight?'

'It's a shortcut. Better than going all the way around.'

Leonie couldn't picture the maze of corridors clearly enough to know whether he was bullshitting or not. 'You wanted to kill everyone with carfentanil.'

'I don't even know what that is.' He paused, as though he was going to say something but thought better of it. Then the internal battle appeared to have been won, because he said, 'You know, I want to kill you. I want to hurt you for what you and Amy have done. One year in prison. One whole year of my life. My career gone. All I ever wanted to do was help patients. I wasn't in it for the money or the glory. And look where it landed me.' He looked down at her with pitiless eyes. 'I just wish you'd been the one to get shot.'

'Fuck you.'

'I'm sorry I couldn't save him,' was all he said, before turning on his heel, leaving through the glass fire door next to the revolving doors, and disappearing into the black night.

Leonie felt detached from her body, reality, time. She pulled out her phone to check the emergency push notification. There was indeed a map. She zoomed in to see that the court building was within the hatched area, which was marked as 'cleaned'.

They had been so close, minutes away from being able to leave. If only she'd argued with Diren a bit longer before agreeing to his plan, he might still be alive.

There was something she had to check before leaving. She made the long journey back to the corridor where she'd found Amy's body. When she approached the spot, she felt a tickling sensation at the base of her skull. The fine hairs on the back of her neck lifted.

She started opening doors along the corridor. *Where was she?*

The chair had been put back against the wall. With no clue as to where along the corridor they'd found her, she looked for a sign.

The more Leonie thought about it, the more she realized that she couldn't remember the scene vividly. She'd been on autopilot, willing to do anything to get Amy down. She hadn't checked her pulse. But Amy had hanged herself. And there had been no signs of her breathing. Then Leonie hadn't been looking for signs. She had barely been able to look at Amy's body at all.

There were two things she remembered. One was how warm Amy's body had been. That didn't mean anything, just that she'd died not long before they got there. The second was how quickly she had been released when Leonie wasn't sure what she'd done to release her.

Leonie found the light fitting which Amy had used. The door to where Leonie had put the body was a couple of metres away. She opened it. Amy's body wasn't there.

*

Leonie kissed Diren goodbye, told him that she was going to find help and that everything would be okay.

She left out of the front of the court building and walked in a daze, shell-shocked.

She headed in a vaguely northerly direction. If she could find the towpath, it would take her the right way. She'd be home in an hour. Other people were also ambling along, looking zombified. Her trench coat was covered in Diren's blood. People gave her a wide berth.

She continued to wander down the dark street, feeling like a refugee in her own city, though she was returning to her home rather than fleeing from it. Finally, she reached the edge of what had been the quarantine zone.

People in hazmat suits directed her at gunpoint to the decontamination booths.

'You did this,' she told them, gesturing at the blood on her coat. 'You shot Diren. This is his blood.'

She was bellowed at from a loudspeaker. 'Put your clothes in a plastic bag and shower thoroughly. Anything you are wearing could be contaminated.'

After being washed down in a temporary white plastic tent, she was allowed to leave the cordon wearing the thin, papery boiler suit they'd given her in place of her confiscated clothes.

On the other side, officials with clipboards were helping people find their way home. They asked her where she lived before directing her to a minibus where ten people all dressed in the same boiler suits were already waiting impatiently to be taken home. Once she and a couple of others climbed aboard, the minibus pulled away.

The deserted streets were eerily quiet as they retraced Leonie's morning bus journey. She looked up and watched street lamps flashing overhead and found the rhythm of it strangely comforting.

The minibus took them through the studenty part of town. Acid Rain posters for the aborted concert still littered the place. She found herself wondering what had happened to the children who had walked so innocently into school that day. If she focused on any of those things for too long, it was overwhelming. All she could think about was getting home to safety.

The bus stopped at the end of her street. She walked the last few hundred metres back to her large Victorian house and was overwhelmed by tiredness. The gravel drive crunched beneath her feet.

The first noise that greeted Leonie upon entry to the house was the sound of Ollie's accusatory meows.

'No, Ollie, not yet.'

He tried to wind his way around Leonie's legs.

She showered first. The shower in the white tent had been cold and harsh and corrosive. She needed warmth. She needed to drown herself in the water.

After showering, she buried her face in a fluffy towel and climbed gratefully into some comfortable loungewear. Diren should have been there with her. He should have been wearing her pink dressing gown, handsome as ever.

Leonie's next port of call was to feed and cuddle Ollie, who purred gratefully and seemed genuinely relieved to have his errant owner home.

After that, she sat in silence, staring into space, until finally she crawled into a cold bed.

Leonie was in the supermarket when she saw a familiar profile peering at the label on a can of tinned soup. She approached slowly, as though browsing, trying not to alert the other person to her presence.

'Hello.'

Wynona jumped and turned to look at Leonie. As soon as she registered who it was, her pupils dilated in panic. If Wynona tried to run, Leonie would grab her arm, but she didn't even attempt it. She was rooted to the spot.

'I know what you did,' said Wynona quickly.

'Well that's good because I know about Geoff.'

Wynona's cheeks paled.

'Yes. So it's mutual assured destruction.' Leonie waited for Wynona's reaction, allowed the silence to stretch out until it became uncomfortable. 'Tell me why.'

'Why what?'

'Why you pushed Geoff.'

Wynona looked down. Leonie could tell she was weighing up what to say next. 'We'd been promised by Quinn that he'd be able to get us out—in one of the prison vans—so we could see our children.'

Leonie remembered Wynona's volte-face from being desperate to get out to wanting to stay put. 'Did this cosy little chat happen when you went missing? After we went looking for Susan?'

She nodded.

'Why did he handcuff Geoff to a radiator, then?' asked Leonie. 'If he was your ticket out of there?'

'He didn't. That was Susan. She was worried that Geoff was going to help Quinn escape.'

'Who told you that?'

'Geoff did.'

'He lied to us about Quinn doing it?'

'Yes. Quinn was trying to find Geoff, but he couldn't. It was only after Anthony and Tanbir released him that Quinn bumped into him, but Geoff had lied about being able to get us out. There were no more prison vans.'

'Why did he lie?'

'Rob offered him money, gave him all of the cash he had on him as a sort of deposit.'

'And that's why you were upset with him? You'd spent hours believing he was going to get you out so you could see your kids?'

Wynona nodded.

Leonie mulled this over for a long time.

'You look different,' said Wynona.

It was true. Leonie hadn't been keeping up with her Botox appointments. She'd allowed her face to thaw a little. She wasn't ageing gracefully as such. Just ageing.

'So do you,' said Leonie.

Wynona's chin dropped, showing three inches of grey roots.

'Did Quinn tell you what happened to Susan?' asked Leonie.

Wynona looked non-plussed. 'No.'

Leonie believed her. She picked up a tin of spaghetti hoops and walked away, feeling Wynona's eyes on her as she left the aisle.

*

She had a window seat. Her rucksack sat beside her, laden with the week's shop. When she peered out at the world from the moving bus, it was to see the world slowly returning to normal. At a smart-looking house not far from her own, she spotted bricklayers building an extension. She shook her head. Didn't the owners realize? Didn't they know things wouldn't be the same now? She couldn't imagine a future where an extension would be of any use, especially not one resembling a glass box. The effort it would take to line the Crittall windows…

The bus arrived at her stop. As she made her way down the street, her rucksack clanked with every step. Once inside the house, she relieved herself of its burden. Ollie began to cry as soon as she closed the door behind her. She ignored him and set about lining her pantry with tinned food. Following her time in the courthouse Leonie had begun to compulsively keep track of the food provisions nearby and how long they'd last. Every week, she went to the supermarket to collect more tins and stored them here.

After she'd finished stowing away this week's haul, she pulled a tin of tuna from one of the shelves and decanted half of it into Ollie's food bowl. He meowed at her heels as she moved between the kitchen counter and his mat on the floor.

After feeding Ollie, she felt the urge to take off her contaminated clothes and scrub her skin. Her weekly brush with the outside world left her feeling like noxious spores had stuck to her clothes like lint. Snatches of conversation about inane topics like football or celebrities, discussions about geopolitical events, her chat with Wynona. *I know what you did…* How much did she know? And did she have any proof?

Through the French doors she could see that the buds on her apple tree were starting to open. Whether she'd ever see them bear fruit, she didn't know. A part of her—a long-dormant part of her—felt the old itch to commit this thought to writing, to crystallize it and make it eternal. But nothing felt permanent anymore, especially not art.

Instead of looking out of the window at the sprouting trees, she pulled the curtains closed and darkness cloaked the room.

ACKNOWLEDGEMENTS

I dedicated this novel to my cousin, Elaine, without whom I probably wouldn't have developed such a deep love of reading. She gave me stories that I wanted to read and let me borrow her copies. I still haven't given all of them back. As well as being the most avid reader I know, she has spent her career as a psychiatric nurse looking after some of the most vulnerable and misunderstood patients. Though this novel features a very unpleasant nurse (to put it mildly), I have enormous respect for anyone in the medical profession. I was hospitalized at the start of 2024, and it is only due to the care and expertise of the doctors, nurses and healthcare assistants who looked after me that I was discharged in time for the publication of my debut novel. I've only ever been treated with patience and kindness by healthcare workers and owe them so much.

Speaking of patience, this was quite a difficult novel to write and was in need of a great deal of editing after being handed in. I owe a huge debt of gratitude to Laura Macaulay and Anna Michaels for their time and energy in editing this book, as well as countless others at both Pushkin Press and Poisoned Pen Press for their careful attention to multiple drafts. It was only thanks to their insight and shrewd notes that I was able to knock this into some sort of shape. Juliet Garcia's careful attention to the manuscript in its final stages was also invaluable.

I'm forever grateful to the wider team at Pushkin including Tom Martland, Rima Rashid, and Nikki Mander in the marketing and publicity departments. Huge thanks also to Basia Ossowaka and Kate Quarry for assistance with copyedits.

Dan Mogford designs covers for some of the biggest names in crime fiction, including a couple of my personal favourites. It's a real pleasure to have him design mine.

I would also like to thank Paul Ardoin, James Cassidy, Gavin Ralph, and Sarah Wakefield for reading early and later drafts of this novel. Particular thanks to Alan Killip, who read the first and final draft, the latter when I was in a bit of a panic.

Many thanks also go to all past and present members of the BXP Team who've listened to my moans and tales of woe when I'm manifesting my tendency to be a bit dramatic. Similarly, the Debut Authors 2024 WhatsApp group has been a source of comfort while we've all been tackling the difficult second book.

Most of this novel was written while I was quite unwell. I'd like to thank my wonderful parents and boyfriend, Bleddyn, who looked after me while I was convalescing and ensured that Coral was fed. My friend, Liz Hanson, also deserves special mention for keeping me sane and persuading me not to discharge myself contrary to medical advice.

Finally, to my agent, Jenny Savill, thank you as ever for your sage advice and words of encouragement.

AVAILABLE AND COMING SOON
FROM PUSHKIN VERTIGO

Jonathan Ames

You Were Never Really Here
A Man Named Doll
The Wheel of Doll

Simone Campos

Nothing Can Hurt You Now

Zijin Chen

Bad Kids

Maxine Mei-Fung Chung

The Eighth Girl

Candas Jane Dorsey

The Adventures of Isabel
What's the Matter with Mary Jane?

Margot Douaihy

Scorched Grace

Joey Hartstone

The Local

Seraina Kobler

Deep Dark Blue

Elizabeth Little

Pretty as a Picture

Jack Lutz

London in Black

Steven Maxwell

All Was Lost

Callum McSorley

Squeaky Clean

Louise Mey

The Second Woman

John Kåre Raake

The Ice

RV Raman

A Will to Kill
Grave Intentions
Praying Mantis

Paula Rodríguez

Urgent Matters

Nilanjana Roy

Black River

John Vercher

Three-Fifths
After the Lights Go Out

Emma Viskic

Resurrection Bay
And Fire Came Down
Darkness for Light
Those Who Perish

Yulia Yakovleva

Punishment of a Hunter
Death of the Red Rider